Y0-CBB-914

"So gritty, vivid, and original that it flaunts one of the greatest qualities of good fantasy: utter believability."
—*New York Times* bestselling author Vicki Pettersson

THE HOUR OF DUST AND ASHES

"Excellent. . . . The best book in the Charlie Madigan series. . . . It seems the author is leading up to a terrific finale."

—*Fantasy Book Critic*

"With a compelling heroine, sarcastic humor, and gritty action, *The Hour of Dust and Ashes* is perfection! A fabulous book and a great series . . . one of the best in urban fantasy today. Unique, intense . . . Bring on the road trip to Elysia!"

—*Night Owl*

"Sizzling. . . . A whirlwind of suspense, tension, and action. . . . Dark and gritty urban fantasy. . . . The chemistry between [Charlie and her partner, Hank] is sexy and hot and the dialogue is humorous with a sensual undertone. . . . The conclusion is heart stopping."

—*Smexy Books*

"Exciting. . . . An excellent, character driven tale."

—*Alternative Worlds*

"Halle-freakin'-lujah! Thank you, book gods. . . . I was truly smitten. . . . If you are an action junkie and a fan of urban fantasy, I would definitely recommend giving this series a try. It's full of intriguing and unique characters, and the story keeps getting better and more exciting with each new installment."

—*Clockwork Reverie*

"Every single thing about the Charlie Madigan series gets better with each book. In *The Hour of Dust and Ashes*, the mythology expands, the romance deepens, and the characters come much closer to actually breathing air. . . . All I can say is bring on the next one!"

—*All Things Urban Fantasy*

THE DARKEST EDGE OF DAWN

"What do you do when your first book is one of the most highly praised urban fantasy debuts of the year? If you're Kelly Gay, you follow up *The Better Part of Darkness* with *The Darkest Edge of Dawn,* and force reviewers everywhere to try and find a better way to describe *amazing*."

—*All Things Urban Fantasy*

"The second book in Kelly Gay's gritty Atlanta-set urban fantasy series is even better than the first! Charlie is a vastly intriguing and likeable heroine. . . . Tight plotting keeps the pace brisk and the action exciting. This author is definitely on the rise!"

—*Romantic Times* (4½ stars)

SHADOWS BEFORE THE SUN

KELLY GAY

POCKET BOOKS

New York   London   Toronto   Sydney   New Delhi

Pocket Books
A Division of Simon & Schuster, Inc.
1230 Avenue of the Americas
New York, NY 10020

First Pocket Books paperback edition August 2012

POCKET and colophon are registered trademarks of Simon & Schuster, Inc.

For information about special discounts for bulk purchases, please contact Simon & Schuster Special Sales at 1-866-506-1949 or business@simonandschuster.com.

The Simon & Schuster Speakers Bureau can bring authors to your live event. For more information or to book an event, contact the Simon & Schuster Speakers Bureau at 1-866-248-3049 or visit our website at www.simonspeakers.com.

Manufactured in the United States of America

10 9 8 7 6 5 4 3 2 1

ISBN 978-1-5011-3764-8
ISBN 978-1-4516-2550-9 (ebook)

THE BETTER PART OF DARKNESS

"This gritty urban fantasy . . . is extraordinary."

—*Booklist*

"Captivating urban fantasy. . . . Intricate world-building and richly complex characters mix with a fast-paced plot to create a standout start to a new series."

—*Publishers Weekly*

"Kelly Gay is a star on the rise. . . . What sets this book apart, besides the great writing and the unique world-building, is the fact that our heroine is a single mom. . . . The love and protectiveness of a mother for her child as well as her family just gave so much depth to the situation as well as a real sense of urgency."

—*Night Owl*

"Charlie Madigan is an awesome character. . . . I could not put this book down."

—*Fallen Angel Reviews*

"A strong debut . . . dark and gritty, with plenty of mystery and treachery thrown in. . . . An excellent start to an electrifying new series!"

—*Romantic Times* (4 stars)

"Solid, action-packed with a kick-ass heroine. . . . Kelly Gay knows her craft!"

—Lilith Saintcrow

SHADOWS

BEFORE

THE

SUN

Prologue

THE SIREN CITY OF FIALLAN

"Again."

His muscles tensed, going rock hard as the whip sliced through the air with a long, brutal sigh. The glowing barb flashed over the walls of the chamber and struck his left shoulder blade, sinking in deep and then ripping flesh as its power burned like acid through the wound.

A shocked gasp lodged in his throat. The pain strung his body taut, frozen, as though time itself had paused to acknowledge the vicious blow.

In a blink, time moved on and the barb withdrew, catching and slicing the flesh over his hip as his breath returned in a great, shaky rush. His head fell forward, hanging low between his shoulders and pulling down painfully on his arms. Shackles held his wrists high above his head—so high only the balls of his bare feet touched the cold stone floor.

"A lash for every year you denied us." The voice was so

beautiful and pure, so powerful and deep, like nothing he'd ever heard from a siren before.

The initial strike of the whip had clouded his vision with pain, but his sight cleared and he saw them; the three witches who held sway over the king and the entire city of Fiallan. The Circe.

All three were similar in height and looks except for the color of their eyes. Some said they were sisters, some said triplets, but there was no one left alive who knew for sure. Their regal bearing and siren looks were deceptive, though. They clung greedily to their power with ancient, iron fists, still denying the natural deaths that should have taken them eons ago.

"Two hundred fourteen in all," the one on the right spoke, green eyes lighting in earnestness.

He growled at them, adrenaline fueling his wrath and dulling his pain for a brief moment. The arcane barb on the end of the whip would impede his natural ability to heal, to knit his wounds back together. That many strokes might kill him. The old bitches were ensuring he would suffer before he died.

"Oh, but sisters . . ." the one on the left said excitedly. "He has denied each of us."

Oh shit.

He wrapped his hands around the chain above him, cursing his inability to attack, to summon his power, to call upon his voice. The helplessness burned through him as harsh and bitter as the barb that had opened his flesh.

"Ah, yes."

"True. Very true."

"Two hundred fourteen leashes for each of us, then."

Rage urged him to fight, to kill. And yet he could do nothing. He struggled and tried to speak, to curse them, to show his complete and utter hatred, but he could not. Nothing came. His words were hindered by the Circe's magic, so he growled between ragged breaths, promising them with his eyes that they'd pay.

Oh, they'd pay. Even if he had to come back from the dead, he'd see them pay for every Malakim they'd destroyed, every life they stole. This was not finished.

"Stop when he loses consciousness," the Circe told the whip master. "And continue your count when he wakes. He must feel every lash."

The middle one stepped closer, her head only coming to the height of his heart. She lifted her chin. "Do not waste your time praying for death. You will not die, Malakim. Every time your body gives up and your soul prepares to leave, it will be forced to endure until the final lash is struck."

The second one stepped up to join her sister. "And once it has, perhaps then we will grant you leave to meet your family in the afterlife."

The third joined in. "Welcome home, Niérian, strongest of the Malakim sirens. Welcome home, traitor. With you the great house of Elekti-Kairos comes to an end."

They watched him, eyes wide and eager and . . . waiting.

Waiting until he understood, until he realized the implications of their words. Cold crept over his skin. The last of his family? That could not be true. When he'd left, his family was large, joined of the two great Malakim houses of Elekti and Kairos through marriage. It had been filled with sons and daughters, nieces and nephews . . .

The Circe smiled in eerie tandem as the truth hit him harder than any barb they could ever wield.

"And now you understand the depth of your betrayal."

"Someone had to pay, after all."

"All gone. Every last one, but you."

They left him then.

A scream of despair, bleak and cold, pushed on his chest, but he was unable to release it. Unable to do a goddamned thing. His pulse came rapid and erratic. Only a wounded, angry groan issued from his throat, finding its way past gritted teeth and out through lips wet from tears.

They were gone. All of them. Wiped out.

Because he had dishonored them.

Because he had escaped from the tower where he had gone willingly and proudly as a child, where his power had helped feed the four rings of protection that strengthened the inner wall around Fiallan.

Being a Malakim, a guardian, was a thousand-year-old tradition and the highest honor one could receive in Fiallan. But it was all a lie. A horrible, horrible lie.

The Malakim never asked to stay in the towers after their seven years of service was done. There was never any choice, never an escape or a survivor who could tell the truth about the Circe's towers.

Until him.

He'd found a way to disconnect himself from the grid—as he called it. He alone knew the truth.

Once he escaped, his ring fell, alerting the Circe and the king. They fought in the tower and, somehow, he'd managed *to throw the king into the grid, a move that eventually cost the king his life.*

Then he'd fled. Branded a traitor and murderer, the first ever in a long line of guardians to dishonor his family.

He had no knowledge of how to care for himself, how to eat, what to eat; the basics were unknown to him, as the grid had taken care of him in the way that power does.

For two hundred years, he lived in the sidhé forests of Gorsedd, learning, growing in strength, and finally leaving to make his own way, always training, learning, and preparing to one day return and liberate the Malakim once and for all.

Only that day had come sooner than he'd planned . . .

He never imagined his family would pay for his desertion; that an entire lineage would end with him.

While he was learning and growing and, in the end, thriving, they were dying.

Christ. They were all dead.

The lash whispered through the air once again and this time when it hit, he accepted the excruciating pain as his due.

I

"I'm serious, Charlie. I think I'm becoming tele-pathic."

"Tele*pathetic* is more like it," I muttered.

Rex's tone went flat. "Funny."

I slowed my vehicle to a stop at the light, and then took a sip of coffee, meeting Rex's dark, sleep-deprived scowl over the rim of the cup. He was un-shaven and needed a haircut. And, yeah, he might be the biggest goofball I'd ever met, but now that he knew who he was and where he came from, he'd become edgier and fiercer than before when he was simply a Revenant occupying the body of my ex-husband, Will.

"What?" He stared at me with one eyebrow cocked.

"Nothing." I looked out my side window for a sec-ond and then back at him. "Your eyes are different."

"Noticed that, did you?"

"Hard not to," I admitted.

Will Garrity's gorgeous gray-blue eyes that had always put me in mind of stormy skies were now changed—once I'd pulled his soul from his body, releasing him to find peace as he'd asked, it had allowed Rex's jinn spirit to lay claim, to knit itself into Will's physical form in a way that was beyond possession, in a way that was permanent and complete.

As a result, small jinn signatures began to manifest, changing things on the inside and the outside. The gray-blue color of Will's eyes was still there, but now it was shaded in the violet indicative of the jinn race, turning them into a strange but beautiful lavender shade.

"I look like a fucking girl," Rex grumbled as I accelerated through the intersection.

Somebody shoot me.

From the time Rex had gotten into the passenger seat, I'd had to listen to him detail every ache and pain, his every claim and suspicion about what he thought was taking place inside of him. "You don't look like a girl," I said. "Your eyes are . . . pretty." Which I knew would set him off, but I had a certain payback quota to fill when it came to Rex.

His finger punched the air. "Exactly! Pretty. Not masculine. Not dark and mysterious. Fucking pretty."

"Oh please. Women love guys with beautiful eyes. Trust me. I think you're good."

He thought about it for a moment, calculating. "How good, exactly?"

I laughed and saw he was grinning. Will had a smile so warm it could melt snow and in Rex's possession . . . well, the female population of Atlanta was in for a treat if Rex decided to start prowling.

"You shouldn't fish for compliments, you know," I said, parking along the curb and then cutting the engine. "It kind of breaks the whole thing you got going on with the scruff and the leather jacket."

Rex might look good on the outside, but inside he was a contradiction convention. Arrogant, yet unsure. Extremely intelligent, yet would veg out in front of Nick Jr. like a four year old. A warrior at heart who walked around the kitchen in a cherry print apron reciting Shakespeare sonnets.

He had a devil-may-care attitude that came from thousands of years as a spirit, one who couldn't be killed, one who had seen it all and done it all within host after host of willing bodies. Until he fell in with the Madigan clan. Until he met my daughter and felt the stirrings of the one thing he hadn't done in life: be a father. Part of a family.

We got out and proceeded down the sidewalk, which ran alongside the tall fence surrounding the Grove. I ducked my shoulders against the light mist of rain and silently cursed the weather. The off-world darkness I'd summoned months ago still churned above Atlanta like a living shroud, but the rain was even worse. It carried some of the darkness to the ground, creating a thin off-world fog and causing my Charbydon genes to go haywire from all the raw arcane energy in the air.

Ahead, ITF cruisers blocked the 10th Street entrance to the Grove and two officers stood nearby talking. I'd been one of them once, proudly wearing the Integration Task Force uniform and dealing with the influx of beings from the dimensions of Elysia and Charbydon. Eventually, I'd moved on to detective, where I dealt with crime in the off-world communities in and around Atlanta, usually in Underground, the biggest off-world neighborhood in the city.

But those days, like everything else, seemed like a lifetime away, when I'd been human, when I had an identity I was sure of. I supposed in a way, Rex and I were both having our own identity crisis. We were just approaching it differently.

Rex bumped me with his shoulder then lifted his chin a notch so I could get a good, clean look at him. "So besides the eyes, do I seem different to you? Like on a sensory level?"

Yeah, *totally* different approaches.

It wasn't even nine o'clock and Rex was already getting under my skin. "For the hundredth time, no."

"Well, I feel different."

"No shit, Rex," I finally said, exasperated. "You've been floating around for thousands of years as a Revenant, occupying one body after another. Always a bridesmaid, never a bride. Now you have a body all your own and it's bound to feel different for a while. Look, you'll get used to it." I took another sip from my paper cup. "You kind of have to, since you're stuck with it."

He rolled his eyes. "Gee, thanks. Promise me you won't accept any speaking engagements, or start counseling, or writing self-help books. Really. Stick to killing things because your motivational skills suck ass."

I shrugged. "We each have our talents." And I was perfectly fine at giving pep talks when the situation called for them, and this one didn't. I wasn't about to feed Rex's imagination. "But I've always thought about writing a book one day . . . maybe something like *How to Deal with Overemotional, Highly Delusional Revenants* or maybe I'll just shorten it to *Revenants for Dummies.*"

Rex gave a humorless laugh. "No, yours would be *Don't Let Life Get You Down, Let Charlie Do It Instead.*"

I shot him an eye roll, unclipped the badge from my belt, and flashed my credentials at one of the two uniformed officers standing before the open gate. Somewhere beyond that gate in the home of the Kinfolk, the city's largest population of nymphs, was a dead body.

As we stepped around the officers and into the Grove, unease slid down my back. Gone were the concrete paths, the benches, the water fountains, and the public restrooms that existed here years ago when this was Piedmont Park. In their place was an ancient forest, thick and dark—spurred into old growth by the nymphs' magic. The forest of the Grove was dark even on the sunniest day, but now, beneath a cover of living darkness, it took on a sinister feel. And when the nymphs said *stay on the path, don't stray from the path,* one tended to listen.

Torches lined the path that cut through the forest from the gate all the way to the shores of Clara Meer Lake and the nymphs' colossal wooden temple. The only things that kept me from feeling like I'd just stepped back in time by a few thousand years were the skyscrapers and city lights surrounding the park.

"This is . . . rural," Rex said as we kept to the path.

"The nymphs' private playground." The only beings born with the power to shift into an animal form—without the use of spells and crafting—the park gave the nymphs ample room to run and play and hunt. "They built their own Stonehenge on the hill there," I said, gesturing to Oak Hill.

Rex stared at it for a few steps. "Looks creepy as hell."

"It's even creepier when it's being used."

The stones sat silent for now, ghostly monoliths that could pulse with power so strong and deep it had once made me momentarily deaf and extremely nauseous.

"You know I'm changing, Charlie, or I wouldn't be here to help with the investigation," Rex said at length.

"I know, Rex. But you're just regaining some of your old jinn traits. You're not developing powers beyond what a jinn is naturally capable of. And telepathy is not a jinn trait. I brought you with me because of what a jinn can naturally do."

"I can only tell you if I sense a jinn presence at the crime scene, so I'm not sure how much that's going to help."

"It'll help a lot. It'll rule them out. The only eye-witness says he saw a large gray-skinned being near the lake." And since the jinn had skin that ran the spectrum of medium gray to dark gray, and were built like linebackers, they were the first to come to mind, unfortunately. There was also the darkling fae, but they were thin, sinewy beings and definitely didn't fit into the "large" category.

But a jinn? That spelled all sorts of trouble. Nymphs were from Elysia. Jinn were from Charbydon. They weren't known for being friendly since the beings of "heaven" and "hell" had continually warred for eons. Here in Atlanta, the ITF and local representatives from all the races made sure peace was maintained and treaty laws adhered to—a sort of neutral ground for all beings. But none of that stopped years of bias and hate. And when it came to the boss of the local jinn tribe, Grigori Tennin, and the nymphs' Druid King . . . well, those two made fire and water look like friends.

So, yeah, a jinn here in nymph territory? Not good. A jinn murdering a nymph within said territory? Monumentally *bad*. Not to mention the highly disturbing suspicion that if a jinn was really here, he or she might've been in the Grove for a very specific purpose. And the subject of that "purpose" was already whispering a welcome in my mind. The soft, feminine tone flowed through my mind, relaxing some of the tension in my shoulders.

Ahkneri's words were usually too distant to understand, and they were brushed with a sadness that made me ache. I had a strange connection with the divine being hidden beneath the lake—weird dreams, the ability to sometimes sense her emotions, understand her language. The First Ones were supposed to be a myth and to most people they were. But to some, like Grigori Tennin and the Sons of Dawn cult, she was their ticket to starting a three-world war. He'd stop at nothing to find her.

The First Ones were the ancestors to humans, Elysian Adonai, and the Charbydon nobles. Their existence would prove to the worlds that the nobles were related to the Adonai, and that they were indeed cast out of Elysia in the forgotten past. If the nobles were to learn the truth, they'd launch an all-out war against the Adonai to take back their true homeland. It would leave the jinn in charge of Charbydon, free from noble oppression, and Earth in the middle of a war we'd no doubt get sucked into.

For the sake of all three worlds, Ahkneri had to stay hidden.

If Rex said there was no jinn signature anywhere near the body, one crisis averted. If not, I didn't even want to think about it, especially since I was supposed to be leaving for Elysia and the siren city of Fiallan tomorrow.

As we drew closer to the colossal wooden structure rising up through the trees, the temperature dropped slightly and the air became cooler and scented with lake water. Rex whistled in appreciation, his steps slowing as he ogled the nymphs' temple with its huge wooden columns the size of California redwoods. I kept moving, going through the structure, the main courtyard, and to the dock that stretched out over the lake.

Liz and her crew were already on the shoreline near the dock. "The chief fill you in?" she asked as I approached.

"A little while ago. I hear we have a body in the lake and one highly uncooperative Druid King."

The ITF's lead medical examiner and gifted necromancer snorted at that. "Highly uncooperative is being nice." She glared at the figure at the end of the dock through horn-rimmed eyeglasses.

"Careful," I said, smiling. "You keep shooting eye missiles at him like that you're going to melt your lenses."

Liz frowned, and then shoved her glasses up the bridge of her nose. "He *irks* me."

"I noticed. If it makes you feel any better, he does that to everyone. Here, hold this." I handed her my coffee cup, which she took but didn't know what the hell to do with, and said, "Wish me luck."

My boots echoed on the wooden planks as I approached the Kinfolk's spiritual leader, enforcer, protector, and all-around badass. And those titles were *more* than accurate to describe Pendaran.

He stood at the end of the dock, alone, hands tucked into his pants pockets, a white T-shirt stretching over his broad back, and his black hair just touching the collar. His focus was on the scene in the lake as two search-and-rescue officers in a dinghy pulled a corpse to shore. Liz hurried closer to the waterline.

A soundless flash of green in the undulating gray mass above us illuminated the dark water and its corpse for a split second. I felt for the nymphs. The Grove was a sanctuary, a home with defined borders patrolled day and night. One of their own had been killed within those borders. And as far as I knew, that had never happened before.

I walked into a thick wave of rage, strong enough to knock the unprepared back a few steps. But I expected Pen's wrath. I stopped next to him at the end of the dock, watching the scene unfold for a moment, letting him get used to my presence. "I'm sorry for your loss, Pen. The chief said you have an eyewitness?"

At first he didn't reply. He continued to stare at the scene, his profile hard as granite. The winding Celtic-style tattoo, which I knew to encompass the entire left side of his body—toes to hand to temple—was stark against the exposed skin; pale not from fear, but from blinding rage.

I went to repeat the question, but he turned.

And didn't even spare me a glance because his gaze zeroed in on Rex like predator to prey.

Oh shit.

It dawned on me then what a huge mistake I'd made. Of course Pen would know, would sense that despite the human figure walking down the dock, it was a jinn coming toward us.

I stepped in front of the Druid King. Probably not the wisest of moves, but I didn't really have a choice. My hand eased back my jacket to rest on the grip of my right sidearm. "Stop, Pen," I warned. "Don't do it."

His nostrils flared. A shimmer of abalone color filtered over Pen's irises, the same color I knew was on the underside of his enormous black wings. If Pen turned dragon and went after what he saw as a jinn coming toward him, we were screwed.

The Druid had nearly declared war on Grigori Tennin and the jinn when Daya, one of his Kinfolk, had died, caught up as she was in Tennin's plan to reveal Ahkneri to the world. Now Pen believed a jinn had invaded his territory and killed another one of his kin. And to add insult to injury, a jinn was coming down the dock.

Pen's features had turned from harsh to downright homicidal.

My vision went cloudy. Heart pounding, I did everything I could to prevent my own power from rising in response. "He's with me. He's here to tell us if your eyewitness really saw a jinn. Rex was a Revenant, Pen. He hasn't *been* a jinn for thousands of years. He doesn't act like them or even think like them. He watches cartoons, for Chrissakes . . ."

But Pen wasn't listening, and Rex had stopped still, like a mouse caught in the gaze of a cobra.

"He lives in my house," I went on. "He's in the body of my ex-husband and my kid loves him. I swear to God if you go after him," I promised with a conviction that came from the depths of my soul, "I'll do whatever it takes to stop you."

No one moved for the longest time, which was good because I needed everything I had to keep a lid on my power as Pen struggled to regain control, his dragon and his grief warring with his own good sense.

He looked down at my hand pressed flatly and firmly against his chest. I hadn't even realized he'd moved forward or that I had touched him. My other hand was still wrapped around the grip of my gun. A raven eyebrow arched. The alpha, the ruler, in him would never move back, so I dropped both hands and took one step back.

"Keep him away from me," he snarled in a deep voice brimming with power.

Crisis averted. I let out a shaky breath. "Okay. No problem. I can do that." I walked back to Rex on shaky legs. "Go to the courtyard and wait for me there."

A muscle in Rex's jaw flexed. He leaned forward. "What an ungrateful piece of work. Why should I help him when all he wants to do is tear me apart?"

"Keep your voice down. One of his kin just died. God, Rex. He thinks a jinn is responsible. You do the math. Just go wait and I'll come get you when I'm done, okay?"

He tossed an evil look at Pen's back and marched away, muttering about staying in bed and demented, homicidal nymphs.

2

I waited until Rex was out of sight before heading back to Pendaran's side. Once there, I let out a loud sigh, knowing just how close we'd come to a bloodbath.

"Thank you," I told him. "For showing restraint. I know that was hard."

"You know nothing."

I didn't rise to the bait. "Look, if you just point me to the witness in question, I'll get out of your hair."

"Doubtful," he muttered. "Since your witness is standing before you, Detective."

I stared blankly at him for a moment. Pen was the witness. Perfect.

"It *was* a jinn." His tone was low and deep and full of soft menace. No wonder he'd nearly gone medieval on Rex. He knew what he saw and believed it.

"Tell me what you saw."

Pen shoved his hands back in his pockets and turned once again to stare out at the water. "I saw," he began in a condescending tone, "a jinn."

"Yeah, already got that part. What else did you see?"

His highly imperious expression said he'd already answered my question and was done. I was dismissed.

I plastered a thin smile on my face and tapped into my Mommy Calm. "If you say 'a jinn' one more time, I'll have to turn into Bad Charlie. We don't want that, do we? I have a brand-new shirt on today that I happen to like, and my favorite boots, so let's not soil them with ye ole dragon's blood and tears, which is what'll happen if you don't start co-operating, so . . ."

An eye roll and the relaxing of his jaw gave me the opening I was hoping for. "Look, Pen. I want to help here, but I can't do it unless you go through the motions with me. That means giving me every minute detail even if it seems unrelated or mundane to you. Let me do my job, okay? You trusted me once when Daya was killed. You have to trust me again."

Well, he'd sort of trusted me. Ordering Orin and Killian to follow me around as I investigated Daya's murder and giving me that insane ultimatum to solve the case on *his* timetable wasn't exactly trusting, but he hadn't interfered, and he'd come through when I needed him. His trust didn't come easy, but I felt we had something of a relationship now, one forged on the battlefield atop Helios Tower against the Sons of Dawn and Grigori Tennin, one forged on common goals and secrets that could shatter worlds.

"I was sleeping in the lake, in the cave . . ." The cave which held the agate sarcophagus containing Ahkneri. Pen cleared his throat. "Killian was on patrol on the east side of the Grove."

My stomach dropped. "Not Killian."

But Pen didn't react to my outburst; he stared straight ahead, lost in his memories, while my chest burned and my fists clenched. Goddammit . . . *No, no, not Killian!*

"There was no scent," Pen went on, "no disturbance, or identifiers. I should've been able to smell an intruder, to feel a presence other than nymph. Even beneath the water, I know who comes and goes. I am the protector of my kin. . . ." Frustration and guilt edged his deep voice. After a long moment, he continued. "The only thing I did notice was the scent of adrenaline and then Killian howling. I shot from the lake, knowing he was already dead." He pointed to the eastern shore. "And I saw a gray-skinned being throw a wolf into the water. The wolf changed to nymph as Killian's spirit left him. I gave chase, but it was like chasing a shadow. The speed was incredible, a blur. There was no scent to follow . . . nothing."

"Did you see the eyes?"

Pen paused and I could tell he really wanted to say yes. A jinn's eyes glowed a reddish violet when they fought or experienced rage. There'd be no way one could've fought and killed Killian without his or her eyes turning. And they were the only off-worlders with that specific trait.

"No. But the build was very large, tall and bulky, like a jinn."

"What about hair? The males are bald and the women usually have braids . . ."

He shook his head. "I didn't notice the hair or lack thereof. I only noticed the shape and body color. And," he added with a heavy sigh, "the scent of death as I returned to the Grove."

"Did you or anyone else try to get him out of the water?" It's every investigator's hope that a victim remained untouched, but the fact that Killian had stayed in the lake, that no one had tried to save him or resuscitate him, bothered me. He was a good guy. He'd put himself in harm's way helping me in the battle on Helios Tower . . . He was quiet, capable, sarcastic. He deserved an attempt, at least.

"He was dead before he hit the water, Charlie. Nothing could've changed that. I went after the jinn. I called your chief from a borrowed cell phone after I gave up the search, and by the time I got back, your medical examiner was already here and"—he glared at Liz as Killian's body was being pulled onto the shore—"that tiny Asian necromancer wouldn't allow me near the body."

"That's Liz for you," I said quietly. "She's always been possessive about her work."

"She *shoved* me."

I blinked at that. Liz had a razor-sharp tongue and balls of steel, but I'd never known her to get physical. And I certainly couldn't picture her small frame squaring off against a six-foot-four wall of off-world power and muscle. "If she pushed you, my guess is you probably deserved it. No offense."

His deepening frown told me I was right. "She's a menace."

I let out a tired sigh, trying to explain without scolding him. "Because *you* made such a menace of yourself when Daya died, calling the morgue every day and making unreasonable demands instead of letting her do her job. Otherwise," I said gently, "she might've gone easier on you today."

His eyes narrowed on me and the imperialism was back. "Are you *scolding* me, Detective?" he asked softly. "You overstep. Again."

"Yet another one of my gifts."

Pen shook his head as though I was a lost cause, but I liked to think that underneath his gruffness, he admired the fact that I poked holes in his I-was-once-worshipped-as-a-Celtic-god complex.

"Look . . . I really am sorry about Killian. I . . . liked him. He was a good guy. I understand where you're coming from. I do. But try to ease up a little and let us do our jobs. I'll keep you in the loop with whatever we find out." I took a chance and gave his big shoulder a pat, which only resulted in him looking at me like I'd gone mad. "I'm going to get Rex to take a look at things. I'll let you know what he says."

"How can you trust anything he says? He's a jinn. He'd never incriminate his own kind."

"Rex has no ties to Tennin's tribe or any other. His only tie is to me, me and my daughter . . . *We're* his tribe now. Go get some rest, talk to your kin, grab something to eat. I'll check in with you later."

I began to walk away, but he called my name. I turned back toward him with a questioning look.

"I hear you're going to Fiallan tomorrow to retrieve the siren."

A sudden lightness spread through my belly at the words. "That's right."

Pen nodded, his grim face unreadable, but his eyes taking on a sincere light. "Good luck."

The corner of my mouth lifted. "Thanks."

As I left the dock, I watched Liz on the shore as she gently pulled Killian over onto his back. His skin was marble white, stark against his usual dark clothes and wet black hair. Grief squeezed my throat and my shoulders sagged in sadness.

I had to leave tomorrow, and I *hated* the idea of leaving Killian's case in the hands of someone else. But nothing short of a family emergency would stop me from bringing Hank home. The siren wasn't only my partner; he was my family, too, the person who'd had my back from day one. Hank and I . . . we'd grown from partners to friends to something more, something that felt like it had real possibilities. But fate seemed hell-bent on keeping us from figuring out exactly what those possibilities were.

I found Rex in the temple courtyard, reclining back on a chaise lounge, eyes closed, ankles crossed, and hands tucked behind his head.

He's a work in progress, I told myself in a rare moment of optimism.

Drawing in a steadying breath to get my mind back on task, I nudged Rex's feet off the side of the lounge with my boot. "Stop goofing off, we have work to do."

His eyes cracked open. "I have decided I want a consultant fee."

My brow lifted. Rex actually bringing home a paycheck? Now *that* would be a novelty I'd welcome. "I'll submit a request to the chief. Come on, we have work to do."

I led Rex to the shore of the lake where Liz was making her first necromantic pass over the body, trying to pick up any residual traces of crafting or imprints on the body. If the perp was a crafter, she'd be able to tell. Her hand moved over his torso, palm down, a couple inches over the body. Her glossy black bob was tucked behind both ears, allowing me to see the frown pulling down her mouth.

I dropped onto my haunches on Killian's other side. "Anything?"

Using her knuckle, she pushed her glasses up the bridge of her nose. "Nothing. The water doesn't help." Her gaze turned to Rex. "You sure he can pick up something?"

Rex scoffed. "He's sure."

Liz didn't bother hiding her dubious expression.

But she stood and stepped back from the body. "No touching."

"Don't need to. I can tell you already, there wasn't a jinn around this guy."

Liz folded her arms over her chest. "Just like that."

"Just like that."

"And how does that work, exactly?"

Rex shrugged. "Like any other animal that can scent their own kind. If a jinn fought with him, I'd be able to tell."

And if Killian had been killed by a jinn, there was no doubt in my mind he would've put up one hell of a fight. A jinn scent would be all over him, water or not.

"Hmm. We'll see." Liz cast a glare over at the dock where Pen made no secret about watching our every move. "You think you can keep *His Highness* off my back for a couple days?"

"I'll try. But give him a break. He's lost two of his own in the last few weeks. I'm taking Rex over to where Pen saw Killian being thrown into the water. Keep me posted."

"As always. Who's going to take point on this when you leave tomorrow? And please, please, please don't say Ashton."

"Okay, I won't." At her look, I apologized. "Sorry, I know he rubs you the wrong way, too. If I had my way, it would be Thompson or Lesley, but they're both up to their eyeballs in the crap Tennin's been pulling lately in Underground—small-time stuff, I know, but I think it's the jinn boss's idea of breaking them in."

"Naw, I think ole GT just misses you and wants you back patrolling Underground as usual, so he's making a fuss."

I chuckled at that. "Right. I'll get the chief to brief Ashton and tell him to tone it down and not push so many buttons with the Kinfolk and Pen. Tensions will be running high enough already . . ."

Liz resumed her necromantic check over Killian's body as Rex wandered to the shoreline. "Well, it sucks you have to leave at a time like this, but thank God you're going in to get Hank. The thought of him being in that grid . . . How do you think talks will go?"

"In our favor, I hope. The delegates have been there for two days already, so let's pray they've made some progress. I'd like to have the way cleared for Titus to work on releasing Hank from the grid."

"Nice having the most famous scientist in the world on your side." Liz called over her shoulder for a body bag. "You'll bring him home," she told me, sounding certain. She stood. "Then you two can finally stop hedging."

"Hedging?"

She gave me that smart-ass look of hers, which I returned in kind. "It means stop being a chickenshit and take a chance. You and Hank are good for each other. God knows you deserve some happiness." Her apprentice/assistant returned with a bag. I hadn't seen him for a couple months, but he still looked ten years old to me.

"Hey, Charlie."

"Hi, Elliot. How's middle school treating you?"

His grin went deep. "Haha." He rolled his eyes and moved to help Liz with the bag.

I stared down at Killian, sobering. "Take care of my friend here."

"We will," Liz said. "Good luck tomorrow."

"Thanks."

Rex and I made our way around the lake. It took longer than it should have due to the docks, temples, and homes we had to go around. The shore where Killian had most likely died was already taped off and a couple of uniformed officers and Kinfolk were walking in a grid pattern over the ground, looking for any evidence that might have dropped to the soft cushion of grass and leaves.

Signs of the fight were everywhere along this portion of the wooded shoreline. Deep ruts had been torn into the ground. A few branches on the trees were broken. Blood splatters . . . Killian had put up a damned good fight—as to be expected from one of the Druid King's enforcers.

"Anything?" I asked Rex.

He shook his head. "Nothing. I don't know what the Druid saw, but it wasn't a jinn. If there was any signature, it would be here of all places."

Which was an enormous relief. But now we were left back at square one.

"You can always get a rogue jinn in here for a second opinion," Rex said, mistaking my silence as questioning his ability.

"Do I need a second opinion?"

"No. Just thought it might make you feel better. I'm gonna walk around a little bit."

"All right. Go slow. And watch your step. If you see anything that shouldn't be here—footprints, clothing, trash, anything—call out, *don't* touch it."

"I got it. No touching."

As he walked off I asked, "You need a flashlight?"

He smiled over his shoulder, shook his head, and then continued into the darkness of the woods. Guess he had his jinn night vision back as well.

Alone now, I moved slowly toward the water. Even though beams of flashlights darted through the trees and small sounds from the officers reached me, I suddenly felt very isolated. Even the temperature felt colder than it had seconds ago. The sounds of the city beyond and the activity from across the lake faded into the background, making the lapping of the water against the shore louder.

The marks on my right arm ached—a weird stinging burn, the intensity coming and going. I stopped, the toes of my boots inches from the water, wondering if it was because I was so close to Ahkneri and her divine weapon—the thing had nearly burned my hand and arm to a crisp, leaving behind the strange markings that Aaron, the Magnus mage, believed to be the language of the First Ones.

Well, the language fucking hurt.

I kneaded my forearm, trying to find some relief as I stared at the dark lake and the city lights reflecting off its surface like a million tiny gems. If I listened hard enough Ahkneri's ancient whispers would become clearer. If I let my guard down I could hear *more* than her. I could hear strangers, bits and pieces of conversations that meant nothing to me, that just seemed to filter in like I was some sort of transistor radio. Occasionally my reality would really screw up and things I shouldn't be able to see through or into, I suddenly could.

I turned away from the lake and resumed my study of the area. I might've missed the long, arcing scar in the tree if it hadn't been eye level and a sliver of bark missing to reveal the lighter wood beneath. The cut was thin and clean. Razor-sharp, too. A breeze stirred the woods and a flash of movement caught my eye. I stepped closer to the tree to find a long white hair caught in the corner of the scar.

Killian had black hair.

Male jinn were bald. And no female jinn had long white hair unless they were elderly. The exception was Sian, the human/jinn female currently working as our office assistant. She also happened to be Grigori Tennin's daughter, but while Tennin was harsh, demanding, and confrontational, Sian was soft, timid, and kind. If Pen had seen a huge, dark figure, I was pretty sure I could rule out both an elderly jinn female and Sian. The only other race of beings that came to mind were the sidhé fae warriors who had appeared in the oracle's club on New Year's Eve, looking for me and the sarcophagus. Albeit they had light gray skin, not dark, but anything in these woods would seem darker than normal . . .

"There was a jinn here."

Rex's voice nearly gave me a heart attack. I swung around, heart in my throat. And then his words sank in. "A jinn was here? Where?"

"Came over the fence, through the woods. Stopped a few feet back from the scene and that's it. Like he watched and then went home."

"Are you sure?"

"Positive."

"Shit." So the jinn *were* snooping around in nymph territory. Near the lake. Near Ahkneri. Could be, if the hair belonged to a sidhé fae, the jinn had merely followed the fae. Tennin's goons had been at the club that night, too. The fae hadn't exactly made their purpose a secret, either. Tennin would be smart to stick a tail on them just in case they found the sarcophagus before Tennin did. I glanced down at the hair strand knowing it could just as easily be human or any number of beings, but . . .

Christ, this is a mess. I parked my hands on my hips and watched Rex wander along the lake's edge, head down, occasionally bending over to look at something.

How do they know you're here? I asked, more to myself than to the being in the lake, but her voice flowed through my mind with an answer.

They follow the signs.
What signs?
The call of power. The wakening. And . . . you.
Me?
. . . Perhaps.

I glared at the lake. Ahkneri should've been in league with the oracle using a cryptic answer like that. A straight answer, for once, just once, would've been nice.

Laughter breezed through my mind. *That was a straight answer. You are an . . . uncertainty. A divine being, made not born, imbued with the blood of the three noble races my kind created. You are like us, but not. An unknown. A confusion.*

I knew several people who would totally agree with those words, and I was one of them. Ever since I'd been brought back to life a year ago, the Adonai and Charbydon noble genes I was given were fusing with my own human code. I was becoming like those who had seeded the three races. The First Ones. That was the theory, anyway.

"Who are they? Who follows the signs?" I asked her.

"So is that like a rhetorical question or do you really want me to answer?" Rex stood beside me, staring at the lake as if trying to figure out who I was talking to. Apparently I'd asked my questions aloud.

"Not unless you know more about those sidhé fae we ran into at the oracle's club," I said, pulling a set of plastic gloves from my pocket.

"You mean the night I kicked ass?" Rex's mouth

twitched. "It kills you that I have skills, doesn't it?"

"Yeah." I shot him an eye roll and handed him the small plastic evidence bag and extra pair of gloves Liz had given to me earlier. "Here. Put these on and hold this open. Skills or not, you shouldn't be fighting. If Will's body takes a mortal blow, you'll be heading straight to the Afterlife. No wandering around until you find another body. You'll be gone. Finished. Game over."

"And your worry for me comes out of a deep, unwavering love, is that it?" I went to reply, but he cut me off, saying, "I knew I was growing on you."

Whatever I was about to say deflated and I was left shaking my head. I gently removed the hair from the tree. There was no need to deny it; Rex was growing on me. Already had, in fact. He'd become an indispensable part of my family and a huge part of my daughter's life. I'd thought living with him would be strange and uncomfortable, and at first it was. Now, I couldn't imagine him gone.

Once the hair was in the bag, Rex sealed it. "To answer your question, no, I don't know any more about those puffed up old faeries than I did before. I thought you asked Sian of the Beautiful White Hair to dig around."

"I did." Rex fell in step beside me as I headed back to the main temple to deliver my find. "She hasn't turned up much other than a few vague mentions about a very old, very secretive warrior sect. And as we all know, legends turn out to be true in most cases. Those guys were definitely old school . . . And speaking of Sian, is it really necessary to call her every day? You do know she's not interested in guys, right?" The memory of finding Sian clutching Daya's photo came to mind. From the moment Rex had seen Sian, when she'd pulled a gun on me and shoved me into an alley in Underground, he'd been smitten, too smitten to even come to my aid—not that I'd needed him to. But still. It was the principle . . .

"I'm just being friendly," he said defensively. "Nothing wrong with chatting and getting to know someone. Consider it therapy," he said, amused by his logic.

"And what? You're the doctor of the shy and introverted?"

He laughed. "Sure, if you want to call it that. I'm helping her come out of her shell a little, all pro bono, of course. And who knows. She might swing both ways."

"Rex!"

He was grinning like a damned idiot. I wasn't sure whether he was being serious or just giving me a hard time like usual. But I decided not to proceed down that particular road. If Rex wanted to beat himself up against the impenetrable shell that was Sian, then he'd do it whether I advised against it or not.

After giving the bag to Liz, Rex and I left the Grove. Pen wasn't in sight, and I didn't go in search of him. I'd call him later. He wouldn't see having a possible jinn witness to Killian's murder as a positive thing. In fact, he'd most likely scour the jinn underground to find said witness and end up causing a war we didn't need.

I dropped Rex off at the house and then drove back to the station to file a report and talk to the chief about handing the case over to Ashton Perry, a.k.a. "Asston," and his crew. They'd have to be briefed on Pen's sometimes volatile nature, and the current state of relations between him and Tennin.

As I exited the elevator onto the fifth floor and headed down the hall, Sian stepped out of our office, saw me, and froze like a thief caught red-handed.

Immediately, I knew something was wrong.

Her hand was still on the doorknob, holding it ajar, but her eyes were pinned on me and her pale gray skin went paler. Slowly, her expression went from shocked to sad. What the hell?

"Sian," I said, approaching. "What's wrong?"

My voice was like a jolt. She jumped, blinked, and then stammered. She was such a contradiction, this tall, beautiful creature with indigo eyes, a cascade of white hair, and a body that wouldn't quit. Her hand shook as she smoothed down a black pencil skirt.

"What happened? What is it?"

"Charlie, it's . . ." Normally she exuded a calming vibe that could lull even the most aggressive creature and yet I wasn't getting that from her. "I'm so sorry, they—"

The chief peered around the door.

"Chief," I said slowly, starting to feel scared, "what the hell's going on?"

He held the door wider. Sian stepped back and looked at the ground. "Come on in, Charlie," he said gently, too gently for the chief. The guy was a bulldozer of a man, in looks, in speech, in everything he did. He didn't do anything *gently*.

I followed him through the maze of discarded office equipment that made up the front portion of our work space. We'd cleared out a large corner near the kitchenette, made a private office for the chief, and claimed the open area where Hank, Sian, and I had our desks.

It was also where six delegates made up of civil rights attorneys, Federation representatives, and ITF officials happened to be standing—the same six who were *supposed* to be in Fiallan working toward the release of my partner.

That they were here now . . .

Oh, God.

3

"Charlie, calm down. Breathe."

My eyelids slid closed at the chief's words. *If only I could.*

I let my forehead rest on the drywall near my left hand, palm pressed flat against the surface. My other hand was sunk deep into the hole I'd just made. Pain radiated from the center of my chest in a burn so acute it felt as though my entire torso had become a boiling, poisonous cavity.

Breathe.

Just give me a minute, I wanted to say, but nothing came out. Just a minute to myself where all eyes weren't on me. To regroup. To allow my wildly beating heart time to slow down. But they weren't going to walk away until I accepted the complete and utter bullshit they were trying to feed me.

I jerked my fist from the hole in the drywall and turned to face them, these vile people, these . . . liars.

This isn't happening.

This. Isn't. Fucking. Happening.

I bit down hard on the inside of my cheek, needing to hurt, to ground myself and force some focus into this nightmare. I glared at the small assembly crammed into our office and repeated what I'd said earlier, right before I hit the wall. "I don't care what you say. You don't have a single bit of evidence. No proof. Nothing at all to back this up."

Argue with that, assholes.

But argue they did, softly and with pity. The arguing I could take, but the pity—not so much.

My gaze found the chief and latched on. He leaned back against the small kitchen counter and wiped the inside corner of his eye, his large shoulders sagging in defeat. My fists closed tightly. I wanted to scream at him. How could he give up so easily and accept what they were saying?

A woman stepped forward. Human. Classy. One of the attorneys, I remembered. Her hesitant look to my left where our resident ITF psychologist, Doctor Berkowitz, stood almost made me laugh. Like Berk could do anything. Like Berk could protect them if I went psycho.

"We're truly sorry, Detective Madigan," the attorney said. "I know your source identified Hank as being in one of the towers, but the Circe took us into each one. Your partner was not there. He was exec—"

"Don't. Don't say it. Just . . . *don't*."

But she pressed on. "Without Hank's testimony, we have nothing to put pressure on Fiallan and the Circe to end the Malakim practice. Nor do we have any cause to bring a case against them for the execution of someone they consider a known traitor and murderer. One of the things that enables the Federation to function is respecting the cultures, customs, and laws of its members . . ."

Blah, blah, blah.

All I could focus on was the fact that she said the one word I told her not to say. What did she not understand about *Don't say it*? I wanted to kill her for that, wanted to wrap my bare hands around her throat and choke off the lies spewing from her painted lips. It would feel good and right, justifiable after they just left him there and—

"Charlie."

An echo, a whisper of my name, nothing more. I shrugged it out of my head and went back to considering murder.

A gentle hand touched my shoulder. I shrugged that off, too.

A second hand landed on my other shoulder. Hurt and anger filled me with a rush that stole my breath. A crash sounded somewhere far off. Power pushed at me, filling me, searing me from the inside out.

And, for once, I didn't care.

I didn't care that my power had become a beacon. Let Sachâth come. The weird shadow being I'd first encountered back in the oracle's club was drawn to my power like a heat-seeking missile. Chances were good it'd knock me out and everything would turn into blackness like before. And blackness would be an easy escape.

No, some inner part of me rose up and said. *Hank deserves more than you falling down now, Charlie. Stand and fight.*

I tried to concentrate, to think, to battle against the sorrow and listen to that inner voice. I had to figure out what went wrong and fix it.

Had to fix it.

Because the idea that Hank was gone and would never come back . . .

Hot grief stabbed my chest as their words breached my defenses. *We're sorry to inform you, your partner was executed upon his arrival in Fiallan. There was nothing we could do . . .*

A sharp pinch to my bicep made me flinch. I swatted at it, wishing they'd all just shut up and leave me alone. My face was wet and hot. I couldn't see, couldn't get enough air into my lungs.

They didn't understand how it was. The bond of friends and partners, the things we'd been through, facing down death together, what that meant. If they were right . . . he didn't deserve to go out like that. Not like that. Like a criminal. *Hank . . .*

The ache . . . the squeezing wouldn't stop. I dropped to my knees. I leaned over until my forehead touched the carpet. My nails dug into the fibers. "It's too short.

This carpet is too short." I couldn't even grab it, pull at it.

"Charlie. Listen to me." Berk placed her hand on my back. "You're going to be all right."

A wet laugh burst from my lips. *Right.* I fell slowly to the side until my face pressed into the floor.

"I gave you a shot, a sedative, something to calm you down."

Someone sat down behind me and pulled the hair back from my wet face, and I knew it was Sian. She'd stayed in the corner, watching, always trying so hard to not draw attention to herself. But now she was here on the floor next to me, her lavender scent filling my nose and her strange, calming vibe working alongside the sedative.

And I just lay there. On the office floor, eyes open but unable to see.

He's not dead. He's not dead. He's not dead.

"Momma?"

Emma's soft voice jerked me awake. I stayed still, the side of my head deep into my pillow, my brain feeling as heavy and overworked as a wrecking ball.

"Mom?"

"Yeah," I forced out through scrunched lips.

The bed dipped with her weight as she sat behind me and put her hand on the comforter covering my hip. "How do you feel?"

"Peachy." *Just peachy.* My gut clenched into an

empty sour ball and I groaned. Once the romance wore off, sedatives and I had a hate/hate relationship. "Can you grab me some saltines?"

After she left, I rolled onto my back, threw off the comforter for cooler air, and cracked open my eyes to the sound of panting. Brim's bald gray head rested on the mattress, his expression pathetic, worried, and hopeful. His tiny ears twitched as if trying to determine my state, and his rear end swayed back and forth as he wagged a tail he didn't have.

I lifted my hand. Immediately the hellhound rooted my palm with his wet nose. "I'm fine, you big stinky beast."

Emma returned and tossed me a half-eaten pack of crackers. I caught them with my left hand, scooted back against the headboard, and stuck a dry saltine in my equally dry mouth.

A parental sigh came out of my daughter's lips, the sound completely at odds with her twelve-year-old self. Her wavy brown hair had been pulled back into the usual ponytail and her round brown eyes rolled skyward. "Hold on. I'll get you some water."

"Thank you. Can you bring me a wet washcloth and the hand gel on the sink, please?"

Em returned, sat on the bed, and handed me a cup of water. "Here."

"Thanks." I washed the lump of cracker down my throat and then took the hand gel to remove the evidence of Brim's loving nose and tongue bath. "My head is killing me." I glanced at the clock. "Can't believe how late it is. It's Saturday, right? Please tell me I haven't been out for more than a day."

The clock on my night table said it was nearing noon, but who knew what day it was or how much power Berk had packed into that sedative. Hell, I could've been out for days.

"It's Saturday. You missed dinner and breakfast, though, so Rex is bringing up some food for you."

Thank God. Not too long at all.

Emma grabbed my wrist and turned my arm so she could look at the markings that had been emblazoned there after I'd wielded the First One's divine sword, Urzenemelech. Anguish by Fire. Aptly named. It had cleaved the Adonai serial killer, Llyran, in two, burning him to ashes as it went, and it had left me with bluish markings that ran from my hand all the way to my shoulder.

I'd told Emma only what was safe to know, only what she had to know. The same thing that was in the official report: the sarcophagus contained dust and bone fragments and the sword, all of which were destroyed. There was no such thing as a First One. And if those bones in the coffin were something from myth and legend, then they were long since gone from the world.

I didn't like lying to my kid, but the lies came easier when it meant her safety.

"I wish we knew what this said," she remarked in a wistful tone, releasing my arm.

"Probably something like: *She Who Was Dumb Enough To Wield The Sword . . .*"

Em laughed. "You have to put more gloom and doom into your voice when you say it."

I smiled and shoved her gently with my foot as Rex entered the room with a tray of food and drink. "I see the grizzly is awake."

"Rex said you snored like a drunken grizzly. But I thought it was more like a jackhammer turning on and off. On and off. On and off . . ."

"Great. Thanks a lot." I made a face at both of them. Rex busied himself with the tray. "Sedatives can do that to anyone, you know."

"Whatever you say, Momma Bear," he said with a smile. The smell of coffee made my stomach grumble. Rex turned with a mug and handed it to me.

"Thank you."

He set the tray on the bed near my knee. "Bagels. Turkey sammy with provolone. Some leftover macaroni salad from yesterday. That should hold you and your divinely morphing self a couple hours."

I set the coffee on the bedside table and picked up the sandwich. Ever since I began evolving, as Aaron put it, my metabolism had skyrocketed. My body was working overtime to readjust to the new DNA that had been introduced to my system. That introduction had saved my life, but it had also enabled me to call darkness over the city for the madman who'd engineered me. I'd done it to save Emma, and would do so again if need be, but would that I could find a way to fix things. *Would that you could fix a lot of things.*

When I glanced up, Rex and Emma were staring at me. Worry and sadness etched their faces. They knew about Hank. Of course they knew.

"He's not dead," I said, chewing.

But they didn't say anything, just stared at me. Tears sprung to my eyes. I set down the sandwich.

"Momma, please don't cry." Emma walked on her knees over the mattress to hug me. My arm slipped around her and I hugged her to my side, kissed the top of her head, and then drew in her familiar scent.

My exhale was rather shaky, but I proceeded on. "I'm sure the chief told you all about it . . . what they said about Hank. But he's not dead."

For a long moment, we just stared at each other. They loved Hank, too. Emma, certainly. Rex would in time. Right now he was having too much fun playing the protector. It wasn't so much that Rex thought I needed protecting, but more that he found it vastly entertaining to give "the siren" a hard time.

"So here's the way I see it," Rex broke the silence. "We have two choices. Accept the official government drivel, or give them the official Madigan salute."

"The official Madigan salute?" I was almost afraid to ask.

He rolled his eyes like I should be following (like it was ever easy to follow Rex's Crazy Train of thoughts). "Emma, dear one, close your eyes." She snorted, but did as he asked. Then he turned to me and said, "Let me introduce you to your new response to any and all comers who spew this particular party line." He made a grand gesture of lifting his hand, folding his fingers down, and popping up his middle finger. "Voilà."

"I know what you're doing," Em said dryly. "I *have* seen the middle finger before."

Rex gave her a gentle shove. "Already she's a juvenile delinquent. What are they teaching you at this school of yours?"

"A bunch of boring stuff," she muttered, falling back behind me, drawing in her knees, and crossing one leg over the other, so that her knee rested against my shoulder. Brim's nose lifted her hand in a bid to be rubbed.

Emma had gotten a partial scholarship to attend the League of Mages' school in Atlanta, a very private, very expensive school that taught gifted children, human and off-worlder, how to craft and best grow their powers. They also, to Emma's great dismay and my delight, were keen instructors of math, science, grammar, languages, and believed in laying a solid foundation to crafting long *before* students were able to actually craft.

"Since you were going into Fiallan anyway and Bryn and Miss Marti are already watching me for the week, I think you should stick to the plan. Still go."

Rex joined in. "The chief is still cool with giving you the week off to go to Fiallan if you want to. He wanted me to tell you that. Thinks you need closure, to see for yourself or you'll always have doubts.

And you already have the necessary paperwork to travel . . . Everything is still on, Charlie. Only question is, when are you leaving?"

A feeling of such relief and hope erupted inside of me. They weren't going to take anyone's word for it, either. They'd stand by me, by Hank, no matter what.

"Well?" Rex prompted.

My stomach was doing somersaults. Right. Okay. "Well, as soon as I get a shower and pack then," I heard myself say.

Rex slapped his hands on his knees and then stood. "Awesome. I picture you walking out the Circe's door with the siren thrown over your shoulder, giving your new salute as you go."

Emma laughed. "That'd be so cool. You totally have to do that."

"Yeah, I'm sure Hank would love to be thrown over my shoulder and rescued like a sack of potatoes."

"Oh, but that's the beauty of it," Rex said with longing. "He'd never live it down and I could spend *years* reminding him of it." He looked off into nothingness. "Good times. Good times."

I got off the bed. "You guys are nuts." But they believed in me. Believed in Hank. And I was fine living on the funny farm as long as I had them in my corner. I leaned down, grabbed my daughter's face, and kissed her on the forehead. "I love you. I'm taking a shower." I turned to walk away.

"Uh, hello? What about me? What the heck kind

of gratitude is that? Why don't I get kisses on my forehead and I love yous?"

"Aww, what's wrong, Wexie Poo?" Emma teased. "Are your whittle feel-wins hurt? I bet Brim will kiss you, won't you, Brim."

Rex's eyes narrowed. "Don't you *dare* tell that hound to kiss me."

I stopped by the bathroom door. That was the thing about my kid. She could communicate with the hellhound, and poor Rex was about to get slimed.

Rex stood on one side of the bed and Brim was on the other, attention fixed on Rex with perked-up ears and a drooling mouth. The look on my daughter's face was priceless. She *so* wanted to do it. Like she was on the edge and already falling.

Rex must've realized she was a goner. "You realize I will get you back for this evil," he told her.

Her grin was wide. "I know, but it'll be worth it," she said, right before pointing at Rex and commanding, "Smooch!"

Happy to oblige, Brim leapt onto my bed and off the other side, tackling Rex to the floor. He fell with a loud oomph and screamed like a girl, vowing revenge as Brim laid wet kisses on his face. I couldn't help but laugh. Em rolled on the bed, holding her stomach and yelling that she was going to pee her pants.

"Don't pee on my bed!" I said, laughing as she jumped off and called Brim after her, running for cover, thumping down the stairs and out the back door.

Rex moaned from the floor, arms flat out, panting, face screwed up and wet. "Call 911. Hurry. I'm not . . . gonna . . . make it. Tell my wife . . . I lov—" he gasped dramatically, lifted his hand to some unseen apparition, and then died a painful, glorious pretend death on my floor.

"Nuts," I muttered, shutting the bathroom door. "I live in a house full of nuts."

I hadn't thought beyond the shock of what the delegates claimed, beyond the denial, but with everything already taken care of and the path cleared for me to go into Elysia, the idea settled easily into place.

I hurried through the shower, dried off, wrapped a towel around me, and then brushed my teeth. When I was done rinsing and glanced into the mirror, I paused. The face staring back at me was weary and pale, a drawn shadow of what I used to be. I couldn't look at this face and not acknowledge the worry and the question I refused to allow anyone else to see. My eyes stared back at me with grief, broadcasting my greatest fear.

What if it was true? What if he's really gone?

No. I couldn't think like that. If I was going, I had to go strong and with purpose. With belief. Otherwise, I might as well have given up right then.

I squared my shoulders, giving myself a long, hard scowl, trying to make the determination brewing inside match the worried face that stared back. God, I looked so tired. And sad. *Acknowledge it and move on.*

Dwelling on the fear and grief wouldn't do me any good, I knew that.

I dipped my shoulder, turning in order to get a good look at my shoulder blade and the mark Hank had given to me during our fight in his apartment.

I'd given him the same arrow-shaped symbol with two slashes and a dot on his chest. The Throne Tree ink now embedded into my skin was used in ceremonial markings, bindings, and, once upon a time—and now highly illegal—death markings.

I hadn't had the mark all that long, about three or four weeks and—

Goose bumps erupted all over my arms and thighs. The mark.

Images seemed to emerge from the mirror. Me lying on the grass in Stone Mountain as my mark warmed and Hank knelt down beside me. Going down the steps into Underground and the mark warming even before I saw Hank stand from his seat on the fountain ledge.

I could find him. The mark connected us. I had my own built-in radar system right here, embedded into my skin. Before all this, I hadn't given it much thought. I hadn't needed to. Hank wasn't lost; he was in the grid. I'd known exactly where to go. But now that he was missing, the mark would be instrumental. If Hank was in the city, I'd find him.

All I had to do was get into Fiallan, tour every inch of the place if I had to, and see if the mark warmed. And when it did, the Circe and I would have a nice little chat from the end of my fist.

Feeling more hopeful than I had since the delegation invaded my office the day before, I hurried into my bedroom and found a pair of clean cargo pants and a black T-shirt. I gave my hair a quick blow-dry in front of the mirror; it had grown since being chopped off in the black crafting ritual that saved Aaron's life, and could now be worn in a ponytail that actually stayed—mostly. The bangs still slipped out of the band to curve around my chin. I'd have to dye it, I realized suddenly.

The game had changed. The sirens who had apprehended Hank behind Station One had seen me. Sure, they'd seen me covered in blood, grime, and the gray sand of Charbydon, and while I doubted any of them could pick me in a lineup, I didn't want to take any chances. I flicked the ends, remembering when Hank had done the same after it had been chopped, remembering the crooked grin he gave me when he did it. My throat grew thick. Determined to see that grin again, I looked away from the mirror and finished getting ready.

I jogged downstairs and asked Rex to run to the drugstore for a box of dye, while I pulled on my boots and then selected weapons from my own personal arsenal.

After Rex returned, Emma helped me bleach and then dye my dark reddish brown hair to a dirty blonde. "Why not a glamour spell?" she asked from behind me, working the dye into my hair as I sat on the vanity stool.

I watched her through the mirror. "Because the Circe are said to be very powerful. If they see through the glamour, they'll wonder who I am and why I'm trying to hide behind it."

Once my hair was done—and no one liked the new color; Brim even growled at me—I stood at the front door and hugged my kid tightly, kissed her several times on her forehead, breathed her into my lungs, and prayed for her safety and my safe return. I threw caution to the wind and kissed Rex on the cheek, gave Brim a ruffle on the head, and then left the house, reminding Em to eat well and do all of her homework.

4

I gazed out the window of the taxi as it entered Hartsfield-Jackson airport, a place that had once seen two million people pass through its terminals every year. Now those giant buildings were silent and dark, locked up along with all the hangars, offices, and other buildings until the day the darkness lifted and air travel safely resumed.

The darkness above had no effect on inter-dimensional travel, however, so the off-world terminals continued operating as usual. Atlanta was the city where genius scientist Titus Mott discovered the other dimensions of Elysia and Charbydon. The first official portal into those worlds had been built here at Hartsfield-Jackson. Other terminals eventually followed: New York, L.A., London, Paris . . . But ours remained the busiest and our

city housed one of the largest off-world popula-
tions around.

As the taxi swept along the curve of the road, the
terminal came into view. Made of glass and steel, it
shone brightly like a beacon rising from a world of
darkness.

Instead of entering through the security wing, I
had the taxi driver drop me off at Arrivals and entered through the main doors. My backpack was filled
with a couple changes of clothes, a shower bag, and
essentials. The small black duffel I carried over one
shoulder held backup clips for my Hefties, additional
rounds for my firearm, and capsules for my Nitro-gun
just in case I ran into any Charbydons—which wasn't
likely since only two Charbydons had ever set foot in
Elysia since the discovery of worlds. And those two
were delegates of the Federation. But, it never hurt
to be prepared . . .

My actual weapons were secured on my person.
9mm on my hip. The Nitro-gun snug against my
right rib cage. The Hefty tucked against my left. I
was right-handed, and depending on what perp I was
going after, I liked to keep the most effective weapon
on my left, so I could grab it easily with my right
hand. The Hefty was extremely effective at subduing
Elysians. The High Frequency Tag emitted a sound
wave capable of dropping most any from that world.
The Adonai, however, proved a little harder to de-
tain, but still we managed.

Game face on, armed to the maximum allowance

by law for an officer engaged in inter-dimensional travel, I strode through the automatic doors and into the terminal.

The center of the long rectangular terminal where I entered was the hub of activity. There was seating, a few kiosks selling books and maps, a café, coffee shop, and bakery . . . The center area was pretty much neutral, designed to be comfortable to beings of all three worlds. But walk left or right and things began to change. To the right was the Charbydon ticket counter and checkpoint for those traveling to the city of Telmath, the capital city of Charbydon. There was seating and a few more kiosks run by goblins and then the final security checkpoint before the giant blue sphere glowing at the end of the terminal.

Been there, done that. I swung a left and headed toward the glowing sphere that occupied the other end of the terminal—a two-story sphere lit with swirling pinks and oranges.

Every world, every planet, had its own unique frequency, a natural emission of electromagnetic sound waves. Its own "music." Titus Mott's harmonic resonance generator had accidentally dialed into the unique frequency of Elysia, creating a portal into a world that had inspired our myths and ideas of heavenly paradise, a world where the beings within could no longer hide, no longer deny they'd been visiting us for eons, meddling, and inspiring myths of gods, angels, faeries, and other paranormal creatures. The discovery of "hell" or Charbydon as it was called,

wasn't far behind and we were to learn the same—
the nobles, jinn, ghouls, darkling fae; they were the
beings behind the legends and fears of demons, mon-
sters, and dark gods.

And though it wasn't the biblical Revelation,
the term had stuck. Fourteen years ago, the world
changed. Laws and policies were put into place, and
the Federation of Worlds was created along with the
Integration Task Force, ITF, which policed and moni-
tored the influx of new beings into our society.

Now there were terminals in several major world
cities. But unlike air travel where you could leave from
one place and arrive in most any chosen location, the
spheres were only connected to one location apiece.
Atlanta's Charbydon gate only took you to Telmath.
The Elysian gate only opened to the Adonai's capital
city of Ithonia. Yet another reason Atlanta was the
hub for off-world travel and immigrants—we had the
only two spheres that lead to both off-world capital
cities.

Unfortunately, this meant I wouldn't be arriving
directly into Fiallan. I had to go to Ithonia first and
then contact a Magnus-level mage to whisk me to my
final destination. And they didn't come cheap, either.

Since I already had my government travel arrangements, I bypassed the ticket counter and headed
straight for the main gate guarded by a gate agent,
a highly trained security expert with loaded weapons beneath his desk and a license to take down any
threat.

The terminal in Ithonia had been created with much reluctance on the Adonai's part. They considered their city and land pristine. They thought any influx of off-worlders would pollute the beauty and sanctity of their world. Never mind that they'd been coming to our world since the dawn of civilization, using Earth as a battleground in their war with the nobles.

Travel to Ithonia was limited by visa and stays longer than a week required special permission. Ridiculous given that terms were different should any Adonai want to come to Earth.

The Adonai took entrance into their city very seriously, so I wasn't surprised to find the agent was an Adonai, a tall, blond-haired, undeniably beautiful male. Easy to see why they'd been called gods and angels by early mankind. And it probably killed him every time he had to allow a human to pass through the gate.

"ID and papers," he said, holding out an expectant hand.

I gave him my travel papers and then set my ID on his desk. His brow rose at what he read, and then he took a moment to compare the face on the photo to mine, the hair color having thrown him off. He set the paper and ID down and pierced me with an unimpressed, arrogant look that instantly got under my skin. I returned his lovely welcome with a smile that dripped smart-ass.

He slid my information back to me. "Bags on the counter."

I rolled my eyes. "Really?" My credentials and permits were in order. He didn't have to search my stuff, but in the end it was the prerogative of the gate agent, and not something I could or would argue about. Even so, it annoyed me because I knew he wasn't holding me up due to any threat or suspicion I posed, but because he apparently got off on being a jerk.

With a martyred sigh, I lugged my duffel onto his desk followed by my backpack. "Enjoy yourself. The underwear is near the bottom." I turned, intending to plop myself dramatically onto one of the seats against the opposite wall.

I froze midstride.

It took several seconds to wrap my brain around the sight of the veiled person sitting there, radiating power without even trying. Her hands moved with speed and grace, bright red nails flashing.

I stepped closer to the oracle. "Alessandra. Are you . . . knitting?"

Her hands stilled and her chin lifted a notch. The veil dropped back slightly, revealing more of her features than I'd ever seen in the smoky haze and dark lighting of her theater where she held court like the Queen of Underground, dispensing riddles and prophecies at a hefty price.

Alessandra and I weren't friends. In fact, she seemed to take great pleasure in making things as difficult as possible whenever I procured her services—which I always thought a huge waste of time since she made the department pay dearly and then never gave us much but cryptic answers and sarcasm. The one time I'd used her prophetic services for personal reasons, to find out if my sister Bryn was possessed, she'd been little help.

The oracle was actually quite pretty, her coloring—otherworldly mossy green eyes, deep red lips, and curly raven hair—vivid against pale skin. Of course, this was Sandra, so her expression was the usual sly amusement and the monumental smugness that came from two thousand years of being a world-renowned know-it-all.

"Yes, I'm knitting, blondie. It calms my mind," she said, setting the blob of fuzzy pink and white yarn into an open bag next to her. "Sit down, Charlie."

I glanced over my shoulder. The agent was setting all my clips on the counter. If he decided to count every one, we'd be here forever.

"Going on a little excursion?" I asked, taking a seat. "Family visit?"

Her smile hiked at the corners as she angled in her seat to face me, her veil dropping in a slow fall of fabric to her shoulders. "Trying to discover my background, are we?"

I shrugged, glaring at the gate agent. "Thought I'd give it a try." He began to dig through my shower bag. "So what's with all the secrecy, anyway?"

"Not secrecy. There are those who have been around since my emergence. My past is not hidden. But it is mine. Mine to share if I choose."

The Adonai jerkwad held up my bra with two fingers like it was radioactive. I crossed my arms over my chest as my cheeks grew warm. "Is that really necessary?" I griped loudly, but he simply ignored me. "There's a blue one, too."

I wanted to sink my fist into the superior expression he gave me. My teeth clenched.

Sandra tsked. "You always rise to the bait, Charlie. You're so predictable."

I snorted. "Everything is predictable to you." Others would say I was the opposite—they never knew what I'd do next.

"Not everything."

It was something in her voice, a resignation, a worry, that got my attention. Her eyes swam with something I'd never seen from her before. Fear, I realized. And then it was gone. Before I could digest that, her next words completely bowled me over. "I'm not visiting anyone in Ithonia, Charlie. I am here to escort you into Fiallan to find your siren."

I blinked, frowned, then frowned some more . . . And then I scanned the terminal for a hidden camera because the Oracle of All Oracles showing up here, to help me—me of all people, who made it a point to give Alessandra as good as she gave—was just a little too bizarre to comprehend.

She stared with one eyebrow cocked as I grappled. Finally I found my voice, but she cut me off. "I know what you're going to say, of course. And I don't need to be an oracle to know that much. I'm going with you. I don't like it. But I'm going. So you might as well get over it." She glanced at the gate agent and gathered her things. "He's done. You ready?"

Then a thought occurred to me and I hurried after her. "Wait. Are you saying Hank is alive?"

"Oracle," the agent greeted her, making a respectful bow. She nodded serenely and took the small disposable earplugs he offered her. "Please proceed through the sphere without stopping. May your journey be safe and prosperous."

Alessandra was honored; I would never be, even though I was law enforcement, even though I put my ass on the line for the beings of all three worlds.

Prosperous, my ass.

The gate agent tossed a pair of earplugs onto the counter. I grabbed the small plastic bag and returned his glare before catching up to Sandra. "Damn it, Sandra, wait."

She finally stopped at the steps, her head tilting up as she stared at the sphere hovering less than an inch above the copper alloy platform. It dwarfed her, making her look so small, like a child. The giant ball of pink and orange energy swirled and changed like a shifting sea of colors, and the drone coming from it pulsed through my entire body. As awe-inspiring as it was, it didn't hold my attention long.

"Did you see him? Did you see Hank in one of your visions? Sandra." I grabbed her arm, tugging it so she'd look at me. "Do you know where he is? Just tell me; I can move quicker by myself and—"

"No, Charlie, I must go. And as for your siren . . . I don't know."

"You know everything. What do you mean, you don't know?"

There was that look again, the flash of fear, and it made me cold. "I can't see the future. Yours. Hank's." Tears pricked her eyes. "I can't see any of it." Alessandra fled up the steps and disappeared into the sphere.

I picked my jaw off the floor, inserted the earplugs, grabbed my stuff, and hurried after her.

5

I'd passed through a sphere before. I knew to keep walking. I knew not to stop. But Sandra's bombshell left me completely off-kilter and I forgot to prepare myself. The portal's intense energy field hit me like a sledgehammer. I stumbled to a stop.

You're not supposed to stop.

The ends of my hair lifted and the fine hairs on my skin stood straight. The earplugs prevented my eardrums from bursting, but it did nothing to ease the heartbeatlike drone of thick energy pulsating through every molecule of my being, so strong and overwhelming that my teeth clinked together in time.

Keep walking.

Disorientation crept in. I tried to move, to put one foot in front of the other, but I felt so sluggish. The drone encompassed all until it seemed as though I'd become a part of it, part of the energy, part of—

Warm fingers wrapped tightly around my wrist and yanked me forward so hard that my neck snapped back.

The next thing I knew I was tumbling down the steps, coming to a stop flat on my back, blinking up at a high marble ceiling where fuzzy marble sea creatures stretched out and then snapped into sharp focus.

I had arrived. And in style no less.

Deep muttering curses filtered into the ear where the plug had come partway out. I groaned and pulled them both from my ears as my gut rolled sickly.

"Of all the stupid . . . Human. I should've known."

A face moved into my line of sight. A highly annoyed Adonai glared down at me. "I should let you wallow in IDT sickness." But he placed his palm over my forehead and muttered some disgruntled words. Heat spread over my skin. The fuzz began to clear from my mind and the intense nausea in my gut eased.

Most humans experienced a minor level of Inter-Dimensional Travel Sickness, but prolonged exposure in the spheres or taking an illegal form of travel was like having a hangover while still drunk.

A small crowd had formed. Alessandra peered over the agent's shoulder with an expression of relief, amusement, and contrition. The gate agent ran his fingers through his hair and let out a heavy sigh, then looked up at the crowd. "And that is why we tell you not to stop in the portal. Never stop in the portal. Ever."

With that lesson delivered, he stood, reached inside of my jacket to get my ID and papers, and then went back to his desk.

Alessandra offered me a slim hand. "Really, Charlie, I thought you knew better."

"I did. Next time save the bombshells for after we jump worlds." I slid my hand into hers and got to my feet, my bags sliding off my shoulders to remain on the floor. "Ugh. Dizzy."

"Nasty things, those gates." Sandra patted me awkwardly on the shoulder. "I remember the old way of travel," she said wistfully.

"The old way?"

"Preparation, ritual, communing with primal gods, becoming one with nature . . ."

"Stop, you're making me want to hug a tree."

"Ha ha. The dizziness will go away in a minute. You're lucky you escaped."

I didn't say anything as I dragged my bags to the agent's desk and hefted them onto the counter. He refolded my papers and slid them to the edge. "You're lucky to escape."

"So I hear." I shoved my papers back inside of my jacket. The thing was, I did know better and it embarrassed me to the point that my cheeks got hot. I drew in a deep breath and looked at him. "Thank you."

He stared at me for a long moment and then nodded. "Just doing my job."

"Not something you have to do very often, I'm sure."

He shrugged. "A few times a month, but if it makes you feel any better, never had a repeat from those who've gotten . . . stuck."

"Yeah, definitely a lesson one never forgets."

After he completed a cursory inspection of my bags, he handed my ID back and set me on my way. "Stay out of trouble."

I let out a soft laugh. "Would be a first." Trouble and I had a way of finding each other.

His lips twitched. He shook his head as a couple came through the sphere and his attention went back to work.

"You need to sit for a minute?" Sandra asked as I caught up with her.

"No, I'm fine. Let's go." I glanced back at the Adonai. He wasn't so bad. Definitely not a jerk like the other one. Maybe people were just in a better mood on this side of the gate, being in paradise and all.

Sandra followed my gaze and my train of thought apparently. "They're still full of themselves," she said as we continued on, walking past high marble columns that lined each side of the terminal. "The Adonai's arrogance is somewhat justifiable, I suppose. They are, after all, the most powerful race in Elysia."

"Yes, but there are others . . . just as powerful or more so."

"True. But as a group, as a whole, they are stronger, more organized and disciplined. Their power shows in every facet of their existence. Once we clear those doors, you'll see what I mean."

She swept ahead of me toward a shaft of golden light that spilled through two-story-tall double doors, which were held open by two giant statues of armored warriors.

It was like walking toward the gates of Saint Peter. My pulse picked up. What existed outside of those doors was the model for heaven. *Heaven.*

I wasn't deeply religious, but I did believe there existed a higher power—undefined and beyond our understanding. I was well aware the land beyond the golden light wasn't a place of eternal rest, a place where souls found peace and reward. I knew all that, but it didn't stop me from experiencing a profound sense of wonder as we drew closer to the wide shaft of light.

People passed in and out of the light, not even noting the beauty of it. And when I did the same, when I passed through that golden light, I came out onto a scene that took my breath away.

My first view of Ithonia was framed by massive white columns, part of a long colonnade stretching to the left and right. I moved to the marble railing built between each column and stood there taking it all in. From our higher vantage point, the city of Ithonia sprawled out in a gentle slope below us. In the distance, far beyond the city, a sun hovered just above green mountains. The white marble walls, streets, and buildings glowed.

I thought of Emma and Rex, of Bryn and my

parents—if only they could see what I was seeing. I thought of Will and wondered if the Afterlife was as beautiful as this, and I prayed that it was.

"Ithonia." Admiration filled Alessandra's soft whisper.

"I never thought I'd see this. Never thought it'd live up to the hype, to the picture I had in my mind, but it does." *A hundred times over, it does.*

"For once, we are in agreement," she said with a genuine smile. "Many of the ancient civilizations around the Mediterranean—the Minoans, the ancient Greeks, the Etruscans—were influenced mostly by the Adonai and sirens who visited your world in ancient times. The architecture here will seem familiar to you because of this."

For so long the mystery existed of how early humans jumped so quickly from being hunter gatherers to building monumental cities with cultures rich in art, religion, writing . . . For so long historians wondered about gods, Star People, the Annunaki, fallen angels; those ancient myths of beings who arrived from another world to teach mankind. Those beings turned out to be the Elysians and Charbydons. The nobles had inspired the Mesopotamians and early Central Americans. The nymphs and fae inspired much of the Celtic pantheon, and so on . . .

It made one wonder what mankind would have been like had they *not* come.

"This was the model for the mythical Mount Olympus, the Elysian Fields, heaven . . ." Sandra added.

I dragged my gaze away from the splendor of Ithonia and stared at the oracle. She was smaller than me by almost a head, but her presence well made up for her size. Granted, I didn't know much about her personally, and she liked it that way, but I did know the oracle never did anything without a price.

"Why are you here, Sandra? So you can't see my future or Hank's; it doesn't explain why you felt the need to come."

"I told you already." She moved back from the view and began walking down the long colonnade, so tall and colossal it made us look like ants. "The mages' league isn't far from here. We should head straight to Fiallan. We'll be detained outside of the inner walls until we're cleared for admittance, so we might as well wait there instead of wasting time here."

"No, you didn't tell me already. Not really." Her steps had gone swifter, until I was almost jogging to keep up. "Sandra. Slow down." And still she went. "Will you just stop for a minute?"

Several passersby stopped—at least they listened—appalled by my raised voice. Guess that didn't happen too much in paradise. But Sandra had stopped, too, so I ignored the curious looks thrown our way and edged us over to one of the columns, lowering my voice. "My partner is missing, dead if you want to believe the Circe, and right now he's probably wishing he was. This isn't a game or an adventure or whatever it is to you . . . and you can't keep running away from giving me a straight answer.

There's too much at stake not to know your intentions. I won't be going in blind like this."

Frustration ballooned inside of me. Alessandra was two thousand years old. Did she even appreciate how precious time was for those of us whose life span was so small? Did she understand loyalty and love and family? Before we went further, I had to know her objective.

I heard whispers from people who passed by us. *Oracle. The oracle.* Clearly she was known here. Clearly from the tone, she was revered here.

Sandra pulled me deeper into the shadow of the column, her eyes glowing brighter than before. Ah. There it was. That Pissed Off Green I knew so well. "Okay. Fine. Here's the truth. The only time I'm not able to see another's future is when their fate is intertwined with mine in a significant way." She let that sink in. "Our fates have collided. Mine, yours, Hank's. I'm here because I must play whatever part Fate has laid out for me. That is the law of the oracle. And as much as I'd rather be back in my temple knitting a sweater for my python, I cannot break Fate's Decree, trust me on that." Her voice broke for the briefest of seconds. Then, she squared her shoulders. "Fate requires me to come and face my destiny and so that is what I must do. And, for the record, I'm not enjoying this any more than you."

"So what if you refused to play your part, what then?"

"That never works, Charlie. Trust me. I'm old

enough to know and let's just leave it at that. I cannot escape my destiny. Neither can you." She glared at me, daring me to challenge her.

And then it hit me. "You tried once before, didn't you?"

"What?"

"To not follow this decree. You tried and failed. I can see it in your eyes."

Her expression went stony, and her hands curled into fists. Then, she seemed to regain some control because her eyes went narrow and shrewd. "You are the most irritating human I have ever known. And let me put that into perspective for you: I'm two thousand years old."

Yeah, a two-thousand-year-old know-it-all, I wanted to say back.

She swept around me, proceeded to the end of the colonnade, and then went swiftly down the wide marble steps.

"Well, that's quite an achievement," I mumbled, feeling a little offended. "Maybe I should add that to my resume."

We went the rest of the way through the city in silence, which was fine by me. It was all very Utopian. Wide, clean streets. No machines or pollution. Gorgeous architecture that surpassed the great temples of ancient Greece and Rome. Only these buildings weren't in ruins; they were majestic and pristine.

Don't let the landscape fool you.

This place was a paradise, no doubt, but I was well

aware that evil existed here just as good existed in the hellish realm of Charbydon. Looks were deceiving and I knew better than to be influenced by my surroundings.

"This is it," Sandra said, veering across a wide square to a massive templelike building that took up one side of the entire square. "Your mage should be here."

We jogged up the steps. The doors were open like they were back at the terminal—the weather here was always beautiful—and while the mage's headquarters held priceless artifacts, books, and powers beyond belief, no need for a lock; the Elders here had other measures in place to secure their treasures.

Inside was a long main gallery, both sides lined with statues of mages holding staffs, books, orbs, and other arcane devices. The tall columns that supported the roof and lined the gallery were black as were the walls. Arched doorways led into rooms off the gallery, but it was the marble floor that commanded my attention and awe. It spread out like a perfect photograph of the night sky, like someone had stretched the universe flat and laid it on the ground, twinkling stars and all. The lofty ceiling was a mirror image of the floor.

Low voices, the soft swish of robes, and echoes filled the place, but it was all tempered by the space, a space designed to make one feel small and yet part of something greater, part of the cosmos, and open to the mysteries that lay within. Sandra, in her veil and robes, with those strange eyes, fit right in.

The delegates had been here, had employed the services of the mages who knew how to manipulate matter and energy, to take a person from one place to the next in the blink of an eye. For a hefty price, of course. There might be portals from one *world* to another, but there were no portals that linked cities within worlds. You traveled the old-fashioned way— by foot, by horse, by flight, by crafting, or you hired a mage.

I pulled out the itinerary Sian had originally pre-pared for me and Titus, using the same travel tem-plate the delegates had used, and proceeded toward the appointed room.

We were stopped several times by mages who recognized Sandra and greeted her with a reverence I knew she adored. And every time we moved on, she gave me a superior smirk, making me wonder which she loved more, the attention or getting on my nerves. "I'm surprised they aren't asking for your au-tograph," I said after the last admirer left us.

"Elysians might be godlike, but one gift they do not possess is divination. They have come to me for ages to get a peek at the future, and they've paid in riches you cannot even imagine in your paltry human mind."

"Which," I pointed out, "makes one wonder why you set up shop in Underground Atlanta of all places. Why not buy a small country and live like a queen?"

"Well, that particular information would cost you, now wouldn't it?"

"Do you do anything without a price, Sandra?"

"I'm doing it right now."

We passed libraries, apothecaries, classrooms, and with all the interruptions, I was pretty sure we missed our destination. I scanned the paper. "I think we were supposed to stop at the room we just passed . . ."

Sandra stopped suddenly and held out her hand.

"What?"

"Your itinerary. Give it to me."

I gave it over, pointing at the paper. "That's what it says for travel, it's the ninth door down on the right. That's also where they sell the *grimwyrd* I'll need to . . ." She tore the paper and threw the pieces into the air. They floated down to the polished floor. "What are you doing?"

"Forget about the schedule, and the *grimwyrd*. You really want to shove a needle in your arm every day you're in Fiallan? You're traveling in style now. Watch and see what being celebrated three worlds over gets you. Perhaps then you will develop some respect for your elders."

I gave her an unimpressed look. "Doubtful."

Her lips quirked into a faint smile. "I knew you'd say that."

She continued on as I glanced around, expecting someone to appear and give us hell about littering on the amazing floor. But the paper stirred as though a breeze had come, though none had, and fire ate up the paper in a soft whoosh until it ceased to exist—ashes and all. Just like that.

A self-cleaning floor. God, these mages are brilliant.

I caught up to Sandra, wondering if my crafting sister knew how to make a floor clean itself, and wondering how the hell to get around the human/siren issue if not a daily injection of *grimwyrd*.

"Okay, so if not *grimwyrd* then what exactly? It's what the human delegates used. It's what every human going into siren territory uses."

"You'll see," was all the answer Sandra deigned to give.

On Earth, sirens were required by law to wear voice-mods to subdue their natural lure and insanely potent voices. Sirens gladly wore the device since the idea of being followed around by a bunch of drooling men, women, children, and some animals was not exactly their idea of a good time. But here, things were different. This was *their* world where humans were a very small minority. It was up to the human traveler to protect themselves.

Because of my otherworldly genes, I was developing a partial immunity to the natural siren lure, but I didn't want to chance it. I needed my wits about me, and *grimwyrd* was the only thing that blocked the lure.

The gallery dead-ended at a tall arched doorway. The hallway split, going left and right. Before we came to the intersection, the massive doors opened and three mages swept toward us. The two on the left and right were male, fit, with strawberry blond hair and dark, intelligent-looking eyes. Brothers,

maybe even twins. They both wore the long forest green robes that signified their level as Magnus,
which put them at a couple hundred years old even
though they looked to be in their mid-thirties. The
only level above Magnus was Elder, and the Magni
had a couple hundred years *more* of study and training to reach that distinction, if ever. The woman who
stepped from the middle with her hands reached out
to Sandra's in greeting, however, already had. She was
an Elder.

Whatever she said to Sandra was lost on me because she spoke in the common tongue of Elysia, but
it gave me time to study the newcomer. The woman
had a kind face, hair on the blonder side of strawberry that had gone white at the temples pulled back
into a high bun. Her robe was white, without a single
embellishment. She was nearly as tall as me, and attractive with high cheekbones and proud nose.

"Forgive me," she said, turning in my direction.
"Sometimes I forget not everyone can understand our
language. I'm Edainnué Lightwater."

I held out my hand. "Charlie Madigan."

Her smile grew wider, and she seemed so pleased.
"Oh, I know. I know who you are, dear." She introduced her nephews, Brell and Trahern Lightwater,
and then invited us into her private study beyond the
massive doors.

"I can't tell you how delighted I am to see you,
oracle. It has been too long, much too long. And to
come with this one! A surprise to be sure. Tell me,

Charlie Madigan," she said as she sat down behind a low marble desk, "how do you feel?"

I was halfway down to one of the chairs opposite the desk when the odd question made me pause for a second. "I'm fine. How is it you know me exactly?"

"Hard not to know the person who called primordial darkness from one world to another." She leaned against the high back of her chair and steepled her fingers under her chin, her shrewd bright blue eyes intent and curious. "It's quite a feat, what you did. Some claimed impossible until you proved them wrong."

I thought of Emma; I'd move mountains for her if I could. I ended up moving darkness. "It could've been anyone," I said. "I just happened to be in the right place at the right time."

"Dead, I hear, when you were given gifts of the noble and Adonai. Not what I would call the right time, eh?"

As nice as Edainnué Lightwater seemed, I hadn't come to Ithonia to be interviewed or to chat about all the things that had happened to me. I'd come for my partner. "I survived. I see that as being in the right."

Lightwater laughed and said to Sandra, "She does have spirit, you're right."

Sandra leaned over the arm of her chair toward me. "Just so you know, *spirited* is not the word I used to describe you."

This made Lightwater laugh again, and my impatience rose. "I don't mean to be rude, Ms. Lightwater, but—"

"Right, right. Fiallan, I know. Reclusive, the sirens of Fiallan, even from their own kind. Quite cut off from the rest of the world. Though, they choose to be that way. I will have Trahern and Brell take you both, but first you will need a few things for your journey and I would beg an audience with the oracle in return."

"Accepted," Sandra said, not giving me a chance to speak.

My cheeks grew warm and I squeezed my fists tightly. How long was an audience? Hank could be in trouble, hurt, dying for all we knew and they wanted to hang out and chat about the future?

"Charlie." Sandra's voice pulled me out of my internal tirade. Lightwater was eyeing me with interest, and her nephews stared at me with concern. "Your hand."

I glanced down and saw the symbols on my right fist were beginning to glow. Shit. I pulled my hand back into the sleeve of my jacket and drew in a steadying breath. "It . . . does that sometimes," I tried to explain, but it just sounded lame. "It's just that . . . time is crucial, and I have to get to Fiallan as soon as possible."

"You have the right of it, to want to move quickly. I understand. Your delegates came through a few days ago, and I believe they were attempting to free a siren who was wrongly accused, though the specifics were not told to me." Lightwater studied me with ancient eyes, wise and knowing. "You will need a few things, of course."

She stood, pushed her chair aside, and then bent to root in the large cabinet behind her. "First," she said over her shoulder, "a cloak of the apprentice, and then . . . ah, there it is." Lightwater gathered her finds and came around her massive desk, setting them on the corner. "Here, put this on." She handed me a dark blue robe. "Fiallan doesn't get many foreigners, but the occasional human student of the arcane isn't unheard of."

I stood and took the robe, grateful and suspicious at the same time. There was no reason for her to help me. True, the Adonai had no love for the sirens of Fiallan—even sirens from other cities had no care for their brothers and sisters—but to offer all this. Was it because of Sandra or some other reason?

"And this." Lightwater presented an amulet.

I took it and examined the tear-shaped milky blue stone etched with a spiral of symbols from top to bottom. "What is it?"

"You're about to enter the land of the sirens, Charlie. They wear no voice-mods like they must in the human world. You might be changing, evolving into a being capable of withstanding their voices like we do, but you're not there yet, so let's just play it safe and wear this at all times." Ah, so here was the Elder's version of *grimwyrd*.

"Wouldn't want you drooling after every siren who crosses our path," Sandra quipped.

I shot her a hard glare. "I'd *planned* to buy some *grimwyrd*."

Lightwater only chuckled. "Two spirited ones, I'd say. And this is for language." The Elder came at me with her pointer finger.

Instinctively, I stepped back. "What are you doing?"

"She's making it so you can understand and converse in all languages," Sandra said with a sigh. "Really, Charlie, try to keep up. It's a simple syndialexi spell. Relax. Travelers do it all the time."

Lightwater gave me a motherly smile. "It won't hurt a bit." Her pointer finger pressed against my temple as she muttered words unknown to me. Warmth radiated from her touch and spread through my skin. Gentle and un-intrusive and then it was gone almost as soon as it began.

"There. Now you may talk and understand."

She was close to me, so close I could smell lavender and sage on her skin. "Why are you helping me?"

Lightwater leaned her hip on the edge of the desk and folded her hands in front of her. "Because I want something in return."

Ah, there it is.

"After you have obtained your goal, set things to right, and have had time to recuperate from your journey, I would ask you to return here to Ithonia and grant me two days." My eyes narrowed. "To study you. To learn. I will have you answer any question posed to you and demonstrate your gifts to the best of your ability."

The cloak I could've gotten. The *grimwyrd* I

could've gotten in place of the amulet. The mages to take me into Fiallan, could've gotten that, too. The language spell was helpful, but travelers also employed translators. So, Lightwater really hadn't offered me anything I couldn't have gotten myself.

"You give me two days, Charlie Madigan, and I will grant you one marker in return."

"A marker," I repeated.

"A promise. One. To put all my power, all the knowledge at my disposal, to completing one task, solving one dilemma, or granting a desire you ask. To the best of my ability and as long as it harms none, of course."

Sandra let out a low whistle. "Never offered me a marker."

Lightwater turned a kind eye to Alessandra. "There is nothing I can offer the oracle that she does not already have. And that which she does not have and desires is unobtainable. This you know."

Sandra huffed as I slipped the amulet over my head, deciding to accept the offer. "I accept your terms, as long as the two days I'm here harms none as well."

The Elder flashed a grin. "Of course. The deal has been struck." She moved back to her seat. "Trahern and Brell will take you now."

Sandra stood, said her good-byes to the Elder, and then faced me. "Ready?"

Trahern stepped next to me and curved his hand around my elbow as Brell did the same to Sandra. And then they vanished. I had a half second to see them blink out before the ground dropped out from under me.

I'd traveled this way before courtesy of Aaron, so I knew what to expect, but it sure as hell didn't stop that brief flash of panic as my body dispersed into energy and then re-formed moments later in a new place, feeling about a hundred pounds heavier.

Yep, I thought. The sensation of going from weightless to weight? Still hated it.

6

He'd always thought going back into the grid would be a fate worse than death.

He was wrong.

Leave it to those fucking old hags to come up with something worse.

His laugh turned to coughs. He lifted his head a fraction to relieve the hard bite of the stone floor against his cheekbones and the side of his skull. He was naked and cold, chained facedown on the floor, arms straight out, held there by manacles on his wrists, neck, and ankles.

They wouldn't let him die. And every time he did, every time his body gave out and his soul departed, their vicious spell would lasso it back, drag it back into his broken body. To endure. He'd seen the fucking light so many times it was making him mad, those glimpses of peace, the feeling it gave him, the brief absence of pain.

There was pure, soft, welcoming light. And then it would begin to dim, growing smaller and smaller and smaller, until he was surrounded in darkness and screaming to go back. This was a dark, despicable magic; one of the most heinous of spells, tethering a soul to a dying or dead body.

Returning to his broken body was a torture the like of which he couldn't comprehend. The shock of it, the utter contrast between peace and pain . . . It was a sensation worse than the grid, worse than the whippings. It was a horror so unique that it fucked with his mind.

He was losing his hold on reality. He craved his own demise. They were turning him into a madman. His lust for death was only overshadowed by his hunger to kill the Circe, to exact the cruelest, most prolonged, most vulgar kind of end imaginable.

Over time, as he lay there, his pathetic body would actually try to heal, to knit some of his wounds back together. To give the whip master something else to tear back down. But nothing could repair his psyche, his mind, his tired soul. There was no healing for that. The sane part of him knew it and no longer cared.

As he went in and out of consciousness, visions of a former life flashed through his mind, of the forest of Gorsedd and the sidhé fae hermit who taught him, of a life that meant something, of a smiling child with big brown eyes, of a woman so fierce and loyal and beautiful that she took his breath away. He'd tried to hold on to those images, tried not to miss a single detail that played through his weary mind.

But they were all disjointed and random. All part of

a shattered life, one that he'd been stupid, idiotic to believe could ever be his.

The most painful, intense regret filled him in the lucid moments after those flashes. It burned through him, searing his chest, his heart, his throat. And sometimes it burned so raw and fierce that he couldn't hold it in and he dug his fingernails into the stone and roared in pain and rage.

He was no longer siren. He was animal. A crazed thing to be toyed with and tortured and lost. An animal that would ravage its keepers as soon as the slightest opportunity arose. Kill or be killed.

He laughed again, the sound ragged and thin. He laughed at that because he had *been killed. Over and over and over again.*

Red washed across his cloudy vision, and he could almost smell the iron tang, and feel its heat and thickness. Red, all of it red in Circe blood and Malakim vengeance.

The highly unpleasant sensation of losing all physical sense and then becoming whole again paled in comparison to opening my eyes and knowing I was there. In Fiallan. In Hank's city. So close. *I'm here, Hank.* I squeezed my eyelids closed and forced down the emotion. I was here, and I was damned well going to succeed.

Trahern's hand fell from my elbow. He stepped back, bowed to me, and then blinked out. Behind him stood Sandra; Brell was already gone.

We stood on a large platform, a wall rising behind

us and a market spread out in front of us. I could smell the sea and, beyond the murmur of many voices and activity, I thought I heard it, too. The aroma of fresh bread and seafood mingled with the salty air and the faint scent of the stones warmed by the sun. I tipped my head to the sky and let it bathe my skin in warmth. It was easy, after a while, to get used to the darkness back home. The only times I acknowledged how much I missed the light were times like these.

Sandra stepped off the block. I followed her, walking backward to get a good look at the wall. It was two stories tall, broken by an arched gate manned by guards. Through this break, I'd guess the wall was at least fifteen feet thick. There were two towers far in each direction. The Malakim towers. I'd envisioned them looking more medieval, but they were actually obelisk in shape, made of smooth cream-colored stone, and rising at least five stories high. The remaining two towers weren't visible from my standpoint, and I saw no rings of power, no visible force field of any kind.

I let out a disbelieving breath and turned around in a circle. I was in Fiallan, the inner wall in front of me and the outer wall—which was built after the city had expanded its old boundaries—far behind us. Both walls were shaped like a horseshoe, enclosing the city to all but the sea.

I knew from my earlier preparations to go into the city that a request had to be made at the gate in order to enter the old city. As I took in my fill of the large market, the gate, and the four streets that fanned off of this central area, I noticed Sandra straightening her veil, lifting her chin, and gliding toward the main gate. *Request in progress.*

I stayed back, allowing her to do her thing, knowing she'd accomplish the task with ease. And that was fine by me. The less notice I gained the better.

I turned away from the gate where Sandra held court and scanned the large marketplace and the crowd, gauging the mood, the threat level, and just letting myself become accustomed to the environment. What I knew of the Circe conflicted with the energetic, happy mood of the place. But then there were few who knew of the lies and heinous practice going on around them.

Eventually, I felt Sandra's presence. "Now we wait." And then she breezed past me.

There were mostly sirens, but some nymphs, a few imps and fae, and one or two humans in the market. Vines and flowers bloomed from railings and over pergolas, creating shaded spots under which tables and chairs had been placed. Streets fanned out from the market, lined with whitewashed buildings no higher than three stories. Brightly painted pottery decorated corners of buildings and doorways, filled with flowers, plants, and seashells.

It was all strangely . . . idyllic, completely at odds with the darkness I'd attributed to this place.

I lost Sandra, but found her again as she neared the building on the corner. It had a bright blue door, whitewashed stone walls, and flowering vines attached to one corner. Her head turned; the flash of her eyes in the shadow of her veil found me and waved me over. I caught the door before it closed, stepping inside behind her.

I'd heard for the normal traveler, it could take a day or more to get approval, but government officials and celebrities like the oracle—it might only take an hour or two.

After Sandra spoke to the innkeeper, we were led to a private room with a window that overlooked the market. As soon as we entered the bright room, Sandra shrugged off her veil and sank into one of the couches. The window was open, one side framed in blooms that crawled up the outside of the building.

I let my bags slide off my shoulders and stared out at the market scene, itching to do something, itching for a fight, honestly. To do what I knew best. I was out of my element, in another dimension that looked like some Mediterranean paradise while all I wanted to do was bust some heads, exact some revenge, and get my partner the hell out of there.

I let out a loud exhale.

"Nothing like Charbydon, is it?" Sandra asked.

I glanced over my shoulder. "No. Nothing like." I turned back to the scene outside. "It's beautiful here." Which pissed me off; it shouldn't *be* beautiful. It didn't seem right, not when children had died to protect this place. "Have you seen the city, Sandra, in your visions?"

When she didn't answer, I moved away from the window. She was watching me, her expression blank. I stopped by the arm of the empty couch across from hers. "Have you?"

I waited, wondering if I'd be able to detect a lie if she told one. Alessandra was a lot of things. Greedy. Haughty. Prideful. Sarcastic. But for some reason, she didn't strike me as dishonest. Oh, she milked her clients for every penny she could, but as far as I knew she never told things she did not see. She was more the type to deliver the brutal truth or simply not answer at all. This time, she chose the latter, which meant she *had* seen this place in a vision.

"Sit down, Charlie. Relax. If you start pacing, I might throw something at you." Her eyes drifted closed and her head fell back against the cushion. "I'm already getting a headache."

I sat down. "I've been thinking about what you said . . . If you can't see Hank's future because it's intertwined with ours, that means he's alive, right? He's part of all this. Otherwise you'd be able to see."

Her chest rose and fell. Her eyes opened and she looked at me with a mixture of exasperation and pity. "Well if he's dead, I wouldn't be able to see him, either."

I winced, her words slicing between my ribs as effortlessly as a surgical knife and straight into my heart. Sandra had a way of hitting me where it hurt, and this time was no exception. I gazed out the window, knowing that pressing her wasn't going to get me anywhere, but I'd needed to do it anyway, needed some hope or reassurance . . . something.

"I'm sorry, that was insensitive of me, Charlie. I'm just . . ." She searched for the right words, but none seemed to come.

"Pissed off that you can't see the future?"

Her eyes glowed and her tiny form seemed to vibrate with energy. "You could say that. It's not enjoyable to . . . *wonder* what will come."

The soft knock at the door came in just under an hour. *Must be a record,* I thought as Sandra stood and shot me a superior smirk before answering the door.

"Oracle!" A tall siren dropped to his knees, grabbed the hem of her robe, and brought it to his lips. "Fiallan is honored by your presence, simply honored."

"Please, stand."

I didn't miss the note of discomfort in her voice, which was surprising. Guess after a while, groveling grew old even for the oracle. Who knew?

The siren straightened. He was handsome, a bit on the thin side with a straight nose, long chin, and thick dark-blond eyebrows. Like all sirens, he was blond and blue-eyed.

"Your name, siren," Sandra prompted him with patience.

He colored. "Pelos, Emissary to the Royal House of Akleion. I offer greetings from King Aersis himself and bid you welcome to Fiallan. You would bestow a great honor upon us to accept the king's invitation to stay at the palace during your visit to our fair city by the sea."

"Well spoke, Pelos." Sandra turned to me, an eyebrow arched.

"Your servant—" His gaze swept over my insignificant self until it landed on my weapons, visible since I'd removed the robe. "Pardon, your guard is most welcome, too, of course."

"She is both, as it happens. It is always wise, dear Pelos, to employ those with multiple talents. Will her weapons be permitted inside of the palace?"

Pelos stumbled. It was clear by the red creeping in his cheeks that they were not.

"Of course," Sandra continued on, "there is no need for protection within the royal house, but my . . . popularity, you see . . . Once word reaches the masses, well, as you can imagine my presence requires protections from those more . . . ardent seekers of the future, and I am so attached to my guard and rely on her greatly."

His eyes grew wide and he was nodding before he probably even realized he was. "Oh, of course. I had not considered that. You must need protecting at all costs. I'm sure the king will permit this protection on your behalf."

Sandra bestowed a glorious smile on poor Pelos. "That is wonderful news! We shall accept his invitation with the highest gratitude."

Pelos turned and motioned to someone behind

him. A siren guard, dressed like those at the gate, stepped inside of the room and picked up Sandra's bag. I waited for him to pick up mine, but no. They were already walking out the door, leaving me to shrug back into the robe, toss my backpack over one shoulder and my duffel over the other.

The emissary fawned over the oracle as we were escorted past the wall and into the inner city or old city as it was also called. As my subservient role required, I followed directly behind them.

The old city of Fiallan sloped gently down toward the sea. Houses had been built snugly into the rocky landscape, packed tightly together or with narrow alleys between them. It was no wonder the sirens took an interest in the Greeks—their land was familiar, from the rocky landscape to the blue sea and the pebble beaches.

The city was made of marble and whitewashed stone that seemed to glow in the sunlight. The main streets were wide and paved with smooth flagstones, and the houses all faced the sea with balconies and fluttering curtains waving in the breeze.

We walked through the meandering streets, Sandra chatting idly with Pelos while I took in my surroundings. Seabirds cried. The sound of the waves mixed with the sounds of everyday life. It was all so familiar and yet . . . not.

I couldn't help but think of Hank as a child, growing up here. His roots were here, his family, his people. I spied the other two towers rising in the distance—

needles jutting up from where the wall turned into sheer cliffs rising straight up from the sea. Goose bumps sprouted along my arms at the contrast of beauty and the evil I knew to lurk there. Sometimes that was the worst kind of danger, the kind veiled in beauty, the unsuspecting kind.

Pelos pointed out areas of interest as we went— the way to a sacred spring, the baths, the market, and the temples to the sirens' primal sea deities, Merses, and his consort, Panopé.

"And those magnificent towers," Sandra said. "Framed on either side of the cliffs, they look like gateways to the sea itself."

"There are two more on the wall behind us. We have four in all. They are the Malakim Towers, built during the war with the Adonai, a thousand years ago."

"Is it true there are children guarding the towers?"

Pelos didn't miss a beat, and I remembered what Hank had told me about the Malakim being so old and so ingrained in his people's customs that no one questioned it. It was just something that had always been. "Oh yes, and they are the bravest of our people," Pelos was eager to share. "The practice, you see, began during the war with the Adonai when the city of Fiallan nearly fell. The Circe, old even then, saved our fair city by creating the four towers and the spell by which four sons—children of its mightiest warriors who were off fighting the Adonai—would release their power, link together, and form the rings of protection around the city. It worked. The city was saved from an Adonai attack. The young guardians became heroes.

"Once peace was reached seven years later, the Circe entered the towers to remove the children. Only, the sons of its warriors proved strong and proud. They asked to continue their guardianship and thus became Malakim. Every seven years, they would be approached again, and yet again refuse."

"Such bravery is rare indeed," Sandra said. "But surely your fair city is safe. There has been no threat from the Adonai since the peace."

"Oh, but the Circe say we must be ever vigilant. There are threats always lurking, always waiting for a weakness to show itself. The towers and the Malakim protect us to this day." He glanced back at my stony face. "Much like your protector guards you."

"Indeed," Sandra said lightly as Pelos moved on to another subject, but the quick look she shot over her shoulder was incensed.

I wanted to grab Pelos by the collar and shake some sense into him, but a calmer side of me played devil's advocate. The siren people had been duped by the Circe for so long. There was no one left alive from the war, and the entire population had been born into the Malakim practice and into the Circe's control. They knew no other way. And they had no idea what had really happened in that tower when Hank freed himself. No, the blame lay squarely on the Circe's shoulders.

Eventually, we came to the palace. It had been

built at the southern edge of the inner city on an out-
cropping of craggy rock, a vast complex of straight
lines with large, long rectangular buildings supporting smaller ones, like building blocks stacked wherever there was room. It had a commanding view of
the sea and everywhere there were smooth columns
painted red and black. They lined entire buildings,
framed entranceways, or held up balcony roofs, and
there were several sets of stone stairs leading to balconies on varying levels.

It wasn't heavily guarded or fortified, but I supposed it didn't have to be seeing as there were the
towers and walls and the Circe to contend with. Fiallan was remote, separated from the nearest siren city
of Murias by Gorsedd, a forest the size of Texas. It
made me wonder why the sirens had built a city here
to begin with and why they'd warred with the Adonai
in their early days. What could the Adonai possibly
want with such a remote city?

The main courtyard was huge, rectangular and
paved with smooth stones inlaid with mosaics depicting sea creatures of the natural and mythical kind.
Steps that ran the entire length of the courtyard led
into a gallery with a line of red columns with black
bases. The far wall was brightly painted in reds,
blues, and sea green.

We passed through what appeared to be a main hall
and then through a confusing maze of hallways, levels, and atriums before finally coming to our rooms.

"I hope the rooms are to your liking, oracle." Pelos

pushed the door open and stepped inside. "You have a main lounge, two bedrooms on either side with bath chamber, and a private balcony with views of the sea."

"It's lovely. Please extend our thanks."

"Of course. We have already dined, but I'd be happy to bring something to eat if you're hungry."

"That would be most welcome, thank you, Pelos. You are an excellent emissary. I will be sure to tell the king."

Pelos looked like he was going to burst into song, but he held himself straight and still. "You are too kind. I shall return shortly."

Once he was gone, I said, "Laying it on a little thick, aren't you?"

"A requirement when one plays with royalty. Be glad you have me along."

"As much as it pains me to say it," I admitted with a small smile, "I am glad. And grateful."

Sandra clutched her chest, her eyes squinting in humor. "Be still."

I ignored her and wandered around the room, taking in the luxurious appointments and the way the open balcony, which ran the length of the entire room, framed the blue sea. White curtains hung on either end and they moved ever so softly in the warm breeze.

"Is it just me or does this place have a bad vibe?" I asked, eyeing the view.

"Like being in a nest of vipers." She rubbed her arms. "With a gorgeous view."

The sky was striped with indigo, orange, and pinks from the setting sun. One of the towers by the sea was in the frame of that beautiful picture. Had Hank been there? Was he still there?

"I'm taking this room!" Sandra's voice echoed from one of the bedrooms. No doubt, it was the larger of the two. But I didn't care. What did it matter? I wasn't here to vacation; I was here to save my partner.

I leaned my shoulder against the column that framed each side of the balcony, crossed my arms over my chest, thinking I might just take a little night stroll through the city . . .

7

I walked the streets alone, passing sirens and other visitors. Lanterns and open fires burned, lighting the streets and the market, which had yet to close down. Waves crashed against the rocks and lapped gently into the shallow curves of beaches. But nowhere did I feel the warmth of my mark.

Sounds were all around me, but distant. Inside I felt silent and dark and alone, so still that every step I took, every breath I made sounded like thunder to my ears.

I followed the long curve of the inner wall, stopping at the base of each tower. I placed my hand on the warm, smooth stone, and felt nothing. At the end of the north tower, I could go no more unless I wanted to drop off the massive cliff into the sea below, so I went down the winding walking path that led to the shore.

For a long time I stood on the pebble beach, listening to the waves and feeling an absence of emotion, of hope. Voices in melody seemed to go in and out with the waves, sounding faintly hypnotic and encouraging—inviting me into the sea. But those were most likely from the people on the docks and in the market.

Finally, I moved away from the water and continued my search.

In the center of the city was a massive square with an impressive fountain and a statue of a mermaid sunbathing on a rock. Stone dolphins surrounded her like sentinels, water pouring from their open mouths.

I went slowly, past every building, every temple. The city hall. The treasury—and still nothing. My mark did not react.

I had no idea where prisoners were kept—if there was even such a building. And it seemed with every step, my hopes grew fainter.

I headed up a winding street toward the palace and then swung a left to where colossal houses were tucked against a sloping curve in the land that led back toward the sea. It was a dark area of the city. Old. Private. Wealthy. Commanding high vistas over the water.

The breeze turned cooler. I walked beneath a tree with gnarled limbs reaching over the street. A gate's rusty hinges whined in the silence. Unlike most of the low walls that defined the property of the wealthy homes I'd passed, the wall I came to next was overgrown and crumbling. The gate was open. And down the drive, I could see the dark shape of a sprawling ruin.

It was a lot like the palace, only smaller. Columns were faded and broken. Weeds and vines grew unchecked. The courtyard was cracked and strewn with dead leaves. The doors were open, so I *had* to go inside. It was more than the usual curiosity, I thought as I went. Something inside of me related to the house, the desolation, the sadness.

Inside, it was hollow and gutted, except for a few broken bits of pottery. Scenes painted onto the walls were faded or chipped away. It was easy to imagine a family living there, the place filled with voices, the running feet of children, of gatherings. A home this large should be filled with family.

But now it was empty, the shutters on the windows gone or hanging askew, left open to the elements, the wind and leaves, the insects and birds . . .

The clip of boots sounded on the stones behind me and then stopped.

I stilled, a zing of alarm sliding up my spine.

Several seconds passed. I didn't move. The visitor didn't move.

Then, slowly I turned to see a man leaning against the wall, arms folded over his chest, regarding me with an even but curious expression. Could've been a siren or an Adonai. He certainly had the looks—tall, golden brown hair, muscular build—but I wouldn't be able to tell for sure until he spoke.

One thing, however, I could tell. He was one *powerful* sonofabitch.

"When visitors come to Fiallan," he said in a deep baritone, "this usually isn't on the sightseeing list."

I didn't feel threatened . . . just wary and on guard. He, on the other hand, projected a calm indifference, and his aura was astounding—a rainbow of colors snapping like an energy field around him. Hadn't seen *that* before.

"It wasn't locked," I responded.

He didn't move, didn't answer, just kept staring at me with one corner of his mouth turned up in a faintly mocking smile.

"What is this place?" I asked, trying to get a better feel for him. "Seems a shame to leave it abandoned. The view is incredible." I glanced at the wide terrace. Columns framed out either side. It was completely open, no doors, no curtains . . . but it was similar to the room Pelos had given us in the palace. I could hear the sea from where I stood. It was easy to imagine it as it might have been, framing the view like a massive picture window, maybe soft sheer curtains blowing in a breeze, a fire burning in the basins beyond each corner of the pool, now dried up and crusted with algae.

The stranger pushed off the wall and strode to the opposite side of the opening where he stared out at the sea, giving me a better view of him. Nice profile. Straight nose, stubborn chin, hair that had a bit of wave to it, the length brushing the collar of the thin leather jacket he wore over a white dress shirt. The shirt was open at the neck and he wore faded jeans.

Well, one thing was sure; he'd been around humans for a while.

He drew back the sides of his jacket and shoved his hands into the front pockets of his jeans. "This was the house of Elekti-Kairos. A place of grave dishonor. Of horrors better left in the shadows." He turned to look at me, his eyes a startling golden brown. "Left like this as a reminder."

"A reminder of what?"

"What brings you here, to this place in particular?"

I had no good answer for that. "Curiosity, I guess. You?"

His lips curved up again into that same mocking smile. "Following you."

Inside my senses were screaming *red alert!* but at the same time, I knew there was no imminent danger, no menace or malice coming from him.

"Confusing, isn't it?" His grin grew wider. "On a primal level, your body is telling you I'm a threat. I'm predator, you're prey. Yet, your signals are crossing." He shrugged in a casual yet arrogant manner. "Confuses the enemy. Lets me strike at will. Useful, no?"

Point taken, I wanted to say, but instead moved on. "So what happened to the people who lived here?" I stepped off the main floor to the terrace stones and then sat down, angling myself to see the stranger as he stood at the far column. I wanted the chance to get a deeper read on him, to figure out if he was friend or foe, and show him that I wasn't interested in a battle of wills or powers.

"Bad things. Very bad things." He leaned against the column behind him, hands still shoved in his pockets. Very relaxed, it appeared. "Tell me, Charlie Madigan, if you find Niérian is dead, will you leave or stay to right the wrong that was done here, in his home?"

His words were like a stun gun to my brain. Thank God I was sitting down because I might have fallen. My mind scrambled to get past the shock and process what he'd said.

Oh God. I was in Hank's home. He had changed his name when he came to our world, to start fresh, make a new life for himself . . . Christ. I was in his fucking house. *The house of Elekti-Kairos. A place of dishonor.*

This guy knew my name and why I was here, which meant I couldn't let him leave. Guess I was getting that fight I was itching for, after all. I stood slowly, shaking on the inside but calm on the outside. My hand moved back the cloak and rested on the grip of the Hefty. "Who are you?"

He eyed me for a long, calculating moment. "You're definitely making a name for yourself in . . . certain circles."

"What else is new?" I said dryly. "You have about three seconds to answer my question before being in a world of hurt."

A light of humor appeared in his eyes, making the gold seem brighter, as though it was lit from within.

"Threats already?" He pushed off the column, removing his hands from his pockets, and moved toward me with an easy, deadly stride. In an instant, his expression went from humorous to predatory. "I can be friend or foe." The smooth warning gave me chills. "The choice is yours."

"Not interested in either, thanks."

"Oh come, now. You're too involved now *not* to choose sides. And if you don't . . . well, wild cards always get hunted and killed."

Now I was getting mad. I moved toward him, not stopping until we met in the middle of the room. "Are you threatening me?"

"Seems fair."

I pulled my Hefty and aimed it at his heart. "I'm going to ask you one more time, who are you, and how do you know about me?"

He regarded my weapon as though I was pointing a pencil at him, and sighed as if in pain, like he'd rather be anywhere but here. "My name is Leander. I err on the side of good. Usually. As long as I get to kill things. I'm here to"—he glanced down the length of my body and up again, his eyes meeting mine with an arrogant light—"feel you out and see if you're worthy of my offer. And I must say, I prefer your natural hair color better. You had a beautiful shade, like polished mahogany."

"How do you know Hank?"

"First I must complete your interview."

"Well, let me help you speed things up."

I pulled the trigger, done with whatever weird-ass game he was playing. The tag would stun him for only a moment, but it'd be long enough for me to subdue him—hopefully.

The tag embedded in his chest, shuddering through him. His eyes fluttered closed and his arms spread wide as though he *liked* what the sound wave did to him. Psycho. His arms went down, his eyes opened, and he grinned. "They said you were a hothead. My favorite kind."

I didn't ask who "they" were, nor did I want to know his "favorite kind" of what.

He snapped his fingers. A sheer dome surrounded us, its edges sparking until it was completely enclosed, and then shimmered like thin glass with millions of tiny air bubbles. I could see through it, but was pretty sure I couldn't *go* through it.

Cool air hit my skin, followed by warmth. Odd. I glanced down and saw that my cloak and weapons were missing.

Okay, *now* I was pissed.

The fucker did *not* just put me in a black leather bodysuit. Except, he did. And the fact that he was standing there grinning like a damned fool was more than I could take. "You are so going down."

"Be glad I didn't opt for more skin."

I shook my head, thoroughly disgusted and feeling the hot sweep of power tingle through my veins. We began circling each other. "So what, you like getting your ass kicked by chicks in leather, is that it?"

He laughed. "Depends on the chick. You know, I wasn't happy about coming here, but now . . . I'm going to enjoy seeing what you're made of. What all the fuss is about."

"Which won't ever happen if you don't stop yapping," I pointed out. "You gonna talk or fight?"

"I do love you humans and your penchant for trash talking. No one does it better."

He cracked his knuckles. A maniacal gleam entered his eyes. He made a motion so quickly I couldn't follow it and then a bolt of blue energy shot from his hands and hit me square in the chest. I slammed into the sphere. All the breath went out of my lungs and a sizzling vibe radiated through me, lighting every nerve with pain.

Shit, that hurt. I slid down to my feet, knees bending until my hands hit the floor. Head down, one steadying breath, and then I glanced up.

How the hell did I fight him with no weapons of my own, unable to use my powers, and only reliant on my physical abilities?

I rose slowly and then charged him. Another bolt shot from his hand as I used my momentum to slide like a runner hitting home plate. The bolt slid an inch over my head. I slammed into him, taking him out. He fell forward over me. I rolled, popped to my feet, and roundhouse kicked him in the jaw as he tried to rise. He flipped to his side, rolled, and got to his feet. His hand went to the corner of his mouth and pulled away blood.

"You can't take me in a physical fight," I taunted him. Probably wasn't the case, but if I could get him to physically engage, get my hands on him without him using his power . . .

"You have no idea how much I'm holding back already."

I laughed. "Anyone who has to point that out tends to think they're stronger than they really are."

He came at me. God, he was fast. Every punch I blocked knocked me back several feet. And it was true; he was holding back. Way back. As long as I made him bleed, I didn't care. I'd learned a thing or two in my training on the job. I'd been fighting off-worlders for years, criminals who didn't fight fair and ITF trainers who did.

A punch to my side left me gasping for air and back-pedaling. He pressed relentlessly. I went to grab his shoulder, but he grabbed both of my wrists as I knew he would, leaving the rest of his torso unprotected. I brought my knee up and slammed it into his groin, then spun out of his hold and slugged him as hard as I could in the jaw with both fists locked together. Before he could react, I grabbed his shoulders, dropped all my weight backward, and pulled him down. With my boots in his gut, I launched him over me.

He slammed upside down into the sphere, catching himself from landing on his head and flipping to his feet, but satisfactorily bent over due to the pain in his groin.

I could barely breathe, but I got to my feet, staying

crouched over, holding my side, pretty sure one of my ribs was cracked. "Hope you weren't planning on having babies anytime soon."

"My ability to do that is just fine," he ground out. "It'd better be."

"You know, you didn't need this dome. I don't run from a fight."

He smirked. "It's not to keep you from running. It's so you can use your power without Death coming for you."

My jaw dropped. One, because he knew about Sachâth. And two, because all this time, I could've been using my power, power that I'd had pent up for what felt like years. The idea of being able to release it almost made me weep. I forgot about the pain and stood. "Don't fight fair, do you?"

"People who do are stupid and don't live very long."

"Did I mention you're an ass?"

"Did you? When a woman speaks, it just goes in one ear and out the other, especially when they're dressed in leather."

I made a face at him. I was going to *love* putting the hurt on this guy. Everything came flooding to the forefront; all the caged energy leapt and built, eager to find release. It burned hot and cold, fighting, wanting out. There was no way I could control it, not this time. This time I didn't have to.

Leander was about to taste a little divine retribution.

My arms and limbs tingled all the way to my toes, fingertips, and my scalp. I clapped my hands together and threw out both arms. Bolts of blue and red shot out as Leander's own power leapt forward to collide with mine.

It ate his up, wrapped around it, scurried down its length, and absorbed it all while speeding its way toward him and finally slamming into him.

He flew back into the dome as my power exploded, radiating around the perimeter and then shattering the dome in a shower of sparks and a boom so loud it shook the house. I fell to my knees.

Leander landed on his feet in a crouch. Now he looked serious. Now he looked deadly. Shit. I straightened.

The breeze once again blew in from the sea and we stood there staring at each other.

Leander's scowl was dark and menacing. He spoke in a tongue I had never heard before at the same time moving his arms and hands in a graceful set of gestures, as though pulling some invisible force to him. The air warbled as he spoke. Even with the spell Lightwater had given me, I couldn't understand the words. They were deep and so powerful it felt like all the air had left the house. He made a swirling motion with his arms and spun. Light shot out in all directions, and then came back in again, bringing with it sparks and colors, all condensing down to where we stood. Leander released another word and the dome went back up and my power blew through me as it erupted inside of the sphere and then dissipated.

I ended up on my ass, breathing heavily, eyes wide with shock.

Leander knelt in the center of the circle, one forearm draped over his bent knee and his head hanging low.

My brain scrambled to make sense of what had happened. I'd never seen anything like that before. Never even heard of anything like that before. "What the hell are you?"

His head lifted. His eyes glowed and then slowly faded.

He stood, brushed off his jacket, and then regarded me with a curt expression. "And that concludes this portion of the interview."

I rolled my eyes and got up. Leander wasn't too bad at trash talk and sarcasm, either. "Can I have my clothes and weapons back now?"

He snapped his fingers and everything was back where it had been.

"So what exactly was the light show about?" I had an idea but I wanted to hear it from him, mainly because it seemed so impossible.

"I have business to discuss with you. Your power escaped the confinement circle. Sachâth coming here would've delayed proceedings. I hate delays. You should make a note of that."

"So you brought it back. My power. You pulled it back and manifested the circle to contain it. Are you a siren?" I'd seen beings manipulate powers that weren't their own, but this . . . this was *commanding* my energy with voice and word. And if Leander could do that, then he could've kicked my ass anytime he chose. I was lucky to be breathing.

He lifted an eyebrow. "Done yet?"

"No, not yet." I was too intrigued to stop now, and if the guy had wanted me dead, he'd have done it by now. "How do you even know about Sachâth? And how do you know about me? And Hank? Is he alive?"

"I know many things, Charlie Madigan. *How* I know them is not important. I will tell you this . . . your partner lives." My knees went weak. "And dies."

I blinked. "What?"

Leander walked closer to the column to stare out at the dark blue sky. Only a few slashes of muted orange remained. "Putting it mildly, the Circe can be . . . cruel." He smiled ruefully, his voice dropping low. He turned to me and there was a brief look of empathy in his eyes. "Death might be the most merciful option for Niérian now."

I swallowed, my throat suddenly dry and my heart pounding. Before I knew it, I was next to Leander, grabbing his arm and jerking him around to face me. "Where is he?" My voice broke.

Leander said nothing. His hand covered my own and instead of removing the death grip my finger had on his bicep, he closed his hands over mine. "Surviving the NecroNaMoria is . . . rare. I'm sorry."

I flung his hand away and released him, stepping

back. "Then you don't know Hank. If I can get to him in time, he'll heal from this . . . Necro thing. He'll sleep for a long time and then he'll be fine, he'll . . ." Leander's eyes turned sad, resigned, as though Hank was already gone, and it pissed me off, this sympathy. "Fuck you. I'm not giving up. That might be how you do things, but not me. And not Hank." A tear slipped from my eye and I wiped it away angrily. "You're going to tell me where he is or I swear to God I will unleash everything I have until nothing remains of this house or you."

His look said *yeah, right*. "I don't know where your partner is being held, but I know he is here and I know of the NecroNaMoria because that kind of crafting defiles a place, corrupts the energy of this world like a slow disease. No matter how hard they try to hide it . . . Once you've tasted soul crafting, you never forget the stench it leaves behind."

"And the NecroNaMoria, what's it do?"

"It's a spell that tethers a soul to a body that has died. It forces the soul back from the very edges of paradise and into a world of pain. If the body is in a condition to heal and resurrect, it does. Then, the torture can start all over again."

And that's what Hank was going through. Right now. All this time. *God.*

Numbly, I walked to the step between the main floor and the terrace and sat down. For a long moment, I stared at nothing, feeling like I burned from the inside out. Burned because I was here and he was there, and I couldn't do a damned thing about it. I wanted to scream.

"Since you seem to be familiar with this kind of crafting, you can help him," I said at length, glancing over at Leander. "Whatever business you think you have with me, whatever it is you want from me, won't happen unless you help me."

"That I cannot do. Once the NecroNaMoria is begun, there is little one can do to stop it."

"Then I guess we're done here." I got up to leave.

"I need you to retrieve an object from the Circe."

I kept walking.

"Retrieve it and I give you something in return."

I turned around at the front door, pissed that I was crying, angry that he couldn't help me after everything he'd put me through, angry that I was standing there in Hank's home not getting anywhere. "Don't you get it? There is nothing else you could offer."

"There is, Charlie. Otherwise I would not be here." He paused as if best deciding how to proceed and then it seemed he decided for bluntness. "I have the antidote to *ash*."

Time screeched to a sudden stop. I wasn't sure how long I stood there, staring at him, my mind trying to catalog his words in the midst of my grief.

"Whether or not you can save your partner"—he shrugged—"I don't know. But I do know you can save your sister and the others in your city. Does this not interest you?"

My mouth worked and I finally found my voice. "You have the antidote to *ash*."

"I have something you need. The Circe have something I need. You plan to gain access to their domain to save Niérian. A little detour to retrieve the tablet and your sister's drug problem is solved. This is what they call a win-win."

And you're what I call a smart-ass.

I wiped the wetness from my face with my arm and regarded him for a long moment. My thoughts cleared. "What's the object?"

"It's a rectangular stone tablet." He held out his hand and cupped it slightly. "The size of a small book. Rounded corners. The front and back are also rounded like dough that has just started to rise. On the tablet are hundreds of small symbols pressed into both sides. It is the color of dried mud and looks worthless to the untrained eye."

"But the symbols are not," I surmised.

"No, they are not. They were priceless enough to start a war."

"And what do you plan to do with the tablet?" Visions of Llyran and Grigori Tennin flashed before my eyes. "Because I can tell you, I'm up to here with psychos out to rule the world via ancient relics and weapons."

Leander's lips curled into a genuine smile, which turned into a laugh. It was a rich sound, warm and deep. He opened his hands in a sign of innocence, though his expression was cocky and anything but.

"The tablet holds information about the First Ones and their Disciples."

I pinched the bridge of my nose. I let out a loud sigh. Why did it always come back to them? "First Ones I know, but Disciples . . . never heard of them."

"They are beings imbued with the power to serve and protect their lord, a First One, as myths call them—we call them Archons. When the Archons slept, the Disciples stood guard until one day they, too, slept."

"And the tablet is necessary because?"

His look became impatient. "Oh, I don't know, maybe because stacking the odds in our favor would be a good fucking idea. Because if we don't and the Circe figure out what they've got, then we're *all* going to the Afterlife. Is that reason enough for you, Madigan?"

I rubbed a hand down my face. Leander grabbed my arm. Power radiated from him. His fingers dug hard into my muscle. "We need that tablet or we're fucked, and it's only a matter of time until the shit storm arrives."

I winced and tried to pull away but he held me firmly. "How do you know about me? About Sachâth?"

"I know all about Ahkneri and her sword. You think those anonymous politicians in Washington don't answer to someone higher? You think your new *job* and everyone else like you are there for the hell of it? Think Tennin and the Sons of Dawn are bad? You ain't seen the shit I deal with on a daily basis. You're living in a bubble, Madigan. Think on that."

"Who are you?"

"One who knows what's coming. Do we have a deal or not?"

"We'll exchange in Atlanta. My terms. If the antidote works, you get your rock."

"I'll wait in the city. Contact me when you're ready." He shoved a business card into my hand, released my arm, and stepped around me, bumping my shoulder.

Jerk.

After he left, I glanced down. No name on the card, just an address and a number. The address I committed to memory, not that it was difficult; I'd been there numerous times.

Helios Tower.

8

I'd returned to a palace illuminated. Fires burned in basins at the corners of balconies and courtyards. Light spilled from rooms open to the night air. The entire complex shone above the city like a beacon.

A beacon to getting lost, maybe.

The guards had recognized me, so getting in hadn't been the problem. It was finding my damned room that proved to be a challenge. It eluded me at every turn, every hallway, atrium, and level. The entire palace was one giant labyrinth, and I was beginning to suspect the design served a purpose—an ingenious one, from a defensive standpoint.

I got lost, turned around, repeated steps, and might've kicked a statue or two in frustration. Finally, I leaned back against the wall before I did some real damage, and, thankfully, at that moment, Pelos hurried by, stopped, and came back. He regarded me with a knowing expression. "Lost, are you?"

"That obvious?"

He smiled. "Happens all the time. Come along. I'll take you back to your room."

"The builders were pretty smart," I said as we walked down the dimly lit corridor, "to design a palace like this."

"It started out small. Every king made his mark, adding to the palace, connecting levels in different ways. Most confusing to visitors and enemies alike. If you live here, you get to know all the passages and levels. We in the palace could escape while the enemy would get lost, like you did, and give our soldiers a chance to attack."

The only real enemy would lie from within, I thought. Someone who knew the palace. But I kept that thought to myself as we passed a hallway I'd previously come down, and through a courtyard I recognized, up a level and then finally to the room. "There you are. In a day or two, finding your way back here will come easier."

The light by the door was bright compared to the passageways, and as Pelos opened the door and stood aside, he gasped. "What happened to your face?"

I hadn't forgotten about the fight with Leander, but I'd given little thought to my appearance. No wonder the guards had given me an odd look as I hurried inside the palace. "I ran into that statue of the griffin, the one we passed in the first courtyard. Or was it the second." I touched a sore spot over my left eyebrow. "Hurts. That's what I get for getting lost and turned around."

He winced on my behalf. "We have excellent healers. If you'd like I could—"

"No. But thank you. I can take care of it."

"As you will. There is food waiting in your room."

I gave him a nod of thanks and entered a wonderful place filled with the smell of roasted fowl of some sort and breads, cheeses, and fish.

Bone tired, I shrugged off the cloak, filled a plate from the buffet, and then sat on the long couch to eat, wondering if Sandra had already gone to bed for the night. That notion was stifled when she walked in the front door.

"Oh, good, you're back. I was doing a little recon and—"

I nearly choked. "Recon?"

She patted me hard on the back and then proceeded to the buffet. "Of course. The sooner we achieve whatever task fate has set out for us, the sooner I'll be able to return to normal."

I snorted at that. She glared over her shoulder, brought her plate to the opposite couch, and sat down, where she studied me for a long moment with those creepy earthy green eyes of hers. "Nice bruises. Fighting already, are we? We're supposed to keep a low profile."

"Believe me, no one saw the fight. And, for the record, I didn't start it."

"You never do, do you?" She didn't wait for me to

answer. "Did you go to the towers? Did you feel your siren in residence?"

My chest went tight. The food in my stomach turned heavy and Leander's information swirled in the forefront of my mind. "No. I didn't feel anything." I pushed my food around the plate with my fork.

"That's too bad. Maybe tomorrow you'll have better luck. Everyone here is locked up tight, lips sealed, you know? I tried small talk with a few visiting dignitaries who have been here for two weeks— two weeks!—and they look at me like I am asking them to take a trip to the moon. No one wants to talk about the Circe. Like they're the boogeyman or something . . ."

"Sandra."

She shoved an olive in her mouth. "Hmm?"

"What is Sachâth exactly?"

Her chewing motion froze and we just stared at each other.

She wasn't on her stage high on laurel smoke, and I wasn't a paying customer. We'd gone beyond client and oracle to something different. Sitting here like this, more casual and intimate than we'd ever been . . . it smacked of the beginnings of, maybe not a friendship, but a relationship nonetheless.

She reached for her drink, took a few gulps, before setting her plate down beside her. "There are certain paths, certain decisions people must make for themselves. My job as oracle is not to change a person's destiny, but give them foresight so they might fulfill the fate set out for them."

"So what's the point, then?"

"What do you mean?"

"If there's no changing or altering this predetermined path we're all supposedly on, then why bother living at all, why struggle, why get a job, and fight the good fight? If all of our decisions come around to one single end, no matter what we do . . ." I shook my head. "I don't buy it."

"You don't have to. There are many paths, many decisions that alter one's life. Fate does not have a life planned out to a tee. It's the journey that makes life worth living, but there *are* roads we must cross, people we must interact with, things we must or must not do in order for the bigger picture to play out as it should. Take you, for instance . . ."

I set my plate on the cushion beside me.

"And your daughter, Emma. There would've been nothing you could've done to prevent her from being conceived or from being born. She needed to be here and so she is. The Revenant coming into her life was also destiny, since he will impact her life in a way that shapes her and her future."

"And Sachâth? You called it Death. Will it kill me, then?" She opened her mouth and then thought better of answering.

"Why the hell can't you tell me?"

"Because I don't know!" She got up and started pacing, wringing her hands together. "You have no idea how stressful my calling is. No idea. To have to make these decisions, to decide what to tell and what not to tell, what small bit of information might change a life or even end it."

"Well, be confident in the knowledge that whatever you say, Fate has decreed that you would and should say exactly what you end up saying!"

She stopped and leveled a glare my way. "There are lives that don't play a part in Fate's bigger picture, Charlie. Lives that play supporting roles, sacrificial roles, roles to move things along to the endgame, lives that don't seem to matter at all," she said quietly.

Annoyed and yet feeling sorry for the burdens she obviously bore, I got up and carried my plate to the buffet, stopping to get hers. "Done?"

She nodded, handed me her plate, and then walked out onto the balcony.

I disposed of our dishes and then went into the bath chamber—it was too enormous to be called a simple bathroom. Normal bathrooms didn't have columns and a sunken pool filled with steaming water. I washed my hands in the sink and noticed the yellow bruising around my left eye and the nice purple mark on my chin.

I just stood there, staring into the mirror, wondering how in the hell I was going to find Hank, and what Sandra's inability to see him really meant. And all this fate craziness was mind-numbing; I could only imagine what it must be like for Sandra, day in day out, vision after vision. . . . I huffed at my reflection. "Go make peace."

It had grown cooler since my earlier foray outside. The sky was dark and littered with stars. Waves crashed against rocks in the distance, the ever-present sound mingling with echoes from the harbor, the market, and the music and voices from the palace.

Sandra reclined on a white chaise lounge, her knees drawn up, head back, and eyes closed. She didn't move when I sat down on the end of the lounge. "So this whole fate thing . . . it pretty much sucks."

Her surprised laugh made me smile. She sat up, tucked a black curl behind her ear, and then wrapped her arms around her knees. "*Sucks* doesn't come close." She went silent and thoughtful, before saying, "I've had visions of you that have since come to pass—flashes, moments of crisis, of pain, or happiness. My visions are never linear, never from one moment to the next, so I must interpret what they mean, put them into a context . . .

"I like to say I know all, like to push people's buttons, but the truth is," she admitted, "I live a life of confusion, addiction . . . I gamble every time I open my mouth and relay my visions. What should I tell and not tell? There was a time when the gift of prophecy was relayed verbatim, but sometimes oracles see things too clearly, things which should not be shared.

And sometimes we must interpret what we see and hope our interpretations are pure."

She gave me a sidelong glance. "I'd think I knew what choices you'd make and then you'd surprise me. It's not often I'm surprised."

I stared out at the sea, the stars from above reflecting off its dark surface. "But nothing surprises All-knowing Fate, is that it?"

"For the most part, probably not. Sometimes I wonder if Fate gets a kick out of changing things, out of screwing with me, gathering information like some kind of super computer and then changing outcomes or courses to suit some end no one can see, not even me."

"So this not being able to see your own path . . . that has happened to you before?"

She rested her chin on her hands. The gesture made her look small and impossibly young. When she spoke, her voice was softer. "It didn't end well. Someone always loses."

So she kept herself apart from others, didn't want to get involved. As unnerving as it was, Sandra was starting to make sense and I was beginning to see her in a more complex light. "Well I don't plan on losing. Neither should you. The only ones losing this time are the Circe. I believe we make our own fate. No offense."

She looked amused. "None taken."

We stayed like that for a while, the sound of the water creating a sense of peace—false though it was.

Even so, I breathed it in and savored it. When I went to stand, Sandra stopped me before I could rise, her expression suddenly determined, as though she'd made a weighty decision.

"Sachâth is drawn to your power because it is reminiscent of divine power. You have the genes of the three noble races inside of you now, Charlie. Just like the First Ones."

I sat back down, careful not to show my surprise; I didn't want to give her any reason to change her mind.

"When the Creator decided it was time to withdraw from the worlds, some of the First Ones refused to go; they'd become attached, you see, to the worlds and to their offspring. To the Creator, their job was done; they had seeded the worlds. They found themselves for the first time in opposition. The rebellious First Ones fled and Sachâth was designed specifically to hunt them down. It is drawn to their unique power—only theirs and none other.

"Some of the First Ones went into hiding, trying to stay one step ahead of this creature. Some interred themselves into tombs of agate to mask their power. Sachâth awakens when this power flares. It senses your power. But because you are not quite there yet, in terms of your evolution, it becomes confused; it doesn't know what you are. It is only supposed to kill First Ones. There are no judgment calls, no maybes. And when it gets close enough to strike at you, it knows you are not quite what you should be and therefore withdraws."

Disbelief slid past my lips in a cold rush. That thing, that shadowy creature that vibrated with power so deep and ancient, was a killing machine made by the Creator. I could only imagine the strength and power it must have in order to kill the First Ones.

"That morning on Helios Tower," I said, remembering when Ahkneri's tomb had been taken by the Sons of Dawn to the top of the tower, and Llyran pulling down the darkness to open the lid. The power surge that had escaped had been astonishing.

"Yes. For the first time in many thousands of years, Sachâth woke. But when it arrived at the source, the battle was over, the lid was back on, and the Druid King had hidden the sarcophagus in the lake. There was nothing to be found. But the creature is a hunter. It scoured the city, looking. And then you used your power in my club and it felt it. I suspect had her tomb not been opened, your power wouldn't have been strong enough to call to it as it slept. But it was already in the city."

I rubbed both hands down my face. "God." I laughed through my fingers in defeat. "My timing really sucks."

Every time Sachâth had approached me, I'd felt its confusion, felt its curiosity and hesitation. And that was a sobering thought. I'd been dodging a fucking divine assassin, and it was just a matter of time before it finally recognized me and went to work doing what it was created to do.

"Well, at least for now, I can still use my power if I need to. It'll show up, but it won't kill me."

"Yet."

"Thanks for adding that," I said with a wry smile.

"No problem."

"How many people would know about Sachâth? Even to most Elysians and Charbydons, the First Ones are merely legend."

"A few. Sachâth is even more obscure than the First Ones. As is, not much exists in the prehistorical artifacts and writings, and what does exist is interpreted as mythology. But, as you know, there are those who search for the truth and those who inadvertently discover it. And there are those who still exist from the time of the First Ones." She laughed at my stunned look. "If your Ahkneri still exists and this creature, then the idea is not so impossible, is it?"

"No, I guess not. It's just . . ."

"A lot to digest. I know." As I went to stand up, Sandra stopped me again. "I'd advise against tiptoeing through the palace at night. Going in and out, or taking a stroll before bed is one thing, but sneaking around in the middle of the night is another. We're in a good position. The royal family trusts me. The Circe have no reason to suspect us. I know you want to find your partner, but to do that we must find their inner sanctum and it's not in the palace."

"I have to try. I came here to try. I can't just do nothing."

"That's exactly what you're going to do. Nothing." Alessandra turned on the lounge and placed her feet on the ground. "We've been invited to a banquet tomorrow with the royal family. The Circe will be there. They will ask me to consult the Fates. I'll say I'll need a private sanctuary, a holy place, close to the gods, close to the things important to the Circe. We won't have to search for their inner sanctum. They're going to invite us in." She let that simmer in the air for a moment. "As long as you don't go snooping around and screw it up."

I woke just before dawn, my right arm aching and hot. My room was open to the balcony and the thin linen curtains swayed in a languid dance. The air was cool and clean, the ever present salty breeze and the sound of the sea playing like a soft lullaby. It felt as though I'd woken from one dream only to find myself in another, in another world, heaven, Elysia, home of the gods . . .

But, as much as I wished it otherwise, this wasn't a dream.

As my vision adjusted, the mural on the high ceiling began to take shape—brightly colored depictions of fish, dolphins, flowers, reeds, waves, griffins . . .

I'd dreamt of Ahkneri again, of some faraway land, of speeding over valleys, plains, and mountains, across the same vast desert and to the colossal temple rising up from the sand and the glittering river beyond.

I knew the dialogue that followed by heart, felt her cries and her heartbreak as if they were my own. As if it was me kneeling on that floor, knowing I was pleading in vain and yet trying anyway.

Our purpose is at an end . . . It was always meant to be like this.

As I lay there gazing vacantly up at the ceiling, I understood now—thanks to Alessandra—what the recurring dream meant, and with no small amount of astonishment, I realized I'd heard the Creator's voice answering Ahkneri's plea.

She'd wanted to remain on Earth; she wasn't ready to leave, to fade from physical existence. Rebelling was her only option, and she'd felt betrayed by the Creator. She wasn't a slave, wasn't a *thing*. Yet she and those like her weren't given a choice, weren't allowed life after they had seeded it, after they had created it.

And they'd been hunted by Sachâth.

It was a sad irony for the First Ones like Ahkneri who had been forced to entomb themselves. Being alone, asleep, gone from the world they so desperately wanted to be a part of was the very thing they'd tried to avoid.

I sat up and swung my legs over the side of the bed. My arm hurt so much; a deep ache that burned from my fingertips to my shoulder. Slowly, I worked the arm, opening and closing my fingers, rolling my shoulder, using my other hand to knead my bicep. As I did, I stared out into the predawn sky, watching it grow lighter.

I missed my kid.

I wasn't sure what kind of time difference existed in Fiallan compared to Atlanta, but it didn't stop me from picturing Emma asleep, skinny arms thrown wide, mouth parted . . . My chest tightened with the need to hold her, my daughter.

"Ugh. Get it together, Charlie."

With a heavy sigh, I forced those thoughts away, knowing how easy it'd be to make myself homesick. I had a job to do, had to stay focused on finding Hank. I stood and headed for the bath chamber, deciding to slip into the bath, shake the depression, and, hopefully, ease the ache in my arm.

I showered first and then stepped into the hot salt-water pool, the steam parting for me as I went. The sirens' penchant for open-air living was growing on me. There was about twelve feet of stone floor separating the bath from the outside. I could soak and watch the dawn transition into day.

I swam to the edge of the pool, rested my elbows on the ledge, let my head fall on my good arm, and closed my eyes with thoughts of the banquet, the Circe, and Hank.

Sometimes he dreamt.

After the lashes, after his death and resurrection, when he was left naked on the floor to heal for the next go-round, he slipped into unconsciousness. And he dreamt.

Mostly they were nightmares, repetition of his torture,

of his tired soul being pulled back into his broken body. But some were relished, like those of death, blood, and vengeance against the Circe.

And some were more painful than all the others.

The good ones were the worst.

The good ones left him waking up to the reality where nothing good existed. He hated the good ones.

Yet, they would come, like they did now, and he would find himself in another time, another place where his mind and body were healthy, where his gaze was currently fixed on the hypnotic sight before him, of the woman who slept in a steaming bath overlooking the sea.

The water pressed and flowed over his skin as he moved toward her. Droplets fell from the ends of her hair and ran down the curve of her back, disappearing into the water that hugged her hips.

He wanted to touch her, to lay his rough palm on her smooth skin, to feel the contrast and make a connection, forge a link, to claim her—all of her. Body. Mind. Heart.

His heart pounded. He felt powerful. But she was more so because she could reduce him to this . . . need.

The water lapped at her back as he moved behind her. He could smell her skin, her hair, hear her soft breathing. A sudden tenderness went through him, making him pause as he went to touch her.

No, he was not tender. Not kind or good.

He was fucked up. Changed. And he didn't care anymore. He didn't care if she cared.

He reached out and slid his fingertips over her hip and then around the curve until he held her. He swallowed hard. Her skin was hot like the water. Silky. Damp. He stepped closer, moving his other hand up her back and then curling it over her shoulder.

Christ, it hurt, being so close, yet not close enough.

He bent over and kissed her shoulder. She stirred, releasing a soft female sigh that made his fingers dig into her hip. He held on as though his life depended on it. As if letting go would shatter him into a million pieces.

His lips brushed back and forth against her skin and then moved to the spot where her shoulder met her neck. He smiled against her warmth. He liked this spot. He wanted to tell her how he felt, what he wanted to do to her, how his body was about to break apart because of her.

So he did.

He wrapped his arms around her, his big hands splayed over her bare stomach, dipped his head, and spoke softly, just below her ear, the deep power of his words giving life to his thoughts, his wants, his driving need. He told her everything.

She straightened, finally waking like Aphrodite rising from the sea. Her back pressed into his chest. Her hands settled over the top of his, holding him to her as her head dropped back, exposing more of her neck as though she wanted more, wanted him.

Accepted him.

9

The knock at the bathroom door heralding breakfast jerked me out of the dream so fast I almost sucked in a mouthful of water. My heart beat like a jackhammer, and my body practically hummed. I coughed several times and then swallowed hard, trying to reclaim some control over myself, but it was pretty damned difficult.

That dream . . . God.

Feeling dazed and shaky, I left the pool and dressed quickly to the sound of servants bringing in the morning meal, setting the small buffet, and Alessandra's muted voice.

As I sat down on the end of the bed to pull on my boots, I was still reeling. Still shaking. Cheeks still flushed and warm.

Hottest dream on record. Period.

Hank's deep, exotic voice echoed in my mind and whispered against my skin.

The mark on my shoulder, however, was still unresponsive, and that realization cooled me off considerably. Thankfully, the ache in my arm was nearly gone. And in a few hours, I'd meet the infamous Circe, start making headway into finding Hank, and proving those delegates *wrong*.

He was here. He had to be.

Shaking off the last shreds of the dream, I stepped into the main room. Sandra took one look at me and said, "We need to do something about your wardrobe."

"Gee, thanks. Good morning to you, too." I went to the table to pick up a slice of warm bread, feeling edgy and frustratingly unsatisfied. "There is nothing wrong with my clothes."

"I didn't say that. But you can't exactly wear that outfit to the banquet. And this"—she gestured from my toes to my head with a wild flourish of her hand—"just doesn't cut it."

"Well, let's see . . ." I lifted a foot. "Steel-toed boots." I stuck out my hip. "Cargo pants for ease of movement." I slapped a hand on my weapon strapped to my waist. "ITF-issued High Frequency Tag gun; otherwise known as a Hefty." I spun around so she could get the full effect. "Outfit designed to maximize that ass-kicking edge . . . priceless."

Alessandra huffed. "You're such a smart-ass."

"So are you. You're just a better morning person

than me. Which is annoying by the way." I sat down on the couch.

"You might be my personal bodyguard, but within the confines of the palace, attending meals and meetings, to carry a weapon is to suggest the place unsafe. It would be an offense to our host to attend the banquet armed. And you can't go dressed like my bodyguard."

"All of which I do know." I shoved the last bite of bread into my mouth.

"Good. Then let's go shopping."

The hall was lit with small lanterns set into niches in the walls. Alessandra walked ahead of me, the fine material of her midnight blue gown flowing out behind her and making shadowy waves on the walls. Wind and string instruments echoed down the passageway in an exotic melody.

And even though the sights and sounds were beautiful and mesmerizing, I was unarmed and feeling completely exposed and antsy.

Don't attack the Circe on sight, I repeated, knowing myself and knowing as soon as I laid eyes on the old bitches I'd want to rip their collective throats out. *Don't kill the Circe. Don't react at all.*

"They are eerily insightful," Sandra had counseled me as we got ready—her in some kind of traditional gown with yards of gauzy fabric and me in loose pants that fell like cool silk and matching tunic with long, flowing sides. "They pick up the smallest vibes. Think of them as a pack of drug-sniffing dogs, and we just lit up a joint back in our room."

I'd just stared at her with a you-did-*not*-just-say-that look. She sniffed and returned to the mirror to fix her hair. "Oh, please. Like you never smoked a bowl back in the day."

"Oh my God." I couldn't help it. I buried my face in my hands and started laughing. Sandra responded with a chuckle that caught fire until she was laughing as hard as me, holding her side and getting teary-eyed.

I was beginning to think Sandra and Rex would make the perfect couple. They both were walking contradictions and both came up with the most off-the-wall shit. Like most off-worlders, they were a unique blend of ancient being and pop-culture junkie. They stayed true to their identities, but they embraced human culture and all the fun things like fashion, entertainment, technology . . .

Alessandra's choice of analogy might be light-hearted, but she was right. I had to play my part; had to be a simple observer on a pleasant trip with my benevolent—as Sandra had put it—boss.

The hallway emptied into a massive covered courtyard, the roof supported by giant round columns set in a rectangular pattern that followed the shape of the courtyard. A large fire burned in the center of the room and there was a wide circular opening in the roof above it.

Long tables ringed three sides of the room, the fourth was left bare and completely open to the outside. People milled about under the roof and in the open courtyard.

As we moved deeper into the area, a wave of silence suddenly flowed from one end of the room to the other. Everyone dropped to one knee. Except me. Because I was frozen. Not by the sight of the sirens sweeping into the room, but by the two creatures walking on either side of a handler.

Short-haired and as tall as Great Danes, bodies sleek and muscular and colored like lions. Wings folded back against their sides with feathers ticked with a succession of tan, brown, reddish brown, and finally red at the tips. They wore thick leather collars and had heads like an eagle only ten times bigger. And ears tipped with the same red as their feathers.

Sandra yanked me down with a glare. "They're just griffins," she whispered as though seen-one-seen-them-all. Uh, yeah. Not this human.

I went down on one knee, totally missing the announcement part of the royal entrance. I knew the worlds of Elysia and Charbydon were full of creatures we'd never seen before and some that we'd seen carved and painted all over ancient walls of our past. Lions, birds, dolphins, goats, snakes . . . these animals had been depicted all over the Mediterranean right alongside griffins, sphinxes, mermaids, and other mythical creatures.

I knew they existed in Elysia and had once existed

in our world, but to see not one but two, in the flesh, being led to a spot behind the table where they sat like regal statues, was extraordinary. *Em would love to see this.*

Activity resumed. Music, laughter, conversation mingled with the clink of glasses and the snap of the fire. We were led toward the far side of the room where the royals had taken up position behind their table. Toward the majestic griffins.

Pelos found us, led us the rest of the way through the crowd, and made introductions to the royal family. While Sandra chatted with the royals, I scanned the assembly, searching for the three old hags until Sandra pulled me next to her. "My assistant is captivated by your griffins, my lord. They are truly magnificent. I have not seen one in quite some time."

"Are they not extraordinary?" The siren king, Aersis, beamed, casting a glance behind him. "And so rare. These two are the last mating pair in this part of Elysia." He eyed me. "Would you like an introduction?"

I blanched. "Thank you for the offer, but . . . I think I'll admire them from here if that's okay." At a safe distance.

The king laughed. "A most wise decision." I wasn't sure if he was messing with me or if he was serious, but I definitely didn't want to find out.

As Sandra spoke with the king and his queen, I returned to my search. No hags in attendance as far as I could see, though my gaze did snag on something. Someone. Shit. Not good.

I recognized one of the sirens who had traveled to Atlanta to apprehend Hank. The same one who had grabbed me in the parking lot when I was travel drunk. He stood with a group of male sirens and they all looked deadly and ready to meet any challenge or threat.

At the time of our altercation, I'd just gotten back from Charbydon. I was bloodied, bruised, covered in gray sand and grit. Now I was healed, washed, my hair was dyed, and Sandra had convinced me to pull it back and to dress in feminine attire. I didn't look anything like the woman who had stumbled out of Charbydon. And more important, I had to act my part.

He, too, was scanning the crowd, and inevitably, his gaze came to me. I was human. He was siren. As such it'd be natural for me to acknowledge him because that's what humans did, they admired sirens, and that was putting it lightly. He gave me a brief, unimpressed once-over and then moved on.

Asshole.

We followed the king and Pelos down the table. Sandra's fingers dug sharply into my skin as we stopped. I went still and focused, getting her message loud and clear: Circe dead ahead. I began my chant from earlier.

Don't kill the Circe. Don't kill the Circe.

"May I present our beloved advisors," the king said, moving aside. "Arethusa, Calliadne, and Ephyra."

They weren't what I'd expected. Not old or bent

over or cackling like Halloween witches. No, the Circe were beautiful. Flawless. Regal. Nearly identical in size, height, and looks, except for eye color and small differences in the fullness of lips, the slant of the eyes . . . All three were decked out in deep burgundy gowns. Their hair, so pale a blonde it looked nearly white, was piled onto their heads and draped with jewels.

A creepy sense of unease replaced the initial shock. At first, I couldn't figure out what it was and then as I studied them, I began to realize that their beauty was deceptive. Unnatural. Something I knew on a sensory level was wrong.

"Honored," Arethusa said to Alessandra.

"Yes, honored." Calliadne.

"To have you here." Ephyra.

Oh God. A shiver went down my spine, and I had to concentrate on not shuddering at the sound of their voices. The singsong quality was so profound, so exquisitely beautiful it made me want to weep. They were so powerful the amulet Lightwater had given to me burned against my chest. I could only imagine what it would've been like without that protection.

Alessandra made a respectful bow. "As I am honored to be here." She straightened and moved a bit to the side. "May I present my assistant . . ." Oh shit. We hadn't actually discussed an alias. "Carly Madison."

I coughed in reaction. Her head whipped around, eyes widening in warning and irritation. I recovered, offering apologies, and bowed my head, acknowledging the Circe with all the feigned respect I could muster.

Carly Madison? Really? I half expected someone to slap handcuffs on me or shoot me with a lightning bolt right then and there.

The weight of the Circe's regard felt like a boulder on my submissive shoulders. But it was only a second before their attention returned to the oracle.

Arethusa, of the sharp green eyes, swept Alessandra with a measuring gaze. "Your reputation precedes you, prophetess."

"We hear your gift is astonishingly accurate," Calliadne added, her blue eyes narrowing as if trying to ascertain that fact for herself.

"Matching that of the first oracle of Delphi," the last Circe completed the triple play. Ephyra's eyes were a strange yellow-brown and they relayed a humor the others hadn't—all malevolence and bad intentions like a hungry cat deciding how best to enjoy its meal.

"Surpassing it, actually," Alessandra answered.

"Ah, yes."

"And, thus, you were blessed with immortality."

"Whereas your mother was not."

They spoke in the same order as before, so I pegged Arethusa as either the eldest, the strongest, or the smartest of the group. Possibly all three.

The music stopped once more and a deep bell preceded servers spilling into the room with food. The banquet had begun.

"Enjoy your meal."

"We shall talk more after."

"Yes, more."

Alessandra and I were shown our seats, which were thankfully on the other side of the royal family, away from the Circe. Food was laid out in front of us—platters of fruits, vegetables, roasted meats, fresh breads . . .

And none of it was appealing. My stomach was in knots. It had taken everything I had to stand there, right there, in the Circe's presence and not do a thing. But it was done. Sandra had gotten us this far, and soon we'd be invited into their inner sanctum. *Soon, Hank. Soon.*

Once the food and drinks were deposited, female performers swept into the center of the room and made a circle around the fire pit. They were dressed in sheer gowns, their light hair long and loose. They wore shell necklaces and anklets.

"Ah, fabulous!" Sandra exclaimed, leaning closer to the shoulder of the king. "It has been quite some time since I've enjoyed this type of entertainment, and in such magnificent company."

Go, Sandra. Schmoozing with royalty was apparently no problem for the oracle, but then she'd been around for two thousand years, give or take, gaining influence, respect, reputation. If nothing else, she'd definitely earned the outrageous confidence and ego.

Her words pleased the siren king. "Then this shall be a memorable occasion for you." The music began.

"The Song of Panopé commemorates the primal goddess of the sea gifting us, her creation, with the Source Words. It is a dance you won't see anywhere but here in Fiallan."

While sirens could manipulate energy, heal themselves, and have extraordinarily long lives just like most races of Elysia and Charbydon, their true and unique gift lay in their voice, and in speaking words of power. But I'd never heard of Source Words before. The only time I'd ever witnessed a siren using a word of power was when Hank had used one on the roof of Helios Tower. It had flattened everything and everyone, but it had cost him a week's worth of recuperating time.

The dancers twirled around the fire, their movements fast and frenzied, in sync with the loud drumbeats. "It begins with Panopé waging war against the fire deity to claim the land around the sea. It was hers by right since it rose from the sea itself during the time of Chaos," the king translated in between mouthfuls of meat.

The drums stopped. The dancers faced the fire, bent over, hands out to the flames, flames that gradually turned to water. The music turned soft and ethereal. They straightened, moving around the water as it rose and gathered shape into a vague semblance of a female. I had to admit it was breathtaking to watch.

"From the essence of the sea and the deity, we were then created to hold the land. She gifted us life, gave us her song, and won us this land. We are the true heirs of Elysia."

"I'm sure the Adonai would disagree with that," Alessandra said, neutrally.

The king spat. "This world existed long before the Creator chose it as the home for his . . . *experiments*. The sirens, nymphs, fae . . . we are all born of this world, all rose from it as children of the primal deities who resided here in the sea, the earth, the air. We, as their descendants, are the rightful heirs of this land. Just as the jinn are to Charbydon and the Neanderthals were to Earth." He waved a hand, and it was pretty clear this particular tirade was a favorite. "Noble races. Ha! There is nothing *noble* about settling a land that is not your own with some master race designed to rule it."

He proceeded to curse the Adonai.

All this was prehistory, of course. And some would argue that the Adonai had as much claim as anyone else. When they came to Elysia, the place was devoid of any civilizations. The beings that did inhabit the world were on par with cave-dwelling mankind, or so the story went. The Adonai had lived in Elysia so long that there weren't many who'd consider them "settlers," exactly.

"Here is where the deity gifted us with the Source Words," the king said as the magically dancing water began to sparkle, small dots of light took shape, and they linked together to coil around the watery form in what appeared to be a long strand of starry pearls. Only the pearls I knew didn't possess a burning inner light. "The words were given to us, inscribed on the jewels of the sea." I realized that the glow wasn't coming from inside the pearly "jewels" but from small inscriptions on each one. "Had not the words been lost, we might have defeated the Adonai and ruled supreme."

I waited for Sandra to inquire what had happened to the words, but she simply nodded; she already knew. I, however, was in the dark, so I couldn't help leaning over my plate to ask, "What happened to the words?"

The king drained his wine and then set it down hard on the table, leaning past Sandra to pierce me with a cold blue stare. "Stolen."

"Not all of them," Sandra amended, glancing to me. "But the most powerful ones disappeared shortly after they were given. Many believed Panopé took them back, the words being too powerful to be in such young hands. Others believed the Adonai stole them."

It was obvious from the king's dark look which one he believed.

"Is that what started the war?" I asked.

"Not specifically, no," Sandra answered as the king's attention was drawn away by his wife. "The war came thousands of years later when the sirens stole a relic from the Adonai. Many believed the theft was in retaliation for the theft of their Source Words."

"Long time to hold a grudge," I said as Sandra bit into a grape. "If they knew the Source Words, though, why couldn't they use them to defeat the

Adonai? Wouldn't the words be passed down orally anyway?"

"To understand, you must know siren history. When the sirens were given their power and the Source Words, each family was given a specific word. The study of each word shaped the abilities and the contribution each siren family made to the community. As time passed, the words became embedded into the very essence of their lineage and power. Think of it in terms of the Greek gods. You have gods of love, war, hate, beauty, nature, air, thunder, wisdom . . . This idea came from the sirens, from their control of an attribute and the ability to wield it in all its varied forms.

"There are some who believe that each siren family was already preprogrammed to bond with the word given to them. It was built into their DNA, if you will. But with some of the words gone, certain families did not develop as others did. They did, however, triumph, becoming great warriors instead. They trained fanatically in physical combat and they employed mages to train them in the arcane. When war with the Adonai finally did come, they were ready, and they became instrumental."

It wasn't a leap to figure it out. "The Malakim came from those families." And Hank was one of them.

Alessandra nodded.

"What were the words that were stolen?"

"Creation, Chaos, and Destruction."

Goose bumps spread up my arms. I could see why

the deity might have taken them back. And, if they were stolen by the Adonai, their motive was pretty clear. Taking away the sirens' most powerful weapons despite the fact that the Adonai couldn't wield them was a damned good strategy.

I was betting on the Adonai. "So what do you think happened?"

She shrugged, her attention on the food and the dancers. "It's not something I have foreseen."

The dance ended. Applause filled the room. But it all seemed to fade into the background as my thoughts turned inward. Maybe it was a good thing the sirens lost their words. Things might be very different today had they not.

I'd actually been in the house of a Malakim family, one who had, despite the theft of their words, risen to become significant players in the history of their world. And the Circe had chosen them, or their children to be specific, to protect the city. Why them? Hadn't they done enough? But I already knew even as the questions came. The Circe had chosen them because of what lay dormant inside of them.

The Malakim might've been lacking their own words, but inside they had to be extremely powerful, powerful enough to wield the stolen Source Words. If a choice had to be made, if all the warriors were off fighting against the Adonai and the city was threatened, who better to choose than the powerful sons of those warriors?

But why continue the practice? That was a question only the Circe could answer. Their creation of the towers secured them a spot as advisors to the royal family. But they'd continued to breed fear into the hearts of the siren people—always keeping the threat of another Adonai war in the forefront of their minds. And no one questioned this after all this time. The royal family had become nothing but figureheads with no real power at all.

10

Sandra had been preening for the last half hour, ever since we'd returned from the banquet wherein I did *not,* in fact, kill the Circe. My restraint, however, put me in a piss poor mood; I was more frustrated and impatient than ever.

"If you say I told you so one more time, I swear to God, Sandra, I will choke the words right out of you." I propped my feet on the edge of the table in front of the couch.

"Touchy, aren't we?" She dropped onto the cushion across from me. "But I did say so, didn't I? They played right into my hands. It was perfect, and now we have our invitation into the Circe's inner sanctum to take part in their Panopéic rites, an honor rarely granted, after which I will do my thing and read the leaves." She stopped her self-adulation and pierced me with a flat look. "You should be happy. Why aren't you happy?"

"Well, it's kind of hard to feel happy given the situation Hank is in. But I am glad we're making progress."

"*I* made progress," she corrected. "You just gawked at the griffins." After a long moment of silent regard, she asked, "You really care so much for this siren of yours, then?"

"Of course I do." My response was immediate. "You should know."

"I know you care enough for him to risk your life, but that's not what I'm asking. The last time I read you there was quite a bit of baggage mixed with your feelings for Hank. A lot of desire, too. And struggle. And hurt. Do you love him? Romantically?"

That was a subject I wasn't ready to think on, but her question stuck anyway. Did I love him? Yes, without question. Romantically? We hadn't got that far. The newer, more potent feelings I was developing for Hank were tangled up in the feelings I already had for him, for our friendship, the loyalty we had to each other, the trust . . . But all that didn't equate to romantic love and it certainly didn't mean those feelings would develop into love, either. For me or for him. But knowing all that, there was an indefinable aura about this *thing* between us, like it was something bigger, more significant than simple lust and friendship.

"Charlie?"

I blinked.

"The question. Do you love him?"

"No." *Not yet.* "There is something, though . . . I don't know . . . But I want the chance to find out, whatever it is." And to explain it all to Sandra would take forever and make me feel like a wishy-washy idiot, so I left it at that.

She considered my response. "You are so certain he lives."

"I know he does." I hadn't told her about my run-in with Leander and now was as good a time as any to see what she thought about that. "What do you know about the NecroNaMoria?"

Her eyes grew wide and she straightened her posture. "How do you know of this?"

"Well, I don't know much, but I know it's happening to Hank . . . that the Circe are torturing him with it."

She just stared at me for a long moment before sinking back into the cushions. "Torture is too mild a term. I think I need a drink." She went to the side table to pour a glass of wine, then leaned against the table and gulped down three long swallows. "Gods, Charlie . . . I know of it. But first tell me why you think this is happening to your siren."

I watched her carefully. "Leander told me."

Her face went white. The glass slipped from her fingers and crashed onto the floor. And still she didn't move. Her stunned expression finally shifted into one of intense thought. "When? When did you see him? Is he here in the city?"

"He was. I don't think he stuck around. Why?"

"Because if he was"—her eyes turned cold—"I would kill him." I went to speak, to question her, but she cut me off. "It's none of your business, Charlie. Don't make the mistake of thinking we're friends, that we *share*. I don't share my past with anyone."

With that she stepped over the spilled wine and stormed out the door and into the hallway.

"Well, that didn't exactly go as planned, did it?" I said to the empty room.

And, damn it, I never got my answer to the NecroNaMoria.

I was standing on the balcony, leaning against the stone wall that separated me from the cliffs below, when I heard Sandra return. The short clip of her heels on the stone told me she was still pissed, or at the very least intent.

The sound came through the main room and right up behind me, where it stopped. I supposed she wanted me to turn around, but I continued to watch the stars in the night sky and listen to the sea. "You know, all that negativity you're throwing around is kind of ruining a perfectly good moment here." I glanced over my shoulder.

Her eyes rolled. "Pot, meet kettle." She took up a spot next to me and watched the stars for a long beat. "I'm not exactly good with people."

I smiled. "And now you're preaching to the choir."

"Yes, that is true. Your people skills *are* exceptionally bad. Far worse than mine."

"Thanks," I said dryly.

We watched the sky for a while before she spoke again. "About what I said before . . . the friend thing . . . You see, it's . . . well . . ."

"Don't sweat it, Sandra," I said with the bizarre realization that she and I were actually similar in a lot of ways—except when she was like Rex. "If you can't let off a little steam with friends, then when can you, right?"

A soft sigh went out of her that sounded suspiciously like relief, but she joked, "Since when are we friends? I don't even like you."

"Yeah, well, right back atcha."

"Good. I'm glad that's settled," she said with humor in her voice. We settled into a companionable silence. And it was nice. Until she said, "So you want to know about the NecroNaMoria."

I turned away from the view, let my hip rest against the stone, and crossed my arms over my chest. As much as I knew I wouldn't like what she said, I had to know. I drew in a readying breath. "Yeah, I need to know what he's going through."

"The NecroNaMoria is the blackest, vilest kind of crafting. Only a few exist who have the knowledge and power to defy the very nature of the soul. It's a spell that tethers a soul to its body even if that body dies. With a siren, able to heal from his wounds, the spell becomes a cycle that is beyond comprehension."

"In what way?" I prompted.

"The body dies and the soul is released. Peace in the Afterlife is at hand. But the tether prevents it from entering that resting place. The soul is pulled back into the body. Imagine that kind of freedom and then being forced back into a dark, damaged, foul container, a prison where every ache and pain is felt a trillion times more intensely, as if for the very first time. The worst thing about the NecroNaMoria is that this can be done indefinitely, over and over again, until the spell is released."

"And once it's released. What happens to the victim?"

"It depends on when the spell is ended. If it's while the soul is out of the body, the person is finally granted death and the soul continues on to the Afterlife. If it happens when the soul is within the body, the person heals eventually, but . . ."

"But what?"

"The toll on the psyche is often irreparable. It is difficult to come back from that, Charlie. Maybe if it's done once or twice, but to experience this over and over again . . . I'm sorry," Sandra said softly.

A wall went up inside of me. "It's not the end, Sandra. There is always a way to fix things, always a loophole . . ." Which sounded lame even to my ears, but on I forged. "If there are people who know things like the NecroNaMoria then there are those who know how to heal from it. I'm not sure how much, but Leander knows something about it. Lightwater might know about it, too."

"Well, I can tell you Leander wouldn't help you even if he could." Her green eyes narrowed on me. "He doesn't offer information for free. He wouldn't just show up and tell you this about Hank; that wouldn't even approach his level of interest." Her arms crossed over her chest, and she lifted her brow. "So out with it. What's his angle? What did he ask in return for this information?"

My first reaction was not to say anything, but it wasn't like I had anything to lose by confiding in her. Despite what she'd like me to believe, Sandra was good, that much I could tell from the short time we'd already spent together. She cared about right and wrong. And she was a fount of information. If I shared with her, she'd be more comfortable sharing things with me. "He wants me to retrieve a stone tablet from the Circe, one he said was priceless enough to start a war. I think he wants the same thing the sirens stole from the Adonai all those years ago. Makes sense based on what you told me about the theft and the war that followed."

She gave a bitter laugh. "For all his power, he is unerringly predictable. Tell him I said that if you see him again. The tablet was stolen by the siren in retaliation for the suspected theft of the Source Words. Neither side will claim responsibility in either theft. Neither side knows how to use what they stole, but each has been trying to regain what they lost for ages."

"The Source Words went missing way before the

tablet was stolen, though, right? Why would the sirens wait that long to retaliate?"

"They simply weren't powerful enough. There were a couple thousand years between the two thefts. The early sirens always suspected the Adonai of coming in and stealing their most powerful words while the sirens were still in their civilization's infancy. This sentiment grew and grew, passing from one generation to the next. When the opportunity arose to steal the tablet, the sirens couldn't resist. And, thus, the war began. Did Leander tell you what the tablet does?"

"It tells about the Disciples. Apparently they were guardians of the First Ones; Archons, as he called them."

"I always wondered what made the tablet so valuable." Her shoulders slumped. A vulnerable, weary look overtook her features. "Some things are coming to pass, then."

"He has the cure for *ash*," I explained, trying to assuage my own guilty conscience—because what if I turned the tablet over to someone who'd cause more damage than *ash* ever could? But my sister Amanda, the others . . . *ash* was slowly killing them; the drug was designed to make their will step aside, to make them weak, shadows of themselves so Grigori Tennin's cult had vessels to control. Withdrawal meant death—once *ash* was in your system, you took it forever or you died. If Leander really did have the cure . . .

"As you say, 'don't sweat it,' Charlie. The tablet in Leander's care is the safest place for it. He is, as much as I *despise* saying it with every breath in my body, on the right side for once."

"The right side being?" Adonai? Siren? Human?

"The side of life."

The ominous reply was spoken with such sadness that it sent a flare of unease through me. "Do you know what's coming, why Leander is preparing?"

She glanced at me and gave a halfhearted attempt at a smile. "I have seen only the random scenes the Fates wish for me to see. It is difficult to put them into context at this time."

As frustrating as that answer was, I didn't press her because right then, the oracle looked like she had the weight of the worlds on her small shoulders.

I pushed away from the balcony's wall and headed for the main room. "Come on. I need a drink. All this talk about doom and gloom makes me want a stiff one."

Her heels clicked behind me. "So when you say 'stiff one' . . . does that refer to a drink or a di—" I spun around, mouth dropping open.

Sandra came up short. "What?"

"I can't believe you just said that."

"Well, technically, I didn't get to finish. I didn't peg you for a prude, Charlie Madigan. And I believe, and I'm not mistaken, that the *gutter* has come out of your mouth more times than anyone can count."

"Yes, but that's me," I said with a laugh as we continued inside. "Hearing the infamous oracle about to say the word *dick* is . . . nothing short of spectacular in my book." And like Rex, I was starting to expect the unexpected when it came to Alessandra.

As she went to sit down, I made for the sideboard to fill two glasses of wine. *What I wouldn't give for a cold beer right now . . .*

"Still, you haven't answered the question," she said over the back of the couch. "So which is it?"

"Well," I answered, pouring the second glass. "Depends on the guy."

A wistful sigh blew from her lips. "I have several propositions to consider for tonight, so at least one of us will be getting lucky."

I lifted an eyebrow and gathered the glasses. "Oh, really?"

"Mmm. A few rather exceptional sirens from the banquet." She took a glass from me as I passed her to sit down. "The sirens"—her eyes went starry—"as I'm sure you can imagine, are incredible lovers. They turn the whole talking during sex thing into a religious experience. It's . . ."—she saluted me with her glass—"out of this world."

I'd just bet it was. I gave her a salute of my own, the Madigan salute, though I delivered it with a smile before downing a large gulp of wine. Sandra's laughter left me feeling a bit disgruntled that she was going to get lucky and I wasn't. And it wasn't really the sex part; it was just being with someone, connecting, being wrapped up in strong arms and feeling safe enough to cast aside the constant guard and just relax.

Oddly enough, I did get a visit from a siren that night.

I slept hard and was deep into the usual Ahkneri dream when a burning in my lungs woke me.

Hand over my face. Large hand, cutting off my airway.

Immediately, adrenaline and panic poured into me. My pulse lurched and then began a loud, rapid pounding against my ribs and through my eardrums. I struggled, my legs tangling in the sheets.

A large shadow loomed over me, and as my vision adjusted to the dark, my senses also kicked in. Siren. And if he didn't release me soon I was going to pass out.

He leaned down. "Whore. Think you can hide." He removed his hand, grabbed me by the throat as I gasped for air, jerked me out of the bed, and then slammed me against the wall. My skull cracked against the stone.

Moonlight and darkness bled together as the room spun in a kaleidoscope of shapes and shades. A moment of stark fear swept through me, bitter and frigid and more painful than what the siren had just done to me. This could not be how it ended! We were so close. The Circe's ritual was in a few hours . . .

"Come here to save your traitor . . ." His fingers

dug into my neck. His nose brushed mine as he leaned in. "You're too late. He's dead. And soon you will join him . . . Detective Madigan."

"Dang," I wheezed. "You found me out." Apparently, he didn't appreciate my sarcasm; he head-butted me in the face. Pain exploded in the front and the back of my head as it hit the wall from the force. He'd gotten me on the bridge of my nose. Hot pain pulsed out across my cheekbones. *Fucking hell.*

The siren released me, ripping the amulet from my neck as I slid down the wall, gasping for air and blinking back tears.

"*K'Analath.*"

The instant he spoke, my will took a backseat to his command. A cold sweat broke out on my skin as I fought against it. My body moved, getting to its knees in supplication. *No.*

"You whored for a traitor. You can whore for me before you die."

I realized being under the lure of a siren didn't mean I lost my ability to think or reason because I was keenly aware of what I was doing. I just couldn't control my actions. From the sound of his voice, this wasn't about pleasure; this was all about punishing and demeaning me. My hands shook as I lifted them and reached for the button on his pants. *Don't do this, Charlie. Don't do this.* My stomach turned when my fingers touched the flesh of his belly. I undid the first button. *Goddamn it, stop!* But I didn't stop. The first button popped open and I moved to the second.

I had to use my power. It was the only thing left to me. Risking a physical fight to subdue this guy would be messy and loud—not that it mattered, since he had me enthralled, but even if I could fight him I knew it'd be a mistake. I couldn't risk bringing the guards. My power, however, was another story. Sachâth or not, I didn't see much of a choice, and I desperately wanted to stop doing what I was doing and kick this guy's ass into next week.

Having Death pay me a little visit would be worth it.

I was pretty sure the siren standing over me was the one who had made eye contact at the banquet, and the fact that he was here alone suggested that he hadn't told anyone else of his discovery. Yet. Guess he wanted that glory all to himself. His mistake.

His buttons were undone. My hand dipped inside and curled around him. He was hard and warm, despite his aversion to me. The compulsion was there, urging my body to take him into my mouth.

I shook, trying with everything I had to stop. My heartbeat was frantic. I was sweating with the effort to stop, and every nerve was lit with energy.

No. This was not going to happen.

Okay, Sachâth, rise and shine . . .

I withdrew inside of myself, concentrating on how my nerves felt, how the energy seemed to lick and snap like the flames of a raging fire. I imagined the floodgates opening and letting the powers I possessed pour into my center, the powers of both the Charbydon nobles and the Elysian Adonai. Unlike before when these powers warred with each other, they now mingled and combined, fuel to my fire—my evolution at work, and something that drove me that much closer to being divine.

As the power built and filled me, it pushed the will of the siren from my body like it was nothing. I was back in control. And the siren was about to be in a world of hurt.

I squeezed hard, twisted, and stood up, spinning both of us around and shoving him into the wall as he had done to me. One hand choking him, the other squeezing the life out of his penis. My amulet dropped from his hand, clattering to the floor.

The energy inside of me hummed so loud and consuming and angry I was lost in it, swept away. The symbols on my right arm began to glow. Vaguely I felt the siren struggling, heard him trying to speak, but he was immobile, unable to release any of his power against me. I was holding him and his power back.

The siren's blue gaze locked with mine and spoke of hatred and death. He said something, his lips moving, but I didn't hear a thing. The glowing symbols on my arm intensified and the same burn I'd felt holding Ahkneri's divine sword blazed down my arm, though this time it didn't hurt. But I wanted him to hurt. I wanted him to burn for what he'd tried to do to me. That was all that mattered.

Something changed in his expression. Fear replaced the hatred in his eyes. He struggled and kicked and pulled at my hand around his throat. I squeezed harder, with both hands, wanting to finish this. To make him go away. *Make him go away.* A surge of energy went through my right arm, down my hand, and into his now-soft penis.

His eyes rolled into the back of his head.

And he burned up, from his dick, to his groin, to his torso; he simply burned up like paper being eaten away by blue fire.

I stumbled back, wide-eyed and panting. The symbols on my arm and hand slowly dimmed and a familiar hot ache took over.

There was nothing left but ashes on the floor. Nothing left. I didn't know how long I stood there gaping at what should've been impossible, and trying to come to terms with what I'd done, what had come out of me.

Just like Llyran. Just like the sword that had cut him in two and burned him as it went. My eyes were dry and hot, stinging with unshed tears. *What the fuck was—?*

I was picked up and thrown across the room, landing out on the balcony on my back, the breath knocked out of me. Stars twinkled in the dark sky and the half-moon was large and bright. The smell and sound of the sea . . . it was . . . peaceful. I laughed at the ridiculousness of it as tears slipped from the corners of my eyes.

In my shock, I'd forgotten Sachâth would come.

A dark cloud blocked out the night sky, swirling above me, condensing into a vague shape—head, shoulders, arms that became wispy and translucent as the thing moved. But in the very heart of it was the same horrifying black void I remembered. The shape moved closer.

I was empty and spent; all the power surrounding us was Sachâth, not me, and it was heavier and denser than anything I'd felt before. It made me sick to my stomach. Tendrils of the gray, swirling matter floated toward me, over me, around me, snaking around my body as though hugging me, lifting me up, and pulling me into the black void.

And then the voice. Ancient and deep, imbued with such power that my teeth clattered together with every syllable. The words I didn't understand, despite Lightwater's syndialexi spell, but the frustrated restraint in them was unmistakable.

Then, it released me. I was weightless for three seconds before my back hit the stone floor of the balcony again. Stars dotted my vision and I faded into darkness.

II

I regained consciousness sometime before dawn. The cool air had worked its way into my bones, and my muscles were tight and trembling, trying to create some heat within my body. My skull and shoulder blades ached, and my arm burned. Overhead, the stars were giving way to a purple sky.

Christ, I hurt.

Carefully, I rolled onto one side and pulled my knees to my chest, giving myself time to adjust, time to think and come to terms with what I'd done.

I didn't enjoy ending someone's existence, didn't enjoy the kill, and didn't seek it out unless it was absolutely necessary. At heart, my goal was to protect. If that meant engaging a foe, defending others, or stopping a murderous creature, then I would. I loved a good fight, sure. I loved feeling like I made a difference, and knowing that I helped people who couldn't make a stand. But there was no thrill in what I'd done.

I'd defended myself. In moments like those when shit is coming at you faster than you can process, you do what you have to do to survive. I acted on instinct, which wasn't anything new—my response had been the normal Charlie MO. It was the *way* I'd killed him that I had a hard time with.

Eventually, I got up and shuffled stiffly into the bedroom where I cleaned up the ashes of the siren and then dumped them over the balcony into the sideways breeze.

I needed to get out of the palace and away from the reminders of last night, so I dressed slowly and then attempted the maze of hallways beyond my room until I found myself outside. The guards gave me a nod of recognition, which I returned before proceeding down the steps toward the sea, not stopping until I came to the market.

I bought a small loaf of warm spiced bread and took it past the dock to the beach, where I walked for a while, taking in the fresh air, the views, and the sunlight. I climbed the path to the cliffs beneath one of the towers and found a good spot to eat.

I needed this . . . peace, this solitary time, and the mindless distraction of the sea as it splashed against the tall, jagged rocks below me. I watched the birds dive from the cliffs and into the sea for breakfast. I watched the sky change colors. And eventually all those things helped clean away the darkness inside me.

My gaze turned to the tower across the bay. The obelisk's pointed top caught the first rays of the sun and sparked bright enough to make me shield my eyes. And then I saw it; the rings of power that made the wall of Fiallan impenetrable. Just a glimpse, like a shimmering mirage and then . . . gone.

I drew my knees in, wrapping my good arm around them, and rested my chin on top. No matter what had happened last night, my goal hadn't changed. The siren had come in secret, of that I was sure. But his disappearance would be noted at some point. They'd start searching, they'd be alert, and eventually they'd make their way to us. The outsiders. But we'd be inside the inner sanctum long before that happened. I hoped.

I stayed a few more minutes, and then headed back toward the palace to attend the Panopéic rites.

"I really don't see why I have to be bare-ass naked in front of everyone!" I whispered vehemently. "*You're* the one who was invited."

Sandra had neglected to mention that being invited to the Circe's Panopéic rites also involved a cleansing—a nude, arctic, freeze your fucking ass off cleansing. I didn't appreciate the non-warning, nor did I appreciate the fact she hadn't stopped flaunting her amazing night of lovemaking ever since I'd returned from my morning walk. In reality, if I thought parading naked through Fiallan whistling "Dixie" would get me closer to Hank, I'd do it in a heartbeat. But I didn't have to like it or the company.

Sandra and I were the last of the all-female procession to shed our clothes and step into the sacred spring. I was allowed to keep my amulet, but I worried about the mark on my shoulder blade and the symbols on my arm being visible. But more so about the mark, as it was identical to the one on Hank's chest. We had squabbled at length with the priestesses, trying to forgo this part of the ritual, to the point they threatened to bring the Circe to back them up. We'd considered Sandra going in alone and then reporting back, but then we learned once the procession was over, no one was ever permitted inside of the sanctum. Sandra felt sure she would not be invited back again, and I might miss my chance to get inside.

In the end, we decided this was our moment. We had to take it whatever the risk.

"You can't come unless you're purified in the spring," Sandra sang over her shoulder.

I shot daggers at her back as a gazillion icy goose bumps swept up my legs and arms. A siren attendant filled a bowl with water and lifted it to my shoulders. I braced myself as cold liquid hit my skin. "Sweet Baby Jesus!"

The only good thing about that moment was watching Sandra get the same treatment, though it was hard to really enjoy her shock since I was in the process of becoming a human Popsicle.

The group in front of us received their gowns and began walking down the shallow stream that led out of the pool.

The grotto and spring tucked into a high rock was, according to Alessandra, supposedly the sacred spring where the deity Panopé had appeared to the Circe and given them the vision of how to save the city from the Adonai. Panopé was also called the Witch of the Sea, which I thought appropriate given her association with the three hags I planned on killing.

Males were prohibited from taking part in the Panopéic rites. Good thing. As it was, my poor brain felt permanently damaged at having to see Alessandra in all her bare-naked glory. Like most Elysians, she wasn't shy when it came to baring all; they often gathered in the baths naked as the day they were born, eating, conversing, as though nothing was out of the ordinary—though for them nothing was.

It made me wonder about her origins. Some race of Elysian, possibly? The fact that nudity didn't faze her was a clue I cataloged with all the others.

Sandra took the gown offered to her. "Besides, Charlie, it wouldn't kill you to let your feminine side out once in a while."

"Uh . . . I believe my feminine side is out right now for all the world to see," I grumbled. "And what the hell is that supposed to mean anyway?"

She laughed. "You're just grumpy because I had fun last night and you didn't."

My glare was cut short by water over my head. I stopped myself halfway into spinning around and decking the attendant. Fuck, that was cold! I swiped a hand down my face. "I hate you," I told the oracle with as much menace as I could manage.

She tossed a cocky look over her bare shoulder. "It was good, too."

I rolled my eyes and pulled the gown over my head. Yeah, if only she knew the night I had. Hers obviously had been nothing but pleasure while mine had been . . . brutal. Whatever. I refused to let her bait me and tried to ignore her constant hints at her *amazing* night.

As I tugged the gown over my wet skin and arranged it correctly, I realized it left part of my mark visible. I glanced over my shoulder, trying to see how much was actually exposed.

"Charlie." Sandra stood downstream, waiting in the bend.

For a moment I was struck by the scene: her wet black hair spilling down her back, the white gown with its hem floating in the water around her calves, the blossoms in her hand, the trees that lined the mossy banks with their thin, fragile-looking limbs and the delicate leaves . . . Like a painting, a scene straight out of some Renaissance artist's dream of goddesses and ancient rites.

Then her eyebrow arched and one corner of her

red lips dipped down, ruining the whole picture. The attendant handed me a bowl filled with white blossoms, which I was to carry down the winding stream, releasing them as I contemplated the gifts of the goddess, asked for her blessing, and offered her my gratitude. Blah, blah, blah.

I tugged on the shoulder of the gown with one hand and balanced the bowl in the other. *Well, at least we were the last to go,* I thought as I picked my way along the mostly sandy bottom of the stream. And I sure as hell wasn't backing out now.

Once I caught up to Sandra, who looked as though she was taking instructions seriously, I poked her in the back to get her attention.

"What?"

"How well can you see my mark?" I asked, turning around.

"Fairly well. But I'm standing right by you. Don't sweat it," Sandra said, moving on. "You're the least important person here, so you'll be in the back where no one will notice you."

Gee, don't mince words, Sandra.

"Now, hush. We're supposed to reflect on the goddess and the connection we make from us to the water and to the sea."

The chant of Tibetan monks came to mind and I couldn't help but say, "Should I start Om-ing?"

She tossed a flat, unamused look my way and then returned her attention to the procession. After a few minutes, Sandra said thoughtfully as she walked, "I want your word on something, Charlie." She glanced over her shoulder to make sure I was listening. "If anything were to happen to me . . . Promise to take me back home to Atlanta. Tuni will know what to do."

The goose bumps that slid over my skin had nothing to do with the cold. Sandra was worried, which was understandable, especially for someone who could always see the future and now couldn't. "I will," I promised.

"You *swear*?" Her eyes narrowed as she stopped to look at me.

"I swear. Cross my heart and everything. Will you do the same for me if you can?"

"Of course."

As we continued walking, I mulled over her request. Did she know something she wasn't saying? Or was she just concerned? Neither thought was comforting.

Eventually, we came to a high rocky ridge topped with trees where the stream disappeared into the large opening of a cave. My feet were completely numb from the cold.

"We're close to the sea now," Sandra said over her shoulder, though it was unnecessary. As soon as we entered into the dark cave, I smelled the salt water and heard the faint echo of waves from some distant place up ahead.

At first it was pitch-black inside, and I was glad the sandy bottom allowed us to walk without much trouble. Light soon came, however, in the form of sunlight, which shot through random holes in the cave ceiling, making gossamer shafts straight to the water. The small waves our passing made reflected light in ripples on the water and along the caves walls.

The mood changed, taking on a quiet reverence. Occasional murmurs from the procession goers drifted back to us in solemn tones.

My senses sharpened. We had to be getting closer to the Circe now. I took the opportunity to scan the cave walls, looking for any passageways and hoping—waiting—for my mark to warm. We were entering the Circe's lair, where they did their dirty work, where Hank most likely was being held.

A song had begun, rising softly over the sound of the waves, the natural acoustics of the cave giving it added volume and significance.

Finally, the proverbial light at the end of a tunnel slowly appeared and we came to an enormous chamber the size of a large department store. The main source of light was a massive opening at the far end of the cave that extended into the sea itself. A few stories high and wide, it provided plenty of light and allowed in the constant push and ebb of the sea. Rocks and ledges jutted up from the seafloor, creating pools within the cave that stayed filled with water. Time had eroded a small beachlike area where the floor of the cave met one of the large pools.

Some of the calmer pools were crystal clear and the

bottoms glittered. The closer I came, I realized why. Gold, jewels, and other treasures littered the sandy floor.

Sandra tugged on my arm. We moved out of the stream where it met with the sea and onto the smooth flat rock that made up about half the chamber's natural floor.

Tucked back against the wall was an altar behind which the Circe had gathered, but my attention locked almost immediately onto the narrow opening behind them. Without a doubt, I knew I had to get inside that passageway.

What followed next was a tediously slow sequence of events. First came a song—a beautiful *long* song. After the song, offerings were made to the deity, which explained all the underwater treasure. Alessandra and I tossed our flowers into the sea, and they floated with the hundreds of others, making a pretty web of white blossoms on the water.

Once the rites were over, the procession filed out of the cave, going back up the stream the way it had come. The Circe crossed the floor, heading our way.

"Thank you for coming, oracle," Arethusa said.

Calliadne took her turn. "Your presence pleases Panopé."

"Come. Let us retire to our sanctum." Ephyra gestured toward the passageway.

"I am likewise honored to take part in the rites. Your hospitality is most kind." Alessandra turned to me and the question not voiced was what they were going to do with me: invite me along or make me wait in the chamber?

The Circe exchanged glances, odd ones that made me wonder if they communicated telepathically. And then they stared at my arm and warnings fired through my brain.

"Your servant's markings." Their eyes didn't stray from my right arm. "Where did she get them?"

"They are . . . unusual."

Alessandra didn't miss a beat—and after the whole "Carly Madison" thing, I feared what would come out of her mouth next. "They were given to her by the jinn who trained her to be my bodyguard. They are ancient jinn markings."

Relief slid down my spine. *Well done, Sandra. Well done.* Using the jinn was genius because very few Elysians ever bothered themselves with Charbydon practices and rites.

"She may accompany you," Calliadne said at length, "but must wait outside the sanctum once we enter."

Alessandra and I bowed. "Most kind," she said.

I followed them into the passageway. *Finally.* It took most of my focus to bank my emotions and aura so the Circe wouldn't feel anything suspicious coming from me, and concentrate on my surroundings.

Dressed only in the gown, I was at a serious disadvantage. The length could easily get tangled in my legs. I had no shoes, no weapons, no power to draw on unless I wanted a visit from Sachâth. So that pretty much left my fists, my training, and my ability to think on my feet.

The passageway made a serpentine path through the gray rock. The air was cool and damp, but it warmed the farther we went back into the earth. I found it strange, if this was indeed the Circe's dwelling, that there were no guards and no real security system—well, at least the kind I could see; crafting was another matter entirely. They could have this entire place protected with wards and traps.

Unless they had gotten complacent. In the thousand years since the Circe had risen to fame and control, there hadn't really been any challenges to their power. Who did they need protection from? Everyone here adored them. And, maybe, the lack of guards was for a reason. Like the fact that they didn't want anyone knowing the evil they did down here.

We walked single file until we came to a round chamber. There were three doors facing us. Calliadne opened the center door and motioned to Alessandra. "Our sanctum is this way."

Ephyra turned to me. "You must wait here."

I wasn't surprised by this, but I *was* shocked at the level of worry I felt for Sandra. The idea of her being alone with the Circe filled me with a very real, very acute sense of dread. I made a step forward. She couldn't go alone. I was her bodyguard, after all, and—

She stepped in front of me, pressing a hand into my shoulder. The smile of encouragement she tried to give me failed miserably. "I'll be fine. There's a bench there by the wall. Just *wait* for me here." She was trying to hide it, but she was afraid. I knew her well enough now to know that, and I knew her well enough to care. And I felt very strongly about not wanting her to go. "Sit and rest," Alessandra went on, squaring her shoulders and taking on an imperious tone. "There is much work for you to do when I return."

I dipped my head and moved back, not liking it one bit. It went against every single protective instinct I had. My fists closed tightly and I clenched my teeth so I wouldn't say anything out of character for an oracle employee. But, God, I wanted to.

Sandra couldn't see her fate or mine; she had no way of knowing if she'd be safe. But we did know we were too close now to screw things up. With that thought holding me back, I remained silent. As the Circe ushered her through the door, Sandra glanced over her shoulder and the look in her otherworldly eyes gave me chills. Regret. Resignation. Friendship.

We'd truly become friends. And she'd just left with three of the most powerful creatures in siren history.

Fuck. I rubbed a hand down my face, eyeing the room and trying to figure out what the hell to do next. I paced. The absence of intel made me bristle. If I knew where Hank was being held, how many guards patrolled the area, I could make a plan. But as

Law.
Vermont

American Literature

1st ed. - vg. but X lib'n
laid down dj.
Credited w/ first
American written &
American produced
comedy and other
literary achievements
all the more remarkable
because his occupation
was in the law

45⁰

4434102303

was/East B-2

Royall Tyler

Royall Tyler

G. THOMAS TANSELLE

HARVARD UNIVERSITY PRESS

Cambridge, Massachusetts

1 9 6 7

TO MY

MOTHER AND FATHER

Preface

Royall TYLER once said of biographers, "I do not thank the author who pursues his hero into the recesses of domestic life, and exhibits the disgusting infirmities of our common nature." He also described, in verse, the scholar who looks on his musty manuscripts, "cites and quotes, / On illustration clear intent; / And in the margin gravely notes / A thousand meanings — never meant." [1] But perhaps he would pardon this intrusion on his privacy, however many unintended meanings it discloses, for the time has surely come, after a century and a half, when further abstinence would be a matter not of propriety but of neglect. If Tyler is not a major figure in the story of American literature, he is an important one historically, both in his accomplishments and in what he represents. He has long been accorded a line in literary histories for his play *The Contrast* (1787), the first native comedy professionally produced; but his efforts to encourage a truly American literature, in the formative years of the new republic, embraced fiction, poetry, and the essay as well, and his own productions in these areas, if less well-known, are equally significant. A study of Tyler not only encompasses nearly all the aspects of the literary world of his time but illustrates the dilemma faced by literary men of the young nation. Literature was not a profession, only a pastime; Tyler was a lawyer and man of affairs first, a writer second. But his dedication, in principle and in practice, to the idea of a native literature makes his story particularly worth record-

[1] *The Yankey in London* (New York, 1809), p. 53; *The Chestnut Tree* (North Montpelier, 1931), lines 625–628.

vii

ing; and it is that story which I have attempted to sketch here.

That this should be, only now, the first book on a man who has been called "one of the most interesting minds of his day" [2] is owing to a number of circumstances, chief among them the difficulty of gaining access to the Tyler papers. It is not, however, the result of a lack of interest in Tyler, for commentators have repeatedly remarked that he deserved closer study, almost from the time of his death in 1826. One obituary declared that "some of his fugitive productions were among the most animating effusions of the eventful days of the second, third, and fourth Presidents," and another said that his novel *The Algerine Captive*, "unquestionably one of the most original and brilliant productions of this generation, will forever secure him a high rank among American writers." [3] Three years later Samuel Kettell, in his *Specimens of American Poetry*, included six of Tyler's poems and a biographical sketch.[4] Then William Dunlap, in his pioneer *History of the American Theatre* (1832), gave a brief account of *The Contrast* and of Tyler, and Joseph T. Buckingham devoted eight pages of his *Specimens of Newspaper Literature* (1850) to the "Colon & Spondee" pieces.[5] Tyler's poetry was discussed in some detail by Pliny H. White, speaking before the Vermont Historical

[2] Alexander Cowie, *The Rise of the American Novel* (New York, 1948), p. 60.

[3] Boston *Columbian Centinel*, 23 August 1826; the second quotation is quoted by the *Centinel* from the Brattleboro *Messenger* (cf. *Northern Sentinel*, 8 September 1826). A contemporary estimate (though admittedly a conventional compliment) is found in James Elliot's *Poetical and Miscellaneous Works* (Greenfield, Mass., 1798), in the last four stanzas (16 lines) of his poem "The Autumnal Season, Addressed to Royal Tyler, Esq." (pp. 43–45): in Tyler he finds "the fruits of early knowledge shine" and "the graces and the virtues blend"; nature has given Tyler "Art, eloquence and taste, alike to grace / The bar, the senate or the studious shade," and Tyler deserves the "meed of genius and the poet's bays."

[4] Samuel Kettell, *Specimens of American Poetry* (Boston, 1829), II, 47–54.

[5] William Dunlap, *History of the American Theatre* (New York, 1832), pp. 71–74; Joseph T. Buckingham, *Specimens of Newspaper Literature* (Boston, 1850), II, 202–210.

Society on 18 October 1860,[6] and his newspaper columns were noticed by Andrew Peabody in 1889.[7] Those two large collections, the Duyckincks' *Cyclopaedia of American Literature* (1855) and Stedman and Hutchinson's *Library of American Literature* (1888), contained sections on Tyler, and the facts of his life were recounted in *Appleton's Cyclopaedia of American Biography* (1889) and in the *National Cyclopaedia* (1892).[8] The Duyckincks went so far as to say, "His life certainly deserves to be narrated with more particularity than it has yet received. His writings, too, should be collected and placed in an accessible form. American literature cannot be charged with poverty while it has such valuables uninvested in its forgotten repositories."

For several generations scholars have repeated essentially the same statement,[9] without producing either the biography or the "posthumous and elegant edition" (which one of Tyler's friends predicted in 1797).[10] A beginning was made by Thomas Pickman Tyler, who wrote a long memoir of his father, incorporating many letters and documents; though never published, it served as the basis for his paper before the

[6] Published as "Early Poets of Vermont" in the *Proceedings of the Vermont Historical Society, 1917–1918* (1920), pp. 93–125 (pp. 108–119 on Tyler).

[7] In an article on the *Farmer's Weekly Museum* in the *Proceedings of the American Antiquarian Society*, n.s. VI (1889), 106–129 (see pp. 115–116).

[8] Evert A. and George L. Duyckinck, *Cyclopaedia of American Literature* (Philadelphia, 1855), I, 432–437; E. C. Stedman and E. M. Hutchinson, *A Library of American Literature* (New York, 1888), IV, 92–106; *Appleton's Cyclopaedia of American Biography*, VI (New York, 1889), 201; *National Cyclopaedia of American Biography*, VI (New York, 1892), 39.

[9] A contrary point of view is represented by William P. Trent, who described Tyler, in his *History of American Literature* (New York, 1903), as "a versatile American who deserves to be respected, though hardly to have his works republished" (pp. 200–202); and George O. Seilhamer, in his *History of the American Theatre* (New York, 1888–1891), had said that Tyler's works were "deservedly forgotten" (II, 239).

[10] William Coleman to Tyler, 24 September 1797, in Tyler memoir (cf. Chapter 1, note 4, below), p. 103.

Preface

Vermont Bar Association on 20 October 1879 and for Henry Burnham's extensive account of Tyler in his book on Brattleboro (1880).[11] A mark of this renewed and serious interest was Thomas J. McKee's edition of *The Contrast* in 1887 (its first printing since 1790), as the first publication of the Dunlap Society. Since that time the fortunes of Tyler have been in the hands of a few devoted researchers with either a family or a Vermont connection. Helen Tyler Brown, Tyler's great-granddaughter, spent much of her life doing an enormous amount of genealogical and historical research on the family and had ambitious plans for a full-scale biography and edition. She worked closely with Professor Frederick Tupper of the University of Vermont, and together they edited the reminiscences of Tyler's wife, published in 1925 as *Grandmother Tyler's Book*. Also she contributed an introduction to James B. Wilbur's elegant limited edition of *The Contrast* in 1920, and Tupper read a general paper on Tyler before the Vermont Historical Society on 7 July 1927.[12] Walter J. Coates, with his Driftwind Press of North Montpelier, took an interest in Tyler, published his long poem *The Chestnut Tree* in a limited edition in 1931, included a checklist in *Driftwind* in 1932, and edited several anthologies of Vermont verse which contained Tyler poems.[13] Four years later Arthur Hobson Quinn wrote, for the *Dictionary of American Biography*, the most scholarly biographical account that had appeared. Next came two scholars from Norwich University in Northfield, Vermont — Arthur W. Peach and George F. Newbrough. In 1941 they edited from the Tyler Papers four unpublished plays for the Princeton series of "America's Lost

---

[11] Tyler, "Royall Tyler," *Proceedings of the Vermont Bar Association*, I (1878–1881), 44–62; Burnham, *Brattleboro, Windham County, Vermont* (Brattleboro, 1880), pp. 83–101.

[12] *Proceedings of the Vermont Historical Society*, IV (1928), 65–101.

[13] *Favorite Vermont Poems, Series One* (North Montpelier, 1928), pp. 5–9; *Series Five* (1934), pp. 18–19; and, with Tupper, *Vermont Verse: An Anthology* (Brattleboro, 1932), pp. 25–27.

Plays"; but their plans, announced in that volume, for a complete edition and a definitive biography did not reach fruition. One of Tupper's graduate students, Bertrand W. Chapman, wrote a master's thesis on Tyler's "nativism" in 1933; and in 1962 Marius B. Péladeau prepared an edition of Tyler's poetry for his Georgetown master's degree. Beyond this, there has been virtually no work on Tyler, other than a few popular magazine articles (usually on *The Contrast*) and brief accounts in standard surveys. Arthur Peach wrote in 1936, "It is an interesting, if not a somewhat tragic fact, that the literary history of America has been lacking in any adequate consideration of the work of the writer of the first American comedy, acted in professional theaters, and the author of the first American novel to be republished in England." [14]

There is no doubt that much of Tyler's work is difficult to come by — scattered anonymous pieces in scarce newspapers or editions of which only a few copies survive — but this situation is equally true of certain of Tyler's contemporaries, like Joseph Dennie and Thomas Green Fessenden, who were the subjects of biographies fifty years ago. The main reason for Tyler's neglect has been the peculiar, but not altogether unusual, situation surrounding the family papers. Because the family had a strong sense of its heritage, various members have hoped to write their own accounts before the materials were released to outsiders. Helen Tyler Brown, attempting to carry on the work of Thomas Pickman Tyler, did allow certain scholars — particularly Tupper and Peach — to work with her, but she wanted to produce an "official" family biography of Royall Tyler. As time passed, and the quantity of research notes increased, she began to deposit them (through the early 1930's) in the Vermont Historical Society, but with the understanding that they be closed to the public until her

---

[14] "The Royall Tyler Collection," *Proceedings of the Vermont Historical Society*, n.s. IV (1936), 3-4.

biography was completed. Before her death in 1935, she appointed three trustees (Tupper, Henry S. Wardner, and Mary R. Cabot, later replaced by Peach), who would have exclusive use of the papers until a biography and an edition could be published. They managed to get out the *Four Plays*, but nothing else, before they died (within a few years of each other), leaving no instructions about who was to continue the work. The Vermont Historical Society was thus left with a legal problem; scholars asked to see the papers, but the Society, acting under the terms of Helen Tyler Brown's will, was not free to admit them. The papers remained inaccessible for twenty years, until the Society, working with Judge Beatrice J. Brown of the Marlboro District Probate Court and the heirs, was finally able, in May 1964, to open them to qualified scholars.[15] The good intentions of Helen Tyler Brown had the effect, in the end, of turning scholarly attention away from her great-grandfather — even of stimulating wild speculations, as the repeated contemporary references to his youthful indiscretions, followed by a descendant who closely guards the family papers, were bound to do.

The Tyler Papers should be of great usefulness to the historian, the economist, and the genealogist of nineteenth-century New England, for the ten large boxes of material are fullest in the accumulations of notebooks, letters, and sermons of Tyler's children and grandchildren and in material relating to Helen Tyler Brown's research. The papers of Tyler himself are unfortunately few in number, and many exist only in later typed copies; but what there is can now be examined, and a major impediment to research has been re-

---

[15] The text of the agreement between the heirs and the Society, opening the papers to scholarly use, is in the Vermont Historical Society *News and Notes*, XV (July 1964), 84–86. For other information about the Tyler Papers, see *Proceedings of the Vermont Historical Society*, n.s. IV (1936), 3–4, 22, 27, 29, 35, 39, 43; V (1937), 44.

Preface

moved. It is time to sift the remains and to complete the task begun over a century ago by Thomas Pickman Tyler. If a definitive edition and biography of Royall Tyler could appear in a 1952 list of the desiderata for scholarship in English and American literature,[16] they would still be on the list. I have tried to assemble some of the facts about Tyler and to assess his literary career, not to produce the authorized account Helen Tyler Brown hoped for, but to provide a starting point for the further research which she knew was justified.[17]

G.T.T.

Madison, Wisconsin
Lebanon, Indiana
June 1965

[16] Chauncey Sanders, *An Introduction to Research in English Literary History* (New York, 1952), p. 124.

[17] I wish to express my gratitude to the Graduate School of the University of Wisconsin for providing the grants necessary to carry out part of the research for this book.

Contents

Illustrations

A photograph showing some of the material in the Tyler Papers, as displayed in 1929, is reproduced in *The Earliest Diary of John Adams*, ed. L. H. Butterfield *et al.* (Cambridge: Harvard University Press, 1966), facing p. 43. Portraits of other members of the Tyler family are reproduced in *Grandmother Tyler's Book*.

Royall Tyler

❧ I ❧

Lawyer and Wit

BOSTON in the middle of the eighteenth century was a bustling settlement of something less than fifteen thousand inhabitants, a commercial center that exuded the atmosphere of being at the heart of important events. It was to become an even more exciting place in the next two decades, though the Bostonians who followed the activities of Braddock, Shirley, and Montcalm in the 1750's could not know that the steps leading to a break with England would occur virtually in their front yards only a few years later. The Stamp Act in 1765 brought about the organized resistance of the Sons of Liberty and the Boston merchants, who again voiced their protest, in 1767, to the Townshend Acts; the next year Boston customs officials were attacked when they tried to collect duty on the cargo of the *Liberty*, and the merchants agreed on a firmer policy of nonimportation. There followed the quartering of troops in Boston, continual skirmishes with these soldiers leading to the "Boston Massacre," Sam Adams' organization of "committees of correspondence," the Boston Tea Party, and eventually the battles at Lexington and Concord.

If the air everywhere was full of whispered conversations and secret plans, it was especially so in the center of Boston. Among the successful merchants there, who profited from war contracts and who met with Sam Adams and the patriots of the "Long Room Club" over Edes & Gill's printing office, was Royall Tyler, Sr. He lived in Ann Street, in the shadow

I

of Faneuil Hall, and operated his importing business from an adjacent storeroom that faced the wharf. Ambitious in politics, he was called "Pug Sly" and was well versed in the art of giving elaborate dinners and in all the hypocrisies of gaining public favor (the fine points of which he taught to his Harvard classmate James Otis). He served on innumerable town committees and worked his way up, through Justice of the Peace and Overseer of the Poor, to a seat in the House of Representatives (1759–1764) and then to a position on the King's Council, which he held from 1764 until his death in 1771. Fond of the limelight, he found himself there frequently — as, in 1754, when he refused to testify upon being questioned about a pamphlet ridiculing the House (he even sued Speaker Hubbard for imagining that he could be connected with it); or when, in 1768, he led the committee which demanded the withdrawal of the British fleet from the harbor and the troops from the city; or when, at a meeting after the Boston Massacre, he spoke so rashly about driving out the British soldiers that he turned his fellow Whigs against him.[1]

This active figure was a member of an established Boston family, settled there in 1680 by his grandfather, Captain Thomas Tyler, son of a Devonshire merchant-ship captain. One of Thomas' four sons, William (born 15 March 1688), had married Sarah Royall on 7 December 1710; and the patriot Royall, born on 8 September 1724, was one of their ten children. Rejecting the practice of law after his graduation from Harvard in 1743 to take over his father's business, he had married Mary Steele, daughter of Captain John Steele, on 24 December 1747, and the couple had four children.[2] One can imagine no more exciting place for a child to grow up than in Boston's Ann Street of the 1760's, where the happenings in the harbor could be clearly viewed. It is perhaps not surprising that one of these children, who could watch his father and other patriots in daily activities that led to revolution and who had roots in Boston going back four generations, would be among the first to use native American materials in works of literature and to express his patriotism as naturally in belles-lettres as in more direct service to his government.

College, War, and Love

The youngest child of Royall and Mary Steele Tyler was born on 18 July 1757, ten years after their marriage. He was named William Clark, but following his father's death the name was changed by an act of the General Court, at his mother's request, to Royall.[3] We are told that he was "more studious and thoughtful" as a child than his brother, John Steele [4] (there were two older daughters, Mary and Jane), and in 1765 he entered the South Latin School in Boston (under Tory principal John Lovell). One can picture him walking to school from Ann Street, by Faneuil Hall, along the thoroughfare of Cornhill, past the State House, to the Latin School on School Street near King's Chapel. On this route he must have witnessed hurried conferences between patriots and occasional fights when the British troops arrived, and he must have spent many after-school hours watching the activities in the harbor or listening to the bells that announced the Boston Massacre or the repeal of the Stamp Act,[5] although he was to make very little reference to Revolutionary events in his later writings. But the Boston of his childhood did furnish material for certain passages in "The Bay Boy," especially his description of a typical Boston street scene on a Saturday and Sunday, with the street cleaners replaced by the church crowds. No doubt he had sat through many a Sunday afternoon service, in which "every pew exhibited drowsiness in all its dozing attitudes" — the "witty maiden," for example, sleeping "serenely under the covert of her hat or bonnet unconscious that her waving plumes by their abrupt noddings betrayed the secret she so artfully attempted to conceal."

And perhaps, like the hero of "The Bay Boy," he kept his eyes on one such maiden at church and found that his "heart thumped like a bass drum."

Just before his fifteenth birthday, Tyler finished the usual seven years' work at Latin School and was ready to enter Harvard, which he did on 15 July 1772. Harvard in these years was just as much a center of revolutionary activity as Ann Street, and Tyler found that his brief journey across the Charles did not take him to a secluded retreat. The student body was anxious to express its patriotism: one way was to abstain from tea (as the seniors had voted to do four years before Tyler's entrance), but a more direct way was to join the student military company, the Marti-Mercurian Band (formed in 1769–70), which had been furnished with weapons only the year before Tyler's arrival. The presence of the General Court meetings in Cambridge (until March 1773) further aroused student feeling, so that by the end of Tyler's freshman year agitation was beginning to mount rapidly. It was not until the end of his second year, however, that British troops occupied Boston to enforce the Boston Port Act and thousands of armed patriots converged in Cambridge, preparatory to besieging Boston. In the midst of such unsettled conditions, college authorities decided not to hold a public commencement that year — nor, as it turned out, was another held until 1781. Students occasionally went into Boston to watch the British drills, but in the spring of 1775, Tyler's junior year, they had an opportunity to see British soldiers in Cambridge, when Lord Percy marched through on his way to give support to the troops at Lexington. As the patriot forces gained strength, the problem of housing them in Cambridge became increasingly acute, despite the availability of the vacated mansions on "Tory Row." The Committee of Safety sent the students home early that year, on 1 May, and the Provincial Congress appropriated the college buildings; even so, tents had to be

4

pitched all over town, and, as winter approached, temporary barracks were constructed in the college Yard and the Common. The college obviously could not operate in Cambridge, and Concord was eventually selected as the place where classes would resume on 4 October 1775. Tyler spent his senior year there, until 21 June 1776, when the depleted student body (probably fewer than one hundred students) returned to Cambridge.[6]

Tyler attended Harvard in the years just after certain important changes in policy were made. In 1766, for instance, the practice of having separate tutors for each subject was instituted (instead of one tutor who taught all subjects to each class); and at the beginning of Tyler's stay, under the administration of Samuel Locke, the ranking of students according to social and financial standing was changed to a listing in alphabetical order. The revised 1767 laws stipulated that "No one shall be admitted, unless he can translate the Greek and Latin Authors in common use, . . . understands the Rules of Grammar, can write Latin correctly, and hath a good moral Character." The Latin School had furnished Tyler with these accomplishments, and the moral character presumably was to be perpetuated by the required morning and evening chapel. A more interesting article in the laws, considering the direction of Tyler's later achievement, read, "If any Undergraduate shall presume to be an Actor in, a Spectator at, or any Ways concerned in any Stage Plays, Interludes or Theatrical Entertainments in the Town of Cambridge or elsewhere, he shall for the first Offence be degraded — & for any repeated Offence shall be rusticated or expelled." [7] Public speaking, on the other hand, was allowed, and both the Speaking Club (formed by Samuel Phillips in 1770) and the Mercurian Club (guided by Fisher Ames of the class of 1774) were in operation during Tyler's first year — with the Speaking Club, at any rate, more interested in literary than political subjects. The two clubs merged in 1773 but became less active as war approached; the group was revived, however, by some of Tyler's classmates and friends, such as Christopher Gore and Rufus King, and Tyler (though not a member) may well have begun at this time to practice the oratory for which he was to become known in the courtroom.

Nineteen years old, Tyler received his degree in July of 1776, just after the Declaration of Independence, in a class that included Gore (later Governor of Massachusetts and a United States Senator) and Samuel Sewall and George Thacher (later Justices of the Massachusetts Supreme Court); for his academic achievement he was also awarded a B.A. from Yale *ad eundem*.[8] Directly before and during Tyler's college years, several events took place in his family: in 1771 his sister Mary died at the age of eighteen; his father died on 20 May of the same year (aged forty-six) and was buried at King's Chapel with elaborate rites befitting his prominence — or notoriety; on 11 October 1772, his mother remarried (again a merchant, William Whitwell) and moved to Jamaica Plain; during the spring of 1775 (Tyler's junior year) this second husband died; and that June Tyler's brother John married their stepsister, Sarah Whitwell. Tyler's father had been successful as a merchant, and, whatever the precise amount of the estate, Tyler's inheritance was large enough to prevent his having any financial worries at this time; it is probable that he spent money with some freedom during his college years and those immediately following.[9] The only incident which family tradition records for Tyler's college career involves his rustication to Maine with his roommate Gore, but not for spending money. It seems that their room was above the door to their building; one day, when they had thrown down a hook and line to catch a pig from among the litter in the yard, they became so engrossed that they did not notice Samuel Langdon (the ineffectual President who had succeeded

Locke in 1774) heading for the door under them, and the hook inevitably caught in his wig.[10] Given Tyler's disposition as revealed in his later writing, his possession of some money, and the general atmosphere (discipline had been notoriously slack under President Locke, and many students boarded in taverns during the Concord period), it is unlikely that all Tyler's escapades were as mild as this one.

After graduation, Tyler began the study of law with Francis Dana of Cambridge, who had just returned from a year and a half in England, having concluded that a peaceful settlement was impossible; when Dana left to attend the Continental Congress in 1777, Tyler continued his legal preparation with Benjamin Hichborn of Boston and perhaps with Oakes Angier, a prominent lawyer who had formerly been a student of John Adams.[11] Whatever reputation for wit and brilliance Tyler had achieved during his Harvard years increased through his association with a group of talented and promising young men who gathered in the rooms of the painter John Trumbull, at what was later 5–9 Scollay Square (previously occupied by John Smibert). Trumbull, of the class of 1773, commented in his autobiography (1841) on this "club . . . of young men fresh from college" (mostly from the classes of 1776 and 1777), which included, besides Tyler, William Eustis (later a member of Congress and minister to Holland), Aaron Dexter (later a Harvard professor of medicine), Rufus King (later a Senator and minister to England), Thomas Dawes (a lawyer), and Christopher Gore. These men, says Trumbull, "regaled themselves with a cup of tea instead of wine, and discussed subjects of literature, politics and war," [12] although their activities were not always so restrained. On 20 October 1777, for example, Tyler, Sewall, and King created a drunken disturbance in Cambridge ("horrid Profanity, riotous & Tumultuous Noises, & breaking of Windows at College") and were summoned before a faculty meeting.

7

According to the faculty records, Tyler responded, "Pray Gentlemen! What right have you to call me before you? I am surprized you should be ingaged in such Business! What Punishment can you inflict upon me? What do I care for a little paltry Degree which may be bought at any time for twenty shillings. If honor in this Country consists in Degrees, you are very welcome Gentlemen to deprive me of yours, for I have two others already." [13] Jeremiah Mason recalls that Tyler (with his "brilliant wit," "amusing conversation," and "natural talents") "entered at once, with great zeal and zest, into the dissipated habits and manners which at that time characterized the young men of Boston." [14] It has been suggested also that Tyler was the father of Royal Morse (born in 1779) by a well-known college "character," the cleaning woman Katharine Morse.[15] Whether or not this particular report is true, Tyler did later refer to these years as his period of "dissipation," and the general tone of the combined testimony is undoubtedly accurate.

Perhaps it was as a result of some of the discussions at Trumbull's "club" during the winter of 1777–78 (the same winter when Burgoyne's surrendered troops were quartered in Cambridge, contributing — in the historian Mercy Warren's view — to the atmosphere of idleness and dissipation) [16] that several of the men joined the Independent Company of soldiers then forming in Boston under Colonel John Hancock. Tyler, as well as King and Trumbull himself, enlisted; Tyler's preceptor Hichborn was the third officer and his brother John Steele the fifth.[17] By late summer of 1778 General John Sullivan had assumed control of the attack on the British at Newport, and Tyler was made an aide to Sullivan, with the rank of major. In August, Sullivan had under his command at Providence a force of ten thousand men and was ready to proceed toward Newport and make a combined attack with the French fleet under d'Estaing. But the French fleet arrived first and, after a skirmish with Howe and the damages of a storm, decided to sail to Boston for repairs, leaving Sullivan's militia without support. Sullivan began to retreat on 28 August; the Battle of Rhode Island (or of Quaker Hill) on 29 August demonstrated that the British were still in control of Newport and ended Sullivan's ill-fated expedition. During the confused retreat, even before the battle, the troops became separated, and it happened (according to the family story) that Tyler and a soldier named Daggett found themselves sharing a barn the night before the combat. They discussed, among other things, the best part of the body in which to receive a bullet; the next day, with a bullet in his lungs, Daggett said, "Ah, Rial, you see I did not have my choice." [18] Such is the extent of Tyler's participation in the war.

Following this interlude, Tyler returned to his legal studies, presumably under Benjamin Hichborn, was granted a master's degree from Harvard in 1779 (after apologizing for his conduct in 1777), and was admitted to the bar (the Inferior Court) on 19 August 1780.[19] Because business in Boston was at a low ebb during this part of the Revolution and commerce was forced to go to Maine, he decided to begin his legal career in Falmouth (now Portland), which was just beginning to recover from a British burning. Although no record of the extent of Tyler's practice at Falmouth survives, one episode is traditionally told: accompanied by the sheriff, he boarded a privateer in the harbor to serve a writ, whereupon the privateer sailed away, pausing only long enough to put Tyler and the sheriff off at Booth Bay.[20] Whether such experiences or the generally more optimistic outlook in Boston was responsible — or whether, as Abigail Adams later said, "his ambition & genious could not brook a retirement like that" [21] — Tyler moved back to the Boston area in the spring of 1782, after less than two years at Falmouth.

Royall Tyler

He took lodgings in Braintree with the family of Richard and Mary Cranch, and opened an office in their house as well. There were two Cranch daughters of eligible age, and it is not to be wondered that a handsome young lawyer, of high promise and great wit, with his scarlet coat and ruffled shirt, should have caused some excitement in the household; indeed, his arrival seems to have been discussed by all the young ladies of the village. Possibly for the very reason that Betsy Cranch and the others invited his attention, he had little interest in them, but an equally cogent reason was that his eye had quickly been caught by the Cranches' niece, seventeen-year-old Nabby Adams, daughter of John Adams, the future President. Mary (Smith) Cranch was a sister of Abigail Adams, and the relationship between the house in Braintree and that in Quincy was an intimate one. During the summer and fall of 1782 Tyler's acquaintance with Abigail and her daughter grew increasingly close, and he found excuses for calling on them — for example, when he had a particularly difficult writ to draw, he would ask if he could borrow a book of forms from Adams' library. By winter he was spending many evenings with them, and the mother, at least, was charmed by him. She could see that he was falling in love with Nabby (as the young Abigail was generally called by her family) and felt somewhat guilty about not having mentioned the situation in her letters to her husband, who had been in Europe since early 1780 negotiating the peace treaty.

Accordingly, on 23 December 1782 she wrote him in detail about this young man with "a sprightly fancy, a warm imagination and an agreable person." Although she felt obliged to mention the fact that there had been a period of dissipation in his life, when he was "rather negligent" in pursuing his professional career, she emphasized the fact that he had now reformed completely. "I am not acquainted with any young Gentleman whose attainments in literature are equal to his, who judges with greater accuracy or discovers a more delicate and refined taste." After commenting on her daughter's reserved nature, which seemed only to attract him the more, she continued, "I know not a young fellow upon the stage whose language is so pure or whose natural disposition is more agreeable — his days are devoted to his office, his Evenings of late to my fire side — his attachment is too obvious to escape notice. I do not think the Lady wholly indifferent; yet her reserve & apparent coldness is such that I know he is in miserable doubt." [22] Exactly a week later Abigail wrote her husband another long letter about Tyler, describing his previous legal career and reporting that he had been conducting his Braintree office with "great steadiness and application," which had "gained the esteem and business of the Town." She found his disposition "exceedingly amiable" and his "attractions perhaps too powerful even to a young Lady possesst with as much apparent coldness and indifference as ever you saw in one character" — with the result that his attention "daily becomes more pleasing" to Nabby.[23] In a third letter, on 10 January 1783, Abigail again alluded to the matter: "I see, what I scarcely believe in my power to prevent without doing violence to Hearts which I hope are honest and good. . . . I wish for your advice and counsel." [24]

John Adams' advice, in no equivocal terms, was prompt in coming, for by 22 January he had received the first of Abigail's letters on the affair and replied, "I confess I dont like the Subject at all. My Child is too young for such Thoughts, and I dont like your word 'Dissipation' at all." Nabby was a "Model," he felt, not to be given to "any, even reformed Rake"; while a lawyer would be his choice, "it must be a Lawyer who spends his Midnights as well as Evenings at his Age over his Books not at any Lady's Fire Side. . . . A youth who has been giddy enough to spend his Fortune or half his Fortune in Gaieties is not the youth for me, let his Person,

Family, Connections and Taste for Poetry be what they will.
I am not looking out for a Poet, nor a Professor of belle
Letters." Tyler's brother in Europe, according to Adams, was
"a detestible Specimen"; Tyler's father, on the other hand,
was "an Honourable Man," although he "had not all those
nice sentiments which I wish." Finally, Adams criticized Abigail for allowing the matter to have advanced so far and for
implying disapproval of Nabby's reserve ("her greatest
Glory"); "I dont like," he added, "this Method of Courting
Mothers." His letters throughout the winter and spring continued to take up the subject — indeed, to belabor it. On
29 January he warned Nabby not to be impressed by superficial accomplishments; on 4 February he said of Tyler, "That
Frivolity of Mind, which breaks out into such Errors in
Youth, never gets out of the Man but shews itself in some
mean Shape or other through Life"; and on 28 March he
summed up his feelings:

My dear Daughters happiness employs my Thought night and
Day. Dont let her form any Connections with any one, who is
not devoted entirely to Study and to Business, — to honour &
Virtue. — If there is a Trait of Frivolity and Dissipation left, I
pray that she may renounce it, forever. I ask not Fortune nor
Favour for mine, but Prudence, Talents, and Labour. She may go
with my Consent wherever she can find enough of these.

He was willing to admit, however, that Tyler seemed to be a
promising young man, except for one "Trait in his Character,
his gaiety" — which made him "but a Prodigal Son." [25]
 Even before she received these letters, Abigail had concluded that it would be prudent "to put a present period . . .
to the Idea of a connection," [26] and Nabby went to Boston
in January to spend the rest of the winter there — though
not, as Abigail assured her husband, because "any of those
Qualities you justly dread have appeared in this gentleman
since his residence in this Town," for "his conduct has been

regular, and his manners pure, nor has he discovered any Love of Gaiety inconsistent even with your Ideas." She admitted "a partiality in his favour," but was happy to be able to report that the affair "is now so far laid aside as gives me reason to think it will never again be renewed." [27] That this conclusion was premature became clear after Nabby had returned from Boston, for Abigail then reported that Tyler "now visits in this family with the freedom of an acquaintance, tho' not with the intimacy of a nearer connection," and she again spoke on his behalf: "he is regular in his liveing, keeps no company with Gay companions, seeks no amusement but in the society of two or 3 families in Town, never goes to Boston but when business calls him there." [28] By July 1783 Tyler had been sworn in as an attorney of the Supreme Judicial Court; [29] by October he had a young schoolmaster named Perkins studying law under him; and by December he had purchased the excellent 108-acre Borland farm [30] — all three facts indicative of his seriousness and desire to settle down, and duly recorded by Abigail. In fact, her confidence in him was great enough that she turned over Adams' account books to him, in case he could collect some of the accounts that had become delinquent since Adams' departure.[31]

Adams, anxious to be reunited with Abigail after their long separation, decided that a trip to Europe for both mother and daughter would not only accomplish the purpose of bringing them all together but perhaps end the connection with Tyler. He set forth this plan once on 14 October: "The Lady comes to Europe with you. — If the Parties preserve their Regard untill they meet again and continue to behave as they ought, they will be still young enough." [32] But by late January 1784 he was more temperate about forcing Nabby to accompany her mother:

if Miss Nabby is attached, to Braintree, and you think, upon advising with your Friends, her object worthy, marry her if you will and leave her with her Companion in your own House, Office, Furniture, Farm & all. His Profession is, the very one I wish. — His Connections are respectable and if he has sown his wild Oats and will study, and mind his Business, he is all I want. . . . I can scarcely think it possible for me to disapprove of her final Judgment formed with deliberation, upon any Thing which so deeply concerns her whole Happiness.[33]

Nevertheless both Abigail and her daughter did sail for England, on board the *Active*, on 20 June 1784. One can imagine the parting scene, as Abigail recounted it: "I have great satisfaction in the behaviour of my daughter. The Struggle of her mind was great, her passions strong, never before calld into opposition; the parting of two persons strongly attached to each other is only to be felt; discription fails." [34] Tyler returned to his room crying, "She is gone! I shall never see her more!" and threw himself upon the couch and wept.[35]

Before this break, Tyler had written to Adams only once, five months before, on 13 January:

I will not presume . . . that my attentions to your Daughter are unknown to you: If you demand why an affair of so much importance to your Domestic Concerns was not communicated by me sooner — I hope that my youth, the early progress of my professional career, and the continued expectation of your daily return to your Family will be accepted as a sufficient Apology. . . . I do not think myself entitled to your Consent to an immediate union yet I cannot suffer this separation without requesting your permission to expect it when ever she shall return to Her native country.

The letter was enclosed in one from Richard Cranch, who commented on Tyler: "he has boarded at our House for near two years past, and, from my acquaintance with him, he appears to me to be possessed of Politeness, Genious, Learning and Virtue; and I think he will make a very respectable Figure in his Profession of the Law. His Business in that Department increases daily." [36] Adams did not receive Tyler's letter until early April but replied immediately in a friendly tone:

Your Connections and Education are too respectable for me to entertain any objections to them: Your Profession is that for which I have the greatest respect and Veneration. The Testimonials I have received of your personal Character and Conduct are such as ought to remove all Scruples upon that head.

He praised Tyler's purchase of land and offered Tyler the use of his library. "But" he added significantly, "the Lady is coming to Europe with her Mother. It would be inconvenient to you to make a Voyage to Europe perhaps." Nevertheless, "you and the young Lady have my Consent to arrange your Plans according to your own Judgments." [37] Two days after receiving this letter, on 27 August, Tyler replied, expressing "all those returns of gratitude, which, a man of Ingenuity may be supposed to render to the person, to whom he shall have been Indebted in a High Degree, for the Principal Enjoyments of his Life." It would have been overly selfish, he piously continued, to have married Nabby before the trip because her filial duties in accompanying her mother across the Atlantic were more important. And he concluded in proper style, "We — I venture to speak for your Daughter — shall chearfully submit to your Inspection and advice, and I hope that our union will afford you and your Lady, that Enviable Satisfaction, which Parents experience when they Perceive their children, Usefull, Worthy, Respectable and Happy." [38]

For a time all was well. Tyler had written two letters to Abigail by 6 November, and she replied at great length on 4 January 1785, describing the daily routine in London and addressing Tyler as "the person to whose care & protection I shall one day resign a beloved and only daughter." Letters from the Cranches in the fall of 1784 refer to the letters Tyler was receiving from Nabby and the picture she had sent; and in January, Mary Cranch could still allude to Tyler with satisfaction: "His business I think increases & as far as I can judge he attends it with steadiness. He has his share at this court." [39] But by June her letters to Abigail contained rumblings that Tyler was not behaving as he should. For one thing, he was not delivering the letters which Nabby had sent to her friends in his care ("She must never wonder why she does not receive answers to her Letters till she is sure they are received. . . . It is one of his whims not to deliver Letters for a long time after he has recv'd them"). [40] In addition, Tyler was apparently not writing to Nabby and did not even answer her May letter asking why he had not written. The vague rumors of Tyler's instability, combined with his seeming lack of attention and with the attractive presence in London of Adams' secretary of legation, Colonel William Stephens Smith, caused Nabby to decide (doubtless with some parental prompting) [41] to break off the match with Tyler. In the late summer of 1785 she wrote him: "Herewith you receive your letters and miniature with my desire that you would return mine to my Uncle Cranch, and my hopes that you are well satisfied with the affair as is / A.A." [42] Ten months later, on 12 June 1786, she and Smith were married.

The standard accounts of this whole episode, certainly one of the most celebrated in Tyler's life, [43] vary according to the conflicting traditions which have grown up in the two families. From the Adams point of view, Tyler had behaved dishonorably, both in his activities in Braintree and in his failure to write to Nabby; from the other side, Tyler was seen as the victim of malicious gossip circulated by Mary Cranch in her jealousy over the fact that Tyler did not court one of her daughters. [44] The truth no doubt lies in between, for there was some justification for dissatisfaction on both sides: it is evident, from Tyler's own admission, that he wrote very few letters to the Adamses in Europe, and it is equally clear, from

Mary Cranch's surviving letters, that she lost no opportunity of putting Tyler in an unfavorable light. In the middle of October 1785, before he had received Nabby's cold note of dismissal, Tyler had managed to write two long and friendly letters, one to John Adams and one to Abigail, full of current news, praise of John Quincy Adams (who had attended the opening of the Supreme Court in Boston with Tyler), and an explanation:

> It has not been without anxiety, that I have refrained from addressing a Letter to you for some months past. But . . . there was but one Subject upon which I could write to you liberally: and I intended to have Desisted from that, until the Completion of my Arrangements should enable me to Discuss it to our mutual Satisfaction. But I am apprehensive, that you may impute to some less pleasing motive, what really originated in Respect: I Reassume my Pen.[45]

Meanwhile Mary Cranch was beginning her long series of letters to Abigail, each letter going into more detail than the last about Tyler's disgraceful behavior. On 8 November she reported that his office had been closed for five weeks, that he was ostentatiously showing Nabby's letters to everyone, and that he was even boasting about the fact that he had received six letters from Nabby before she could have had one from him; on 10 December she accused him of lying about putting letters aboard every ship; on 9 February 1786 she described his refusal to give up Nabby's letters and his announcement that Nabby's dismissal of him was only a misunderstanding created by unfriendly relatives; on 2 April she remarked disapprovingly that Tyler left the Cranch house each day after breakfast and did not return until the family was in bed at night, and that he planned to sail to Europe soon to straighten everything out. And through all these detailed accounts ran protestations that she had given Tyler no reason to be angry with her.[46]

However much credence may be given to Mary Cranch's letters, they were effective, and the general sentiment which prevailed among the Adams relatives, upon the announcement of Nabby's marriage to Smith, was one of relief that an unfortunate connection had been avoided. John Quincy Adams wrote to this effect on 28 December 1785, even though he and Tyler had been on friendly terms for several months before that time; [47] Eliza Shaw, another sister of Abigail's, pitied Tyler but granted that everyone felt the break to be for the best; [48] and Mary Cranch outdid herself in reporting Tyler's dejection:

I most heartily congratulate you all, not only upon your acquisition but upon your escape. — Can he after this delude another Family — must another unsuspecting fair one fall a victim to his vanity. — I have no pity to bestow upon him unless for his folly. He means to brave it I see — he puts on such an air of indifference & gaiety as plainly shows how much he is mortified. . . . How much more pleasure do you feel by introducing a man of such a universally good character into your Family than one exactly opposite to it.[49]

Two months later she could still describe him as "*dismally* mortified," and added, "I cannot help pitying him a little although he has told so many Fibs about me." [50] But the following fall she continued to recount unfavorable stories about Tyler, until Abigail finally asked her not to mention the subject again.[51] Despite the remarkably full documentation available, it is not possible to know the complete story nor to assign the shares of blame accurately; but at least one may say that neither side was wholly blameless — and surely John Adams was pleased that his original plan for avoiding the Tyler connection had worked so well.

Tyler's dejection found one outlet in physical activity, for he worked at improving the Borland farmhouse and even constructed a windmill in the spring of 1786 — which turned out by July to be a fiasco because (according to Mary Cranch) he did not listen to advice.[52] From the spring of 1785 on he had spent an increasingly smaller part of his time at the Cranch establishment, partly because of his suspicions of Mary Cranch's role in the split with the Adamses and partly because lodgings in Boston were more convenient when the court was in session there. While still keeping his room and office at the Cranches', he took another room with the Joseph Palmer family on Beacon Street. Among the lodgers there in the fall of 1785 was the blind Henry Moyes, who was delivering a series of lectures on "natural history" (particularly electricity), and family tradition has it that Tyler assisted him.[53] At any rate, Tyler was scarcely in Braintree at all during October and November. Through the spring of 1786 he generally returned to the Cranch house only to sleep, and by May he was not going there at all, even though he was still serving on some local committees. Early in July, after the word had spread all over town that he had lost Nabby, he stopped in to pick up some of his belongings and left in low spirits for his mother's place in Jamaica Plain.[54] By fall he had returned to his practice in Boston and to the Palmer household; but the work he was having done on his Braintree property was putting him in debt,[55] and he was ready to welcome almost any opportunity which would take him away from these scenes of unpleasant events. Such a chance for escape offered itself the following winter.

Throughout the fall of 1786, there had been agitation among the farmers in the western part of the state as a result of the depression which was especially severe in the rural areas. By January 1787 a group of these discontented men, organized under Daniel Shays, decided that it was useless to expect a peaceful settlement of their grievances, and they planned an attack on the federal arsenal at Springfield. General Benjamin Lincoln, who had conducted an unfortunate campaign in

South Carolina during the Revolution, was appointed leader of the state troops for an expedition against Shays. Tyler joined this force and was made aide-de-camp with the rank of major. In the midst of a severe New England winter, the troops set out to protect the arsenal. Though Shays had intended to meet Luke Day, in charge of another group of insurgents, and make a joint attack, he arrived first, attacked alone, and was defeated by Major General William Shepard's militia (already stationed there) before Lincoln arrived. Lincoln then proceeded against Day, scattered that band, and pursued Shays, who had retreated with some of his followers to Amherst. By the end of January he promised to recommend for pardon any rebels who would surrender, but he had no authority to grant amnesty, as Shays demanded; he therefore continued after Shays and, on 2 February, made his famous surprise attack at Petersham, by marching through a snowstorm at night, and captured many of Shays's remaining men.[56] On one occasion during these maneuvers in the deep Berkshire snows, Tyler, in charge of a troop of cavalry, came upon a number of rebels piously listening to a discourse in a meetinghouse on Sunday — a diatribe about the tyranny of the government. Since the men had left their weapons outside with only one guard, it was a simple task to surround the building and take the entire group prisoners. According to legend, however, Tyler waited until the speaker had finished, marched to the pulpit, and addressed his literally captive audience on the benefits to be derived from allegiance to the government. If it is an overstatement to say, with one nineteenth-century chronicler, that the result was "the instant conversion of the whole band into good citizens," the force of Tyler's eloquence does appear to have swayed the insurgents.[57]

Though the Petersham attack effectually ended the rebellion, certain of the ringleaders had escaped, Shays himself into Vermont. Lincoln asked Tyler to accept the important mission of pursuing these men, a particularly delicate matter, since the governments of the surrounding states were not always sympathetic to the rather autocratic Governor Bowdoin of Massachusetts, and one further complicated by the fact that New York still claimed jurisdiction over the so-called "New Hampshire Grants" in Vermont territory (though Vermont had declared itself independent in 1777). The official request came from Lincoln on 14 February 1787: "I have therefore to solicit, sir, that you would pursue & apprehend these delinquents. And all such farther powers as you may need in executing this commission, You will please to apply to the Governors of the neighboring States for them. To whose countenance you are particularly recommended as a Gentleman to whom the most perfect respect and confidence is due." [58] Tyler set out the next day and made arrangements at Williamstown for Colonel Fay to have his five hundred men ready to move at a minute's notice. On arriving in Bennington, Tyler found the Vermont council (to whom his petition was presented on 17 February) opposed to issuing any warrants for the arrest of the rebels, and Ethan Allen expressed the view that persons fleeing Massachusetts for safety should not be seized. The tact with which Tyler could handle such difficult situations was illustrated soon after his arrival. A number of the leaders in the Vermont government "seemed to feel mortified," as he put it, that the governor of Massachusetts had not formally written to the governor of Vermont about this matter; Tyler then explained that Massachusetts law did indeed require such action, and they "amicably resolved that his Excellency's dispatches must have been intercepted by the rebels." [59]

The nature of Tyler's activities at this time is conveniently summed up in one of his letters to the Palmers, written from Bennington:

My good Friends: How I wish you could look in upon me, and

see your old friend the center, the mainspring of movements, that he once thought would have crazed his brain — this minute, haranguing the governor and Council, and House of Representatives; the next, driving 40 miles into the State of New York, at the head of a party to apprehend Shays: back again in 20 hours: now, closing the passes to Canada: next, writing orders to the frontiers — as thus: "Mr. Officer! have 200 men in readiness." "Messrs. Selectmen! provide sleighs to transport them at a moment's warning." "Pray, where is your Honor going?" — "To Major Tyler. The Commissioners levy!" Will not this make you laugh? — I hope to be home, and bring Shays with me. If the command of a pocket full of money, and 500 choice men will do it; and if this State are not blind to their own interest, I shall do it.[60]

Nevertheless, Tyler's mission was not a success; he captured only Abram Wheeler, who was then rescued by a band of men from New York. But he had spoken so persuasively that, after he left Bennington on 27 February, the Vermont government, following a long debate, issued the very proclamation against aiding fugitives that he had been arguing for. Still, in his official "Memorial" to the Massachusetts legislature on 6 March, he pointed out that "Proclamations . . . can never Coerce the General Sentiment of the People" and that "the Bulk of the People in Vermont are for affording protection to the Rebels." [61] Lincoln wrote to Tyler, "You have done a great deal; we cannot command success; to deserve it has the same merit." [62] Because Tyler had capably conducted the Vermont business, he was asked to pursue several further negotiations in regard to the Shays affair. After reporting to Lincoln at Pittsfield, he was sent to Stockbridge to ascertain the facts of the final rebel attack, which had taken place on 27 February; he then proceeded to Boston, arriving early on the morning of 5 March, sent dispatches to Governor James Bowdoin and Judge Theodore Sedgwick, talked to the Governor the next day, and was asked by the Council to take on another mission, this time to the authorities in New York.[63]

Lawyer and Wit

Setting out on 8 March, he arrived in New York City on 12 March and, with the cooperation of the state government, accomplished his mission. The insurgents asked for pardon, and later in the year amnesty was granted (to all but a few leaders, who were pardoned in 1788). It may have been affairs of state which drew Tyler to New York City, but this man who was too gay and frivolous for John Adams was not one to limit himself to such business. He had not been in New York before, and undoubtedly he was determined to take advantage of the various opportunities for amusement which the city offered — notably, of course, the theater. Such is the background for the most famous moment in Tyler's life. Five weeks after his arrival in New York, he had written a comedy with a native setting and had seen it performed: *The Contrast*, given at the John Street Theatre on 16 April 1787, has the distinction of being the first American comedy produced commercially. Little more than a month later, on 19 May, another work of his was put on the stage, a comic opera called *May Day in Town*. Although Tyler had read widely in English literature and (as we know from the Adams letters and his participation in the Trumbull gatherings) had exhibited some literary inclinations, he had not before been a "literary figure" — a position which he was now enjoying to the full. According to tradition, the handsome young lawyer and Major who could dash off popular plays was, during those two months or so, "petted, caressed, feasted and toasted." [64]

After this triumph it is all the more difficult to understand why Tyler should have fallen into a state of depression and left New York. In fact, almost nothing is known of this period in his life, but he returned to his mother's home in Jamaica Plain for a while, before he resumed his legal practice in Boston, boarding again with the Palmers. Almost the only incident of this time recorded in family tradition, though perhaps apocryphal, at least shows Tyler's interest in protecting the

23

family property on Ann Street and is suggestive of his general impulsiveness: when city officials, over his protests, attempted to move a small building into an alley on the Tyler land, he seized an axe and cut the rope by which several men were pulling the building, causing them to fall abruptly on top of each other.[65] If Tyler seems to have been simply marking time during this period, the course of his future was beginning to take shape. For if he had lost Abigail Adams, he still had little Mary Palmer, eighteen years younger than he, right there in the house where he was boarding. He had first admired her as a child of eight or nine when he took her on his knee and called her "my little wife"; and Mary herself recalled that, "if ever a life-long love was commenced at first sight, it was then done on my part." A new phase of Tyler's life was about to begin.

Mary Palmer and Vermont

The Palmers were not as old a Boston family as the Tylers, but they were an extraordinarily interesting one. Young Mary Palmer's grandfather, Joseph Palmer of Devonshire (1716–1788), came to America in 1746 with his wife, Mary Cranch, and his brother-in-law, Richard Cranch (who later married John Adams' sister-in-law, Mary Smith). The two men, settling in the Germantown part of Braintree, had built by the mid-1750's various factories — notably a glassworks, but also chocolate mills and spermacetti- and saltworks. Palmer, as the overlord of all this activity, constructed an elaborate house, Friendship Hall, in which, it is said, he lived "more like an old fashioned English country gentleman, than any one beside has ever done amongst us." [66] He was gregarious and philanthropic; the Braintree town records reveal him as active in civic affairs from 1755 on and generous in contributing funds to pay the local militia in 1780; and his name appears frequently in the annals of pre-Revolutionary agitation, since he was elected (in early 1775) the Braintree representative to the Massachusetts Provincial Congress and was on the committee of safety. As Brigadier-General of the 1777 Rhode Island expedition, he received a great deal of blame for its failure, but was acquitted in a court-martial held in November of that year. His spirits dashed and his finances depleted, he died before he could put into operation his schemes for rebuilding his fortunes.[67] John Adams wrote in general of both the Palmers and the Cranches, "Those 2 families well deserve the Character they hold of friendly, sensible, and Social. The Men, Women and Children, are all sensible and obliging." [68]

The unusual prominence of the Palmers, however, extends beyond Joseph Palmer and the connection with the Adamses. Palmer had three children, two daughters and a son, Joseph Pearse Palmer (1750–1797), who like his father participated in Revolutionary events, as a secretary of the committee of safety and an "Indian" in the Boston Tea Party. This son married (after parental objections were quieted) Elizabeth Hunt (1755–1838), one of the five daughters of John Hunt of Watertown, who were celebrated for their beauty. Mary Hunt Palmer (1775–1866), whom Tyler eventually married, was one of the nine offspring of this union, but three of her sisters produced distinguished families as well. Elizabeth Palmer married Nathaniel Peabody and thus became the mother of the famous Peabody sisters (Elizabeth Palmer Peabody, the educationalist; Mary, the wife of Horace Mann; Sophia, the wife of Nathaniel Hawthorne); Amelia Palmer gained as a son-in-law the editor and writer Park Benjamin; and Catherine Palmer married Henry Putnam and became the mother of the publisher George Palmer Putnam.[69]

It was into this family that Tyler found himself more and more intimately drawn through the 1780's. He first met the Palmers while he was boarding with the Cranches in Braintree in the winter of 1783–84, and he began to make frequent visits to the house at Germantown. Joseph Pearse Palmer became one of his closest friends; Mary Palmer recalled that the two were "twin souls," and that Tyler was repeatedly their "friend in time of need." General Palmer had returned from the war in financial difficulty, and a quarrel with John Hancock about the depreciation of the currency seemingly caused more pressure to be exerted on him, so that he was forced to give up the Germantown estate; from then on the Palmers occupied a succession of rooming houses in Boston, and Tyler not only paid them rent but at times paid their creditors as well.[70] For several years at the end of the decade and at the beginning of the 1790's, Mary Palmer and Tyler saw little of each other. For one thing, Mary spent the spring and summer of 1789 in New York taking care of the children in the family of Elbridge Gerry — during which time she not only witnessed the inauguration of Washington but also discovered, according to her account, that *The Contrast* was a frequent topic of conversation, as a result of its revival on 10 June 1789.[71] After her return, the Palmers, dissatisfied with their Boston existence, gladly accepted the opportunity of moving to the Hunt farm at Framingham.[72]

At the same time, Tyler had also resolved on a move away from Boston. In the summer of 1790 he stopped at the Palmer house in Framingham and announced that he was on his way to Vermont, which, according to Mary Palmer, was "then considered the outskirts of creation by many, and [an area] where all the rogues and runaways congregated, and for that reason considered a good place for lawyers." [73] It is true that Vermont offered such advantages as cheap land and low taxes, and that statehood and an influx of population were immediate prospects. Even so, it is difficult to fathom Tyler's reasons for leaving an established practice and friends in Boston for the Vermont frontier — or, indeed, for any of his abrupt changes of location and fits of depression. Idle speculation is pointless;

all one can do is to observe that in 1787 he had suddenly abandoned the gaiety of New York social life for his mother's place at Jamaica Plain and that in 1790 he relinquished his Boston life, turned the family property over to his mother, left his brother John Steele to look after her, and set out to begin again in Vermont. There is no doubt that an altercation with his mother was partly responsible, for she objected to his interest in Mary Palmer; and as Mary later said, he "had ever been a spoiled child, and unused to being thwarted in his inclinations."[74] He was always depressed after seeing his mother and refused ever to discuss these visits with Mary. What lay behind his mother's objections, and what other factors were involved, it is now impossible to say.

In any event, Tyler must have remembered from his earlier visit to Vermont in the Shays affair where the best opportunities might lie, for in early 1791 he established himself in Guilford. With 2432 inhabitants[75] (many attracted there by the town's rebelliousness in previously throwing off the yoke of both New Hampshire and Vermont), Guilford was the largest settlement in the state, boasting of two merchants and two doctors, but no other lawyer. Tyler's account book for 1791 shows that his practice flourished and that he was given cases and attended courts in several neighboring counties. He took pride in the fact that he settled some cases which had been dragging on inconclusively before he arrived, and his increasing reputation was evidenced by the eighty-four cases he handled in the June and November terms of 1793.[76]

During these years, between terms, Tyler made periodic trips south to visit the Palmers. He had offered, when he stopped there in 1790 on his way to Vermont, to look for a position for Mary's father, possibly as a teacher, and he wrote to the family on this subject during the winter. In the summer of 1792, after the adjournment of the court at Bennington, he visited Judge Sedgwick at Stockbridge, Massachusetts, and proceeded to New Lebanon, New York, where Mary was staying with her uncle, Ephraim Hunt. Mary was overjoyed at Tyler's surprise visit, after an absence of two years, but she found that considerable explanation was required before her aunt and uncle "could be quite pleased with me for welcoming him in such an extraordinary manner." When they learned who Tyler was, though, they were favorably disposed, since Uncle Ephraim's only reading besides the newspapers was his printed copy of *The Contrast*, which he inflicted on his wife each evening until she had it nearly memorized. Tyler gave Mary the material for a dress on that visit, and his subsequent visits, which became more frequent, were always accompanied by presents, such as a bracelet with two hearts and the motto, "True as steel." [77]

It was probably in the winter of 1793–94, when Mary was eighteen, that Tyler formally proposed marriage and explained that he was about to buy a house, which would be ready for her the following spring.[78] Since he had been elected State's Attorney for Windham County, he had to return to Vermont immediately, but he took Mary's father with him, for he had found employment for Palmer in Windsor, about sixty miles from Guilford. In May 1794 Tyler, after a disturbing visit with his mother, returned to Framingham and asked Mary if she would consent to a secret marriage, not to be announced until the following winter when the snow would make possible a sleigh journey with luggage to Vermont. Mary's own account of this marriage and the ensuing months emphasizes the mysteriousness of Tyler's behavior and the difficulties of her own position, innocent of the reasons for secrecy and forced to reveal the marriage sooner than Tyler intended because of the premature birth in December of their child. Explanations suggest themselves but they must remain mere speculation, for there is no other source of evidence. Whether or not Mary's story is distorted by more than the simple passage of time, all one can do is recite the facts as she gives them. Tyler returned, she says, in February 1795, hoping he could finally take her and the baby to Vermont, but sufficient snow did not fall and she had to wait another year. Understandably this period was difficult, and she describes, in her devoutly religious way, the considerable soul-searching which she went through. Her picture of Tyler stresses his unfailing kindness (in providing the poverty-stricken Palmers with supplies or presenting Mary with such gifts as monogrammed teaspoons) and accepts unquestioningly his peculiar behavior as partly the result of his disagreements with his mother and partly the natural eccentricity of a literary man.

In February of 1796 heavy snow fell at last, so that Tyler could go to Framingham and bring back Mary and fourteen-month-old Royall. Accompanied by Mary's young brother Hampden, now a law student with Tyler, and driven by Tyler's team of horses, Crock and Smut, they entered Guilford after a three-day journey, passing the houses of Dr. Stevens, Major Field, and Dr. Hyde, and descending the hill into the village and their home, where Tyler's housekeeper Molly Clough had all in readiness.[79] Thus began the five years of married life which the Tylers spent in Guilford, years that saw the birth of three more children and the death of Mary's father and her young brother Edward (both in 1797, just a week apart) and, in 1800, of Tyler's mother.[80] Tyler and his mother were never reconciled (though she sent Mary a tablecloth and dishes in 1796 and wrote her a letter), and he was not informed of her death, learning about it only in a newspaper obituary after she was already buried.

If the rhythm of their lives in Guilford was set by births and deaths, by weekly social gatherings at friends' houses, and by Tyler's periodic departures for legal sessions, there was still time enough for occasional writing and the art of

conversation. Soon after his move to Vermont, Tyler had met Joseph Dennie at Charlestown, New Hampshire, and was drawn into a group of intelligent and witty young men, many of them lawyers, who indulged their appetite for literary activity. Out of this association in 1794 came the partnership of "Colon & Spondee" — that is, Dennie and Tyler — which produced a large number of amusing and satiric essays, sketches, and verses appearing in the *Eagle, or Dartmouth Centinel*, then in the *Farmer's Weekly Museum* (published by David Carlisle and Isaiah Thomas in Walpole, New Hampshire), and later in Dennie's *Port Folio*. Tyler had not given up playwriting, either, and knew something of the Boston theater world through his brother, who was managing the Federal Street Theatre. At this time he wrote a comedy called *The Georgia Spec*, produced in Boston on 30 October 1797 and later that year in New York; his other comedies — *The Farm House*, *The Doctor in Spite of Himself*, and *The Island of Barrataria* — may also have been performed at this period, though no record of their production survives. In addition, Tyler found enough leisure to turn out a novel on the timely subject of the Barbary pirates, published pseudonymously in two volumes in the fall of 1797 by Carlisle in Walpole.

After his mother's death, Tyler went to New York to settle the estate and returned with three thousand dollars. Out of this money he purchased, with Mary's encouragement, the Micah Townsend farm in Brattleboro and moved his family on 3 March 1801 to the town which would be his location for the rest of his life. With 1867 inhabitants, this "little collection of houses" (as Timothy Dwight called it) was somewhat smaller than Guilford and was not to grow rapidly, increasing by only 274 in the next three decades. The farm consisted of 150 acres, with several orchards, fields of wheat and rye, a number of cattle, hogs, sheep, chickens, and turkeys, and fruit and vegetable gardens around the house. Situated on the hill where the first meetinghouse in town had been, the farmhouse contained seven rooms downstairs, including an office with an outside door. In a long letter written soon after the family moved in, Tyler noted that the "house is entirely secluded from a view of any neighbors; though on the crown of a hill it is yet in a hollow, but the necessary buildings around it give it the air of being a little neighborhood. . . . I think this place may be made comfortable and even pleasing." [81] That first summer the Tylers held a large dinner party for their new neighbors, and under Mary's skillful management the house was apparently as pleasing as Tyler had predicted. They lived on the farm until 1815, when they moved into town, and, according to Mary's diary, the years passed by in great happiness. Although that diary, written between 1858 and 1863, long after Tyler's death, may romanticize certain hardships of the past, this remarkable and courageous document is fitting testimony of Mary's strength of character and devotion. Throughout the Brattleboro years, she continued to bear and educate children (seven more) and to manage the house with kindness and efficiency.[82]

Mary Tyler was an author, as well as a mother and wife, and *Grandmother Tyler's Book* was not her first effort. No one knew the trials of motherhood better than she, and by June of 1810 she had written her experiences and advice into a book of 291 pages, published anonymously in the fall of 1811 by the New York publisher Isaac Riley, with whom her husband had been dealing.[83] Taking as its motto the dubious maxim, "Every Mother her Child's best Physician," the book is well described by its title page: *The Maternal Physician: A Treatise on the Nurture and Management of Infants, from the Birth until Two Years Old. Being the Result of Sixteen Years' Experience in the Nursery. Illustrated by Extracts from the Most Approved Medical Authors. By an*

American Matron. It went into a second edition in Philadelphia in 1818 (published by Lewis Adams), and James Thacher, in his *American Modern Practice* (1826), referred to its author both as a "sensible writer" and as "a fascinating American writer," and praised the book as "a production replete with interesting matter, and worthy the attention of every nursing family." [84]

The six chapters of the book comprise the early care of infants, education in the use of hands and feet, weaning and discipline, diseases, medicinal plants, and a conclusion. For measles — to take one example of her remedies — she recommends a mixture of rhubarb, cinnamon water, and orange peel. Tyler's influence perhaps shows in her use of literary epigraphs and quotations throughout, but these often create a ludicrous effect. Thus, when she begins to discuss the treatment of children younger than four months, Pope's *Essay on Man* (slightly misquoted) supplies her with "For thee health gushes from a thousand springs" (p. 20); or, in stressing the value of the mother's own milk, she exclaims, "O what a blissful moment to a fond mother! when 'The starting beverage meets the thirsty lip, / 'Tis joy to yield it, and 'tis joy to sip' " (p. 31); or she chooses an epigraph from Drayton's *Idea* sonnets when she gives directions about weaning: "Since there's no help, come let us kiss and part" (p. 140). It is unkind to imagine that Tyler's sense of humor could have led him intentionally to suggest to his wife such misapplications; it is more likely that he accepted the quotations as legitimate embellishments to a highly sentimental and flowery mode of writing.

The cultural and social milieu in which the Tylers lived was one which would tolerate Mary's description of her subject as "the all-important and delightful task of nursing those sweet pledges of connubial love, over whom every good mother watches with tremulous anxiety, and almost painful affection" (p. 6), or as "the preservation of this lovely and interesting portion of society" (p. 100). Her dedication to her mother represents this tradition at its nadir:

Madam,

That helpless babe which reposed on your affrighted bosom when you fled the vicinity of Boston, on the day of the ever memorable battle of Lexington, now a wife, a mother, and near the meridian of life, as a small tribute for all your maternal cares, most respectfully addresses this little volume to your perusal; candidly confessing that all which is valuable in it she derived from you.

For the nurture of my infancy I am *most grateful* — but for my education, and, above all, for the sublime lesson you taught me, *"that the best pleasures of a woman's life are found in the faithful discharge of her maternal duties,"* I owe you more than gratitude.

May you find an ample recompense in the assurance that from your grandchildren I receive that filial love and respect which has ever been rendered you by

Your Daughter
MARY.

Another passage gives a glimpse of the Tylers' home life (and shows Tyler in a more indulgent mood than he often appears in Mary's memoir):

I was here almost tempted to address a word or two of advice to *fathers*; but my own good man, who sits laughing on the sofa, whilst his favourite little Joseph is drawing his watch tied to a string round the carpet for a plaything, and who just now *looked* as if he thought me cruel for refusing the dear enchanting little innocent my ink-standish for a go-cart, might esteem it *too presuming*. (p. 170)

If Mary's writing deserves little attention, at least the fact of her writing is noteworthy, as well as the totality of her experience, encompassing both the Revolution and the Civil War.[85] Her story, especially as she tells it, illustrates the kind of integrity and stability that Tyler was continually holding up as goals for the people of the new republic.

Royall Tyler

Law and Poverty

During these years Tyler was pursuing his vocation and was becoming in the process a celebrated and successful lawyer. He had young men studying under him from time to time[86] and devoted considerable effort to improving his own legal knowledge as well as to handling cases all over the state. For most of the Guilford years, from 1794 until 1801, he served as State's Attorney for Windham County, a position which brought him in touch with many prominent figures. As a result, on 12 October 1801, he was elected one of the three judges of the Vermont Supreme Court. He and Stephen Jacob, a good friend from Windsor, were Assistant Judges; the Chief Justice was Jonathan Robinson, earlier somewhat hostile to Tyler's Federalism and his satiric comments on Republicanism in the *Farmer's Museum*, but after their association on the bench quite friendly and cooperative. On 14 October 1807, after Robinson was elected to the United States Senate, Tyler was made Chief Justice (the ninth in Vermont history). His Federalism seems to have become so mild that he could take office amidst a general Republican victory, but for the same reason could not survive the Federalist victory of 1813.[87] Even so, he served twelve years, longer than any other Supreme Court judge in Vermont prior to Charles K. Williams (whose term began in 1822). He also ran for the United States Senate in 1812, but was defeated by Dudley Chase, 110 votes to 94.[88] Overlapping his court tenure was his service to the University of Vermont: he wrote to his wife on 20 January 1802 that he had accepted appointment as a trustee of the University (a position he held until 1813), and from 1811 to 1814 he was Professor of Jurisprudence there (with a master's degree from Vermont *ad eundem*).[89]

Tyler's success in law was no doubt partly due to his skill in public speaking, and several anecdotes about his oratory survive, such as the story of his meetinghouse speech to the captured men during the Shays pursuit. A similar incident occurred during one of his first winters in Vermont. In Charlestown on legal business, he was asked to serve as lay reader at church one Sunday, in the absence of the minister; he not only read from the prayer book but delivered a sermon of his own composition, based on Luke 2:13–14. The members of the congregation, which included several lawyers in town for the court session, were so enthusiastic about his performance that they requested him to give the Christmas sermon also. After this experience he seriously considered entering the clergy. His wife recalled his comment on the episode: "And in truth it would have been a rest to my soul at that time had I dared [become a preacher], but a consciousness of having lived too gay a life in my youth made me tremble lest I should bring in some way disgrace upon the sacred cause!" [90] This remark, authentic or not, is an indication of Tyler's basically religious nature and another of those persistent allusions to his "dissipated" early behavior. Despite Tyler's enthusiasm as a lawyer, his wife's statement that he "never ceased to regret his decision" (to remain in law rather than take up the ministry) must carry some weight.[91]

Another of Mary Tyler's undoubtedly biased observations is that "few were the audiences who could resist his eloquence. I always thought his power consisted greatly in the remarkably melodious intonation of his voice aided by as remarkable insight into human nature." [92] Tyler himself described his effect on an audience, though the occasion was not a characteristic one; on 22 February 1800 he delivered an oration on the death of George Washington, which had occurred two months before. "The spectators," he wrote to Mary, "were numerous, and my success — was what you might wish. I shall only say here, that the austere Democracy, who came resolved to be displeased; down whose hard unmeaning faces ne'er stole the pitying tear, wept. I never more earnestly wished your presence." His remarks were so highly admired that Governor Tichenor requested their publication, and a sixteen-page pamphlet duly appeared in March, printed by David Carlisle at Walpole for Isaiah Thomas. That Tyler could pronounce such an oration and that his name would be allowed to appear on its title page are further indications of the general taste of the time and the attitude toward literature; for the speech is in the same ornate style as the *Maternal Physician* and, as a useful public discourse, carried enough respectability to be claimed by a professional man. For that matter, there was a professional motive behind it, and the flowery rhetoric may indicate only that Tyler knew what would move the public: "One great inducement I had to deliver this Oration was the hopes of making myself more known in this vicinity; and giving the people a sample of my speaking powers. I have found the good effects of my plan already. In one hour after I left the meeting house, I was engaged in three important causes; and I am told that I shall be in more." [93]

The *Oration*, of about 2500 words, begins with some reflections on human mortality, then asks "ye children of our political father" to "hear the instructive lesson of your parent's life" (p. 4). In a series of parallel rhetorical questions the virtues of Washington — "vigour of mind," "martial courage," equanimity, modesty, and so on — are enumerated as models for emulation: "He taught us how to live" (p. 5). This discussion constitutes the bulk of the oration, but, when Tyler comes to the virtue of "conjugal excellence," he elaborates on the grief which Washington's widow must feel:

Oh! at those solitary moments, when busy, meddling memory, in barbarous succession, musters up the fond endearments of your tender heart; at those cheerless moments when you recollect pressing the clay cold hand of a dying husband, wiping the clammy sweat from his forehead, while his fixed eye balls gave the last look of affection upon you, and closed forever; when you remember that heart rending hour, when you thought all happiness flown from you forever, and you felt yourself alone, and the world was a blank before you; then, while your agonized bosoms throb with anguish at your own loss; think on the pangs of her who mourns a WASHINGTON. (pp. 10–11)

Obviously Tyler had mastered all the techniques of the melodramatic oratory of the time. The speech is full of emotional appeals and balanced constructions: "Such was the man whom we lament; and such was the man whom the world applauds" (p. 11). In the last few pages he emphasizes national unity as one of Washington's fondest hopes: "Thus united in affliction, let us be united in love; and at this moment, while we recline over his bier, let us resolve never more to separate; but to inhabit the goodly heritage, which God has given us, like a band of brothers" (p. 16). The performance is a competent, even skillful, example of the funeral eulogy in this tradition, and it illustrates the quality of Tyler's rhetoric, if not of his thought.[94]

Another trait which stood Tyler in good stead as a lawyer, and especially as a judge, was his human compassion. Writing to Tyler from Washington in 1810, Justice Robinson provides an insight into this aspect of Tyler's nature:

Dear Sir: — You speak well of Bro. Fay, as a judge. I had never any doubt either of his honesty, clearness of perception, legal knowledge or patience, so essential for a judge, but feared he might be too legal, in other words, might give too great weight to technical precision, although useful, yet not wholly essential in administering impartial justice to ignorant but honest suitors. But I knew you and Bro. Herrington would stand as a check. I was always pleased with you more than I ever expressed on that account, because it is a bright gem in the character of a court lawyer, not to lay too much stress on the manner of action or pleading. When we come to be judged for our judgments, my friend, the question will not be whether we pursued legal forms or technical niceties, but have you heard the cry of the poor and relieved them from their oppressors. But I hope that the philanthropy of Bro. Fay and yourself will prevent all unpleasant results because he does not carry the Hopkinsian doctrine to that lofty pinnacle of revelation and philosophy to which you so justly and rationally aspire.

Robinson further characterizes Tyler two years later, in a postscript describing how his own letter would be received among the judges:

Bro. Tyler filled his pipe and said, "Come, Brethren, let us see what Bro. Robinson has to say." Reads. Bro. Fay spits and says, "Bro. Robinson is as cross as the devil." "Well," says Bro. Herrington, "I feel easy about it, it is a pack for their backs, not mine." Bro. Tyler smiled, and filled his second pipe.[95]

These were the qualities which had already been recognized, as early as 1797, by John A. Graham, who published in London his observations on Vermont and included a comment on Tyler:

Mr. *R. Tylor* (formerly of *Boston, Massachusetts*), lives in *Ryegate*; he also was bred to the Law: he possesses a fine turn for poetry, and unites to it the most humane disposition, and a most benevolent heart. — Does misery need an advocate? Mr. *Tylor* eagerly steps forth, its unpurchased champion. Does guilt (when not atrocious) sink down heart-broken and desponding? in Mr. *Tylor* it finds a man, who (though his own morals are irreproachable) feels for the errors of others, pities their vices, and compassionates their wants. How commanding is his oratory when pleading in their behalf! with what resistless power does it assail the hearers! he rouses every sympathizing passion of their souls, attacks them in every vulnerable part; awes, soothes, softens, and finally prevails. Such a character can seldom fail of being considered with due respect. Mr. *Tylor* is looked up to with admiration, affection, and esteem.[96]

Also to Tyler's advantage were his handsome appearance and his ready wit. His sense of humor frequently entered the courtroom. Once, earlier in his Vermont career, he found himself defending a man who, when his lease was up, wanted to remove a barn he had built on rented land. Tyler guessed, from the way the opposing lawyer read his Latin quotations, that he did not really understand them, and he knew that the farmer-judge did not; therefore Tyler cited as his authority the line, "Cujus est solum ejus est usque ad coelum," and translated it for the court as "Who builds a barn on hired land has a right to move it off again." [97] The constant puncturing of pretentiousness found in his writings was a part of his life as well.

Tyler's position as Chief Justice made his name widely known for a time, but a more lasting legal fame resulted from his publication of reports of Vermont Supreme Court cases. Soon after Tyler became Chief Justice, Isaac Riley in New York began communicating with various state courts about the possibility of publishing reports of their cases (eventually bringing out those for Connecticut, Maryland, New York, and Virginia). Tyler, on 8 November 1808, replied, "I can merely state, that, ever since I have been upon the bench, now nine years, I have been collecting reports of decisions of my official labors, to prepare them for the press." He estimated that his material would fill three volumes of six hundred pages each and that he could have one volume ready by the following August. So he set to work, using his spare time and vacations for the extensive revisions necessary, and sent batches of the manuscript to Riley as he got them finished. For every hundred printed pages, he was to receive one hundred twenty dollars plus fifty dollars' worth of books and stationery. Volume I was completed by mid-summer of 1809 and was published late in the year; by the end of 1810 a second volume appeared.[98] Both carried Tyler's name on their title pages, making them his only major work not published anonymously.

The *Reports of Cases Argued and Determined in the Su-*

preme Court of Judicature of the State of Vermont cover, in the two volumes, the cases between January 1800 and February 1803. Though no more were published, Tyler's *Reports* are the only record of Vermont cases in the interval between 1797 and 1813. The legal reports, of all states, were chaotically published during the early years of the republic — and were not published at all except when someone like Tyler had the energy to prepare them. In Vermont, one earlier judge, Nathaniel Chipman, had compiled *Reports* to cover the years 1789–1791; but after Tyler there were no published reports until those of William Brayton (for 1815–1819) and Daniel Chipman (who filled in some cases for 1797 and 1813–1815, before he proceeded with those for 1824, the beginning of the series unbroken to the present). Tyler's *Reports* give evidence of careful compilation, and they provide adequate indexes and marginal headings. Their initial reception seems to have been favorable, if the reaction reported by William A. Palmer, in a letter of 21 July 1810, is typical. Writing to ask Tyler for a copy of the *Reports*, he went on to say, "They are generally spoken highly of; and your *enemies* do you the justice to say that they are not only *accurately*, but *elegantly* reported." Later that summer R. C. Mallory wrote that Vermont jurisprudence had often been ridiculed in the past; "Your Honor, therefore," he continued, "claims the highest esteem for boldly standing forth in defense of its reputation, and lending your talents and influence to rescue it from unmerited reproach." [99] But aspersions continued to be cast, for Chief Justice John Savage of New York remarked in 1825 that "Tyler's Reports are not considered good authority, even in his own state." [100] Other than a vague distrust of Vermont courts on Savage's part, it is difficult to find any basis for this statement. If Tyler took occasional liberties with the transcription of an opinion, he was doing no more than other state reporters of the day. There can be no doubt that his *Reports* were of great usefulness at a time when records of American precedents were sparse, and one can have only praise for the efforts of those few scholarly men dedicated enough to attempt the publication of their cases.

Of the one hundred twenty-five cases in Tyler's two volumes, Tyler himself delivered the opinion or made a statement in eight of them (Robinson was Chief Justice during these years and handed down a majority of the opinions), and is recorded as dissenting or hesitating in five.[101] In some of his statements he expresses his personal opinion about what *should* be true, as "I have long considered that some general rule ought to be adopted . . ." or "it would be desirable that . . ."; in others, he allows himself digressions and irony, as when he points out that James II "had unhappily imbibed opinions of the royal prerogative, which were held by the nation totally incompatible with that portion of liberty which ought to be enjoyed in a limited monarchy." [102] Many of the cases dealt with actions of ejectment and trespass or with promissory notes and debts. In Robbins *v.* Windover and Hopkins (July 1802), Tyler set forth the rule that, in applications for a new trial, the affidavit of a panel member cannot be used to reveal what passed in the jury room. In Harris *v.* Huntington *et al.* (May 1802), he expressed the view, in a long and orderly opinion citing numerous precedents, that statements made by a citizen in a petition to the General Assembly are not actionable for libel — "a question of greater magnitude, and more interesting to the people of *Vermont*," he believed, "than any which has been hitherto agitated in this Court."

But Tyler's most important decision occurred in Selectmen *v.* Jacob (August 1802). Stephen Jacob (one of the Assistant Justices) had brought a slave into the state in 1783, and she worked many years for the town of Windsor; the town was now bringing action to demand that Jacob assume part of the expense of her support in old age. Tyler pointed out that the issue was whether or not the defendant's bill of sale was valid in Vermont; since the Vermont constitution provided that no inhabitant could hold a slave, Tyler reasoned that when a person brings a slave into the state "his bill of sale ceases to operate here." This is true, he said, because the United States Constitution is not involved, and the ruling can be a local one; but he hoped that the people of Vermont would "submit with cheerfulness to the national constitution and laws, which, if we may in some particular wish more congenial to our modes of thinking, yet we must be sensible are productive of numerous and rich blessings to us as individuals, and to the State as an integral of the Union." [103]

Perhaps the other most celebrated case over which Tyler presided was the *Black Snake* affair in the late summer of 1808. The Embargo Act of 1807 had resulted in a flourishing smuggling trade on Lake Champlain, and clashes between customs officials and smugglers occurred repeatedly. One ship, the *Black Snake*, which had been smuggling potash, was captured at Joy's Landing on the Winooski River near Burlington on 3 August, but only after three government men were killed. The crew was indicted for murder, and Tyler, as Chief Justice, was in charge of the grand jury trials held in a special session of the court at Burlington, beginning 23 August. His main apprehension was that strong partisan feelings might triumph over justice; in his charge to the jury, therefore, he addressed himself to that subject, and his remarks are said to have achieved a wide contemporary reputation:

The awful and melancholy occasion of our present meeting must be a subject of deep and lasting regret to every upright and feeling mind: it is so considered by this Court; we doubt not it is so viewed by you. We officially learn, by the verdict of the Jury of inquest, that three of our peaceable, unoffending citizens have been wilfully murdered: that our once peaceful and happy land has been polluted with human gore; and the voice of the blood of our brethren crieth from the ground. . . . In a word, if you are assailed by hatred or malice; by fear, favor, affection, or hope of reward, repair to your oath. Remember it is not merely your guide now, but can be your only justification to your consciences hereafter.

A verdict of guilty was returned in the case of eight men, but only one of them, Cyrus B. Dean, was executed (on 11 November 1808); the others were sentenced to prison terms. Tyler worked over the records of these trials to prepare them for publication and late in 1808 Samuel Mills of Burlington brought out *The Trial of Cyrus B. Dean for the Murder of Jonathan Ormsby and Asa Marsh*. Though the 48-page pamphlet does not include the jury charge, it does provide a good sample of Tyler's sustained legal argument, in his denial on 16 September of the appeal made by Dean's counsel. At the end, after discussing states' rights and state citizenship, he must have been thinking of his own life when he said that "this state is emphatically a land of emigrants, the language of our constitution is inviting to all to come and fertilize our soil." [104]

If legal affairs had always caused Tyler to be away from home a great deal, his tenure on the Supreme Court kept him away even more. A typical year (such as 1802) found him in both Chittenden and Addison counties for the January and June terms, in Rutland County in February and July, in Bennington in February and May, in Windham and Windsor in August, and in Orange and Caledonia in September; [105] every year he twice made the circuit up the Connecticut River and down the west side of the state with his horse and sulky. Mary was left with the main responsibility for household affairs and rearing the children (five were born during these twelve years). Tyler wrote to her frequently, in letters full of affectionate yearnings for home and family. On one occasion, during the February term of 1802 in Rutland, he saw a man from Guilford in the audience and wondered if the man had brought letters from Mary; he could hardly wait until court was adjourned, at which time he "leapt from the bench," he says, "with a skip and a jump, rather inconsistent with the gravity of a Judge," to ask for news from home. His letter of 8 February 1802 is characteristic:

My dearest Friend: I have just returned from spending an hour with Mrs. Blake, to whom I have delivered a hasty line for you; but I cannot go to bed before I write a few more lines, though I have nothing to communicate, but the evidence that I have the wish to convince you that I am not content with merely writing because it is proper, but that I take a pleasure in conversing with you. Indeed, amidst the hurry of business, when I can get a moment to you, it seems to be a refreshing retirement from the world, and brings you, and home, and the children, and happiness nearer to me. Do you consider that it is but a few weeks, and this tedious circuit will be ended, and we shall have two whole months to be together; and, what though the weather may be cloudy and the roads deep, shall we not have all the joys of our fireside to comfort us; all the pleasures of our children to gratify; and all the blessings of our affection to bless us? And what shall we want more? And when the miry season's over, we can mount our horses, and go a visiting; and stroll the fields, and inhale the breath of spring.

Many letters report purchases for Mary — silk for a cloak, a new bonnet, and "some good furs for your tippit." The theme is always the pleasures of home versus the duties of business: "Do not think, my love, that I forget you, or home, or the children one moment. I think always of you, and frequently catch myself in audible ejaculations for your health, happiness and safety; but if I think too much on the subject, I cannot perform these public duties." [106]

The public duties ended for him (at the age of fifty-six) with the October elections of 1813, and, within a year or two, Tyler found his private practice, though not lucrative, more profitable than his thousand-dollar annual salary as Chief

Justice.[107] During his time on the bench he had begun to suffer from a skin cancer which was developing on the left side of his nose near the eye; he now decided to wear a black silk patch on his face to hide the spot. An instance of his undaunted spirit and his flair for courtroom drama concerns this patch. It was a jury trial in the Newfane court, with a Mr. Richardson as his client. The opposing lawyer suggested that Tyler would never have brought the case to court if he had been in good health and that the court must overlook Tyler's actions in his present condition. When Tyler's turn came to address the jury, he began by saying, "Richardson! go home! there is no use of your staying here! I thought you had a good case." He then summed up all the points of the case and concluded, "But I was mistaken in supposing you had any rights that could be maintained. It appears you have no case because my faculties are failing, and what is worse, you have no case at all, because I have this patch on my nose. Go home! go home! I can't be expected to say a word to the jury under such circumstances." The other lawyers were astounded at his performance, and Richardson gained a favorable verdict.[108]

During all Tyler's main years of legal activity, however, he did not neglect his writing, and the *Reports* were not his only publication. Simultaneously with the first volume of reports he worked on a book of essays about English customs, supposedly written by an American visiting England; it was published anonymously by Riley in 1809 as *A Yankey in London*. Even earlier, in one of his first Vermont years, 1793, he published (anonymously) a poem called *The Origin of Evil*, and a *Christmas Hymn* was issued in broadside the same year. At the turn of the century he had the idea of writing a work to be called "Moral Tales for American Youth" and also a comic grammar; he did actually write substantial parts of them, but publishing plans seemed never to develop. In

1810 he wrote to Riley that he would like to do an "American Law Dictionary," which would be "entirely original, excepting as to the definitions of some English law terms"; he estimated its size as "two quarto volumes," but "much remains to be done to complete it for the press." [109] It was never completed, for his cancer made writing increasingly difficult. In 1817 he worked on *The Touchstone, or A Humble Modest Inquiry into the Nature of Religious Intolerance*, but only a part of it was ever printed. His three religious plays may be products of these later years, and he was preparing "The Bay Boy," a semi-autobiographical narrative, for the press when he died. One cannot estimate how important these unfulfilled projects might have been, but they bear testimony to a continuously active mind.

The last two of Tyler's eleven children were born in the years after his retirement from the bench, in 1815 and 1818. The oldest of his children, Royall, Jr. (1794–1813), and the second oldest, John Steele (1796–1876), approached university age during Tyler's last years as Chief Justice, but his salary would not permit him to send both to college; John Steele accordingly went to Boston in 1810 and entered the business of his uncle, George Palmer, while Royall, Jr., in the fall of 1811, became a freshman at the University in Burlington. He was a promising student and followed his father in writing a poem ("The Present Age") and a play ("Quackery" or "The Dumb Gent," performed at the college in 1812), but he died of typhoid fever at the beginning of his junior year. The youngest child, Abiel Winship (1818–1832), also died in his teens, but most of the other children lived long and active lives: Mary Whitwell (1798–1874), kindergarten teacher; Edward Royall (1800–1848), Yale graduate, minister, and editor of the *New Englander*; William Clark (1802–1882), Boston merchant; Joseph Dennie (1804–1852), Yale graduate, Episcopal clergyman, and head of the Virginia Deaf and Dumb

Asylum; Amelia Sophia (1807–1878), dedicated teacher.
trained by Elizabeth Palmer Peabody; George Palmer (1809–
1896), graduate of Yale and Union Theological Seminary,
and Congregational pastor; Royall [Charles] (1812–1896),
Harvard graduate and Vermont lawyer; Thomas Pickman
(1815–1892), Trinity (Hartford) graduate and Episcopal
pastor.[110]

Perhaps the most depressing period in Tyler's life was the
fall of 1813, when, in sudden succession, he lost his judgeship,
learned of his oldest son's death, and returned home to find
creditors clamoring for his property (since his steady source
of income was now stopped). It was some time before he
recovered from this triple blow: he raised some money by
selling the farm and moving into town, and, through the
kindness of Judge Gilbert Denison,[111] he was made Register
of Probate for Windham County (beginning in December
1815) and managed to reestablish his private practice. Nevertheless, the ensuing years were not easy, and the children,
particularly John, contributed to their parents' support; it
was John who established them in a house on Putney Street in
Brattleboro in 1821.[112] Soon afterward, the severity of Tyler's
cancer began to prevent his attending to probate duties, and
in December of 1822 he was removed from that position.
Earlier the same year John's business in Boston had failed,
and the Brattleboro property had to be signed over to other
hands. From that time, the Tylers became objects of public
charity.

Mary Tyler began keeping a journal in 1821, and its entries
through 1826 tell a story of unrelieved poverty and sickness.[113]
The children would make visits and contribute what they
could afford; anonymous letters enclosing five dollars would
arrive; friends would join together and donate fifty dollars;
and neighbors would supply butter, rice, sugar, turkeys, and
other food. Tyler's cancer eventually reached into his eye,[114]

47

and he sat with the window shades drawn while Mary read to him from the Bible, Cooper, Scott, Maria Edgeworth, Byron, Cellini, Josephus, and many others. Pathetically he still held the hope of publishing more of his own writings. Mary records that, in 1822, he wrote "several beautiful little poems" and that, by late 1824, he was in the midst of revising *The Algerine Captive*; he also wrote a play, "Five Pumpkins," for the children of a local school, and, as late as April 1825, sent the manuscript of his collection of tales for children, "Utile Dulci," to New York.

The theme of Mary's journal is expressed in her entry for 28 May 1822: "Support us O God! under this and every dispensation of thy providence!" Doctors and friends struggled vainly to suggest remedies that would at least ease the pain, and Tyler tried them all in turn — copperas curd, yellow dock root, pokeberry salve, rhubarb, and magnesia. Only opium and laudanum gave much relief, and on some days he took between seventy and eighty drops of laudanum. Mary's entry of 20 July 1826 presages the end: "This day as a last resort my afflicted husband consented after much persuasion to try injections, which relieved him but kept him uneasy and restless the chief of the night." Finally, on 26 August 1826, she wrote: "On Wednesday the 16th my husband was released from his sufferings. . . . My husband died with perfect composure and resignation and surely he passed from Death into Life! . . . May I be enabled to do my duty in my new situation." He was buried in Prospect Hill Cemetery, in the east village of Brattleboro, under this epitaph: "ROYALL TYLER / Reip. V. Mont. Cur. Sup. Jurid., / Princ. / Mortem Obiit / Die XVI. Aug. Anno Domini / MDCCCXXVI / Etatis Suae / LXVIII / Uxor et liberi / ejus / Hoc saxum ponendum. / Curaverunt." [115] As in life, he was officially known for his judicial services, while his literary productions, unannounced, continued to attract attention.

·❧ II ❧·

Dramatist: The Contrast

W HEN Tyler, after his unsuccessful pursuit of Shays in Vermont, was sent to New York by Governor Bowdoin in the spring of 1787, just two months before the opening of the Constitutional Convention in Philadelphia, he had probably never had an opportunity to witness a professional dramatic performance. Before the Revolution — in fact, as early as 1749 — professional troupes had appeared in such cities as Philadelphia, New York, Williamsburg, and Charleston; but the religious climate (influenced partly by a view of the Restoration stage, linking it with dissipation, but particularly by the Puritan heritage) was hostile to the theater, and laws were passed in some colonies prohibiting, or restricting, such entertainment. In the Boston of Tyler's youth the prejudice against the theater was particularly strong, reflected in the Harvard regulations and in Tyler's own description of the conditions under which Boston amateur groups had to struggle:

The front door of the store was closed and every crack and keyhole carefully stopped with paper or cotton that no glimmering light might alarm the passing watchman; the entrance was through a bye lane into a door in the backyard, and such was the caution observed that but one person was admitted at a time, while two, one at each end of the lane, were on the watch to see if the person to be admitted had been noticed. No knocking was permitted, but a slight scratch announced the approach of the initiated. . . . A Panic seized the whole assembly [upon the approach of the watchman;] . . . the lights were extinguished or put under a bushel, but the voice of the watchman as he chanted his midnight ditty distancing as he passed on, we took new courage and the play proceeded.[1]

Any progress which the drama had made in America, despite such difficulties, was halted on 20 October 1774, when, in view of the impending war, a resolution of the Continental Congress banned all plays and public entertainments. At that time only one play by an American had been produced.

It was inevitable, however, that playwriting would begin to flourish, despite the ban, for a period of revolution and national crisis always stimulates the corrective of satire. Writers like Mercy Warren turned out plays on patriotic or national themes, printed when they could not be produced. By August of 1785, about two years before Tyler's arrival in New York, the American Company under Lewis Hallam had reopened the John Street Theatre, though the restrictions were not to be relinquished in some cities for another decade. The kind of theater which Tyler encountered in 1787 was different from the pre-Revolutionary one: attended by all classes of people, it was a force for national unity and, with its plays on political subjects, has been called "spoken journalism." [2] But the principal fare was still imported drama, and in the first few weeks after his arrival Tyler could have attended productions of *Much Ado About Nothing*, *Cymbeline*, *Richard III*, *The Clandestine Marriage*, *The Jealous Wife*, *She Stoops to Conquer*, and, most important, *The School for Scandal* (on 21 March). Whether or not he saw these plays, he was able to construct, by 16 April, a work of his own which treated a native subject, for the first time, in a comedy produced on the stage and which helped to demonstrate, in so doing, a value and a future for the drama in America.

Dramatist: The Contrast

Misconceptions and Disagreements

Because of its early position among American plays, *The Contrast* has received much comment over the years, particularly at the hands of anthologists and literary historians who wish to fill in the background with a few hurried sentences. A tradition quickly becomes established, each writer making the same points without bothering to check on their authenticity. If, then, one is to approach the play with a clear mind, one must be aware of several misconceptions that have become established in this way. Though it may not be possible to ascertain the truth in every instance, one should at least realize that certain points have not been resolved.

The largest of these muddled areas has to do with the dating of the play and its relative position in American drama. Because William Dunlap, in his pioneer *History of the American Theatre* (1832), made an unfortunate error in recording the date of the first performance, many nineteenth-century commentaries place it on 16 April 1786.[3] Thomas P. Tyler, doing research on his father's life, believed that this date was in error but argued that the correct date was 16 April 1789 and the place the Park Street Theatre.[4] The play was actually performed, as Joseph Ireland had recognized as early as 1866, on 16 April 1787 at the John Street Theatre in New York.[5] The accuracy of this date is clear from numerous contemporary advertisements and references. The New York *Daily Advertiser*, on 14 and 16 April 1787, announced a comedy, "Never [before] Performed," by "a Citizen of the United States," entitled *The Contrast*, to be acted on Monday, 16 April, along with "the English Burletta, Called *Midas*"; it was reviewed at length in the same paper on 18 April.[6] On the 17th and 18th the advertisements were repeated, for a second performance on the 18th; both performances were mentioned in the review in the *Worcester Magazine*, which did not appear until the first week of May. Then on 1 May the play was announced for a third performance on Wednesday, 2 May — this one reviewed on 5 May in the *Independent Journal*. Finally, on 12 May, came a benefit performance, "at the particular request of the Author," to help those suffering from the Boston fire.[7]

It is not necessary to say that the play enjoyed a "run," as some writers do, in order to emphasize its success. Four performances within a month was a record which no other American play had thus far attained, and it would have been unusual even for the most popular of the English plays. Baltimore was next to see *The Contrast*, on 12 August 1787, and on 10 December Thomas Wignell (the comedian of the American Company who made a hit as Jonathan in New York) gave a reading of it in Philadelphia; it was repeated in Baltimore on 19 August 1788 and then in New York, soon after Washington's inauguration, on 10 June 1789. Next came Philadelphia (on 7 July 1790), where a newspaper referred to the "curiosity which has everywhere been expressed respecting this first dramatic production of American genius." [8] It may not be too much to say, therefore, that *The Contrast* was the first commercially successful American play. The question of "firsts," however, which always attracts such zealous interest, is a tricky one, despite the assertion in its dedication that *The Contrast* is "the First Essay of *American* Genius in the Dramatic Art." There should be no doubt on certain points: the play is certainly not the first ever produced in America (it came 125 years too late for that), and it is just as clearly not the first by an American to be produced (a distinction generally assigned to Thomas Godfrey's *The Prince of Parthia*, a full twenty years earlier), nor the first with a native subject (Robert Rogers' *Ponteach*, 1766), nor the first printed in America (Robert Hunter's *Androboros*, 1714).[9] Yet one writer in 1880 entitled an article about *The*

Contrast "The First American Play," and another in 1889 called it "the first play of American authorship that ever appeared on any stage"; as late as 1916 a portrait of Tyler, accompanying an article by Montrose Moses, bore a caption describing him as the author of "the first play to be written by an American," and in 1961 he was referred to as "the first American playwright." [10] Other writers, searching for a safer way to state the case, have used such complicated phrases as "the first American play . . . got up on a regular stage, by a regular company of comedians," "the first public performance in a regular theatre of a play written by a citizen of America," [11] and so on, until it is difficult to see precisely how it has any priority at all. Put most simply, *The Contrast* is the first native comedy to be professionally produced.

Another myth connected with the chronology of the play concerns the date and circumstances of its composition. The extraordinary success of an untutored genius is an appealing concept which, in this case, has been transformed into the legend that Tyler, with no knowledge whatsoever of the theater, wrote in less than three weeks (or, in some versions, a matter of days) a strikingly successful play. It must be admitted that this tradition derives from a source close to Tyler, for Wignell, in the "Advertisement" to the published version of the play, reported that "it was written by one, who never critically studied the rules of the drama, and, indeed, had seen but few of the exhibitions of the stage; it was undertaken and finished in the course of three weeks." Though intended to gain favor for the play by emphasizing the remarkable facts in its composition, this statement is mild compared to some of its later embroiderings, and some recent writers have declared that Tyler "dashed off" his play.[12] This he may have done, but the general tenor of the legend is almost certainly not true. Neither is there evidence to support the idea that Tyler wrote the play during his military service and had it finished when he went to New York.[13] We shall probably never know exactly how many plays Tyler had seen nor exactly when he began to write *The Contrast*. But we do know that he arrived in New York for the first time on 12 March, little more than a month before *The Contrast* was performed, and that *The School for Scandal* was given on 21 March. That Jonathan's famous description of "The School for Scandalization" in the third act of *The Contrast* may be a fictionalized account of Tyler's own first visit to a theater is suggested not only by the Sheridan title but by the reference to "Wig — Wag — Wag-all, Darby Wag-all," since Wignell, for whom Tyler created Jonathan, had taken Darby's role in *The Poor Soldier*, the other play on the same bill. Even so, there is no reason to suppose that Tyler was entirely unacquainted with drama, for amateur or private performances had been given in Boston before that time, and, judging from the breadth of his allusions to English literature in other works, he may well have had a wide reading knowledge of plays. In any event, the play is so overflowing with the devices and themes of eighteenth-century British drama that one may reasonably assume on Tyler's part a more extensive familiarity with theatrical literature than is usually conveyed by accounts of his hurried composition.[14]

One further misconception relating to the circumstances under which the play first appeared has to do with contemporary knowledge of Tyler's authorship. It is all very well for Frederick Tupper to say that Tyler assigned the copyright to Wignell because he did not dare to "link his patrician name with the experiment." [15] That writing was a pastime for Tyler and that he generally published his literary works anonymously is true, but one should not infer that his authorship was thereby concealed. The advertising, to be sure, did not reveal his name, and the title page of the published work three years later, in the spring of 1790, was still maintaining that the author was simply "A Citizen of the United States." But it must have been a very open secret, for the *Independent Journal* review of the 2 May performance took Tyler's authorship for granted, referred casually in the opening sentence to "the new Comedy, written by ROYAL TYLER, Esq.," and concluded with a eulogy that Tyler could hardly have looked upon with disfavor:

America has long boasted successful adventurers in the various walks of literature, the Drama excepted, that path had hitherto remained unexplored — and it must give sincere satisfaction to every lover of his country to find that this, the most difficult of all the works of human genius, has been attempted with such abundant success, and that it is likely from the abilities of this Gentleman, if his other avocations will permit him to cultivate his talent in this species of writing, that America may one day rank a *Tyler* in the Dramatic Line as she already does a *Franklin* and a *West* in those of Philosophy and the Fine Arts.

Similarly the review in the *Worcester Magazine* named "ROYAL TYLER, Esq.; of Boston, *Attorney at Law*, and late *Aid de Camp* to the Hon. Major General Lincoln" as the "author of the truly sentimental entertainment," going on about how he had "just left the active field of MARS" and "was in this city, on business that could not occupy his whole time." When proposals for printing the play were issued, it was called "A *Comedy* written by *Major Tyler*," and by 1797 one of his later plays was openly advertised as "by R. TYLER, Esq. Author of the Contrast, &c." [16] He enjoyed, in other words, a high literary reputation, and his squeamishness about its effect on his legal reputation has sometimes been overemphasized; if recognition could come without his resorting to the ungentlemanly device of appearing to ask for it by signing his work, one may imagine that he was certainly not averse to gathering in the accolades.

A second area in which there is room for disagreement concerns the relative importance of the character Jonathan, the provincial Yankee servingman in *The Contrast*. It has become traditional, following Dunlap, the Duyckincks, Odell, and many others, to point to Jonathan as Tyler's "distinctive contribution to drama" (in the words of Oral Coad) and to speak of that character as the first in a long line of stage Yankees, or "Jonathan-figures." [17] One even hears the suggestion that Tyler's Jonathan was the prototype for Uncle Sam. To attribute much of the success of the play to Jonathan, as Arthur Hornblow does, is an entirely different matter, for it is surely true that, with the popular Thomas Wignell playing the part, this comic role must have been the main attraction in the piece.[18] And there is no question that the stage Yankee became one of the most popular types in American drama, portrayed on the nineteenth-century stage by James H. Hackett and George Hill in a large number of plays, in some of which the character was even named Jonathan (as in Woodworth's *The Forest Rose* of 1825 or Dunlap's *A Trip to Niagara* of 1829). One student of the subject has said that "no satisfactory Yankee characters" appeared in American drama before 1787, but immediately following *The Contrast* came the Yankee servant in Dunlap's *The Modest Soldier* (1787) and the housemaid in his *The Father* (1788), Dolly the country girl in Samuel Low's *The Politician Out-Witted* (1788), and Yorick the Yankee Federalist in *The Better Sort* (1789).[19]

One can, with some justification, think of *The Contrast* as standing at the head of a tradition, but to point to it as the ultimate source of the Jonathan character (or of native characters speaking idiomatic American speech) is to oversimplify, and thus misunderstand, a complex process. For one thing, more than half of the approximately forty native plays written before 1787 contained attempts at realistic American characters, including at least one homespun farmer like Jonathan (Simple in *The Blockheads*, 1776). Further, when one observes that the figure dropped to about a third after that time,[20] one sees not only that Tyler did not stimulate a tradition of native characters but also that the presence of such figures in plays is partly a reflection of nonliterary factors, in this case the nationalistic feelings surrounding the Revolution. In addition, the term "brother Jonathan" had been used pejoratively by Tories even before the Revolution as a synonym for "Yankee," and affectionately later by patriots.[21] It was well enough known that a retired British Army captain, Joseph Atkinson, who had served in the United States during the war, could use the name Jonathen for the Yankee servant of an army officer in his play *A Match for a Widow*, performed in Dublin almost exactly a year before *The Contrast*, on 17 April 1786, and published in 1788. Atkinson's play, based on Joseph Patrat's *L'Heureuse Erreur* (1783), contained a Yankee whose talk resembles Tyler's Jonathan and whose function of showing up affectation by provincialism was similar; and Atkinson declared in his preface that he had, "for the first time, attempted the introduction of a *Yankee* character on the European stage." [22] While Tyler may have heard reports of this play, it was probably not an important source for him since it was not printed until after his own play had been performed; anyhow, it is patently untrue to give Tyler credit for being the first to employ a stage Yankee. In view of these facts, it seems more sensible to think of *The Contrast* as the culmination, not the inauguration, of a tradition; and, for that very reason, it could embody satisfactorily and concretely certain attitudes of Americans toward themselves (previously unformulated and subconscious), so that it served to solidify the type if not to create the symbol, and to stand as a model for later representations.[23] Leaving aside these points, it is unfair to stress Jonathan as the sole important contribution of a play which, unlike most of its American predecessors, is still actable today.

A final source of disagreement is provided by the two songs

in the play. "Yankee Doodle," which Jonathan attempts to sing in Act III, causes little difficulty; though it would be rash to say that no one has ever nominated Tyler the originator of it, there is general agreement that his use of the song popularized the most familiar and traditional version, which was not otherwise printed until much later. The tune, which goes back to the time of Charles I, was first heard in an American play twenty years earlier, in Thomas Forrest's *The Disappointment* (1767); [24] whether or not one wishes to say that Tyler made the first dramatic use of the *text* in America depends on how hard one is straining to find Tyler firsts. The important point is that Tyler saw the dramatic value, both for his characterization of Jonathan and for his nationalistic theme, of including an authentic popular song, sung by the troops and civilians alike, which had accumulated a patriotic emotional charge.

The other song, which the disconsolate Maria is singing as the second scene opens, is a sentimental lyric on the nobility of a dying Indian. The first of its four stanzas illustrates its rhyme and sound patterns and its mood:

> The sun sets in night, and the stars shun the day;
> But glory remains when their lights fade away!
> Begin, ye tormentors! your threats are in vain,
> For the son of Alknomook shall never complain.

The fourth line, with slight variations, becomes a refrain closing each stanza and explains why the song is referred to as "Alknomook." It is perhaps the best surviving example of what is almost a genre in itself, the Indian death song emphasizing the heroic endurance, or simple integrity, of the primitive warrior.[25] The story of its numerous publications, in differing versions, is a complicated one, but the gist of the matter is that it has been variously attributed to three different authors, one of them Tyler. Thomas J. McKee, in 1887, wrote, "After considerable research, I have become convinced that

Alknomook is the offspring of Tyler's genius"; and Arthur Hobson Quinn, thirty-six years later, said, "I see no reason to attribute it to anyone else." [26] The poem appeared anonymously, however, three months before *The Contrast*, in the January 1787 issue of the *American Museum*, the third edition of which (in 1790) assigned it to "P. Freneau." Though Freneau never claimed the poem, others have given it to him; F. L. Pattee, for example, included it in the Princeton edition of Freneau's poetry in 1903.[27] The third candidate is a British poetess, Mrs. Anne Home Hunter, who included the words among her *Poems* in 1802; her right to them was not questioned in a contemporary review nor in her obituary in 1821. Since the first appearance of the poem was in a 1783 British song collection and since the British sheet music of about the same date credited the words to "a Lady," Mrs. Hunter seems to have the strongest claim. Although the printing of the music with *The Contrast* may suggest that the song was not universally known, it was nevertheless extremely popular in both England and America; there is no reason to suppose that Tyler was any more responsible for its composition than he was for "Yankee Doodle." He, like Ann Julia Hatton in *Tammany* (1794), was simply making use of a current lyric — one which contributed to a sentimental characterization and foreshadowed, through that character's own analysis of the words, her later admiration for an equally noble, if superficially different, soldier.[28]

Dramatic Technique

If there is little documentary evidence about Tyler's preparation as a dramatist, one glance at *The Contrast* reveals his familiarity with dramatic conventions. The plot, though less involved, is otherwise reminiscent of eighteenth-century British drama, with its hypocritical rake, gossiping young ladies, and domineering parent. Mr. Van Rough has arranged a marriage for his sentimental daughter Maria, against her wishes; meanwhile, her betrothed, Billy Dimple, equally displeased with the match, pays his respects simultaneously to two of Maria's more sprightly friends, Charlotte and Letitia. When Charlotte's brother, the patriotic Colonel Manly, enters the scene, he and Maria are instantly drawn to one another; and the impediments to their engagement are removed when all of Dimple's treachery is exposed — not only his behavior to Charlotte and Letitia (who, at the end, are also repentant for having encouraged him) but his profligacy (which is the decisive factor for Maria's father). Tyler's lack of experience is shown perhaps in the fact that this basic plot is not elaborated upon; instead, the time is filled with conversations about fashions or patriotism and with scenes involving the servants (which do not, however, constitute a subplot, for there is no intrigue in these scenes — nor do they cause complications in the main plot). The result is a play with a great deal of talk and little action; but, given such a plot, Tyler shows in other ways his awareness of various tricks of the craft.

The play is held together, to an even larger extent than usual, by contrasts and comparisons, and the theme is the contrast of the title, between the polished but hollow and insincere Dimple, with his British affectations, and the forthright, honest Manly, who may have fewer social graces but is a loyal son of liberty. It is only an adaptation, to fit the circumstances of a young republic, of the perennial concern of social comedy — the differentiation of hypocrisy and sincerity, of surface show and inner worth — and the construction of the play is based on these contrasts. The word "contrast" is used twice to make explicit this structure, once in reference to Dimple and Manly and once to their servants, Jessamy and Jonathan. At the end of act II, Jessamy muses, "How sweet will the contrast be, between the blundering Jonathan, and the courtly and accomplished Jessamy!" [29]

Royall Tyler

Mary Hunt Palmer Tyler

Frontispiece to *The Contrast*

THE

CONTRAST,

A

COMEDY;

IN FIVE ACTS:

WRITTEN BY A

CITIZEN OF THE *UNITED STATES;*

Performed with Applaufe at the Theatres in NEW-YORK,
PHILADELPHIA, and MARYLAND;

AND PUBLISHED *(under an Affignment of the Copy-Right)* BY

THOMAS WIGNELL.

Primus ego in patriam
Aonio——deduxi vertice Mufas.
VIRGIL.
(Imitated.)

Firft on our fhores I try THALIA's powers,
And bid the *laughing, ufeful* Maid be ours.

PHILADELPHIA:

FROM THE PRESS OF *PRICHARD & HALL,* IN MARKET STREET,
BETWEEN SECOND AND FRONT STREETS.

M. DEC. XC.

Title Page of *The Contrast*

THE

ALGERINE CAPTIVE;

OR, THE

LIFE AND ADVENTURES

OF

DOCTOR *UPDIKE UNDERHILL:*

SIX YEARS A PRISONER AMONG THE ALGE-
RINES.

—————By your patience,
I will a round unvarnished tale deliver
Of my whole course.—————

SHAKESPEARE.

by Royal Tyler.

VOLUME I.

Published according to ACT *of* CONGRESS.

PRINTED AT *WALPOLE*, NEWHAMPSHIRE,
BY DAVID CARLISLE, JUN.
AND SOLD AT HIS BOOKSTORE.

1797.

Title Page of *The Algerine Captive*

Dimple, in a parallel speech near the end of the play, makes the point even more directly: "Ladies and gentlemen, I take my leave; and you will please to observe, in the case of my deportment, the contrast between a gentleman, who has read Chesterfield and received the polish of Europe, and an unpolished, untravelled American."

One need not be told, either in the title or these speeches, that the play is built on contrasts, for the fact is obvious enough in the methodical balancing of scenes. Tyler not only submitted to the conventional five-act pattern; but, unlike his British models, he divided each act into two roughly equal scenes. The two scenes of act I introduce the three ladies: in the first Charlotte and Letitia are discussing fashions and Dimple; in the second Maria is lamenting the match her father has made for her. Act II begins like act I, with Charlotte and Letitia again discussing fashions, after their return from the shopping trip on which they were just embarking at the end of the first scene; but where Charlotte, in the opening scene, had revealed (in an aside) her attraction to Dimple, Letitia in this scene does the same. We also meet three men in this act: Manly, just arrived in town, enters to greet his sister in the first of the two scenes; and in the second the two servants, Jessamy and Jonathan, having met on the mall, converse about etiquette. The only major character who has not yet appeared is Dimple, so act III opens with him and his servant Jessamy; but Dimple soon leaves, and Jenny (Dimple's maid) and Jonathan enter, making this another scene devoted to the servants. Since the second scene finds Manly and Dimple together in the mall, the structure of act III reverses that of act II, in which the two servants had met on the mall in the second scene. It also illustrates the parallelism of Tyler's method, for we are shown the first meetings of the principal contrasting characters on the mall in the second scenes of two consecutive acts.

Although the first and third, and the fourth and sixth, of these six scenes may be balanced, it cannot be said that there has been much direction to the play thus far. These scenes have served as an uneconomical way of introducing the characters and presenting discussions on certain topics; the only hint of any plot has come in three asides or soliloquies — Charlotte's and Letitia's expressions of interest in a man supposedly engaged (Dimple), and Dimple's exclamation of displeasure upon learning that Manly is Charlotte's brother. Only the last two acts have any plot in the usual sense. Act IV, scene i, brings together for the first time the three ladies and the two gentlemen, and intrigue results not only from Dimple's setting a rendezvous with both Letitia and Charlotte for the same evening but from Maria's recognizing Manly as the person she fell in love with at first sight when he accidentally stepped into her apartment that morning. Tyler's attention to continuity of action is demonstrated in the next two scenes. In IV.ii Maria's father is agitated over the revelations of the banker (whom he was just preparing to see at the end of I.ii); and V.i begins with Jonathan and Jessamy talking over Jonathan's attempt to make love to Jenny in III.i. The banker's information about Dimple's monetary extravagances predisposes Maria's father favorably toward any substitute, and, after the other disclosures of V.ii about Dimple's behavior, no further obstacles stand in the way of Maria and Manly's happiness.

If the plot (which thus exists almost exclusively in two scenes, IV.i and V.ii) is not handled very adroitly, it is clear that Tyler was making an attempt to use various dramatic techniques which had come to his attention. The concern with continuity of time and action, the balancing of scenes, the alternation of scenes on different social levels, the distribution of key speeches among several roles, and the pattern of confrontations among characters are evidence of this. Further, *The School for Scandal* (if not numerous other plays) taught him the usefulness of concealed characters who over-hear conversations, and this device occurs three times in the last three scenes. In IV.ii Van Rough retires to a closet so that he can hear what kind of sentiments Manly expresses to his daughter Maria, and in V.ii Manly first conceals himself in the closet and then Letitia listens at the door. Manly is able to hear Dimple profess his love to Letitia and call Charlotte "that trifling, gay, flighty, coquet, that disagreeable —"; then both Manly and Letitia overhear him making advances to Charlotte, referring to Letitia as "that insipid, wry-mouthed, ugly creature." Also, whether or not Tyler was familiar with his Congreve, he had learned the value of well-timed en-trances, for, just as Dimple is pronouncing his disparaging description of Charlotte, it is Charlotte herself who enters, and Dimple abruptly changes his tone: "My dear Miss Manly, I rejoice to see you; there is a charm in your conversation, that always marks your entrance into company as fortunate."

The theater, too, which so frequently enters in an impor-tant way into English eighteenth-century plays, has its role here. Any play which deals with fashions and hypocrisies, with appearance and reality, finds the metaphor of the theater useful for illustrating a distortion of values and for comparing the acting on-stage with the acting off-stage; in addition, fashions and etiquette are naturally on display at the theater, and the playwright is able to bring his point home all the better because it will be an actual theatrical audience listening to his remarks about the theater. The state of the American the-ater in 1787 and Tyler's own recent introduction to the stage combine to make any theatrical allusions in *The Contrast* of special interest. A few brief references show that the society we are concerned with took the theater for granted, at least enough to use it metaphorically in conversation, as when Charlotte, commenting on her brother's high-flown language, compares him to "a player run mad," his head "filled with old scraps of tragedy" (II.i). Later in the same scene she describes satirically the behavior of a group of ladies who often share a box at the theater, in a passage which surely is not entirely literary in origin and must in part reflect Tyler's acuteness of observation of the post-Revolutionary American theater:

Every thing is conducted with such decorum, — first we bow round to the company in general, then to each one in particular, then we have so many inquiries after each other's health, and we are so happy to meet each other, and it is so many ages since we last had that pleasure, 'and, if a married lady is in company, we have such a sweet dissertation upon her son Bobby's chin-cough;' then the curtain rises, then our sensibility is all awake, and then by the mere force of apprehension, we torture some harmless expression into a double meaning, which the poor author never dreamt of, and then we have recourse to our fans, and then we blush, and then the gentlemen jog one another, peep under the fan, and make the prettiest remarks; and then we giggle and they simper, and they giggle and we simper, and then the curtain drops, and then for nuts and oranges, and then we bow, and it's pray Ma'am take it, and pray Sir keep it, and, oh! not for the world Sir; and then the curtain rises again, and then we blush, and giggle, and simper, and bow, all over again. Oh! the sentimental charms of a side-box conversation!

Then Dimple, in IV.i, comments on American provinciality by referring to the "miserable mummers, whom you call actors," that "murder comedy, and make a farce of tragedy"; he pointedly declares that, the one time he was "tortured" at an American theater, he sat with his back to the stage, "admiring a much better actress than any there; — a lady who played the fine woman to perfection."

But the most elaborate use of the theatrical metaphor is Jonathan's description of his accidental attendance at the theater (III.i), the most famous scene of the play and by all odds the one most frequently anthologized. Jonathan, reflecting the puritanical prejudice against the theater, asserts that he will never be caught in the "devil's drawing-room" where "the devil hangs out the vanities of the world, upon the tenter-hooks of temptation." He then proceeds to describe his disappointment the night before when, after buying a ticket to see the *"hocus pocus* man," he finds nothing but a "great green cloth" which was presently lifted, allowing the audience to "look right into the next neighbour's house"; he wonders if many houses in New York are made in that way, and he judges the family to be "pretty much like other families; — there was a poor, good natured, curse of a husband, and a sad rantipole of a wife." His description of what takes place, as well as his reference to the "School for Scandalization," makes clear what play he was viewing; and his mention of "Darby Wag-all" as the actor's name is a pun the contemporary audiences would have enjoyed, since Wignell himself played Jonathan. The entire scene is not only good comedy — the comedy of naïveté — but an integral and effective part of several larger concerns of the play. For one thing, it enables Tyler unobtrusively to ridicule the absurdity of religious attacks on the theater. The very fact that Jonathan is unable to distinguish the "wicked players" from an ordinary family emphasizes not merely the innocuousness of the theater but, at the same time, the great amount of acting in real life. Even Jonathan is able to make the application on an elementry level, for "Mr. Joseph," in the play, "talked as sober and as pious as a minister; but like some ministers that I know, he was a sly tike in his heart for all that." Furthermore, the naïve viewpoint is an advantage in contrasting common sense with excesses of convention, and the patriotic aspect of the contrast is evident in Jonathan's criticism of Darby's fear of firearms: "Now, I'm a true born Yankee American son of liberty, and I never was afraid of a gun yet in all my life." The Jonathan scenes may not be an essential part of the intrigue, but they form an indispensable foundation for the contrast theme.

Another mark of Tyler's awareness of dramatic technique is his use of asides and soliloquies. Such speeches — as well as disguises (which Tyler does not use) and eavesdropping — are easy ways for the dramatist to reveal hypocrisy in his characters, but their ease can lead to excessive dependence on them. Tyler was familiar with the tradition of asides in Renaissance and Restoration drama, but, just as he relied on hidden characters for the elaboration of his plot, his inexperience as a dramatist resulted in an awkward use of asides. In the opening scene Charlotte delivers an aside of thirty-eight words, which amounts to nothing more than a direct exposition to the audience, explaining how "Letitia little thinks" that Dimple is making himself disagreeable to Maria "in order that she may leave him at liberty to address me." This interpretation is not quite accurate, and it does fit Charlotte's character — but the fact remains that the speech is an interior thought made objective in a framework otherwise composed of externals and that it is a short cut to exposition purchased at the cost of a change of method. The rivalry between Charlotte and Letitia and their desire for Dimple continue to be expressed in asides — Charlotte unnecessarily explains, " 'I'll endeavour to excite her [Maria] to discharge him' " (IV.i), and Letitia later says of Charlotte, "So anxious to get me out! but I'll watch you" (V.ii). A similar kind of awkward exposition occurs when a character is alone on the stage: Maria's exclamation, "Ha! my father's voice," or her long speech about "How deplorable is my situation" (I.ii).[30] It is true that the soliloquies of Maria and Letitia (II.i), at the ends of two consecutive scenes, reinforce the balanced structure and that those of Jessamy and Jonathan, at the ends of the next two scenes (II.ii, III.i), emphasize the contrast theme; but when Dimple closes the following scene (III.ii) in the same way, talking about Manly, one begins to feel that the device is being overworked.

Jonathan's asides, however, are more successful, as are those of Jessamy and Jenny in the scenes with him, because they are more appropriate to the dramatic context and are not the exclusive source of information. That is to say, these speeches are often merely exclamations of a kind that such characters might be expected to make under their breaths, and the information imparted supports what the audience has learned about these characters in other ways. So when Jessamy admires his own choice of a word, asserts that Jonathan ("horrid brute") cannot have read Chesterfield, or admonishes himself for being "guilty of a vile proverb" (II.ii), he is simply reinforcing the traits of affectation he has already demonstrated and is not providing essential exposition. Similarly, Jenny's exclamations of "stupid creature" about Jonathan or Jonathan's confessions of social inadequacy (III.i) are at least harmless, and usually a source of humor, if not actually constructive. There are a few other asides of this kind in the play: Dimple's expressions of self-satisfaction ("I have hit the Bumkin off very tolerably," III.ii), displeasure ("The devil she is! . . . Plague on him!," III.ii), conceit ("an affair of this sort can never prejudice me among the ladies," V.ii), or amused admiration ("How he awes me by the superiority of his sentiments," III.ii); Charlotte's comments on Maria's love for Manly ("some folks . . . can praise a gentleman," "Oh! ho! is that the case," and "A lucky thought," IV.i); and Maria's reactions to a conversation about Manly ("Oh! my heart!" and "His family! But what is it to me," IV.i). The best that can be said of these asides is that they are not objectionable. In *The Contrast* asides are either innocuous exclamations of emotion or awkward announcements of plot; they are not successful in serving the more subtle purpose of revealing complexities of character.

This failure, in any case, is a function of the characterization, for there are few complexities of character to be revealed.

Details of character can be filled in by the audience once the type is known, and Tyler's assemblage of types shows once again his acquaintance with the post-Restoration tradition. There is the unscrupulous rake (Dimple), whose affectation and hypocrisy are an integral part of his double dealings with women; and there are the scheming women (Charlotte and Letitia), full of gossip and ready to exploit their closest friends in order to gain the attentions of a man. Present, too, are their opposites, Manly and Maria, the gallant and serious-minded male and the helpless and unprotected female. Maria states the familiar dilemma succinctly in a soliloquy: "How distressing for a daughter to find her heart militating with her filial duty!" (I.ii). She has the usual intolerant father who is sure that the match he has arranged is best for her, and she makes the usual protestations of helplessness ("Who is it that considers the helpless situation of our sex, that does not see we each moment stand in need of a protector"). Finally, there are servants who reflect certain qualities of their masters and illustrate the theme on another social level.

Manly and Maria are the two most exaggerated character types. Maria's sentimental view of the world is ridiculed not only by the extravagance of speech which the author gives to her but by the other characters as well. Early in the play Charlotte exclaims, "A fig for sentiment" (I.i), and later says to Letitia, "I hope you are not going to turn sentimentalist" (II.i); she refers to "the grave Maria, and her sentimental circle" (I.i) and to the "flow of sentiment meandering through [her and Manly's] conversation like purling streams in modern poetry" (II.i). As in *The School for Scandal*, literature is held partly to blame. Letitia describes how Maria "read Sir Charles Grandison, Clarissa Harlow, Shenstone, and the Sentimental Journey" (I.i) and came to see that, "according to every rule of romance," she should reject a suitor forced on her by a parent. Later Charlotte, speaking to Maria, mocks the sentimental approach: "Why, I should be shut up in my chamber [if I were to be married in a few days]; and my head would so run upon — upon — upon the solemn ceremony that I was to pass through! — I declare it would take me above two hours merely to learn that little monosyllable — *Yes*" (IV.i). Though Maria recognizes this as "raillery," it does not prevent her from saying, " 'Oh! how sweet it is, when the heart is borne down with misfortune, to recline and repose on the bosom of friendship!,' " nor from admiring Manly because "he spoke the language of sentiment."

Manly's language is certainly an extreme and comes in for its share of criticism. His sister likens his conversation to " 'old fashioned brocade' ": " 'it will stand alone; every sentence is a sentiment' " (II.i); she describes his constant lecturing which makes her " 'as melancholy as if I had been at church.' " One is inclined to think her judgment too charitable when Manly enters to pronounce his first words:

My dear Charlotte, I am happy that I once more enfold you within the arms of fraternal affection. I know you are going to ask (amiable impatience!) how our parents do, — the venerable pair transmit you their blessing by me — they totter on the verge of a well-spent life, and wish only to see their children settled in the world, to depart in peace. (II.i)

He continues in the same vein throughout the play, pointing out that "nothing can compensate for the loss of a parent's affection" (IV.ii), emphasizing patriotically that in America "affections are not sacrificed to riches," and, most amusingly, advises Maria to obey her father: "we may be assured, that if we are not happy, we shall, at least, deserve to be so. Adieu! I dare not trust myself longer with you." The sentimentalism of these two characters, though overdone, is functional, because there is a depth of feeling, good sense, and sincerity on their part, brought out by contrast with the usually jeering but superficial Charlotte in her move toward sentiment at the end. When she talks of her "practice of the meanest arts," her violation of "the most sacred rights of friendship," and the "littleness" of her past conduct (V.ii), it becomes evident that there are contrasts to be made in sentiment as in everything else.[31]

That the characters are essentially stock varieties is further supported by Tyler's use of the easy, and widespread, device of naming them suggestively. The choice of "Manly" for the solid American is obvious, but Tyler does not deny himself the occasion for a reinforcing pun and has Maria describe him as "so manly and noble" (IV.i). Manly's opposite, the affected Anglophile, is accordingly "Dimple" (his father is "Van Dumpling"), and Maria's stern father is "Van Rough." But it is for characters who are only alluded to, where a capsule characterization is especially convenient, that these names are applied most profusely: a milliner named Mrs. Catgut, a "rich Carolinian" Mr. Indigo, a matched couple in Miss Lovely and Bob Affable, the fashion-conscious girls Miss Blouze, Sally Slender, and Nancy Brilliant, the gossipy Miss Wasp, the sallow Miss Wan, the bankers Mr. Transfer and Mr. Van Cash, the loan shark John Hazard, the noblemen Colonel Piquet, Lord Lurcher, and Sir Harry Rook — to say nothing of a theater party consisting of Billy Simper, Jack Chassé, Colonel Van Titter, Miss Promonade, and the two Miss Tambours.[32] As with other simple devices, Tyler abuses this one, but the contrast he is making gains force when we observe (though a different principle of suggestiveness is involved) that the girls Jonathan knows are named Tabitha Wymen and Jemima Cawley.

This interest in puns and names is one aspect of a prevading concern with the resources of language. The characters are differentiated by their use of language, from Van Rough's "mind the main chance" to Jonathan's "dogs." But Van Rough's continual repetition of one phrase (four times in one speech in IV.ii) is merely a mechanical use of a hackneyed device — the "tag" line so common in the Restoration and post-Restoration theater [33] — whereas Jonathan's expressions represent, not an imitation of locutions from English drama, but an attempt to create an authentic Yankee. It is true that Jonathan's inventiveness in oaths may partly result from Tyler's possible familiarity with Sheridan's Bob Acres, but one must admit that the oaths, set against Dimple's affectations, give the desired effect. Jonathan will swear "by the living jingo" or simply "swear"; he will say "dang it all," "tarnation," "mercy on my soul," "what the rattle," "smite my timbers," "maple-log seize it," or "swamp it"; he is fond of "what the dogs" or "the dogs a bit"; and, for adjectival oaths, he turns to "cursed," "tarnal," and even "damn'd" (but only to apply to a Tory). He cannot utter a sentence without one of these expressions or a cliché: "the bag to hold," "a burning shame," "kicking up a cursed dust," "every mother's son of us," "as thick as mustard," "pretty dumb rich," "a month's mind," "chock full," or "all that." His speech may be ungrammatical, but his repeated admiration of the "true blue son of liberty," the "true blue Bunker-hill sons of liberty," or the "true born Yankee American son of liberty" is sincere.[34] That a man who says "buss" for "kiss" and "counted" for "thought" is at the same time honest, unassuming, and candid epitomizes the contrast of the entire play between inelegant goodness and polished deceit.

The linguistic basis of this contrast is at times one of the most subtle features of a play not generally known for quiet effects, and it shows that Tyler's perennial attention to the colloquial idiom had already begun. When Jessamy asks if Jonathan blackens his master's boots, Jonathan replies, "Yes; I do grease them a bit sometimes" (II.ii). The shift to "grease," like Jonathan's inability to understand "kiss" or his interpretation of "gallantry" as "girl huntry," is the verbal expression of a more basic lack of communication between the two. Jessamy himself comments on Jonathan's "indelicacy of diction" when he remembers that Jonathan was going to "stretch his legs upon the Mall" (III.i), but we know what Jessamy means by elegant speech, for he has already observed Jonathan's "most prodigious effect upon [his] risibility." His mind has fewer thoughts than Jonathan's, for he avoids clichés only because Lord Chesterfield disapproves of them, and he has no ideas to express anyway except those he parrots. Tyler has given us, then, a sophisticated inversion of the usual situation, to enforce his point — clichés here carry more thought, because used instinctively, than speech which eschews them only out of affectation. Of course Jonathan's language is a principal ingredient of the comedy of the play, but when we observe him speaking nonsense in an attempt to imitate Jessamy (as when he says "cherubim consequences" for Jessamy's "cherub of a consequence"), the comedy is springing from a deep, and serious, source.

Evidence of still other verbal experimentation abounds, from the use of grammatical errors for comic effects (Jonathan says "with I") to the presence of foreign phrases as a suggestion of affectation (Jessamy makes a vain effort to impress Jonathan with his French). Malapropism is practically unavoidable in such a play, and one is surprised not to find more of it — at any rate Jonathan does say "sturgeons" for "insurgents" and "hystrikes" for "hysterics." Unusual words, like "rantipole" (III.i) and "penseroso" (IV.i),[35] as well as enduring colloquialisms like "henpeck" (I.ii), reveal Tyler's delight with language, further displayed in passages of witty repartee and verbal sparring (as when Charlotte assures Manly she will introduce him "to two or three ladies of my acquaintance," and Letitia remarks, "And that will make him acquainted with thirty or forty beaux," II.i). The balancing of lines and sentences is another manifestation of this interest. In the first scene of act II there is a passage of ten short lines spoken alternately by Charlotte and Letitia, a kind of sticho-mythia in which each line plays on the preceding one; and in the opening scene Letitia consciously produces a parallel construction in casual conversation: "the wickedness of Love-lace without his wit, and the politeness of Sir Charles Grandi-son without his generosity." Figurative language appears, too, but chiefly as a means of characterizing Charlotte, who feels, in the first scene, "the rage of simile" upon her and re-marks later that Manly's tours in "the fields of conversation" always end in "the temple of gravity" (IV.i). It is not neces-sary to overemphasize these matters to see that Tyler does have an interest in them, which he goes on to develop more overtly in certain chapters of *The Algerine Captive* and *The Yankey in London.*

The central theme of the play, involving not just the con-trast between affectation and plainness, but also between city and country, hypocrisy and sincerity, can accommodate with ease an emphasis on patriotism and native worth — and it is here that the originality of the play lies. Otherwise its theme strikes one as little different from countless Restoration and eighteenth-century plays, and no less distinguished in execu-tion, despite its stiffness, than many of them. When one comes across a discussion of gossip (with Charlotte saying, "I take care never to report any thing of my acquaintance, especially if it is to their credit, — *discredit,* I mean," I.i), or satire of fashion (Charlotte buys clothing which "will never sit be-comingly" on her only because it is fashionable, II.i), or asides which reveal hypocrisy, or a situation of conflict between parental commands and natural inclinations in love, and so on — when one encounters these in *The Contrast,* one feels comfortably within the familiar English tradition.

Tyler, however, was doing something more. The Revolu-tion had emphasized the perennial problem of artistic independence, and the concomitant heights of patriotic fervor demanded the use of native materials. If he was not able to avoid being imitative in form, he at least was acutely aware of the problem (as his later preface to *The Algerine Captive* shows) and was successful in fitting an American subject into the ready-made framework. Patriotism crops up everywhere, from Charlotte's remark on her brother's constant desire to do "a gallant act in the service of his country" (II.i) and Jonathan's repetitive "true blue son of liberty" to comments on "our illustrious Washington" and on "those inestimable blessings that we now enjoy, our liberty and independence" (III.ii). One may feel that this insistence on patriotism is rather oppressive at times, as when Manly comes on stage to deliver about four hundred words on the theme, "Luxury is surely the bane of a nation." And he takes the ancient Greek states as his principal example of a country ruined by luxury:

They exhibited to the world a noble spectacle, — a number of independent states united by a similarity of language, sentiment, manners, common interest, and common consent, in one grand mutual league of protection. — And, thus united, long might they have continued the cherishers of arts and sciences, the protectors of the oppressed, the scourge of tyrants, and the safe asylum of liberty: But when foreign gold, and still more pernicious, foreign luxury, had crept among them, they sapped the vitals of their virtue. (III.ii)

As if the parallel were not obvious enough, he goes on to explain the dangers of division and concludes, "Oh! that America! Oh! that my country, would in this her day, learn the things which belong to her peace!"

It is evident that Manly is addressing this advice directly to the audience. The important point, though, is not that this element of the play turns the work into a tract or piece of propaganda; rather it is, perhaps surprisingly, the degree to which such a speech (admittedly too long) is dramatically appropriate in the context. We have come to expect Manly to speak in a solemn, didactic, self-righteous way; and it is precisely the "pernicious" "foreign luxury" of which he talks that we have seen operating in the play in contrast to his own stiffly forthright conduct. The speech is not a set piece that intrudes itself, relevant only in terms of historical events external to the play, but it grows directly out of the character and situation. Thus the usual dichotomies take on one further ingredient: surface polish, affectation, and hypocrisy equal the British; honesty, sincerity, but lack of social finish equal the Americans.[36] Everything else falls into place accordingly. The city–country theme becomes the sophistication of Europe versus the provinciality of America, with Jessamy finding the mall wanting in comparison with Ranelagh and Vauxhall (II.ii) and Dimple disparaging the "two or three squeaking fiddles" that New Yorkers consider music and the actors that "make a farce of tragedy" (IV.i). When Dimple predicts that Manly, after visiting the attractions of Europe, "will learn to despise the amusements of this country," Manly replies, "Therefore I do not wish to see them; for I can never esteem that knowledge valuable, which tends to give me a distaste for my native country." He explains that partiality to one's country is "laudable" because it adds to one's happiness without hurting others and leads to "the noble principle of patriotism." Even the question of fashion in clothing can be turned to account, for when Charlotte criticizes Manly's attire, he springs to the defense of his "regimental coat," which he had worn in the service of his country, and reaches the nearly blasphemous extreme of professing that "it is of little consequence to me of what shape my coat is" (II.i).

This statement is shocking, in a world of affectation, for the very reason that it denies the importance of surface appearances. The deceptiveness of surfaces is continually associated with the English–American contrast in the play, as when Jonathan is surprised that Jessamy calls himself a "servant," for, as he says, "you look so topping, I took you for one of the agents to Congress" (II.ii). The word "servant" is, in itself, repugnant to Jonathan, and Manly, too, disapproves of class consciousness based on superficial factors — he says proudly, when wooing Maria, "In our country, the affections are not sacrificed to riches, or family aggrandizement" (IV.i). Both Dimple and Jessamy take Lord Chesterfield as their ideal and regard departures from his sacred words as unworthy of a cilivized being. Jessamy believes that Jonathan "never can have been in a room with a volume of the divine Chesterfield" (II.ii), and Dimple cannot read him without pausing after each sentence to say, "Very true, my lord" (III.i). The result is that they live only by the book: Jenny is criticized because there is "something so execrably natural in her laugh" (III.i), and Jonathan because he laughed at the wrong places in the play he attended (V.i). When he asks, "don't I laugh natural?," Jessamy replies, "That's the very fault." It does not occur to Jessamy and Dimple that in their efforts to become cultivated human beings, they have ceased to be rational beings.

Obviously Tyler knew the English tradition. If his play is to be criticized as the work of a novice, the fault is not that he was unaware of conventions but that he was trying too hard to get them all in. Despite this essential imitativeness, the play can be called original. Tyler found that American characters, speech, settings, and issues would fit the old framework, and he made an important stride forward in the use of native materials for art. Significant as this step was, he had the greater insight of understanding that the patriotic theme grew directly out of the long-repeated themes of English comedy and that, though he was adding something, he was not destroying an organic whole. Questions of personal integrity and of national integrity are inevitably connected; and if what Tyler had to say about the individual in society was particularly cogent and salutary for an audience of the early republic, it has not lost its relevance with the years. Few would say that the play is an unqualified success, but, strangely enough (on second thought, understandably enough), it is limited and dated most by the very elements borrowed or imitated rather stiffly from the British tradition. At the same time, Tyler could not have found a way to express himself with such integrity and coherence if he had not been provided with the accumulated and patterned experience of a convention. His achievements and his limitations are testimony to the nature of the dilemma faced, and the triumph occasionally attained, by the "colonial" (if not "provincial") artist.

Reputation

Contemporary comments on *The Contrast* were, by the standards of 1787, quite full, and the three known reviews show that the main question, from the very beginning, was one of disentangling a consideration of the play's intrinsic merits from a recognition of its historical importance. "Candour," in the *Daily Advertiser*, after providing detailed criticism, said that "the piece, particularly when considered as the first performance does the greatest credit to the author." "Philo. Dramaticus," in the *Independent Journal*, was more specific when he referred to "the partial ardour of [the play's] friends, who have hitherto applauded the novelty of the attempt, in this country, without strictly weighing the merits of its execution," but went on to conclude that, considering the difficulties under which it was produced, "candour must allow its being an extraordinary effort of genius." The *Worcester Magazine* struggled with the same duality most aphoristically: "An American comick production, is a novelty —

therefore it was pleasing . . . this is not the whole truth — the piece has merit, and it will not be denied, that *merit* with *novelty*, forces applause, whereas *novelty* without *merit*, simply attains it." A review of the Baltimore performance, a few months later, declared that the comedy is a "specimen in proof that these new climes are particularly favorable to the cultivation of arts and sciences" and that it "rivals the most celebrated productions of the British muse in elegance of invention, correctness and splendor of diction." [37]

The *Daily Advertiser* had much more to say, to the extent of about nine hundred words. The "greatest defect," according to the reviewer, was "the want of interest and plot," which might have been alleviated by "a scene between Dimple and Maria," an interesting suggestion intended to make Maria's love for Manly seem more believable. Realism, in fact, lay behind most of this critic's comments. After praising the "sentiments" of the play, which were "the effusions of an honest patriot heart expressed with energy and eloquence," he declared that the soliloquies were "seldom so conducted as not to wound probability" and that the dialogue in general, though "easy, sprightly, and often witty," needed "the pruning knife very much." The reviewer's own uncertain critical principles came out in a related remark about Manly: his long soliloquy on America in the second scene of act III creates an entirely unnatural situation, yet "the thoughts are so just, that I should be sorry they were left out entirely." Jessamy received criticism on the same grounds: he "is a closer imitation of his master than is natural, and his language in general is too good for a servant." Other than suggesting that the satire of Chesterfield was somewhat unjust and that Jonathan's part "sometimes degenerates into farce," the reviewer praised in general terms the great merits and "many beauties" of the play, which had received "the unceasing plaudits of the audience." [38]

Dramatist: The Contrast

Tyler gave the copyright for *The Contrast* to Wignell, who issued proposals for printing the play and eventually obtained a sufficient number of subscriptions so that the play could be published, in the spring of 1790, by Prichard & Hall of Philadelphia.[39] A review in the *Universal Asylum* several months later called the dialogue "sprightly, and correct," the servant plot "diverting," and the characters "well drawn," but wished that the play bore "less resemblance to the comedies of Charles II. reign, as there are some passages which border on indelicacy"; still, because it is "the first American attempt at this species of composition," it is "worthy of the public attention."[40] Isaiah Thomas' *Massachusetts Magazine* the same year printed parts of two scenes, act III, scene ii, and act V, scene i.[41] After several revivals in various cities in the 1790's, the play was not performed during most of the nineteenth century, but its occasional mention by critics and inclusion in anthologies suggest that its "novelty" (or historical importance) was deemed greater than its "merit." Dunlap, in his 1832 history, commented on it as "the commencement of the American drama as united with the American theatre," which, though it was "extremely deficient in plot, dialogue, or incident, . . . was relished by an audience gratified by the appearance of home manufacture." Various writers, like the editor Joseph Buckingham, mentioned *The Contrast* in the 1850's, and the Duyckincks included the Jonathan play-scene in their 1855 *Cyclopaedia*,[42] but it was not until the centennial of *The Contrast* that it was accorded much interest. In that year, 1887, the Dunlap Society, dedicated to the study of the early American theater, issued as its first publication an edition of *The Contrast*, with an introduction by Thomas J. McKee, who lamented "the neglect and inattention it has heretofore met with"; though "meager in plot and incident," it contained, he found, "considerable intrinsic merit" as an "acting play." Charles F. Richardson, in his literary history the following year, agreed that, however "crude and imperfect," the play possessed "adaptability for public presentation," and E. C. Stedman included the opening scene in his 1888 anthology.[43] Whether or not these reactions were responsible, the American Academy of Dramatic Art staged a revival of the play in 1894, but it received little other attention until the second decade of the twentieth century.

It was indicative of the fate of Tyler's reputation that when the Drama League of America produced the play (under Arthur Hopkins and Robert Edmond Jones), as one of its American Drama Matinees at the New York Republic Theatre on 22 and 23 January 1917, the author's name could appear on the program as "Royall Taylor." Nevertheless, the play was gaining recognition, having been performed five years before at the Brattleboro festival and given two other productions in 1917. Helen Tyler Brown, enthusiastically pursuing details of her ancestor's life, was responsible for some of this attention, and she wrote an introduction to the limited edition of the play which Houghton Mifflin published in 1920. James B. Wilbur contributed a preface describing a copy belonging to George Washington, whose name had led the list of subscribers to the original 1790 edition and whose copy was the basis for the 1920 edition. *The Contrast* had become a rare book, and the play was accorded the reverence due a key national document.[44]

This interest in the play, part of a general revaluation of our native literature in the 1910's and 1920's, was reinforced by a number of scholars who did not fail to mention the play in their literary histories or studies of the early drama.[45] In the decades which followed, *The Contrast* was given more than a dozen productions,[46] discussed in several scholarly articles and dissertations [47] as well as in popular magazines,[48] and anthologized eight times.[49] It is more widely known than most other literary works of the immediate post-Revolutionary years and is perhaps the most famous American play before the twentieth century. Attractions of "quaintness" and patriotism aside, the play, on the dual grounds of influence and merit, can be said to deserve its fame. If Tyler is usually remembered only as the author of *The Contrast*, it is no doubt largely for the reason implied in the prologue,[50] written "by a Young Gentleman of New-York":

> Yet *one*, whilst imitation bears the sway,
> Aspires to nobler heights, and points the way,
> Be rous'd, my friends! his bold example view;
> Let your own Bards be proud to copy *you*!

Tyler was to use American materials many more times, but the conjunction of circumstances and execution have given this "bold example" a special place. After nearly two centuries, one may find most appropriate the opening of that prologue, which has taken on additional meanings, unintended by the writer: "this night is shewn/A piece, which we may fairly call our own."

Dramatist: Later Plays

T HE success of *The Contrast* encouraged Tyler to continue his playwriting, for his second effort appeared on the
John Street stage a month later, on 19 May 1787. Late April
and early May had seen productions of *The Beaux' Strategem*,
Romeo and Juliet, and *Macbeth*, and 19 May was to be a
benefit for Wignell. The first play of the evening was *The
Recruiting Officer* (performed only five days before for Mrs.
Harper's benefit night), and the second was announced as
"a COMIC OPERA in 2 Acts, (never performed) written
by the Author of the Contrast, (for this night only) called
May Day in Town, or NEW-YORK in an UPROAR." [1]
The music was "compiled from the most eminent Masters.
With an Overture and Accompanyments," and sheets of the
songs were to be sold on the evening of the performance.
One can only speculate on the plot and music of *May Day*,
for neither the play nor the song sheets are extant. It is impossible to know whether Tyler had sufficient musical knowledge to "compile" the score, and, if so, what kind of music
it was, since he shows little interest in music in his other
work; at least someone was having difficulty getting the music
put together, for the opera apparently had to be postponed
one day on this account. [2] The plot, perhaps in the vein of
The Contrast, probably arose from Tyler's own experiences
during his first May in New York, as he saw the city in the
"uproar" caused by the 1 May date for moving households.

The piece was less successful than *The Contrast*, since it was not repeated and did not elicit much comment in the newspapers, and one twentieth-century writer calls it a "trifle" and a "failure." [3] However, a contemporary witness, Congressman William J. Grayson, wrote to James Madison on 24 May admiring this play which "has plott and incident and is as good as several of the English farces"; but he admitted that "it has . . . not succeeded well" and suggested that the explanation was "the author's making his principal character a scold. Some of the New York ladies were alarmed for fear strangers should look upon Mrs. Sanders as the model of the gentle-women of this place." [4]

After these two plays, perfomed only a month apart in the spring of 1787, there is no record of further dramatic activity on Tyler's part for nearly a decade. His move to Vermont possibly was not conducive to writing for the stage, but the fact that his brother, John Steele Tyler, became manager of the Federal Street Theatre, Boston, in November 1795, combined with Dennie's prodding, may have provided adequate motivation for renewed efforts. Dennie wrote to Tyler in his usual style on 2 October 1795:

I perceive by a recent Centinel, that your brother is appointed Manager of the Theater. This information cannot be premature, as the circumstance is corroberated [*sic*] in the Orrery. This revolution in the dramatic world cannot fail to shed select influence upon your plans. I propose residing here for some time. This information may induce you to descend from the mountains, to cooperate with your friend, and *now* to think seriously of writing for the stage; which under present auspices cannot fail to essentially promote your interest. Pray don't defer an instant *doing* on the present occasion. Your predecessor Gay and you have speculated enough in property: realise now fortune invits [*sic*]. The interest I have in your well being & the claims which genius has upon your contemporaries call loudly for that snug annuity, which I swear you can have, and which will give you a couch for your gouty limbs, & Swift's daily pint, to dissipate the "curae edaces" of age. . . .

Whether you choose to have your opera sung or a future *new* comedy acted in great pomp, by his Majesty's servants, & praised by Gardner, heard by Morton, & puffed by me; this is the "mollia tempora." condescend for a day to vacate your indolent room, and entertain stock jobbing ideas. I wish you to receive that most honorable of pensions, which the dunces & knaves of a stupid mart have owed your talents since you first wove the web of fancy.[5]

Whether or not Dennie's persuasion was responsible, a play now attributed to Tyler appeared on the Boston stage five months later, on 6 May 1796. Entitled *The Farm House, or The Female Duellists*, it was announced as the afterpiece for *Every One Has His Fault*. Though no copy of the play survives, comparison of its cast with that of Kemble's 1789 *Farm House* (performed just a year earlier in New York and based in turn on the 1715 *Country Lasses*) suggests that it was an adaptation of Kemble. Tyler's brother had resigned as manager of the theater the month before, but Tyler's son reports, "The Dualists [*sic*] was performed and was especially popular." [6]

A year and a half later the Haymarket Theatre in Boston presented a play that can be assigned to Tyler with greater certainty. Dennie had written in the spring, "If I go to Boston this summer, which I am half resolved to do, I think I can lay a plan to start some Dramatic piece for you." [7] The *Independent Chronicle* duly announced, for 30 October 1797, as an afterpiece to follow *Wives as They Were*, "an original national DRAMA, in three acts, (never performed in any Theatre) entitled, The Georgia SPEC; *Or, Land in the Moon*. Written by R. TYLER, Esq. Author of the Contrast, &c." [8] The title suggests that Tyler was exploiting the current interest in land speculation in Yazoo County, Georgia, and that he was again utilizing native materials as the basis for satire.

84

Newspapers had been ridiculing the whole affair with such pieces as "an Elegy on the death of *Miss Georgia Purchase*"; [9] and the word "spec" was a common abbreviation for "speculation," particularly in connection with property, as in the advertisements for houses headed "A Spec!" [10] The names of the characters, as they appeared in the announced cast, offer a further glimpse into the nature of the play. In addition to "Old Spec" himself, there are Jasper Lunge, Charles Modish, Blunder Bubble, Slap Dash, and Billy Chatter, plus the ladies, Miss Bubble, Miss Prattle, and Miss Glib — and, finally, Old Bunker, identified as a Berkshire farmer. This is another instance of Yankee common sense contrasted with the ridiculous excesses of fashion. The *Columbian Centinel* commented, "It contains a rich diversity of national character and native humor scarcely to be found in any other drama of the language. Replete with incident, enlivened by wit and amply fraught with harmless mirth, the comedy is entitled to the applause of all without wounding the feelings of any." [11] The play moved to New York two months later, where it was performed at the John Street Theatre on 20 and 23 December under the title *A Good Spec: Land in the Moon, Or, The Yankee Turn'd Duellist*; it was given a third time in the New Theatre on 12 February 1798.[12]

One may suspect that Tyler had still further associations with the Boston theater: he did write an "Address" for the opening night of the 1795–96 season (under his brother's management), and as late as 1811 his brother was still asking him for prologues and inviting him to send "your Play which you mean to brush up." [13] It is a paradox (though not entirely unexpected) that the plays of Tyler which were performed have not survived (with the exception of *The Contrast*, which was printed), while those which in all probability were never staged have come down to us in manuscript. Until 1941 *The Contrast* was the only basis for a judgment of Tyler's skill in drama, although persons who had access to his son's memoir knew the titles of these other plays. In that year, however, the texts of four more Tyler plays, found among the Tyler Papers, were edited by A. W. Peach and G. F. Newbrough for the Princeton series of "America's Lost Plays." It may be that these plays do nothing to increase Tyler's stature, and it may be that they are so different in kind from *The Contrast* as to form almost a separate category of his work — but it is futile to wish that some of the produced plays had been saved instead, and in any case one is grateful for what meager material there is, material that does have its importance for an understanding of Tyler.

The Island of Barrataria

The first of the plays in the 1941 volume can be set apart from the other three but seems to fall in the same class with one final nonextant title ascribed to Tyler in that both are adaptations from foreign literature. Though nothing whatever is known about a play entitled *The Doctor in Spite of Himself*, which Tyler's son credits to his father, it appears to be an adapted version of the Molière play and can be dated approximately 1795 from a letter of Tyler's.[14] Similarly, the first of the four 1941 plays, *The Island of Barrataria* [sic], is based on the Barataria episode in *Don Quixote* (especially on chapters 45, 47, 51, and 53 of part II). While the Molière piece may have been little more than a revision of a translation, the Cervantes offers an opportunity for examining Tyler's dramatic technique, since in this case details from a prose work had to be selected and rearranged for dramatic effect. The Barataria sequence had previously been dramatized by Thomas D'Urfey, but if one is to accept Tyler's inscription on the title page of his manuscript, he wrote without a knowledge of previous efforts: "As the author is informed there is a farce in print — on the same subject — and perhaps with the Title first Proposed — the following is suggested as a substitute — Tantalization, Or The Governour of a Day." It has been suggested that the allusion is to Frederick Pilon's version of D'Urfey's *Barataria, or Sancho Panza Turned Governor*, performed at the John Street Theatre on 5 October 1789. Although there is no record that Tyler's play was ever performed, this reference, if correct, provides a *terminus a quo* for the play and suggests that it probably belongs to his second, or "Boston," period of play-writing — an inference supported by Tyler's further comment on his title page: "A Farce in Three Acts never before performed on any Stage [,] by a Bostonian." [15]

A comparison of *The Island of Barrataria* with the relevant chapters of *Don Quixote* reveals the skill which Tyler had acquired as a dramatic craftsman. If the finished play is not as important, nor even as interesting intrinsically, as *The Contrast*, it does show that Tyler knew how to put a play together, for in the course of its composition he had done three things: he had selected the most dramatic episodes from his source and omitted the others (compressing the time from seven days to one); he had added new incidents to create a romantic interest; and he had so arranged these elements as to form two interrelated plots, constituting a true intrigue as opposed to the episodic structure of the *Don Quixote* material. The basis of the intrigue (and Tyler's addition to the Barataria story) is, characteristically, a situation in which two lovers try to outwit an uncooperative father, his objections to the match founded on class consciousness and social pretensions.[16] Alvarez, a wealthy middle-class Baratarian, is determined that his daughter, Julietta, shall marry a nobleman, though she is in love with Carlos. Julietta, disguised, takes the initiative in arranging affairs, and the trick by which she attains her goal provides the main thread of "plot." It so happens that this family crisis occurs at the very time when

Sancho Panza takes over as governor of Barataria, and Tyler not only involves him in the plot but inserts portions of the traditional story into the framework thus provided. The result is that the two stories support each other, and what was an episodic adventure in the picaresque vein becomes a finished plot in the Aristotelian sense, with a beginning, middle, and end.[17]

The beginning shows the two strands before they become related. Of the four scenes in act I, the first and third concern the Alvarez story (Carlos talking with Alvarez, and Carlos and Julietta trying to outwit Alvarez through disguise), while the second and fourth introduce the Sancho Panza part (the Captain of the Guard announcing Sancho's arrival, and his entry itself). The future connection between the two, however, is disclosed at the end of the opening scene when Alvarez suggests the possibility of offering his daughter to the new governor, Sancho Panza (who is to arrive "this morning"), since Sancho is obviously of a noble family if he is to be governor; Carlos' protestations that Sancho is a "mere fool" and a "short thick fat squab boorish looking fellow" (p. 5) have no effect on the snobbery of Alvarez, who sees only that Sancho is a "grandee." The act also builds to a climax with the arrival of Sancho and the closing barrage of gunfire and shouts of the mob to welcome the governor. Tyler saw the theatrical value of pageantry and elaborated on the simple statement in Cervantes that Sancho entered amid pomp and the ringing of bells. He further perceived the usefulness of a comic motif and took a hint from the episode of Cervantes in which Sancho is not permitted to eat; Tyler leads up to that scene, in a degree that Cervantes does not, by emphasizing Sancho's appetite. The second thing Sancho says is, "And then let us go to dinner, for I am very hungry" (p. 10), and practically all his other remarks in the scene relate to food. He is a caricature, but one appropriate to the farcical world of Barataria, and the hunger provides a greater unifying thread than it does in Cervantes.

In act II the emphasis is on Sancho, but Tyler's device for interweaving the two plots makes him a very different figure from the one in *Don Quixote*. In the first scene Julietta, disguised as a page, slanders herself to watch Carlos' reactions and then asks her father (who does not recognize her) to recommend her as a page at the governor's palace. The two of them leave for the palace, which is the setting of the following scene. Although Sancho is still hoping for food (he has "all honour and no porridge"), the striking thing about the scene is his attitude toward his wife. Alvarez offers his daughter, and Sancho first replies that he is "noosed already" and that he "must not forget my good old spouse Terresa"; but when Alvarez mentions the money that will accompany Julietta, Sancho's attitude quickly changes, and he wishes "old Terresa was asleep in Paradise." He not only agrees to abandon Terresa and marry Julietta but accepts Alvarez's seal ring as pledge, though not without some pangs of conscience. He tells Alvarez, with a characteristic simile, to "speak softly that my conscience may not hear you, for it kicks like a mule colt," and he imagines Alvarez to be "a relation of that old gentleman who sometimes for his amusement sports a cloven foot" (p. 15). This Sancho is far removed from the one in Cervantes, who writes to Don Quixote asking him to forward letters from his wife Teresa because he longs for news of her and the children. Tyler's reason for the change appears to be a desire to make even more explicit the satire on rulers: when Sancho asks, "Would it not be wrong to make my spouse Terresa a castaway?," Alvarez assures him, "Wrong in private men, but in great men honourable. . . . a great man's conscience sleeps like himself in down" (p. 15). But the injection of this note weakens — not strengthens — the force of the satire. That the satire is more effective in the Cervantes chapters, or in Brackenridge when Teague O'Reagan is elected to an office for which he is not qualified, results not from the fact that Tyler is too direct, or overtly didactic, but from the more important fact that he has presented Sancho with an ethical dilemma foreign to the world of farce.

This is not to say that marital questions cannot be one of the main sources of farce, but that the heartlessness of Sancho's behavior in this scene, with the allusions to conscience and temptation by the devil, is not in accord with what we otherwise learn of Sancho, or even with the spirit of the entire play. The scene returns to farce at the end, when Sancho questions Carlos about Julietta (especially, "can she make a good dumpling?"), and Carlos replies with a ludicrously unpleasant picture of her — as he explains in an aside, "the fear of losing thee forces me to disparage thee" (p. 16). Julietta, still disguised as a page, is placed in the position of praising herself. Though the scene is not in Cervantes, the idea of describing Julietta as "a beauty if it were not that she is blind of one eye and squints with the other" and a good dancer "if she were not lame" probably comes from the similar (but much longer) description of a country girl in the Barataria section of *Don Quixote* (chapter 47). The whole scene is a crucial one for evaluating Tyler's effort because he is here carefully tying the threads of his plot together (foreshadowing the end with Alvarez's promise that whoever presents the seal ring shall have his daughter) and exploiting the comedy of Sancho's hunger — it fits admirably, that is, into the structure of the play. But in his zeal to comment more directly on the unscrupulousness of rulers, Tyler's method shifts to create the only serious blemish in the play: Sancho's lack of affection for his wife is not in itself objectionable; the problem lies in the approach to the matter. If Tyler is trying to make of Sancho a more complex character facing a serious moral and ethical decision, then he fails to pursue these implications through the rest of the play. The flaw is not in structure but in mood and characterization.

The final scene of act II is the longest in the play and presents the heart of the Barataria story — Sancho's decisions in his court of law. Though the first three cases which come up are from Cervantes, the ritual of the court is not; as a lawyer, Tyler was taking the opportunity to satirize the extravagances and jargon of his profession. After the crier calls the court to order, Don Ignatio Salkedor Ventris Fleta Bracton Comberback presents the first case and opens a roll, ten or fifteen feet long, listing the charges; when Sancho wants to know briefly what the man is accused of, Don Ignatio replies, "that would be against all precident." In the second case Don Ignatio points out that the issue cannot be heard without a formal statement — "the Plaintiff," he says, "should have filed her declaration in haec verba":

Attach Joseph Nunnez of Algazanas in the Province of Andelusia, now resident in Barrataria yeoman, to answer unto Magdeline alias Martha alias Margery alias Dorcas alias Deborah alias Catharine alias Keturah Slammerkin alias Slubberkin alias Slipshins alias Slipshod of Avedo in the Province of Astrinas Spinster in a plea of Trespass on her case — For that the said Joseph at Astrog in Kamskatchka to wit in Barrataria and so forth et cetera and so forth — on the body of her the said Magdaline alias Martha alias Margery, alias Dorcas alias Deborah alias Catharine alias Keturah Slammerkin alias Slubberkin alias Slipshins alias Slipshod with staves clubs swords guns bayonets pistols crowbars Congreve Rockets boarding pikes steam boats masinos and Torpedoes and other deadly weapons — did make an assault and for that the said Joseph, aforesaid at Kamskatchka aforesaid to wit at Barrataria aforesaid — did aforesaid — then aforesaid and aforesaid there aforesaid — her aforesaid — the aforesaid said aforesaid Magdaline aforesaid alias Martha aforesaid alias Margery aforesaid — alias Dorcas aforesaid alias Deborah aforesaid alias Catharine aforesaid alias Keturah aforesaid Slammerkin aforesaid alias Slubberkin aforesaid alias Slipshins aforesaid — alias Slipshod aforesaid and for that also moreover nevertheless and likewise — and so proceed to set forth the Plaintiff's case. Clearness and precision, may it please your Excellency, are the glory of the Law. (pp. 18–19)

Thereupon Don Fabricio, a second lawyer, asserts that this suit should have been presented "by indictment — billa vera, my Lord," and goes on to declare that the only point on which lawyers agree is "that the law has been immutably settled for more than seven hundred years. But then how or in what manner or in which way, it is settled, we have been disputing about ever since." The pragmatic wisdom of Sancho's un-tutored judgment is of course illustrated in Cervantes and follows the immemorial pattern of native insight triumphing over elaborate dialectic; but Tyler's caricature of legal procedures and verbiage makes the incisiveness of Sancho's decisions stand out all the more.

The first case (which is one of the last in Cervantes' account, chapter 51) has to do with travelers on a bridge, each of whom is asked his reason for crossing. If he tells the truth, he may continue; if he lies, he is immediately hanged. The problem is that Lope de Stepaway said he was crossing the bridge for the purpose of being hanged; if he were executed, then, he would have told the truth and should have lived. Sancho answers quickly: "Let the prisoner go free for where the case is doubtful, the judge should always incline to mercy." When Don Ignatio reports that there is no precedent for such a decision, Sancho says, "Then put it in your books, that there may be one page at least an honest soul may love to read" (p. 17). The second case (from chapter 45 of *Don Quixote*, Sancho's second case there) concerns a woman who accuses a man of assaulting her, though the man claims he paid her what she had asked until she saw that he had more money. Sancho's solution is first to award the purse to the woman;

then, when the man tries to take it away from her, she defends it so energetically that Sancho can say, "if you had been as carefull to defend your Jewell as you have the purse, there are not many men in the old or new world who could have rob'd you" (p. 20). Though Tyler's Sancho does not castigate her as much as Cervantes', in both cases the man leaves with his money. The third issue (Sancho's first case in *Don Quixote*, chapter 45) turns on another trick: one peasant, casually handing his staff to a second, swears that he has paid the second peasant his debt; Sancho, after some thought, realizes that the money is concealed inside the staff.

These cases, while not related to the Alvarez plot, serve to reveal Sancho's character before he is faced with a case which does involve the love plot. After the two peasants leave, Julietta enters, disguised as an old woman, and tells Sancho a story about being abandoned by her husband, a story exactly parallel to Sancho's own projected behavior. "Such doings," says Julietta, "may do for emperors & governours & princes but won't do for Christian people" (p. 22). Sancho, who is aware of "a case as like this as two peas," advises her to tell her husband to "resist the devil," for "a good wife and children are the richest comforts a man can possess." Julietta asks for a token, as proof that she has talked to the governor, and Sancho gives her Alvarez's ring. Sancho's character has thus been righted, but dissatisfaction at his ambiguous role is not relieved. His inability to play the part of the unfeeling and corrupt monarch manifests itself in this decision as in the other three: all are consistently part of Tyler's satire on governmental hypocrisy, as brought into focus by naïveté and simplicity. But why did the Sancho who cuts through legal nonsense and refuses to submit to arguments about precedent ever attempt the role of the corrupt ruler or acquiesce to Alvarez's deal in the first place? If this episode is intended as a study of the good man who yields to temptation but sees his error in time, then the play is simply not up to the burden it must carry. Sancho goes through no agonized process of soul-searching, nor is there reason for him to in the world of the play; but one may feel that for a few moments he was in a different world.

The plot, in essence, is contained within those last two scenes of act II, for at the end of the act the ring has passed into Julietta's hands; there remains, in act III, only to make explicit the end of the affair. Of the two scenes in this act, the first is the culmination of the hunger theme. Sancho has not been permitted to eat since his arrival in Barataria, for the governor must traditionally appear at court before he dines. Now at last Sancho is confronted with a magnificent table of food, only to find (as in *Don Quixote*, chapter 47) that each dish he chooses is ruled out as unhealthful by the royal physician Don Pedro Physico Positivo Pulmonic Detergent; even the ale and wine are drunk by the official tasters. In the second scene, set in Sancho's private apartment, he is promised a special repast, but fresh matters of state interfere. First comes the announcement that the enemy is preparing to invade the island; then Julietta, disguised now as a gypsy, gives the ring to Carlos, who gives it in turn to Alvarez, who is forced by his earlier promise to award his daughter to Carlos; and, finally, the invading army arrives, Sancho is bound in armor so that he cannot move, he is trampled upon by soldiers, and at the end he is given credit for gaining the victory (based on chapter 53 of *Don Quixote*). Hypocritical praise is just as distasteful to him as the cant of the lawyers, and he can take no more of it. The play ends with Sancho, "in a sullen mood," delivering the moral to the audience: "I have for some time suspected I was the fool of the play. . . . Sancho is a simpleton I know, but as simple as I am, I have mother wit enough to find out in a brief day that I am unfit for office. But are there not some who govern it for years — bear abuse on abuse and have not wit enough to see that they are the Sancho's of the political play?" (p. 30).[18]

This final speech has no place in the play and may be regarded as a conventional eighteenth-century curtain speech to the audience. Otherwise, except for the wavering in the treatment of Sancho in act II, the play is successful enough to reassure one that Tyler's dramatic ability was not entirely exhausted in *The Contrast*. This play reveals a firmer (and less mechanical) grasp of dramatic structure and unity, and it demonstrates an insight into farcical situations and dialogue (which differ from those in drawing-room comedy). As in *The Contrast*, Tyler's underlying purpose is to deliver a sermon to the new republic, but, however overt, it is not quite so direct as in the earlier play. Even Sancho has been made into a kind of disguised Yankee, with his down-to-earth approach, his similes about peas and colts, and his expressions like "long locrum story" (p. 17), "how she kites it" (p. 23), and "Cork your peepers, good woman, and unstopple your mouth" (p. 18). Tyler's experimentation with words is again evident in colloquialisms, in characters' names, and in puns. Sancho constantly plays on words, particularly to bring the subject back to food — when Julietta is called "the toast of the town," it is inevitable that Sancho will say, "Very comfortable in a noggin of brisk ale" (p. 14).[19] One of his puns well illustrates the patriotic slant of the play: Don Ignatio's mention of a precedent causes Sancho to say, "President? — I never knew but one good President in my life & he is gone to glory" (p. 17).[20] The patriotism, as in *The Contrast* and *The Algerine Captive*, is critical and instructional; it is an attempted corrective of abuses in a system worth preserving. Only episodes from Cervantes' Barataria story which would contribute most directly to a satire of incompetence in high places are chosen (Sancho's "rounds" in chapter 49 are omitted), and a comparison of Cervantes' and Tyler's treatments of Sancho's exits from Barataria shows that Tyler's criticism is harsher and more biting. The unity he gives to Cervantes' incidents corresponds to the coherence of thought lying behind the play. Tyler knew the effectiveness of laughter and labeled his work a "farce" with no frivolous intent.

The Sacred Dramas

If *The Island of Barrataria* is not an unexpected successor to *The Contrast*, the other three plays, which are sacred dramas in blank verse, are so different that one student of Tyler has remarked that they "somehow hardly fit into the picture." [21] Yet the witty and satiric Tyler is not the whole man, as many of his poems show; and one should not be surprised to find a man who almost went into the ministry discovering a literary outlet in Biblical stories. These plays may have been intended as examples of the "coarse fabric" of the American "parnassian looms," which deserve patriotic support because they are "homespun," [22] but they are also the sincere products of a long familiarity with the Bible.

The shortest of the three, *The Judgement of Solomon*, may be taken as an illustration of the method used. This play, scarcely 750 lines, is made up of two approximately equal acts (the first of three scenes, the second of one), with a prologue and an epilogue. Its Biblical source, a short passage in I Kings (3:16–28), is the famous incident in which two women, each claiming a particular child as her own, appear before Solomon for settlement of the dispute. Solomon gives the command to have the child divided into two parts, one for each woman, and from the reactions of the women he determines which is the real mother — for one raises no objection to the division, while the other says she would rather lose custody of the child than see it slain. The latter is of course awarded the child, and the case is taken to represent one of the high points of Solomon's wisdom.

Out of this brief tale Tyler has constructed a well-rounded and dramatic work; he has exploited the conflict and suspense inherent in the story but not utilized in the Biblical version. The first act is of his own invention and serves, in three different episodes, to build up interest in the actual trial scene, which constitutes the second act. The opening scene is a conversation between two elders of Israel, Chalcol and Baanah. Chalcol, renowned for his wisdom, has been gone from Israel for many years in search of knowledge, and now, upon his return, he questions his old friend about the changes that have taken place. After all the strife that had occurred under Saul and David, Chalcol asks how it happens that now "peace and plenty crown this favour'd land" (p. 102); and the answer is that Solomon, "deemed of all mankind / The wisest," now rules. Although Chalcol, wise himself, is somewhat skeptical, Baanah explains that Solomon's wisdom is "from above, the special gift of God" (p. 103). Baanah points out Solomon's temple, and the scene ends as Chalcol amazedly tries to take in all these "genuine fruits of wisdom" (p. 104).

The second scene shifts to the house of the two women, Lernah and Maachah, and shows them quarreling. Whereas in the Biblical account the women are unnamed and undifferentiated, here they assume at least a small degree of personality; whereas in the Bible they simply appear before the King and explain the situation, here their conflict is dramatized, and we learn the dilemma through their quarrel. Lernah, the woman who speaks first and whose baby has supposedly died, is the one who speaks more gently, for the most part, and ultimately triumphs; Maachah, who is on the defensive from the start, is rather too sensitive about the question of whether the baby she is carrying is really hers, and her outbursts of anger suggest a guilty conscience. Tyler has provided in these women the rudiments at least of convincing characterizations. Lernah is determined to reclaim her child, "if in Israel, in God's own land / Justice can yet be had" (p. 106). "I'll fly straightway," she says, "to royal Solomon / And at the footstool of his golden throne / Will cry for justice"; and Maachah follows her.

Like these two scenes, the third has its ultimate focus on Solomon. This scene balances the first, with a conversation between two men, one of whom (like Chalcol in the first) remains to be convinced of Solomon's greatness. Liba, formerly a servant of Mephiboseth, extols Solomon, who has awarded him half of Mephiboseth's property; Shimei, on the other hand, considers Liba an apostate from the house of Saul and curses Solomon and the race that took over Saul's throne. So Liba suggests that they go to court, for that very day a difficult case between two women is to come up, a case in which the wisest men have declared that no justice can be done. The symmetry of the first act is completed when he names Chalcol, "This day return'd," as one of those wise men. All three scenes have pointed toward Solomon and have aroused curiosity (even in those who know the story) about the scene in which Solomon will meet this test of his wisdom.

The second act is set in Solomon's throne room and opens with a herald's announcement that Belkis, the Queen of Sheba, has arrived. Tyler is here joining, for dramatic effect, two separate passages in I Kings, for the visit of the Queen of Sheba (I Kings 10:1–13) is not connected in the Biblical account with the decision in the case of the two women; however, she does come to see if the reports of Solomon's wisdom are true, and thus, in the play, she is another figure like Chalcol and Shimei, doubting until she observes with her own eyes. When the two women enter, Lernah first presents her case, in words close to the King James version (this is the very opening of the Biblical account) — for example, in the King James the first woman explains that "there was no stranger with us in the house, save we two in the house" (3:18); Lernah says, "There were with us no stranger in the house — / No one save us to see our infant babes" (p. 114). Then Maachah argues her side, and Solomon recapitulates the case, asks if there are witnesses, and turns to Baanah to determine whether there is a rule or precedent covering such a situation. The ritual symmetry of the play continues with the interpolated comments of Shimei (who believes that Solomon is baffled) and Liba (who still defends the King), balancing the brief discussion between Baanah and Chalcol just before the two women entered. When Solomon orders the child to be split, Shimei decries the barbarity of the decision, and Tyler continues to put off the climax by having Maachah speak before Lernah (in the Bible the true mother cries out first). There remains only for Solomon to award the child to Lernah and for Belkis, following closely the King James phrasing,[23] to deliver a glowing encomium to Solomon's wisdom.

It is understandable that Tyler should have been drawn to this subject, concerned with the administration of justice, and the Solomon case is only a serious presentation of the kind of legal puzzle that occurs in *The Island of Barrataria*. Furthermore, though overt preaching is kept out of the drama itself, the Prologue and Epilogue make clear the intended application. The Prologue centers on the question, "Has wisdom ceased her cry in modern times?" The answer is No, but modern man has turned to "earthly vanities," to "idols vain," and he may be helped by contemplating "How heavenly wisdom did in ancient days / Inspire the wisest of mankind." The Epilogue then points out that wisdom even greater than Solomon's is still bestowed "on all who rightly seek the Lord / And gain the honor of the Christian name." Finally, it is evident that Tyler knew these Biblical materials well, for all the names (except Belkis and Lernah) occur in the

Royall Tyler

Bible (chiefly in I Kings and I Samuel), and, if the incidents
themselves are not authentic, the identities of most characters
are.[24] The ease with which he sketches in political history
in the third scene — the background of intrigue which led
to Solomon's accession — is added testimony that Tyler had
read his Old Testament more than casually.

To find that Tyler has skillfully employed various dramatic
techniques to turn a short tale into a play is to find no more
than one would expect, after *The Contrast* and *The Island
of Barrataria*; more surprising, perhaps, is the quality of the
verse. Tyler's blank verse reveals itself in this play to be a
flexible, fluid instrument, capable of subtle effects and occasional power. He is in sufficient control of his medium that
he is not afraid to run over certain lines, to vary the caesuras,
or to cut some lines short (especially the last lines of speeches).
The Miltonic patterns, with an attraction to place names, are
illustrated in the seventh speech of the play, by Chalcol:

> In search of knowledge I have travel'd far
> Through Persia, Media and Chaldea's land,
> E'en to the peak of frozen Caucasus.
> Three years I sojourn'd on the banks of Nile;
> Thrice saw its mighty waters rush amain
> O'er Egypt's fertile plain; and three years more
> With wonder I in Babylon survey'd
> The huge remains of that stupendous pile
> Call'd Babel, raised by impious man.
> To mock Omnipotence I likewise climb'd
> The steep ascent of lofty Arrarat
> And hence have brought a piece of shittim wood
> Cut from the ribs of that same wondrous ark
> Which saved the righteous Noah from the flood
> Which delug'd the whole earth. (p. 101)

Alliteration and simile are not to any extent parts of Tyler's
equipment,[25] but the short last line, as here, appeared so
effective to him that it became a trademark of the longer

speeches and emphatic short ones: "But Solomon is deemed of all mankind / The wisest" (p. 102); "To give just judgment in this wondrous case / So dark and intricate" (p. 109); "My Lord the King, I cannot bear to hear / Her lie so basely" (p. 114).

The strengths and weaknesses of Tyler's verse can be seen, at the beginning of act II, in the last lines of the prayer (modeled on the one in I Kings 3:6–9) which Solomon offers up before the trial:

> When I ascend the seat of judgment then,
> Hear thou in heaven, thy dwelling place,
> And me endue with wisdom to discern
> The good from evil, and still to award
> A righteous judgment to thy chosen race. (p. 110)

There is a faltering, as in the second and fourth lines, and occasionally an instance of overregularity, as in the first (with its filler word at the end); but there is also a sense of rhetorical effect, of how to construct and phrase a verse sentence for cumulative power, of combining movement and meaning. Tyler had learned to write by reading the masters, and, if his verse is derivative and filled with conventional expressions, it is not dull. He knew English poetry as well as he knew the Bible, and he practiced his lessons faithfully: his blank verse may not be always stimulating, but it is always competent. To say that much is to say a great deal, when one is speaking about a lawyer of the early republic, writing thirty years before Robert Montgomery Bird and sixty before George Henry Boker.

The other two plays, with a few distinguishing features of their own, manifest the same qualities of adaptation and prosody, and show invariably a flair for the selection and combination of inherently dramatic Biblical episodes. The Esther story is widely regarded as one of the best narratives in the Old Testament, though its brutality and secularism have raised questions about its appropriateness for inclusion in a sacred text. Tyler retells this story in 1150 lines, emphasizing (as the title indicates) the Hebrew celebration which grows out of it, in *The Origin of the Feast of Purim; Or, The Destinies of Haman and Mordecai.* This subtitle, contrasting the haughty Haman with the devout Mordecai, points to another aspect of the tale which Tyler stresses: the defeat of pride by righteousness, suggested by the epigraphs from Proverbs and Psalms [26] and by the concluding didactic lines: "pride and envy, baleful passions, / Altho' awhile they injure righteous men / Upon their base posessor oft recoil / And merge him in the ruin he design'd" (p. 60). A further subtitle suggests a certain amount of eclecticism: "A Sacred Drama in Three Acts Taken Principally from the Book of Esther." If Esther provides the material for the body of the play, the opening and closing choruses draw on the Psalms and some of the prophets. One may surmise that the opening lines of the male chorus were inspired by Jeremiah (see 4:8), but there is no question that the last speech of the female chorus in the opening section is a paraphrase (often repeating the King James wording) of Psalm 137 (pp. 34–35); then the prophet Haggai enters and, alternately with the male chorus, delivers what is in part a close paraphrase of passages in the book of Haggai; [27] and, after the action of the play, the choruses [28] speak again, this time with echoes of Psalms 98 and 100 (and perhaps 66, 81, and 95).

This combination of elements produces an anachronistic plot, since Haggai's attempts to arouse his people to return to Jerusalem and rebuild the Temple occurred about fifty years before the supposed deliverance of the Jews from Ahasuerus by Esther and Mordecai; but the result is greater dramatic effect and a more affirmative story, for Mordecai becomes the hero who not only saves the Jews but who, against his own personal wishes to go to Jerusalem with his friends, stays behind to look after those of his people who remain. The entire tale is given an added dimension, since the intrigue is set against a background of renewed hope and purpose on the part of the Jews. This expanded plot is in turn framed by the choruses, so that it assumes the status of a metaphor. The opening lyric section is a lamentation spoken antiphonally by the men and women, who join nine times to pronounce the refrain:

> Take up the burden of the woeful song:
> The Lord the God of Jacob hides his face;
> His promise to our Fathers is forgot. (pp. 33, 34, 35, 36, 37)

After the salvation of the Jews has been worked out, the closing choral section is a hymn of praise, which repeats its echo of the Psalms six times:

> O make a joyful noise unto the Lord
> Rejoice ye in the God of our Salvation,
> For the Lord hath remembered Jacob
> The Holy one hath redeemed Isra'l. (pp 60, 61, 62)

As in a formal elegy, uncontrolled grief is transformed to serenity and happiness through a creative process which restores order; the activities of Esther and Mordecai against Ahasuerus and Haman become symbolic of the ordering power of righteousness and selflessness in a world that contains pride and vicious conceit.

The intrigue itself follows closely the Biblical pattern, though Esther is already queen when the play opens, and we learn little here about her replacing Vashti (p. 39); it is characteristic of Tyler not to allow us to see the main figure at once, and Esther in fact does not appear until the next to the last scene. Of the three scenes in act I, the first is Haggai's appeal to the "pious remnant of this stubborn race"; the second, also not in the book of Esther, is a conversation between Luzzi and Elam, two who are going back to Jerusalem following Haggai's advice; and the third, a domestic scene between Prince Haman and his wife Geresh,[29] reveals Haman's anger over the failure of Mordecai to make obeisance to him. While Tyler gives Haman's consultations with his wife (in alternating scenes) in far greater detail than does the Bible, we are not shown directly (as in Esther 3:8–15) Haman asking Ahasuerus to destroy all Jews. We learn about this only when Mordecai tells Hatach, Esther's eunuch, in the short second act; using Hatach as go-between, Mordecai persuades Esther to approach the King and plead for the Jews (though visiting the King unbidden can mean death). The other scene of act II, again between Haman and his wife, reveals (following Esther 5:12) Esther's shrewdness in playing on Haman's pride, for he is overjoyed that Esther has invited him and the King to a special banquet.

Act III traces the downfall of Haman, following his false elation. First Ahasuerus remembers that Mordecai once saved his life and asks Haman to do Mordecai honor in the King's name; Tyler sees the dramatic possibilities of the irony and has Haman protest slightly (as he does not in Esther 6:11). Then, after Haman and his wife talk over this unfortunate reversal (scene ii) and after Esther has prayed (scene iii), the banquet takes place in which Esther exposes Haman's treachery and Ahasuerus gives the order that Haman be hanged on the gallows prepared for Mordecai. The play is built on a kind of Sophoclean irony, for Haman thinks he is continually rising higher and still imagines the final banquet an honor to him, even after the Mordecai celebration, in which he had unwittingly arranged his own humiliation. Tyler concludes quickly with Ahasuerus' didactic speech and the Chorus' joyful announcement of the Purim celebration, leaving out entirely the bloody descriptions of Jewish revenge reported in the ninth chapter of Esther. This omission, as well as his decision to elaborate certain scenes to dramatize Haman's

pride, underlines the fact that Tyler's interest is not in a tale
of exciting (and cruel) adventure but in a poem of devout,
yet active, faith.

The remaining play, *Joseph and His Brethren*, is the longest of the three (with about 1250 lines) and tells the familiar
story from Genesis (chapters 37–50). With its long time span
and wide-ranging scenes, the history of Joseph is the most
intractable material Tyler attempted to dramatize. But the
story does have highly dramatic moments, and Tyler wisely
chose to concentrate on them. Act I recounts, in four scenes,
the brothers' hatred of Joseph, their decision to cast him into
a pit, their selling him to merchants, and their reporting to
Jacob that he is dead. Tyler expands the Biblical account of
Joseph's dreams (Genesis 37:3–10) in the opening scene so
that there is some motivation for later action: Joseph's dreams
may at first appear egotistical, but his soliloquy shows him to
be self-sacrificing, and it is apparent that he is the victim of
his brothers' jealousy and irritation, arising from his position
as their father's favorite. Act II jumps to the second year of
the famine; Tyler omits the account of Joseph and Potiphar's
wife, and of Joseph's interpretations of the prisoners' and
then of Pharaoh's dreams, resulting in his rise to power (Genesis 38–41). The seven years of plenty have passed and two of
the famine, and Joseph's brothers now (in the first scene of
act II) appear before him in Egypt asking for food. The second scene shows Jacob giving permission for Benjamin to
go on the second trip, and in the following scene Joseph's
steward welcomes the brothers to Egypt for a second time.
This leaves the five scenes of act III [30] for the climactic action
— Joseph's revelation of his identity (following the stolen
cup trick) and Jacob's reaction to the news that Joseph is
alive. The details of Jacob's later years in Egypt with Joseph
(Genesis 46–50) are entirely omitted, and the play ends,
much more dramatically than the Biblical account, with the

effective scene in which Jacob and Leah are on the threshold
of a new life. The last lines, taken almost without alteration
from Genesis (45:28), are spoken by Jacob: "Joseph, my
son, is yet alive / And I will go and see him ere I die!"

If the choice of scenes shows dramatic skill, the over-all
form is less satisfying. Though there is no prologue, there is a
Chorus of Israelitish Women which intrudes itself between
the first two acts to explain that thirteen years are passing in
this interval. The Chorus' twenty-eight-line speech, oddly
enough, consists of an opening four-line quatrain (*abab*) in
iambic pentameter, followed by twenty-four lines of iambic
tetrameter, rhyming usually in couplets (except for the
rhymes of lines 7 and 10, 13 and 21, 14 and 22). Why the
first lines should be longer than the rest, why indeed the
poem is in rhymed tetrameter at all, is not clear. These jingling
lines, surrounded by blank verse, make the trite sentiments
expressed all the more conspicuous. The Israelitish women
tell us to turn to the Biblical account,

> Compar'd with which the feeble verse
> That our poor actors do rehearse
> On this our mean Scholastic Stage
> Seems dross beside the finest gold. (p. 78)

Surely Tyler did not shift to tetrameter simply in order to
fit sound to sense, for the "feeble verse" of the rest of the
play is above this; in any event the speech is a distracting and
superfluous interlude. There is no similar break between acts
II and III; then, after act III (which seems rather carelessly
planned, with its two brief opening scenes), the Israelitish
chorus pronounces a seventeen-line epilogue in blank verse,
which is unusually didactic:

> . . . neglect not now, wisdom to win
> From these our scenes, and let our drama teach
> The lessons better taught in Holy Writ —
> That God for his own glory governs still

Human events, and turns the crimes of men
To the best good of all mankind. . . . (pp. 95–96)

Perhaps Tyler followed his model too closely in this effort.
In his other two Biblical plays he combined episodes from
different parts of the Bible or invented new scenes, so that,
however closely he paraphrased at times, he was creating a
new entity. In the Joseph play his task was only one of
condensation, and he did not introduce new characters or
scenes; [31] as a result, he perhaps felt that, instead of shaping
something of his own, he was merely producing a weak substitute (as the chorus reiterates). He was not entirely in control of his material.

The point can be illustrated by the verse of the play. More
than in the other two plays, Tyler resorts to inversions and
periphrasis to fill out his lines (as "Ye well do know my wife
to me two sons / Did bear," p. 90) and — a related matter —
follows the King James wording more closely and more
often.[32] The effect is not only dull, routine lines but a greater
tendency toward moralistic pronouncements. Near the be-
gining Joseph takes sixteen lines to explain that God works
in mysterious ways (p. 67); he later indicates the meaning
of the story when he asks God to turn seeming evil into future
good (p. 73); and he points out at length that his earlier
misfortune was part of God's plan to save Jacob's family
(pp. 91–93). When, on the other hand, Tyler's instinct for
drama leads him to elaborate on a hint in the Biblical story,
the verse takes on life and the penetration of character is
quite sharp.[33] For example, Joseph's relation to his brothers
has a sound psychological basis: Levi recognizes a strain of
pompousness in him and calls him "fond babbler" (p. 67),
while Simeon's sarcasm (p. 69) reveals his own jealousy.
Joseph's soliloquy (p. 69) shows him to be thoughtful and
serious, and he emerges from the play a study in kindness

combined with what others might take for pride. But the vigorous lines with which the play opens offer a promise that is not, except in isolated passages, fulfilled.

Tyler never expected that these plays would be performed, unless his reference to "this our mean Scholastic Stage" implies a school performance. They were the literary exercises of a man who gained great pleasure from such experimentation, and they were part of the same impulse that produced adaptations of Molière and Cervantes and projected "moral tales" for the instruction of youth. Both as exercises in adaptation and as materials for instruction, they provided the opportunity to write poetry and to construct dramatic situations. If phrases from the King James Bible account for the dignity of some of the verse, Tyler displays a facility of his own; if the Biblical stories provide a plot, Tyler demonstrates a sense of the dramatic. Tyler should not be measured entirely by these productions; but they are not negligible.

❧ IV ❧

*P*oet

AFTER the early plays, Tyler turned his attention to poetry. It is perhaps natural that a man with literary bent, for whom writing could be only a sideline, should find more occasion for producing verses than longer works. Tyler wrote with facility, however, and did manage to turn out some book-length efforts later; but during the middle 1790's his publications were almost exclusively in periodicals and in verse, and he continued to appear in the journals through the first decade of the nineteenth century. From the 108-line *Origin of Evil*, published separately in 1793, to the last poem for the *Polyanthos* in 1807, he wrote a considerable quantity of verse; nor did his efforts end in 1807 — he continued to write for his own amusement, if not for publication, and his later verse includes his longest poem, the 744-line *Chestnut Tree*, not published until 1931.

Although Tyler wrote verse sporadically during most of his life (at least after 1793), it is by no means clear exactly how much he wrote. Contributions to newspapers and magazines at this time were generally anonymous or pseudonymous, and, in the absence of a record kept by the author himself or by the editor, it is now virtually impossible to establish the complete canon of any particular writer's periodical work. Tyler's name appears on only a handful of poems; other poems may be identified as his through the comments of editors (either in their reminiscences or in marked copies of their publications); still others have been printed posthumously from his papers. Beyond that, there is little one can do, for stylistic tests, unsupported by external evidence, are hazardous, especially since Tyler wrote poetry in several styles, all of which were popular in the periodicals of the day. A further complication is the fact that a contributor might send in a poem, announcing in a prefatory note that it was the work of a poet he admired greatly, and his initial or pseudonym would be printed as the signature to the introductory note; this note would be enough to justify the periodical in labeling both it and the poem "original" (that is, not reprinted from another journal); finally, the poem might be by the contributor, despite his note, if he wanted to add an extra dimension to his protective mask.

With these difficulties, statements about Tyler's poetry must of necessity be approximate rather than precise, though a large enough number of poems can be identified to permit certain generalizations about the characteristics of his work.[1] Of the poems published during his lifetime, about fifty, totaling over 2900 lines, can be attributed to him with a great deal of certainty, and it is possible, with less assurance, to assign to him well over one hundred published poems (aside from that large category which could conceivably be his, or almost anyone else's). This count does not include the blank verse plays, the manuscript poems published since his death, or the fourteen passages used as epigraphs in *The Algerine Captive*. A survey of those fifty-odd poems that are undoubtedly Tyler's shows, beyond all question, that his favorite form was the four-beat iambic line. Fully two-thirds of his poems (amounting to half the total number of lines he published) are in tetrameter, either wholly or predominantly — sometimes arranged into couplets, sometimes into more intricate rhyme schemes with occasional short lines, but most frequently into quatrains rhyming *abab*. The fact that his longest poem (three times as long as any other) is in such tetrameter quatrains indicates his preference for the form. Of the remaining poems, the majority are in iambic pentameter couplets; a few are anapaestic; and those in the sonnet form or in blank verse (other than the plays) are negligible in number. Tyler did not reserve certain verse forms for particular kinds of work, for both serious and comic poems appear in the same metrical schemes; but in general his output does fall into three categories: satire, verse composed for specific occasions, and reflective or moralizing poems.

Publication

The story of the publication of Tyler's poetry begins with his meeting Joseph Dennie. Eleven years Tyler's junior, Dennie was to become one of the best-known essayists and editors of the young republic, but in the early 1790's he was in a position very similar to Tyler's — a graduate of Harvard, with legal training and an attraction to literature, who enjoyed the pleasures of the city but found himself in a small country town. Tyler knew who Dennie was as early as the spring of 1790, when he defended two of Dennie's classmates. In December of that year (a few months before Tyler settled in Vermont) Dennie moved to Charlestown, New Hampshire, to study law with Benjamin West,[2] and it is not surprising, given Tyler's traveling and Dennie's yearning for a literary life, that the two should have met and formed a lasting friendship. Nor was their distance from an urban center a disadvantage, because they discovered other young lawyers who would rather write verses than plead cases, and soon there were local outlets for their work that attracted national attention.

Dennie had published several numbers of his first series of Addisonian essays, "The Farrago," in the Windsor, Vermont, *Morning Ray* in 1792. By the middle of the next year Hanover, New Hampshire, had a four-page weekly paper which was both Federalist in politics and literary in emphasis: *The Eagle, or Dartmouth Centinel*, started on 22 July 1793 by Josiah Dunham, Dartmouth graduate and Hanover printer.[3] Dennie's "Farrago" continued there, and by 1794 Tyler, more immersed in legal business than Dennie, was drawn into the circle of the paper's contributors. "A Christmas Hymn," which he had written for a celebration at Claremont, New Hampshire, the preceding year, appeared in the *Eagle* for 6 January 1794; it was followed, in July, by two serious poems signed "T." And at this time Dennie and Tyler conceived the idea of a collaboration.

It was the custom for newspaper contributors to adopt pseudonyms and to furnish series of essays or poems under that heading. Tyler and Dennie hit on the metaphor of a shop — their column would be a store which purveyed all varieties of prose and verse. They called it "From the Shop of Messrs. Colon & Spondee," and the first "advertisement" for their "wares" appeared in the *Eagle* of 28 July 1794:

Salutatory and Valedictory Orations, Syllogistic and Forensic Disputations and Dialogues among the living and the dead . . . Synaloephas, Elisions, and Ellipses of the newest *cut* — v's added and dove-tailed to their vowels, with a small assortment of the genuine Peloponesian Nasal Twangs — Classic Compliments adapted to all dignities, with superlatives in *o*, and gerunds in *di*, *gratis* . . . Anagrams, Acrostics, Anacreontics; Chronograms, Epigrams, Hudibrastics, & Panegyrics; Rebuses, Charades, Puns and Conundrums, by the *gross*, or *single dozen*. Sonnets, Elegies, Epithalamiums; Bucolics, Georgics, Pastorals; Epic Poems, Dedications, and Adulatory Prefaces, in *verse* and *prose*. . . . Serious Cautions against Whoredom, Drunkenness, &c. and other coarse Wrapping-Paper, *gratis*, to those who buy the smallest article. . . . *On hand a few Tierces of Attic Salt — Also, Cash, and the highest price, given for* RAW WIT, *for the use of the Manufactory, or taken in exchange for the above Articles.*

The metaphor was carried on in the column "To Correspondents" in the same issue: "Just arrived — a BALE OF GOODS from the SHOP *of Messrs. COLON & SPONDEE* — they shall be disposed of, on commission, as directed." The "Colon & Spondee" columns, thus begun, continued (often making elaborate use of the mercantile metaphor) in various journals for a decade. Consisting principally of satire and literary criticism, they quickly became famous for their wit, increased the circulation of the journals they appeared in, and inspired numerous imitators (such as "Messrs. Dactyl and Comma" or "Verbal and Trochee").[4] They represent one of the high points in early American journalism.

As Dennie later indicated, he was "Colon" and Tyler was "Spondee"; he wrote most of the prose and Tyler most of the poetry.[5] In the absence of evidence to the contrary, therefore, one can assume Tyler's authorship of "Colon & Spondee" poems;[6] in some cases they are signed with an "S." for "Spondee," and, indeed, "S." became established as Tyler's signature, even apart from the "Colon & Spondee" columns. By the end of 1794 six "Spondee" poems had been published in the *Eagle*, light verse with such titles as "Anacreontic to Flip," "The Rural Beauty," "The Widower," and "The Test of Conjugal Love." No further work of Tyler's appeared in the *Eagle*, and Dennie's contributions stopped in the spring of 1795, when he decided that he must get back to Boston and start a journal of his own.

At this time Tyler had about 500 lines of verse in print, but he was to increase that figure only a little during the next year. On 20 October 1794 Robert Treat Paine, a Harvard graduate somewhat younger than Dennie, started in Boston his strongly Federalist semi-weekly, the *Federal Orrery*.[7] Dennie published some satiric prose and theatrical criticism in it, and Tyler's main contributions were two theatrical poems, "Occasional Prologue, To the Mistakes of a Night; or, She Stoops to Conquer" (signed "R. Tyler, Esq.") on

29 December 1794 and, nearly a year later (9 November 1795), "An Occasional Address" on the opening of the new theater season (signed "By a Gentleman of Vermont"). By May of 1795 Dennie had arrived in Boston and was launching a small four-page weekly, the *Tablet*. It lasted only thirteen issues, from 19 May to 11 August 1795, and was principally an outlet for Dennie's "Farrago" essays. Some of the "Colon & Spondee" pieces were reprinted, but only one new identifiable Tyler poem appeared, "The Clown and Rose" (in the last issue, signed "S.").[8]

If 1795 was a slack year for Tyler's poetry, 1796 inaugurated the most spectacular period in his poetic career, his association with the *Newhampshire and Vermont Journal: or, the Farmer's Weekly Museum* of Walpole, New Hampshire. The *Farmer's Museum* (as it was later called) had begun on 11 April 1793 and, by 1796, had already reprinted some of Tyler's verse, but it was not until this time that he contributed original work to it. Walpole in these years, a town of 1400 inhabitants, was something of an intellectual center. For one thing, the printing shop of Thomas & Carlisle was turning out handsome volumes in addition to publishing the *Museum*. David Carlisle had been an apprentice of the great printer Isaiah Thomas, who gave him the financial backing in 1793 to set up a bookstore and printing shop in Walpole. Equally important, Walpole was the place frequented by a brilliant coterie of young Harvard lawyers and aspiring writers from the upper Connecticut Valley, who met between the court sessions and, according to Jeremiah Mason, "freely indulged in gambling, excessive drinking, and such like dissipation." Particularly after Major Asa Bullard took over the old Crafts Tavern (next door to Thomas & Carlisle), it became the rendezvous of this Literary Club, which included, besides Dennie and Tyler, Mason, Samuel Hunt, Roger Vose, Samuel West, and Thomas Green Fessenden ("Christopher

Caustic"). Dennie, leaving Boston after the failure of the
Tablet, arrived in Walpole in the early fall of 1795 and became the leader of this group. He began contributing his
"Lay Preacher" essays to the *Museum*, within a few weeks
was directing the literary policy of the paper, and in April
1796 officially became editor. Though a number of important
contributors to the *Museum* were not members of the Literary
Club, much of the copy for the paper was produced next door,
in between games of cards, jokes, drinks, and large meals.
The spirit of the whole enterprise is suggested by one story
about Dennie writing a "Lay Preacher" essay in sections during a game of whist; he finally had to ask Tyler to sit in for
him, so that he could finish the last paragraph, which was
already overdue at the printer's. In another version of the
story Tyler completes the essay for him, with no discernible
shift in Dennie's polished style.[9]

There is no question that, during Dennie's editorship
(1796–1799), the *Farmer's Museum* reached a level rarely attained by a weekly literary and political sheet,[10] and its circulation was national. Its four large pages had a higher proportion of original contributions than most papers of the time,
and its back page, "The Dessert," certainly printed more original poems and literary essays. The quality of the work,
from the pens of John Curtis Chamberlain, David Everett
("Common Sense in Dishabille"), and Isaac Story ("Peter
Quince"), as well as the Crafts Tavern group, was remarkably high for hastily written journalistic satire, and it often
showed considerable learning and wit. The "Colon & Spondee" papers were one of the mainstays of the publication, and
Tyler did his share in keeping Dennie supplied with material.
At least, he published verse with more frequency than was
usual with him, for twenty-five of his poems appeared in the
"Shop of Messrs. Colon & Spondee" during the three years
Dennie was editor — poems that represent Tyler's poetic

range, from the literary satire of the "Address to Della Crusca" to the patriotism of the "Windsor Ode." A score of Tyler's poems were reprinted in the 1801 anthology *The Spirit of the Farmers' Museum*, and Dennie's annotations in the copy now owned by the Boston Public Library provide further assurance in attributing them to Tyler.

The next phase of Tyler's poetic career again follows one of Dennie's moves, for Tyler published no more in the *Museum* after Dennie left it in 1799. By summer of that year Dennie was ready to return to the city, but this time business took him to Philadelphia, where, after contributing to the *Gazette of the United States* for two years, he established in 1801 the *Port Folio*, a weekly of eight pages "in the manner of the Tatler," which became the leading American literary journal.[11] Although the *Port Folio* occupies an important place in the history of American magazines, it is of much less significance for Tyler's story, since he contributed little to it. Whether because Dennie was not able to prod him so much from the distance of Philadelphia or whether Tyler was too occupied with legal duties (these were his first years on the Vermont Supreme Court), he published only a few items in Dennie's journal, one of them the often-quoted "Love and Liberty" (signed "R. Tyler, Esq.") on 20 October 1804. Dennie, however, continued using the "Colon & Spondee" rubric, which now contained prose almost exclusively.

One of Dennie's principle themes in his column "To Readers and Correspondents" became a lament for the absence of Tyler. On 28 February 1801, in the second month of the *Port Folio's* existence, Dennie remarked, "The *poetry* of *Spondee*, was always fashionable, and in constant demand. Our credit will be affected, unless he attend with more diligence to the *business* of literature" (I, 69). Two weeks later he explained that poetry was Spondee's task, but "For some time, the poetical share of this work has been neglected"

(I, 87). On 17 October he sighed, "We hope soon to hear from our fellow-labourer, 'SPONDEE.' The Editor feels himself solitary indeed, without the cheering companion of his literary toils"; and he quoted, "One was our labour, one was our repose, / One social supper did our studies close" (I, 336). Throughout 1802 these pleas continued: on 10 July, "A valued friend, who has often assisted and cheered the Editor in his course, is affectionately addressed . . . , and the Editor hopes that in some pause of *judicial* care, his friend will forget for a moment the eloquence of the *forum*, and turn his 'bright fantastic eye' to every willing muse" (II, 215); a week later, "The Editor hopes soon to hear from his friend, and quondam companion, S. Our invocation to this much loved bard is frequent and fervent" (II, 223); and on 21 August, "S, we hope, will reflect on the following lines from the favorite GIFFORD. . . . 'Say, wilt thou from thy duties pause awhile, / To view my humble labours with a smile?' " (II, 263). But Tyler did not heed the call, and Dennie at last desisted.[12]

A more important magazine for Tyler, and the last major outlet for his verse, was the *Polyanthos*, a Boston monthly founded in late 1805 by Joseph T. Buckingham, who had been an apprentice to David Carlisle in Walpole in 1796 and who thus knew the old *Museum* crowd. It was a literary journal which gave special attention to biographical sketches of notable figures and to the theater. In his reminiscences, Buckingham reports, "Of the several writers, from whom I received aid, Judge Tyler of Vermont was the most liberal in his contributions. The series of numbers entitled 'Trash,' . . . and all poetical fugitives signed S. were supplied by him." Buckingham had written on 22 March 1806 asking for contributions, and Tyler sent one on 3 April, but with reservation: "I must, however, observe that the unvarying condition upon which you are permitted to publish it, must be your solemn promise, that I am not known as the author, either by private communication to your friends, or any public hints to patrons and subscribers." Later Tyler praised Buckingham for making the journal "lively" and criticized other Boston periodicals for being "very wise and very learned, and very dull: — dull, when they should have been witty." [13] Between April 1806 and July 1807 Tyler published thirteen poems in the *Poly-anthos* (and a few prose pieces). These include three long poems in pentameter, two of them important theatrical criticisms and the third an elegy; a long tetrameter fable, "The Wolf and Wooden Beauty"; and some shorter lyrics and epigrams. They were Tyler's last important group of poems published during his lifetime, and they rank near the top of his output.

Tyler's poetry appeared in a few other journals, but generally just as occasional reprints — such as the "Convivial Song" in the Haverhill *Federal Gazette* (8 August 1799) or "Love and Liberty" in the *Columbian Centinel*, Benjamin Russell's Federalist paper in Boston (24 July 1805).[14] Among the poems still in manuscript at Tyler's death, a few were published in the 1920's and 1930's: "Lines on Brattleboro," "The Mantle of Washington," "On the Death of a Little Child," "Upon Seeing a Pair of Scales Suspended in a Justice's Office," [15] and *The Chestnut Tree*; others remained in manuscript until 1967, when the complete edition of Marius B. Péladeau appeared.[16] The publication record of Tyler's poetry emphasizes the fact that publication was not uppermost in Tyler's mind when he wrote; composing verses was an intriguing entertainment, a way to relax between court sessions. The verse had served its purpose before it reached the printed page.

Satiric and Humorous Poems

It is not surprising that the author of *The Contrast* should find his best poetic outlet in light verse or in satires of current fashions. Many of his poems — and those for which he was most famous in his lifetime, aside from his patriotic poems — fall into the category of brisk, lighthearted (even flippant) jingles, lines dashed off rapidly by one who had a knack for rhyme and meter. But they are skillful in their way, they do not moralize, and they often catch the spirit of rural New England:

> Stingo! to thy bar-room skip,
> Make a foaming mug of Flip;
> Make it of our country's staple,
> Rum New-England, Sugar maple.[17]

Most of the light verse has to do with love and marriage and often celebrates sensual joys. "The Rural Beauty, A Village Ode" is characteristic in using irony to hide sentiment:

> Then I whisper wedlock joys;
> Future group of girls and boys;
> — Girls and boys, as fair, as SUE,
> Honest as their father too;
> — Now I feel her pulses beat —
> She burns me with her blushing cheek.

Although this "Ode" contains conventional phrases such as "fleecy sky," "dimpled cheek," and "eyes so blue," the lightness of tone and quickness of movement prevent it from becoming sentimental:

> Yes, I come, my tempting SUE,
> See she smiles to meet me too.
> Now my arms her waist entwine;
> Now her hand is lock'd in mine.[18]

Another poem about "Sue" illustrates the kind of twist that frequently forms the basis of the humor; when a bachelor rejects Sue as a possible wife because she is too young, a neighbor says he must "speak to *clear her reputation*": "She's old enough to be your lady, / For *two years past, she had a baby!*" [19] This ending also shows that Tyler was not particular about his rhymes.

The epigram was a useful form to a man with Tyler's turn of mind and limited time for writing, and he produced several on the marriage theme. One of the best points out that, of the husbands who are "grumble tonians," each probably "chose his *dearest* by the *eye*":

> Ye fools, if you were buying houses,
> You'd be more cautious than in spouses;
> Not one of you would glance the windows,
> And buy with out once entering indoors,
> Nor yet about the doors be dodging,
> But try the house with one night's lodging.
> The house so tippy outside door,
> Might prove within a cursed bore;
> I think, says Tim, that's all I'll say,
> Wives might be chose in SOME SUCH WAY.[20]

The colloquialisms, the feminine rhymes, the risqué metaphor or amusing comparison, all occur in other epigrams. Puns are common, as when Sue, "at a female tea-drinking," asks the girls what business they would like their husbands to be in and declares her own preference for a cooper (that is, T. A. Cooper, the English actor in Boston at the time); this epigram rhymes "pass on" with "parson," "witty" with "pretty," and "tomorrow" with "follow." [21] Another "Epigrammatick Sketch" (which, with forty lines, goes beyond the bounds of an epigram) ridicules the ladies' pursuit of fashion; Tom Tweezer, a devoted husband, is running home with a present for his wife so that he will get it in her hands before it is out of style:

> Stop me not, I must not falter,
> I must hasten to my true one,
> The fashion else I fear will alter,
> And my Duck will want a new one.[22]

Satire of the artificiality in feminine fashions was a favorite eighteenth-century subject on both sides of the Atlantic, and Tyler in these poems is simply carrying on in the tradition of *The Contrast*. Echoing *The Rivals*, "To Miss Flirtilla Languish" enumerates the current cosmetics (paste for the neck, rouge for the cheeks, wigs, and so on) and ends with the beau's wish that Flirtilla would "press *me* to what *once* was her breast." [23] Despite the anapaestic movement, there is a seriousness here not present in the similar poem about Tom Tweezer.

Another set of fashions — those in literature — had been touched on in *The Contrast* and became one of Tyler's main subjects for satiric verse and parody. He chose, as his object for repeated attacks between 1797 and 1799, the work of the Della Cruscan poetasters, who had enjoyed great popularity in England and were being reprinted and imitated in America. Their verse, most of it a parody of itself, was characterized by extreme sentimentality and elaborate, high-flown diction. The group was originally composed of a few Englishmen who gathered in 1784 in the Florence salon of Mrs. Hester Lynch Piozzi.[24] They amused themselves by writing flattering verses to each other, and, as these became known in England, other would-be poets felt the urge to express themselves in similar fashion. Robert Merry, one of the original group, signed his work "Della Crusca" because he was a member of the Florentine Accademia della Crusca, and the name came to be applied to the entire coterie and then to all the writers of newspaper effusions in this vein. Tyler's main targets, besides "Della Crusca" himself, were two of the later followers, Mrs. Hannah Cowley ("Anna Matilda") and Mrs. Charlotte Smith. The attack had already begun in England, led by William Gifford (whom Dennie continually quoted when addressing Tyler in print), and Gifford's second onslaught, the *Maeviad* (1795), had appeared two years before Tyler's first Della Cruscan parody; Dennie and Tyler were the most energetic and influential of the attackers in America. The whole movement represents one of the excesses of romanticism and was an inevitable concomitant to the growing emphasis on personal feelings; it was not, however, solely to blame for all the affected expression in America (like that which Timothy Dwight called the "Boston style" of oratory). In ridiculing these tendencies Tyler was attacking not romanticism but an insidious sentimentalism which had far deeper roots than the Della Cruscan writers.

The *Farmer's Weekly Museum* on 4 April 1797 printed Tyler's first effort along this line, "An Ode to a Pipe of Tobacco, Addressed by Della Yankee, to Anna Jemima," in seventy tetrameter lines, with its obvious parody of Della Cruscan pseudonyms and circumlocution. He vows his eternal faithfulness to his pipe, which becomes his "extatick tube," his "sweet, assuaging tube," and his "lenient solace of dank care." [25] A month later he wrote a more skillful satire, in sixty-six lines of pentameter couplets, entitled "Address to Della Crusca, Humbly Attempted in the Sublime Style of That Fashionable Author." The main part of the poem describes the triumph of Della Crusca in America, with epithets assigned to each Indian tribe:

> Gods how sublime shall Della Crusca rage,
> When ALL NIAGARA CATARACTS THY PAGE.
> What arts? What arms? Unknown to thee belong?
> What ruddy scalps shall deck thy sanguin'd song?
> What fumy calmuts scent the ambient air,
> What love lorn Warhoops, CAPITALS declare.
> Cerulean tomahawks shall grace each line,
> And BLUE EY'D WAMPUM glisten through thy rhyme.

At the end he exclaims, "Proclaim thy sounding page, from shore to shore, / And swear that sense in verse, shall be no more." [26] Four months later, in his "Sonnet to the Indian Muckawiss," Tyler (signing himself "Sensibility") gave an example of an American subject treated in Della Cruscan fashion and parodied the work of Charlotte Smith. The sonnet (Shakespearean in form) is replete with such phrases as "tuneful art," "lorn numbers," "dusky plain," "Child of the sober eve," and "sad delight"; it is followed by a note explaining its particular beauties to the ladies.[27]

In 1799 Tyler wrote two more Della Cruscan sonnets that illustrate his parody at its height. In one he explains that he is going to take a rhyme from the *New England Primer* — "The Cat doth play, / And after slay" — and amplify it in the manner of Charlotte Smith:

Sonnet to an Old Mouser
> Child of lubricious art! of sanguine sport!
> Of PANGFUL MIRTH! sweet ermin'd sprite!
> Who lov'st with silent, VELVET STEP to court
> The bashful bosom of the night.
>
> Whose elfin eyes can pierce night's sable gloom,
> And witch her FAIRY PREY with guile,
> Who sports fell frolic o'er the grisly tomb,
> And gracest death with dimpling smile!
>
> DAUGHTER OF IREFUL MIRTH, sportive in rage,
> Whose joy should shine in sculptur'd bas relief,
> Like Patience, in rapt Shakespear's deathless page,
> Smiling in marble at wan grief:
>
> Oh, come and teach me all thy barb'rous joy,
> To sport with sorrow first and then destroy.[28]

The other sonnet has a prefatory advertisement in which Messrs. Colon & Spondee

inform their kind customers that they brighten the dullest compositions in prose and verse by the apt and judicious insertion of

Royall Tyler

capital letters, italics, asterisks, brackets, apostrophes, carets, hyphens, idiopathics, ichnographics, ellipses, and synalephies, notes manual, digital, and astral, with notes of the interrogation, obnubulation, and admiration, by the gross or dozen.

N.B. They have some capitals of an uncommon large size, for the use of the female muse.

The ensuing "Sonnet to the Turtle Dove" illustrates most of these devices in its opening lines:

SWEET CHILD OF WOE!! who pour'st THY LOVE LORN LAYS
ON THE DULL EAR! of PENSIVE night,
Who with THY sighs protract'st the pitying gale,
WHICH seeks with GOS'MER WING the INFANT LIGHT.[29]

If the Della Cruscan extravagances formed the most repeated subject for Tyler's verse satire, he wrote individual poems ridiculing other literary excesses. In "The Exile," Messrs. Colon & Spondee set up a "Caledonian Loom" and parody Burns and other writers in Scottish dialect; the theme of the poem occurs in lines 7–8: "While Bessy wha is far awa, / Is faithfu' unto me." A glossary is provided and a significant introductory note, which comments ironically on the lack of American nationalism in both literature and business: "we hope to be na farer behint the Europeans, than is common wi' the youthful manufactures of America."[30] Excessive use of alliteration is parodied in "An Alliterative Address" (illustrating also Tyler's love of playing with words), in which each line repeats the same initial sound (it opens, "The sweetest Seraph's softest smile").[31] The "Poetical Paraphrase of our General's Journal" is a skillful if exaggerated mock epic, in heroic couplets, satirizing the *Memoirs* (1798) of Major General William Heath. The General is depicted as rising to announce to his children, in the most elaborate terms ("Shoots of my glory, scions of my name, / Twigs of my hope . . ."), the publication of his reminiscences.[32]

Satire of pedantry is a recurring motif in Tyler's work, and the "Irregular Supplicatory Address to the American Academies of Arts and Sciences" tries (in 112 lines) to deflate the "learned wights, who all the heights / Of science still are soaring, / The comet's tail, or tail of mites / Sagaciously exploring." He explains why he would like to be elected to the Academy and then lists his qualifications — he has several items which should be investigated, such as "a full grown Pumpkin . . . No bigger than a pullets egg." That Tyler could utilize devastating metaphors is evident in the poem: the botanists, he says, "Lasciviously delight to act, / As pandars to the flowers." [33] Finally, one may notice "The Sun and the Bats," a political satire of 120 lines in which the sun is the principle of Federalism, sending good things downward to all, while the bats (Anti-Federalists) are active in the absence of the sun and resent such centralization of power as the sun has.[34] The satire is competent but, with the sun's speech at the end, tends too much toward the overtly didactic — a fault which Tyler usually avoids in his satiric verse.

Occasional Poems

One important category in the Tyler canon consists of poems which he wrote for particular occasions. His talents were well suited to such versifying, for he could produce, at short notice, a smooth and graceful lyric; if it was not particularly striking or profound, it expressed the usual sentiments conveniently and served as a focal point for a celebration, which was all that was expected of it. His first poem in the *Eagle*, "A Christmas Hymn," had been sung at the Claremont services on Christmas 1793. Though in part a conventional hymn praising "the joyous day, / On which our Lord was born," it proceeds to show how the Lord is responsible for the freedom of the United States:

He crown'd fair freedom's cause;
He made our nation great;
The Leader of our wars
He raised to rule our States.
Your voices raise!
To HIM who brings
To earth proud kings,
Be deathless praise.[35]

There are ten such stanzas in the poem, the first four lines of three beats each, rhyming alternately, and the last four of two beats, rhyming *cddc*; the fifth line is the same in every stanza, so that the final word in each case rhymes with "raise." In the satiric poems Tyler did not experiment very widely with verse forms, but the occasional poems show that he could, if necessary, manipulate a variety of stanza patterns with ease. "A Christmas Hymn" was evidently popular, for it was reprinted in broadside many years later, after Tyler had become Chief Justice, with his name on it. In the few cases where Tyler allowed his name to appear on a poem, it was always an occasional poem. Perhaps he felt that, if the authorship were known at the time of the celebration, there was no need to hide it later; but, more important, such poems were serving a socially approved purpose, and a gentleman's name could be openly attached to them.

If the "Christmas Hymn" expresses patriotic sentiments,[36] the poems for Independence Day do so even more. The "Ode Composed for the Fourth of July," which appeared in the *Newhampshire and Vermont Journal* on 19 July 1796, is probably Tyler's most famous poem; certainly it is the one most often reprinted. It is a jolly and fast-moving piece, which sounds like the calling of a square dance:

Squeak the fife, and beat the drum,
INDEPENDENCE DAY has come!!
Let the roasting pig be bled.
Quick twist off the cockerel's head,

Quickly rub the pewter platter,
Heap the nutcakes fried in batter.

. . . .

Sal, put on your ruffel skirt,
Jotham, get your *boughten* shirt,
To day we dance to riddle diddle.
— Here comes Sambo with his fiddle;
Sambo, take a dram of whiskey,
And play up Yankee Doodle frisky.

So it goes for fifty-five lines, building up enthusiasm for the celebration, giving a good picture of late eighteenth-century rural customs, and, at the same time, working in a few references to current social problems:

Sambo, play and dance with quality;
This is the day of blest Equality.
Father and *Mother* are but men,
And Sambo — is a Citizen,

. . . .

Come, one more swig to southern Demos
Who represent our brother negroes.[37]

Another of Tyler's best-known poems, "Love and Liberty," is similar:

In bri'ry dell, or thicket brown,
　On mountain high, in lowly vale,
Or where the thistle sheds its down,
　And sweet-fern scents the passing gale;
　　There hop the birds from bush to tree,
　　Love fills their throats,
　　Love swells their notes,
　Their song is Love and Liberty.[38]

The varied rhythm and well-manipulated sounds make the three stanzas of this poem one of Tyler's most graceful lyrics.

For the Independence Day celebration in Windsor, Vermont, in 1799, Tyler wrote two poems, a serious one, the "Windsor Ode," for the main ceremony, and a lighter "Convivial Song" for the evening festivities; both were published under his own name in the *Farmer's Weekly Museum*.[39] The "Windsor Ode" consists of six ten-line stanzas, mostly tetrameter, with a four-line refrain at the end of each stanza. It begins by praising "Columbia's natal day," then refers to the country's enemies, first the "haughty Britons" and now the "faithless" and "bloody" French, then surveys American heroes and forces, and ends with praise of Adams and Washington. Despite occasional clichés ("blushing east," "warlike swords"), the poem has an honesty and strength, suggested by the refrain (which varies slightly from stanza to stanza):

> Shout, shout Columbia's praise,
> Wide through the world her glory raise,
> Our Independence bravely gain'd,
> Shall full as bravely be maintain'd.

"The Convivial Song," in eight eight-line stanzas of a rather complex metrical and rhyme pattern, is composed of a series of toasts. The first is a general one:

> Come, fill each brimming glass, boys,
>   Red or white has equal joys,
> Come, fill each brimming glass, boys,
>   And toast your country's glory;
> Does any here to fear incline,
> And o'er Columbia's danger whine,
> Why let him quaff this gen'rous wine,
>   He'll tell another story.

There follow toasts to Washington, to the gallant tar, to the native land, to Vermont, and finally to Adams, who with "temp'rate head . . . sits sublime, / And for our good is thinking."

Besides these enthusiastic lyrics which he produced for patriotic celebrations, Tyler wrote verse for theatrical occasions. Just as the prologue to *The Contrast* emphasized that it was a native play, so Tyler's prologues follow the theme of literary nationalism. In his "Occasional Prologue" to *She Stoops to Conquer*, he devotes the entire thirty-eight lines to showing that, despite "Proud *Europe*, and still prouder *Britain*," the liberal arts "have stemmed the atlantic wave":

> Let candor then, imprint this thought alone,
> *The painting, acting, music, are our own.*

He prophesies that a "future *Avon* shall meandering glide" through the Green Mountains and that England, "humbled" and "awed by our success, / In arts and arms, our triumph shall confess." [40] The following year (1795), Tyler wrote "An Occasional Address" for the opening of the Boston Theatre's new season, the first under his brother's management. Again in pentameter couplets (though considerably longer, 118 lines), it takes up where the other left off, even using some of the same lines about England's yielding to American success. After an opening passage praising the culture of America ("*That* land, where genius soars sublimest heights; / Where *Trumbull* painted, and where *Trumbull* writes"), he addresses, in turn, the boxes, the pit, and the upper gallery. The artificiality of the coquettes in the boxes contrasts with the natural laughter from the gallery ("the warm impulse of the glowing heart"); as for the critics in the pit, Tyler speaks to them of a native literature and suggests their duty in fostering it:

> For *me*, sustained by *you* — the task be mine,
> Where native genius droops in shades to find,
> The tender buds from wintery vales to bring,
> To where your bounty sheds perpetual spring.

When this occurs, the "*Charles* shall rival British *Avon's* pride," and there shall be "Columbian *Shakespeares*" and "Yankee *Garricks*." [41]

If these two poems are companion pieces of the 1790's, two later poems, occasioned by the theatrical season of 1805–

1806, are in effect one work. The "Epilogue to the Theatrical Season: Or, A Review of the Thespian Corps" appeared in the *Polyanthos* for April 1806, followed two months later by "An Epistle to My Muse: Or, A Postscript to the Epilogue to the Theatrical Season." [42] Together they total 402 lines of heroic couplets and constitute one of Tyler's major poetic efforts, his only extended attempt at satiric portraits in the grand eighteenth-century manner. After invoking the Muse and her sister Candour, he presents ten vignette portraits of members of the Boston company during the past season, deciding that each is unfit for the laurel, until he comes to T. A. Cooper, who is "beyond all praise." Behind his criticism of most of the actors is a concept of realism: he can always recognize one actor, in whatever role, because of his yellow shoes; another moves like a "clock work man"; and a plump actress ("Great ton of beauty") plays roles not compatible with her physique ("thine is the comick mien / To strike broad humour from the saddest scene"). Since "men of sense" are offended when "virtuous speeches flow from lips impure," those actors are best who play good roles not only on stage but off, so that their acting is natural ("The Voice of Nature is thy mother tongue"). The populace is easily pleased and has little discernment in such matters, but an actress of Mrs. Powell's quality will never overstep "nature's modest aims" to become the "screaming favourite of a tasteless age":

> What though thy scenick pencil oft portrays
> Fine strokes of nature lost to common gaze?
> The purblind many can't read nature's line,
> Unless in lamp-black capitals it shine.
> What though less frequent shouts thy worth reward,
> And the house slumbers when it should applaud?
> Be thine the approving smile of all the chaste,
> Thine the proud plaudit of the man of taste.

Similarly, William Twaits, who played comic roles, is praised for doing what Tyler himself was trying to do: "With squint-eyed satire a bad age reclaim, / And vice and folly laugh to open shame."

This was the harshest attack Tyler had indulged in, and the editor Buckingham, in a prefatory note, admitted that he found some of the portraits "rather too severely handled." In his second installment, the "postscript" to the "epilogue," Tyler capitalized on the stir the earlier part had created. He addresses his Muse, describing how "the Green Room quakes with wild uproar," everyone discussing who was praised, damned, or omitted in the "Epilogue." Beginning with line 60, he announces that he will survey the actors again, this time more gently, although they are all eager for fame and would "rather be lampoon'd than be neglected." But instead of naming individuals, he simply enumerates certain faults common among actors: there is the tragic actor whose grimace is comic (lines 79–92), the actress whose effective anguished pause is caused by her forgetting the line (93–106), the man who exemplifies all the mistakes mentioned in Hamlet's advice to the players (107–132), and actresses who are either overly timid or overly aggressive (133–148). This poem, like the other, is imitative of the tradition of Churchill's *Rosciad* and Lloyd's *The Actor*, but its high spirits, comic rhymes, and witty criticisms make it more than a literary exercise. All the occasional poems are sprightly and, either directly or indirectly, patriotic in intention without being mawkish. To use Tyler's own criterion, it is the naturalness and sincerity of these poems which make them an attractive group.

Reflective Poems

Tyler was at his best in light or satiric verse; when he attempted serious reflective or philosophical poems, he committed most of the faults he ridiculed in others.[43] Although a few redeeming features can be found in some of them (particularly the two long ones), the most that can be said for the rest is that they are mediocre — competent enough for newspaper verse (when compared with others in the same papers), but in no way distinguished. Tyler needed the mask of humor or satire to present serious ideas effectively; his straightforward attempts partook too much of the sentimental cliché, of what was, after all, the accepted mode of popular utterance.

The point is illustrated by some of his didactic verse, which he often called "fables." "The Sensitive Plant," in 120 tetrameter lines, tells of all the qualities (from Venus, Minerva, Cupid, and so on) that contributed to Anna's character, in rhymes that are frequently inexact: "Some seek Arabia's balmy sweets, / To give the fragrance of her breath; / Some dive for pearls old ocean's deeps, / To form the whiteness of her teeth." At length Minerva says that she will root the sensitive plant "deep in Anna's breast," for it removes all "unchaste desires";

> And know, each maid, this plant is yours;
> Each bashful virgin feels its aid;
> For sage Minerva's gift secures,
> The beauties of each virtuous maid.
>
> This plant, the heart, the garden yield;
> Though men have different names assigned;
> Called Sensitive, when in the field,
> And Modesty when in the mind.[44]

The same theme recurs in "The Clown and Rose": Laura is like a rose because she has sweet looks combined with thorny anger to protect her virtue; she will be kind only if approached with an offer of wedlock, just as the rose allows soft breezes to touch its petals but will prick the hand that tries to break off a blossom. The rose speaks at the end and explains the comparison in detail:

> To guard the beauties, nature gave,
>> She all my thousand thorns prepar'd,
> And Laura's lovelier charms to save,
>> Gave Thorny Virtue for a guard.[45]

Similarly, in "The Wolf and Wooden Beauty: An Old Fable New Vamped," a wolf makes advances to a beautiful carved figure and is confounded to discover that she is not real. Though this part is recounted in a jocular fashion, the explanation of the moral — that beauty is the least important quality in a good wife — is entirely serious: "*But she* who fills with nobler pride, / That female throne the fire side" is a "help-meet on life's weary way" who nurtures the children "by her fostering hand," and so on.[46] Another treatment of this idea (occasioned by Proverbs 31:10) is "The Properties of a Good Wife," 102 solemn lines spoken by Israel's King:

> Through all his prosp'rous, joyous days,
> Her virtues shall command his praise,
>> And, though to blame inclin'd,
> No action of her blameless life,
> Shall stain her conduct as a wife,
>> To vex her husband's mind.[47]

Tyler never tired of writing on this subject, but one should turn to his epigrams on marriage rather than to these verses for his best statement of it.

In blank verse, which Tyler always used for serious purposes, he shows himself to be a competent versifier, but, more than anything else, he reveals his familiarity with the tradition of English poetry, for his lines are highly derivative. The seventy-four lines of blank verse labeled "Author's Manuscript Poems" which serve as epigraphs to twelve chapters in *The Algerine Captive* are only fragments, varying from two to nineteen lines in length, but they show his aims in blank verse. The chapter which records a dream of the hero's mother carries an eight-line passage:

> Nor yet alone by day the unerring hand
> Of Providence, unseen directs man's path;
> But, in the boding vision of the night,
> By antic shapes, in gay fantastic dream,
> Gives dubious prospect of the coming good;
> Or, with fell precipice, or deep swoln flood,
> Dank dungeon, or vain flight from savage foe,
> The labouring slumberer warns of future ill.[48]

The varied caesura, the occasional run-over line and alliteration, the elaborate syntax and inversions, and the formal diction all reflect established practice from the time of Milton on; the lines are an exercise in versification more than a piece of poetry. For the other passages the same may be said, with such phrases as "The beaming dignities of man eclipsed," "the dear pledges of their mutual love," "hellish rage," "firm foundations of a Saviour's love," and "the young sighings of a contrite heart." [49] Tyler published in the April 1806 *Polyanthos* a passage of twenty-six lines, which he entitled "Extract from 'The Divine,' A Poem in Six Books." It is an exposition of all the virtues of the Reverend Joseph Buckminster, founder of the Boston Athenaeum, and furnishes in its ending an example of sustained parallelism and inversion:

> From the rich pages of the inspired pen,
> Which mock all human rhetorick to scorn,
> The classick christian breathes the chaste discourse;
> With temperate zeal the wandering sinner warns;
> Sustains the pious with the promis'd grace;
> Confirms the doubting; wakens the secure;
> With mild consoling voice the wretched cheers;
> And, with purest elegance of speech,
> Gives new attraction to the gospel truth.[50]

When the man who so often argued for native literature expresses himself in this fashion, the result must seem ironic. In another of the epigraphs he says, "Still let the faithful pen unerring point / The polar truth" (II, 97); but one cannot help seeing a disparity between the sentiment and the style. That Tyler was familiar enough with the Miltonic tradition to turn in an able performance is a fact for the cultural history of America; that he wrote such lines with greater seriousness than his rhyming genre pictures of New England life is a fact of his own limitations as an artist.

Of the two remaining long poems, one, a 108-line unsigned work entitled *The Origin of Evil: An Elegy*, was published separately as an eight-page pamphlet in 1793 (with no publisher or place indicated on the title page). The main evidence for attributing the poem to Tyler seems to be that the unique copy in the American Antiquarian Society has "By Royal Tyler" written on the title page in a contemporary hand thought to be that of Isaiah Thomas. If it is Tyler's, it precedes his earliest published poem in the *Eagle* and is unlike his other poems in content; but if he could write blank verse plays on Biblical subjects, it is not unlikely that he should have tried his hand at versifying the Adam and Eve story in tetrameter quatrains. Indeed, the poem is semi-dramatic in form, concentrating on one episode presented largely in terms of conversation between the two characters — a method which perhaps owes something to one of the works quoted in the epigraphs, Sébastien Châteillon's *Dialogorum sacrorum* (1543). The "Proem" of three stanzas, with its jingling rhythm, hardly seems an appropriate introduction to the cosmic tragedy to follow:

> Ranting topers, midnight rovers,
> Cease to roar your fleshly lays;
>
> . . . .
> Let each lovely *Miss* and *Madam*,
> Quit the dear joys of carnal sense,
> Weep the *fall* of *Eve* and *Adam*,
> From their first state of Innocence.

The poem deals with the moment when Eve sees the forbid-

den fruit and questions the justice of the divine command.
It is noteworthy only in one respect: the emphasis throughout is sensual, and Eve, foreseeing the consequences of her
action, nevertheless cannot restrain herself from the allure-
ments of sensual pleasure:

> "Threaten'd death will soon o'ertake me,
>   If this forbidden tree I pluck,
> But life itself will soon forsake me,
>   Unless its cordial juice I suck."

Detailed sensuous descriptions recur frequently:

> Her bosom, heaving for caresses,
>   Seem'd blushing berries cast on snow.
>
> . . . .
>
> As *Eve* cast her arms so slender,
>   His brawny chest to fondly stroke;
>
> . . . .
>
> As her arm Eve held him hard in,
>   And toy'd him with her roving hand,
> In the middle of Love's Garden,
>   She saw the Tree of Knowledge stand.

This dramatic juxtaposition suggests a real insight which is
unfortunately obscured by the structure and meter of the
context in which it is set.

The other poem, Tyler's longest production in verse and
the one on which he was working despite his illness near
the end of his life, was not made public until 1931. In that
year Walter J. Coates (who had already printed in the *Driftwind* a few unpublished Tyler poems which Helen Tyler
Brown had given him) brought out, at his Driftwind Press
of North Montpelier, in a limited edition of 250 copies, *The
Chestnut Tree: or, A Sketch of Brattleborough at the Close
of the Twentieth Century, Being an Address to a Horse
Chestnut Presented to the Author by the Rev. A. L. Baury*.
It consists of 186 of Tyler's usual tetrameter quatrains and

takes as its starting point the planting of a chestnut tree, which will still be living long after the present generation has died. The first eighteen stanzas (lines 1–72) [51] introduce the poem by suggesting that "the sorceress Fancy" can lift the veil of the future, reveal the "vista of two hundred years," and depict what will take place under the tree during that time.

The procession of future scenes then begins. People of all kinds (students, businessmen, lovers) rest in the shade of the tree (lines 73–144); the "village Hoyden" climbs the tree (145–156); and a group wanders along laughing at the eighteenth-century fashions in a copy of *The Ladies' Diary* (157–176). Next (177–204) come the sick and diseased ("dropsy's bloated bulk," "gout with crutch and flannel armed," "corroding cancer"), accompanied by two arguing physicians, like those Tyler satirized in *The Algerine Captive*: "I had well hoped this wordy war / Would cease before that distant day." Lawyers, too, are still "wrangling at the noisy bar" (205–224), and there are derelicts thinking of the tree for suicide (225–236). A Quaker couple appears, "firm in noiseless faith" and "stiff in moral rectitude" but acknowledging the power of love (237–272); then the drunkard "with burning breath," a "wilful, lingering suicide" (273–296); and then (297–340) "boisterous youngsters" in "rude athletic play," along with grown men fishing ("solace for a vacant mind") and hunting (the "cruel sportsman" shoots a bird which "bleeds his little life away"). "Manufactory's fetid halls" are responsible for the condition of the "haggard mottled crew" which comes next (341–376), a contrast to the happy group climbing the nearby mountain (377–432). Thirteen stanzas then describe the "female Pauper," a lonely old woman ill-treated by those she had befriended earlier in life (433–484), followed by an extended picture of a lonely man, a "stale bachelor of 42," and a description of the joys of wedlock which he is missing (485–600) — a familiar Tyler theme. The remaining stanzas place side by side the pedant gazing at "a worm-eaten, smoke-dried page" (601–628) and the "studious young divine" learning the "charms of pulpit eloquence" under the old tree (629–652), then a "pensive party" visiting the graveyard (653–692) and youthful lovers sighing vows of "eternal love and truth" (693–708).

After this long succession of visions, Tyler concludes, rather irrelevantly, that his own situation is not unlike that of the chestnut seed, a symbol of immortality:

> Misshapen seed! I too like thee
>   Shall in our parent earth be cast,
> And with new life shall quickened be
>   When the grave's wintry season's past.   (729–732)

The poem as a whole, though it contains many of Tyler's favorite themes, is a disappointing production — perhaps it contains too many themes, for the final effect lacks unity. Several descriptions are obviously given adjacent positions for contrast, and the idea of imagining a tree in the future provides a loose framework; but many of the individual portraits have no connection with the tree, and the ending, stressing a Christian afterlife, has not been prepared for in the social criticism dominant in the bulk of the work. Individual phrases, and even whole stanzas, are effective, such as the satire of the scholar or the description of the bachelor; and occasionally there is a sensitive picture of early nineteenth-century New England life (the mountain-climbing episode, for example). But the tetrameter becomes tiresome, some of the portraits are one-sided and sentimental (like that of the "female Pauper"), and the whole is permeated with stock phrases: "the ravages of time," "quaff the dulcet tide," "sicklied age," "the surge of ocean," "changing like the inconstant moon." There is no firm conception shaping the entire work, and the result has greater value as a social document than as a poem.

Tyler cannot hold rank as a poet, but he himself realized as much. It is enough that in eighteenth-century America he had the background and the inclination to amuse himself by writing verse and at times to put in a public word on behalf of the arts. He personally was unwilling to work harder at poetry, but he knew some of the places to look for shallowness in others. With some justice he has been called "an earlier and coarse Wendell Holmes." [52] At the end of *The Chestnut Tree*, his self-estimate is more than a literary convention:

> When ardent youth crowned life's gay scene
> I could bright fancy's dreams create,
> And from a stubborn flinty theme,
> The flickering sparks could scintillate.
>
> My ebbing mind and troubled head
> Both bid me cease the poet's strains;
> Invention's gone, and fancy fled,
> And naught but chiming rhyme remains.   (713–720)

It may be unkind to point out that the "chiming rhyme" was there all along, but one must admit that so was the "flinty theme" with its sparks.

❦ V ❦

Novelist

ON 17 August 1797, Joseph Nancrede, the Boston publisher and bookseller, inserted an advertisement in the *Independent Chronicle* that concluded with a special note: "*The Algerine Captive*, which has, for a few weeks since excited so much curiosity, and which on perusal, has been pronounced by a *few men of taste*, *The Rabelais* of America, is hourly expected at the above Store." [1] This book, in two well-printed volumes, purporting on the title page to be a factual account of Algerian slavery by Dr. Updike Underhill, had been published at Walpole early in August by David Carlisle, in an edition of 1000 copies. [2] That it was actually the work of Royall Tyler (who knew no more about Algerian slavery than what he had read in newspapers and books) seems to have been recognized from the beginning, for, after Nancrede did obtain copies late in September, he changed his advertisement: "These two volumes, attributed with some foundation, to *Royal Tyler*, Esq. have been pronounced by Gentlemen of taste, to be fully equal to Mr. Tyler's reputation. They are offered to the American Public, as a specimen of indigenous Wit." [3] Joseph Dennie, who was continually prodding Tyler to write and had suggested the idea for the book, echoed these advertisements in a letter from Boston late that August:

Your novel has been examined by the few and approved. It is however extremely difficult for the Bostonians to supply themselves with a book that slumbers in a stall at Walpole, supposed, by the latest and most accurate advertisements, to be situated 400 miles north of their meridian. . . . People are pretty well convinced that you are capable of writing well on any subject, and, for your encouragement, I can assure you, that a taste for letters begins gradually to obtain here.[4]

The Federalist journalist William Coleman, for a time the law partner of Aaron Burr, wrote in a similar vein a month later:

When I have heard you mentioned here, with much tribute of applause, for your literary talents, as I have often; and when I see your publication of the "Algerine" announced with great eclat, as it has repeatedly been in different papers, and "the public curiosity is said to be alive to read it;" I feel proud that I was once so intimately acquainted with the man and the Author.[5]

The book continued to be advertised during the next few months, and it was still listed among the "Fresh Supply of Books," as "an original and entertaining work," in the Walpole paper the following summer.[6]

Interest in the work was, in fact, more prolonged than this, and its contemporary appeal no doubt resulted largely from the widespread public curiosity about the Barbary pirates. Years later, Tyler himself commented on this topicality in a preface he wrote for a proposed new edition of the book:

In the year 1797, when the sufferings of our unfortunate seamen, carried into slavery at Algiers, was the common topic of conversation, and excited the most lively interest throughout the United States, the Author . . . embodied such information as could then be obtained as to the manners, customs, habits and history of those Corsairs in a little work, entitled The Algerine Captive.[7]

Trouble with the Barbary States was one of the most difficult problems faced by the new government. The vessels of a young country, no longer under the protection of England, were a natural target for the privateers; at the same time the situation helped to unify the American states in a single cause, for meeting the challenge was a matter of national pride. Several American seamen had been captured in 1784 and 1785, after the Treaty of Paris, but it was in the fall of 1793 that America suffered most, with eleven ships and 109 men taken in less than two months. At one time in the early 1790's there were 1200 Christian slaves in Algiers, exposed to cruelty and plagues; in 1794 smallpox alone took the lives of 4 American captives. Through the efforts of Joseph Donaldson and Joel Barlow, peace (of sorts) was made in July 1795; the 85 remaining Americans were ransomed, set sail on 13 July 1796, and after further attacks of disease reached home in February 1797, six months before Tyler's book appeared.[8]

The American public was interested in any scrap of information or myth about the Barbary States, and the newspapers were happy to comply.[9] Books also appeared, so many eventually that one may legitimately think of the Algerine captivity narrative as a distinct species of adventure story. Tyler was not the first to use these materials as the basis for a literary and patriotic work: Peter Markoe wrote in 1787 *The Algerine Spy in Pennsylvania; or, Letters Written by a Native of Algiers on the Affairs of the United States of America* (with the early letters set in Gibraltar); Susannah Rowson's first play, *Slaves in Algiers; or, A Struggle for Freedom*, was performed and published late in 1794; and in 1797, besides Tyler's book, a poem in two cantos (695 lines of pentameter couplets) called *The American in Algiers; or, The Patriot of Seventy Six in Capitivity* (which also attacked Negro slavery in America) was published.[10] Tyler's information about Algiers could have been derived from any number of sources. In the same year as his own book James Wilson Stevens' *An Historical and Geographical Account of*

Algiers appeared, as well as the American edition of Donald Campbell's *Journey over Land to India* (which included shipwreck and imprisonment); in 1794 Mathew Carey had published *A Short Account of Algiers*; in 1795 James Leach, *A New and Easy Plan to Redeem the American Captives in Algiers*; and in 1796 Emanuel de Aranda, *The History of Algiers*. In addition, there were many European books on the subject, some of which were probably available to Tyler — works like J. Morgan's *Voyage of the Mathurin Fathers to Algiers and Tunis, for the Redemption of Captives* (1735); Thomas Shaw's *Travels and Observations* (1738); *A Compleat History of the Pyratical States of Barbary* (1750); *The Female Captive* (1769); Alexander Jardine's *Letters from Barbary* (1788); Abbé Poiret's *Travels through Barbary* (1791), and others.[11] Whatever his sources, Tyler epitomized a large amount of material successfully enough that his account became the basis for at least one later work (Thomas Nicholson's *Affecting Narrative*, 1818) [12] and was not completely lost amid the increasing flurry of reminiscences that appeared after the prisoners' return.

Reception

The Algerine Captive is not, as all this might suggest, a work of history. It is a fictional account of Updike Underhill's adventures, the first volume entirely devoted to Updike's American experiences and the second to the Algerian. One of the first commentaries of any substance on the book, a letter to the editor of the *Farmer's Weekly Museum* on 24 April 1798, did call the work a novel but attributed it to "Peter Pencil," another of the paper's regular contributors. Before criticizing some minor faults of the book, the correspondent began with a statement to which exception cannot be taken even today:

An American novel has lately been presented to the public,

from your press, under the title of the Algerine Captive. The subject of this work is well chosen, the publication well timed, and the execution does great credit to the talents and erudition of the writer. In delineating the national character, and in describing the local peculiarities, in manners, customs, and language, of the people of New England, there is no preceding work, either from Europe or America, which can claim the smallest pretence to rivalship.

The faults mentioned are really only two: that "a geographical errour has been committed, in working the voyage of his hero from Gibralter to Algiers; from which the Rover is made to sail a distance of five or six hundred miles in a single night," and that the stress on New England uprightness is a little hypocritical and may be offensive to inhabitants of the South (such as the Southern minister satirized in chapter 24):

In the sympathetic watering of the preceding voyage to Africa, an errour is thought to be committed, by people at the southward, by the use of an ingredient seldom to be met with in those parts, called *yankee conscience*. It has been a subject of common observation, that the industrious people of the northern states, who have so eminently distinguished themselves in this humane traffic, whenever they proceed for the coast of Africa, make a point of leaving this old, and somewhat unfashionable staple of their country at home, to be resumed again at their return, as the decorum of religion or morality should render expedient. . . . I am apprehensive, that the smart of the lash will be felt too severely, by the clergyman of V———a, and that the sympathetic interest of his parishioners may diminish the demand for such valuable wares.

The letter was as much an occasion to comment on the "Colon & Spondee" and the "Peter Pencil" columns as on *The Algerine Captive*, and there was no discussion of the literary quality of the book. But the work was to come in for more, rather than less, comment as the years passed. In early 1802, four and a half years after the book's publication, Dennie quoted in his *Port Folio* a statement from the *Farmer's Museum* (which incidentally takes Tyler's authorship as a matter of fact) to the effect that, while some books receive unjustified praise and some are unaccountably forgotten, others "are only neglected for a while, till their deserts call them from an unjust oblivion. Amongst the latter, may be classed the Algerine Captive, written by R. Tyler, Esq. a work of much humour and merit, and for which we are happy to see a late and increasing demand." Dennie added his own praise, as Tyler's friend:

From our partiality for Mr. Tyler, and our conviction of the ingenuity of his mind, we are much delighted with the above information. A second edition of his work, enlarged to two volumes octavo, and published in the style of "Mordaunt," by Dr. Moore, is greatly wanted, and would afford the author an opportunity to extend his chapters, which are now too brief, and fill a fine outline, with very captivating colours.[13]

The last point is well taken, for the two volumes, totaling only about 65,000 words, are made up of sixty-nine chapters, some of which are no longer than a good-sized paragraph.

But if Tyler was not immediately given the opportunity for an expanded edition, a new edition did appear within a few months after Dennie's remarks. In April 1802 a two-volume edition, printed by S. Hamilton and published by G. and J. Robinson, appeared in London, and as a result *The Algerine Captive* is usually called the first American novel to be reprinted in England. That distinction properly belongs to Charles Brockden Brown's *Ormond*, published in England in 1800,[14] but Tyler's book was one of the earliest, for very few pre-1820 American novels were reprinted there.[15] Although Tyler was later to remark regretfully that this was the period of Sydney Smith's "Who reads an American book?," [16] he at least had little cause for complaint about the way his work was presented. Robinson's two volumes were handsomely printed, and the text was not expurgated, not even the patriotic preface or such references to England as "that haughty exasperated power" (though it did embody nearly 250 alterations of wording — usually for the better — and many hundreds more of punctuation).[17] Unfortunately this edition did not have a large circulation because Hamilton's warehouses and printing office burned down while the edition was stored there, destroying nearly all copies. To remedy the loss, the Robinsons decided to issue the work serially in the *Lady's Magazine*, which they published, and it appeared there in 1804, divided into thirteen installments and adorned with several engraved plates (illustrating such scenes as "A Medical Consultation" or "Updike Underhill seized by the Algerines").[18] A note to the initial installment announced, "The narrative is almost entirely founded on facts; and it is the first genuine American production of the kind that has been published in this country." The text (including the preface) followed the 1802 edition (with a few more changes in punctuation), except for one episode near the beginning, which must have been thought too daring to include in an *Entertaining Companion for the Fair Sex* (as the subtitle of the magazine reads), though it is actually one of Tyler's most amusing sketches. The narrator, telling of his ancestor John Underhill, reports that the venerable man was once charged with adultery because, at a public lecture in Boston, he gazed "stedfastly, and perhaps inordinately," upon Mistress Miriam Wilbore,

who it seems was, at that very time, herself in the breach of the spirit of an existing law, which forbad women to appear in public with uncovered arms and necks, by appearing at the same lecture with a pair of wanton open worked gloves, slit at the thumbs and fingers, for the conveniency of taking snuff; though she was not charged with the latter crime of using tobacco.[19]

At the trial Master Cotton "quoted Gregory Nazianzen upon

good works" and Master Peters averred that "these opennings [in the gloves] were Satan's port holes of firy temptatione." Thus the Robinsons thought best to omit the last three paragraphs of chapter 1 and all of chapter 2, so that their serial version contains sixty-eight chapters, all suitable for ladies.

The London *Monthly Review* devoted eight pages to *The Algerine Captive* in its September 1803 issue, but most of the space was given over to extracts from the book or to plot summary, with the only critical comments coming in the last two paragraphs. The writer predictably finds the book wanting when compared with British or European works — the "management of the story" is below *Robinson Crusoe*, the "exquisite humour" of *Gulliver's Travels* is absent, and the "delicate and refined irony" of the *Lettres Persanes* is not to be found here; nevertheless, the reader is "carried along by a train of probable and touching events," presented with "natural and lively painting" of "the folly or wickedness of human kind." The laudable sentiments in the book — the exposure of the evils of captivity and of the African slave trade, the "able and warm" defense of religious freedom, and the disapproval of certain aspects of European policy — according to the British critic, "may be allowed to atone for partial failures in the execution of [Tyler's] plan." Of the three faults he singled out, one is natural to come from the British viewpoint (that "the moral picture of London is darkened with shading not its own"), and the other two have become almost standard comments (that "the contents of the first volume are more diversified and more amusing than those of the second" and that, in Updike's debate with the Mohammedan priest, "the author too feebly defends that religion which he professes to revere").[20] Dennie's *Port Folio* also commented on the English edition with its usual loyalty: in June 1803 it announced that an "elegant" edition had appeared and asserted that American works received better treatment in England than at home; in April 1804 it commented on the "soothing *triumph* to the ingenious author to learn that his book is perused in the country of his *ancestors*," even though somewhat neglected in his native land.[21]

If the book then passed out of public attention for a time, it did enjoy a more prolonged life than the average publication, for it was still being discussed in 1810 and was reissued in 1816. The Boston *Monthly Anthology*, in one of its "Retrospective Reviews" for 1810, lamented, "This little work is very undeservedly hastening to oblivion. It contains an admirable picture of the manners of the interiour of New England." The book was also to be praised for the instruction that it gave, especially in the matter of children's education, where conceit is too often mistaken for genius. But again there are three flaws, two of them familiar by now. First, Updike's journeys as a doctor form "the most amusing part," and the second volume is "much inferiour," being "a collection of common-place remarks upon the Barbary powers, and a relation of common incidents, accompanied with many trite reflections." Second, the religious debate puts Christianity in too weak a position; and, finally, the "perpetual invective against classical learning" is to be deplored.[22] Though Tyler later expressed wonder that the book could be criticized for infidelity, he must have been pleased with the recurrent interest in the work. There was at least enough demand for it that Peter B. Gleason of Hartford set up a new compact one-volume edition in 1816 (rather carelessly proofread).[23] And Tyler himself, who was working on a revision and expansion of the work in the last years of his life, must have sensed its importance, even if he did not realize that he had failed by only a few degrees to produce something as significant in the history of American fiction as *The Contrast* had been in American drama.

Novelist

The Preface

For a book that purports to tell about a captivity in Algeria, the preface makes some unexpected points about America and American works. This preface is one of the important early manifestoes of American literary independence.[24] The use of native materials and the creation of a distinctive literature, perennial concerns of American writers, had special relevance in the years when the country was becoming politically independent as well, and Tyler's pronouncement is of a piece with those of the Connecticut wits and other gentleman-writers of the young republic. His preface introduces a strain of Americanism — praise of freedom and the glories of America — that recurs continually in the book, like the poets' conventional survey of the country's golden future. He calls for realism at a time when only one or two earlier novels (such as *Modern Chivalry*) could be said to treat the American scene with fidelity, although approximately twenty-five books that qualify in some way as fiction had already been published in the United States. A glance at the titles of other novels of 1797 (Hannah Foster's *Coquette*, Mrs. Patterson's *The Unfortunate Lovers*, Samuel Relf's *Infidelity*, and James Butler's *Fortune's Foot-ball*) shows that sentimentality reigned supreme, even among works which sometimes claimed to be based on fact.[25]

But Tyler's preface is interesting also because it is made an integral part of the book. That is, since the title page announces the work to be an autobiographical narrative by Updike Underhill, Tyler must step into his persona even in the preface and express his views both about fiction in general and American works in particular from the point of view of a contemporary educated New England writer of nonfiction. The nine pages of the preface are divided into three para-

149

graphs which mark the three stages in his argument. Underhill begins, having just returned from his seven years' captivity, by noting how many more books are being read purely for amusement by "all ranks" of New Englanders (whereas formerly such books had been available only in seaports), and he proudly points to American education as the cause of this rapidly increasing "taste for amusing literature" — for in no other country "are there so many people, in proportion to its numbers, who can read and write." Tyler's taste in literature, as well as Underhill's character, is reflected in his description of the reading material previously available to rural communities: "certain funeral discourses, the last words and dying speeches of Bryan Shaheen, and Levi Ames, and some dreary somebody's Day of Doom, formed the most diverting part of the farmer's library." What replaced these works was not always better, because the "social libraries" and "country booksellers" had "filled the whole land with modern Travels, and Novels, almost as incredible" — an oblique comment, if the critics had seen it, on the form of the book itself, for, under these circumstances, the best approach to truth might be a fictitious travelogue. Underhill's description of this shift in taste to frivolous works demonstrates Tyler's allusive style and light touch and is consistent with the Underhill we follow through the book; he explains that all

forsook the sober sermons and Practical Pieties of their fathers, for the gay stories and splendid impieties of the Traveller and the Novelist. The worthy farmer no longer fatigued himself with Bunyan's Pilgrim up the "hill of difficulty" or through the "slough of despond;" but quaffed wine with Brydone in the hermitage of Vesuvius, or sported with Bruce on the fairy land of Abysinia.

If the hired man and the maid no longer wept over sad ballads, they "amused themselves into so agreeable a terrour, with the haunted houses and hobgobblins of Mrs. Ratcliffe, that they were both afraid to sleep alone."

Given this state of affairs, Underhill goes on to point out what is to be "deplored" in it and what can be done to rectify it, observing parenthetically what the function of novels is. The first objection is that these books often "are not of our own manufacture," a fault to be remedied simply by producing "our own books of amusement." The second problem, inseparable from the first, is more serious — since novels present a "picture of the times" and since most of them are British, "the New England reader is insensibly taught to admire the levity, and often the vices of the parent country. While the fancy is enchanted, the heart is corrupted." The argument, then, is not quite the usual appeal for a native literature on patriotic grounds, for here the morality of novels and their practical effects are most important, though these questions do involve patriotism of a more subtle sort:

If the English novel does not inculcate vice, it at least impresses on the young mind [American, presumably] an erroneous idea of the world, in which she is to live. It paints the manners, customs, and habits of a strange country; excites a fondness for false splendour; and renders the homespun habits of her own country disgusting.

The implication is that American customs (as in *The Contrast*) are pure, unaffected, and simple — and therefore more desirable; that novels do have a lasting effect on the behavior of their readers; that novelists reflect the manners and customs around them; and that, as a result, the best novels for Americans to read are novels written by Americans depicting American manners.

Underhill then follows the tradition of pretending that he would not have been so presumptuous as to write his own story if the idea had not been suggested to him by "a friend."

This anonymous friend had told him that an account of his own life would "at least display a portrait of New England manners, hitherto unattempted." This remark brings us, however circuitously, to a rationale for the first volume of the work, for it does portray American (not only New England) manners; yet Underhill's reasoning is still a bit shadowy, since his discussion of the faults of British fiction for American readers leads one to expect him to announce a proper work of American fiction, not an autobiography. The second volume, a large part of which describes the customs of the Algerines, is even more puzzling and is explained only by the statement that "the manners of that ferocious race" are "so little known in our country" — and would therefore at least be "interesting." One can only conclude that it is more dangerous for Americans to read about the customs of the British (for whom a touch of loyalty might yet remain in many minds) than those of the Algerines (for whom there could be no sentimental attachment and about whose evils it would be beneficial for Americans to be informed). Underhill's closing satirical touch is to point out that his work will be just as exciting as fiction to all readers except one like the lady described by Addison, who threw her Plutarch (which she had been enjoying as a novel) aside "with disgust, because a man of letters had inadvertently told her, the work was founded on FACT."

It is characteristic of Tyler, as a Federalist lawyer and amateur man of letters, to write a novel pseudonymously, in the guise of a truthful autobiography, with both a patriotic and a social purpose in mind. The two purposes show through the dedication (dated 20 June 1797) to David Humphreys, a Connecticut wit and a minister to Spain. Underhill (who signs the dedication) first makes a distinction between European dedications (in which "the author oftener looks to the plenitude of the pockets, than the brains of his patron") and those of America (which involve no pecuniary gain and are determined by the "acknowledged merit" of the individual chosen). With exact parallelism (Underhill is "a lover of the Muses" and "a biographer of private life," and Humphreys is "a Poet" and "the Biographer of a Hero" — Israel Putnam), he explains the appropriateness of his dedication in a book about "those miseries of slavery, from which your public energies have principally conduced to liberate hundreds of our fellow citizens." Humphreys' efforts toward a treaty with the Algerines helped correct a social evil and so, Underhill implies, can a book informing the public fully about the situation.

The First Volume

If patriotic and social purposes are present throughout the novel, they operate in different ways in the two volumes. In the second volume the exposure of the evil of Algerine captivity offers the opportunity for occasional remarks on the glories of America; in the first volume the satire of certain American customs is only gentle criticism by one who hopes to make an excellent country even better. The patriotism remains; the social criticism changes. The first volume is light, satirical, and picaresque; the second is humanitarian and informative. Among American works, the first is reminiscent of Brackenridge's *Modern Chivalry*, the second of an Indian captivity narrative. The divergence between the two volumes is too great to be accommodated even in the tradition of the wandering rogue; the two volumes must be considered separately, for they constitute essentially two books.

The first volume, if it is reminiscent of *Modern Chivalry* in its picaresque framework and its satire of American customs, is not so consistent in approach nor methodical in coverage. *Modern Chivalry*, whose method may not be apparent immediately, eventually presents a thorough investigation of

the practice of democracy; *The Algerine Captive* touches
here and there sporadically on many social follies — perhaps
in almost every case related to democracy but not explicitly
so. Tyler, as *The Island of Barrataria* shows, knew his Cervantes as well as Brackenridge, and he makes allusions which
reveal his familiarity with Smollett. But the unity of a picaresque novel requires more than the presence of a hero, and
the individual incidents (about election procedures, for example) in *Modern Chivalry* add up to a coherent whole in a
way those in *The Algerine Captive* do not.

The underlying organization of the first volume is a chron-
ological account of the life of Updike Underhill to the time
when, at the age of twenty-six, he is taken captive by the
Algerines. Inspired in part by stories of the captivity of his
great-uncle Thomas, Tyler traced his hero's ancestry back to
the famous Captain John Underhill, author of *Newes from
America* (1638). After three chapters on the Captain's gallant exploits (following the account in Jeremy Belknap's
History of New-Hampshire), and some brief comment on
his eldest son, Benoni (a fabrication of Tyler's), from whom
Updike is supposedly descended, we come (on page 49) to
a description of the hero's birth on 16 July 1762.[26] This event
is accompanied by the proper omens, for his mother dreams
that Updike is captured by an Indian "playing at foot ball"
with his head, signifying that he would "one day suffer among
savages." His childhood (chapters 5–6) is represented by a
few paragraphs on his attendance at a private school and his
ensuing study of Greek and Latin (which he greatly enjoys),
and soon (chapter 7) he takes a position as country schoolmaster (which he thoroughly dislikes and from which he is
released by a fire that destroys the schoolhouse). By this
time his father has decided that he should be in a profession
(chapter 8), so Updike commences his study of medicine
with a celebrated doctor (chapters 9–15), a process inter-

rupted occasionally by his encounters with polite society (chapters 11–14). His studies completed in June of 1785, at the age of twenty-two, he visits Boston and Harvard (chapters 16–17) for medical supplies and sets out, "full Speed, to seek Practice, Fame, and Fortune, as a Country Practitioner." When he becomes dissatisfied with his first place of residence (chapters 19–21), he decides to move to the South, where he had heard "that the inhabitants were immensely opulent" and "paid high fees with profusion" (chapter 22). Though his journey begins well, with a visit to Benjamin Franklin in Philadelphia (chapter 23), his experiences in the South (chapters 24–25), needless to say, are not as he had anticipated, and he soon accepts an offer to sail as surgeon on a ship bound for England. One chapter (26) is devoted to his impression of London and three (27–29) to Thomas Paine, whom he meets before he sets sail again on 18 July 1788 in the ship *Sympathy*, bound for the coast of Africa to pick up Negro slaves. As physician, it is Updike's duty to inspect the slaves, and, when an epidemic breaks out, he recommends that they be taken ashore to get well (chapters 30–31). While camping there with five slaves who are still recuperating, he is abandoned by his ship and, on 14 November 1788, is captured by the Algerine *Rover*, which eleven days later "hove in sight of the city of Algiers" (chapter 32). It is here, at the beginning of Updike's Algerine captivity, that the first volume ends.

This course of events has been arranged to serve an obvious purpose. Tyler wants to satirize or comment on certain customs and practices, and he plans Updike's life so that they are included. When Updike first tries teaching school and then becomes a doctor, Tyler has the opportunity to say something about two professions; when Updike's ancestry is described, Tyler can comment on the American past and particularly on the Puritans; when Updike goes to the South, Tyler can point out the hypocrisy of aristocratic life and can criticize one part of America for not being American; when the hero finds his way to England, Tyler can make comparisons with the splendors of his native country. The portraits of Franklin and Paine are patriotic and political; the chapter on Harvard is a plea for greater Americanism; and the description of conditions on the slave ship is humanitarian protest. The volume is a kind of anthology of targets for the satirist and scenes of inspiration for the patriot. Tyler seems to have assembled his opinions on almost all subjects in which he was strongly interested and has strung them together on a biographical thread; the result, if not quite inconsistent, is certainly less than unified.

But to say that restraint, shaping, and subordinating would have produced a more coherent whole is not to say that there is no power in individual scenes, for some of the sketches are among the most skillful and amusing in early American literature. Updike's love of Greek, for instance, which could almost be called a motif of the volume, forms the basis of several episodes and serves a double purpose: his recitations at inappropriate moments are part of the general ridiculing of pedantry, and the common people's ignorance of Greek is taken, at the same time, as a mark of their general lack of culture. Both the pedantry and the social gap are evident when Updike, as the country schoolmaster, begins talking to a group of men in a tavern about Achilles' horse (chapter 7) or when, at a women's quilting party, he brings up the subject of Andromache at her loom, and then he speaks of Penelope:

This was received with a stupid stare, until I mentioned the long time the queen of Ulysses was weaving; when a smart young woman observed, that she supposed Miss Penelope's yarn was rotted in whitening, that made her so long: and then told a tedious story of a piece of cotton and linen she had herself woven, under the same circumstances. She had no sooner finished, than, to enforce my observations, I recited above forty lines of Greek, from the Odessey, and then began a dissertation on the *caesura*. (I, 73)

This humor of exaggeration and incongruity is nearly always successful — as when Updike leaves the party:

I was about retiring, fatigued and disgusted, when it was hinted to me, that I might wait on Miss Mima home; but as I could re-collect no word in the Greek, which would construe into *bundling*, or any of Homer's heroes, who *got the bag*, I declined. In the Latin, it is true, that Aeneas and Dido, in the cave, seem something like a precedent. (I, 74)

Earlier (chapter 6), on his father's farm, he "gave Greek names to all our farming tools; and cheered the cattle with hexameter verse":

After I had worked on the farm some months, having killed a fat heifer of my father's, upon which the family depended for their winter's beef, covered it with green boughs, and laid it in the shade to putrify, in order to raise a swarm of bees, after the man-ner of Virgil; which process, notwithstanding I followed closely the directions in the georgics, some how or other, failed, my father consented to my mother's request, that I should renew my career of learning. (I, 65–66)

The comedy of book learning which does not work out in practical life recurs in the volume, as does the device of the anticlimactic twist.

Other branches of learning come in for mild thrusts as well. When Updike, as a child at school (chapter 5), is asked to read from Dilworth's spelling book, he recites as loud as he can "without regard to emphasis or stops." The teacher con-siders Updike his "best scholar," and the minister, "who prided himself on the strength of his own lungs," is so pleased by the volume of Updike's recitation that he recommends college for him (I, 53–54). If this incident reflects on the quality of both the teaching profession and the ministry, Up-dike's own career as a teacher is a commentary at once on the lack of excellence in the country schools and the related lack of interest in education on the part of the people. Updike is not a good teacher, but one feels that he had the ability, if he had not been defeated by the community. To be sure, he is not so dedicated as to rise to the challenge, but he at least has considered the matter seriously: "As I had been once unmercifully whipt, for detecting my master in a false concord, I resolved to be mild in my government, to avoid all manual correction, and doubted not by these means to secure the love and respect of my pupils" (I, 68). In one sentence Tyler has suggested the hypocrisy (or incompetence) of the schoolmasters, the need for more humane treatment of children, and the ironic contrast between a teacher's idealistic intentions and actual experience. The "love and respect" of the pupils never come, and, equally expected, the parents take the children's side. Thus, when Updike is forced to strike a student who will not relinquish the master's chair by the fire, the father of the student soon appears with threats — "the only instance," Updike remarks sarcastically, "of the overwhelming gratitude of parents I received." The public appreciation of education is further reflected in the low salary (tendered in produce each fall) which causes Updike to go into debt. Altogether it is not a very pretty picture of colonial education, and the good humor of the telling (with the exception of Updike's one sarcastic comment) is more effective than an angry protest, though one may wonder occasionally, here and elsewhere, if the comedy is not sometimes indulged in for its own sake and its ostensible purpose lost sight of. In any case, the split between the educated minority and the Philistine majority is just as evident here, if not treated so militantly, as it is in *Main Street* or other works of the 1920's. Doubts about the utility of education are present even in Updike's own family. Although the book does not show us Updike's development enough to be considered a *Bildungsroman*, it does contain an element often present in such works, including recent ones — a mother who is "a little spare woman," interested in the arts and education, and a father who is practical and worldly, "a large bony man" (I, 55).

The minister who appreciates strength of lung more than vitality of thought is a characteristic Tyler clergyman, though religion in *The Algerine Captive* is not simply a subject for ridicule. It is true, however, that references to public worship are usually made with irony and the hypocrisy of divines is repeatedly emphasized. Even Updike's account of his illustrious ancestor alludes to the time "when the zeal of our worthy forefathers burned the hottest against heretics" (I, 32) and includes the glove episode. When Updike's father seeks a professional opinion on the value of Greek (chapter 6), he learns from a Boston clergyman that it is now useless, for there are fashions in divinity as in everything else:

When our forefathers founded the college, at Cambridge, critical knowledge in the mazes and subtleties of school divinity was all the mode. He that could give a new turn to an old text, or detect a mistranslation in the version, was more admired than the man, who invented printing, discovered the magnetic powers. (I, 61)

What appears at first to be a didactic episode (chapter 14) on the importance of Bible-reading — an incident which "contains a lesson, valuable to the reader, if he has penetration enough to discover it, and candour enough to apply it to himself" — ends by connecting religion with monetary gain, for, when Updike belatedly turns to the Bible his mother had given him, a guinea falls out: "[I] resolved that, in gratitude, I would read a chapter in the bible, every remaining day of my life. This resolution I then persevered in, a whole fortnight" (I, 120). The deflating of sentiment present here represents the tone of the first volume, and it is not until the second that the comments on religion, at least, take on a different character.

Another minister in volume I (chapter 24) is criticized

for his behavior, in an episode which also contrasts the solid worth of New England with the frivolous hypocrisy of the South. In a state "south of Philadelphia," the parson arrives at church cursing and beating his slave, only to deliver an "animated" sermon on sinning with one's tongue. When the short service is over and the congregation has "prayed fervently," everyone rushes outside to the horse race, where the parson "descanted, in the language of the turf, upon the points of the two rival horses, and the sleeve of his cassoc was heavy laden, with the principal bets." Updike, the true Yankee, expresses his disapproval in his best dead-pan manner:

> The whole of this extraordinary scene was novel to me. Besides, a certain staple of New England I had with me, called conscience, made my situation, in even the passive part I bore in it, so awkward and uneasy, that I could not refrain from observing to my friend my surprise at the parson's conduct, in chastising his servant immediately before divine service. My friend was so happily influenced by the habits of these liberal, enlightened people, that he could not even comprehend the tendency of my remark. He supposed it levelled at the impropriety, not of the minister, but the man; not at the act, but the severity of the chastisement. (I, 162–163)

The reader is then directed to "interlard those quotations" with oaths, so that the scene will be both more natural and less "tasteless and vapid" to the Southerner.

Tyler's satire of social customs is again effectively expressed through Updike's naïveté, in the episode in which he becomes involved in a duel (chapter 12). Updike had presented an ode, full of classical epithets, to a young lady, one of whose suitors took the description "ox-eyed" as an insult rather than a compliment. In a letter revealing all his lack of education but showing his knowledge of the code of honor, the suitor demands an explanation for "Them there very extraordinary pare of varses." Fooled by the polite tone, the innocent Updike believes it to be a request to discuss the ode, "to be indulged with an explanation of some of its peculiar beauties":

I began to recollect illustrations and parodies, from some favourite passages in the Iliad. But, what we were to do, in wasting a few charges of powder, was utterly inexplicable. At one time, indeed, I thought it an invitation to shoot partridges, and bethought myself of scouring a long barrelled gun, which had descended as an heir loom in our family. . . . Then again, I reflected, that the lower end of a wharf, in a populous town, was not the most probable place, to spring a covey of partridges. But what puzzled me most, was his punctual attention to hours, and even seconds. (I, 104–105)

A fellow student explains the code and advises Updike to accept. The challenger, "a raw lad, from the country," is surprised, and the town officials step in to settle the matter peacefully — Updike escorted "by the high sheriff, two deputies, three constables, and eleven stout assistants . . . guarded by a platoon of the militia, with a colonel at their head." The exaggeration, the piling up of detail, the pose of innocence, the matter-of-fact tone, all contribute to skillful satire of social pretentiousness. After this occurrence, Updike says, "I verily believe that, if I had spouted a whole Iliad, in the ball room, no one would have ventured to interrupt me: for I had proved myself a MAN OF HONOUR."

The most extended satire in the book, however, is not of ministers, teachers, or men about town, but of physicians. Medical jargon is a favorite target (the ninth chapter describes "A Philosophical Detail of the Operation of Couching for the Gutta Serena"), as are the deceptions of quacks. In one town where Updike settles (chapter 19), he encounters a learned doctor (who follows the books, measures out medicine carefully, and is opposed to fresh air), a cheap doctor (who is "careless, daring, and often successful"), a safe doctor ("if he did no good, he never did any harm"), and a musical doctor (that is, "entertaining or facetious"). He also comes across a quack (barely distinguishable from the four preceding) who has captured the faith of the public by making elaborate spiels in his own version of Latin. When Updike meets him (chapter 20), the quack has just "prescribed a gill of burnt brandy, with a pepper pod in it, to keep up the patient's spirits, under the operation, and [takes] another himself, to keep his hand steady" (I, 138). The two work out a successful partnership: Updike provides the knowledge, the quack the clientele; needless to say, the patients attribute all success to the quack. Soon after, when a jockey falls off a horse, the poor man is subjected to a professional consultation by this entire group of practitioners. The learned doctor is not able to venture an opinion since he "had unfortunately left at home his Pringle on contusions," but the safe doctor does not hesitate to propose "brown paper, dipped in rum and cobwebs, to staunch the blood." It is the quack's opinion that the jockey will recover since his soul has not been damaged, a jockey's soul being in his left heel. Finally (chapter 21) one doctor pours "a dose of urine and molasses down the patient's throat: who soon so happily recovered as to pursue his vocation, swop horses three times, play twenty rubbers of all fours, and get dead drunk again before sunset" (I, 150).

As with the double-edged satire of schoolmasters, the criticism here, though good-natured, is by no means limited to the pedantry or incompetence of the physicians themselves, for the gullible public that will support quacks is equally to blame. Updike has a difficult time finding a practice, where the quacks have already gained their patients' confidence, and he discovers (chapter 18) that doctors often command no more respect than schoolmasters:

In the neighbouring town, they did not want [need] a physician, as an experienced itinerant doctor visited the place, every March, when the people had most leisure to be sick and take physic. He practiced with great success, especially in slow consumptions, charged very low, and took his pay in any thing and every thing. Besides, he carried a mould with him, to run pewter spoons, and was equally good at mending a kettle and a constitution. (I, 130–131)

The picture of the medical profession which Tyler presents is just as discouraging as that of the teaching profession. The few good doctors are unrecognized, unrewarded, and driven to odd jobs on the side; the doctors that prevail are ignorant, unscrupulous, and mercenary, playing on an equally ignorant and hypochondriac public. That a serious purpose underlies Tyler's satire becomes evident in several straightforward passages, like the description of a blind man in the process of emerging from a successful operation (chapter 9), the anecdotes of the "celebrated Doctor Moyes" (chapter 10), or Updike's praise of his own teacher, who "possessed all the essence, without the parade of learning" (chapter 15). This combination of the overtly serious with the satiric — and with irony that verges on self-indulgent humor — is characteristic of the kind of mixture found throughout *The Algerine Captive*. But the solemn statement or direct comment is often isolated in a separate chapter and rarely intrudes to break the tone of a satiric sketch; Tyler's gift for comedy, gentle ridicule, and telling social criticism is nowhere better displayed than in these portraits of physicians.

The Second Volume

If the first volume is made up of groups of chapters relating to certain objects of satire, the second must be thought of in terms of topical headings, such as history, religion, law, public ceremonies, language, finance, and so on — for volume II is, more than anything else, a direct and unadorned account, supposedly factual, of the Algerines, their history, their customs, and their country. The text of this volume is longer by

some forty pages than that of the first, but it is likely to seem
even longer to most readers. Its subject matter is remote from
general interest, unenlivened by satire or whimsy except in
a few brilliant passages, and plot is almost nonexistent. The
first volume, a digression from the story of Algerine captivity
which has little plot other than the successive escapades of
the hero, is important historically in its use of native materials
and is still entertaining today. In the second volume, Tyler
is not able adequately to integrate details of an unfamiliar
setting with whatever action is taking place in it, and the resulting passages of description are more irritating than diverting.

Most of the intrigue is concentrated in two chapters near
the end, chapters 30 and 36.[27] Earlier references to what Updike is doing are rarely inserted for themselves; they are employed to put him into situations where other aspects of
Algerine life can be expounded. In this respect the picaresque
plan of volume I is continued, with the course of the hero's life
predetermined by the subjects for discussion; the difference
is in the tone of those discussions, which is factual and expository, not satirical and anecdotal. The volume begins with
a description of the palace of the Dey of Algiers, Vizier
Hassen Bashaw, before whom Updike and the other captives are brought. Since Updike cannot promise ransom, he
is exhibited in the slave market, where he is purchased by
Abdel Melic, who then takes him to his mansion (chapters
2–4). Updike's attempt to help a fellow slave who is being
whipped is an occasion for comment on the freedom of
America (and causes Updike to be assigned to the stone
quarry); his conversation with an Englishman who has
espoused Mohammedanism provides the opportunity for religious commentary (chapter 5), followed by a comparison
with Christianity in his debate with the mullah (chapters
6–7). Upon returning to the quarry after the debate, he

feels more familiar with the language, so we are given a chapter on "The Language of the Algerines" (chapter 8). Although there is a hint of plot in chapter 9, when Updike makes plans to escape, these plans are thwarted by the occurrence of a public celebration, which is duly described in the following chapter.

The trend of the account may be said to take a slight turn with chapter 11, because there we return to the subject of medicine. Chapters 11 through 14 describe Updike's collapse from exhaustion and depression, his stay in the infirmary, his purchase by the head of the hospital (due to his former medical experience), his new duties, his trips for medical supplies (an occasion for comment on Algerine medicine), and his visit to a sick lady. But these four chapters together lack one page of being as long as the next chapter, the longest in the book, a "Sketch of the History of the Algerines," which begins a long expository section that is the center, if not the heart, of the volume. We have a description of the city of Algiers (chapter 16), an account of its government (17), revenue (18), and military forces (19), and a discussion of Algerine dress (20), marriages, and funerals (21); then follows a "Life of the Prophet Mahomet" (22) and two chapters on various sects and religious practices (23–24); an analysis (25) of the sources of Algerine power (why Europeans have not been able to suppress the Algerines) is succeeded by an example of an Algerine lawsuit (26) and an Algerine sermon (27). It is not until chapter 28 that we are given any assurance that Updike has not forgotten his story:

> I have thus given some succinct notices of the history, government, religion, habits, and manners of this ferocious race. I have interspersed reflections, which, I hope, will be received by the learned with candour; and shall now resume the thread of my more appropriate narrative. (II, 178)

Despite this promise, we still have to hear about the position of the Jews in Algiers — an account which, surprisingly, leads us directly into the largely narrative framework of the last nine chapters, for Updike, with his greater freedom as a medical slave, wanders into the Jewish section and makes the acquaintance of Adonah Ben Benjamin, who promises to help him escape.

The only true plot (in the sense of an intrigue in which the order of events makes a difference) occurs in these last chapters, although even there four chapters (31–34) are given over to a description of a pilgrimage to Medina and Mecca. In the space of one chapter (30), Updike makes arrangements with the Jew for his escape, having turned over all his savings, only to call at the Jew's house on the appointed day to find him dead of apoplexy and the Jew's son unwilling to acknowledge any of the money as Updike's. This chapter, if it does nothing to redeem Tyler's sense of narrative proportion, does demonstrate his feeling for melodramatic turns of events. The hero's hopes are built up, and then are destroyed, just before the final happy outcome. Updike is more discouraged than ever until, after he cures the Jew's son of a fever, the son is so grateful that he confesses his perfidy, repays Updike's money, and lends him enough more to make up the ransom (chapters 35–36). Even here Tyler attempts to create suspense by having the son not make the payment at the appointed time, but a day later; and the abrupt vicissitudes continue when Updike, on the ship making his escape, is seized and taken captive by a man from Tunis. After an agonizing forty-eight hours, enlivened by a storm, a Portuguese ship comes alongside and frees Updike and the other slaves. It is then a simple matter for Updike to get to Portugal, to arrange passage to England, and to return to the United States (chapter 37). He lands at Chesapeake Bay on 3 May 1795, after an absence of seven years, buys a horse, and rides to a happy reunion with his parents.

Novelist

In spite of the large amount of expository material, volume II does approach a unity of tone and does make a connection with volume I through its comments on two subjects — religion and American freedom. While one of Tyler's purposes was undoubtedly to alert his fellow countrymen to the evils of the Algerian depredations, another was certainly to inspire patriotism and, to a slighter degree, love of Christianity. The principal motif of the entire work is the glorious freedom of America. In volume I certain American habits may be satirized, in the interests of improvement, but patriotism is always a solemn subject. Even in that anecdote criticizing the religious zeal of early New Englanders, Updike does not fail to mention their "love of liberty, which under God enabled us to obtain our own glorious freedom" (I, 44). When Updike visits Harvard he is indignant that the museum has so few American objects (chapter 17); and he loses no opportunity to make invidious references to England — thus the English took over the land which rightly belonged to John Underhill (chapter 3), and the common man in England, as Updike observes on his visit to London, was "rotting in dungeons, languishing wretched lives in foetid jails, and boasting of the GLORIOUS FREEDOM OF ENGLISHMEN" (chapter 26). Social and economic criticism of the English is intended as indirect praise of America: their "little smoky fire of coals was rendered cheerless by excise, and their daily draught of beer embittered by taxes." Americans, especially New Englanders, also have a greater feeling for justice than other nationalities. So, on the slave ship *Sympathy*, Captain Russell fears that Updike is "moved by some *yankee nonsense about humanity*" (I, 201) and, in the South, Updike is uneasy because of that "staple of New England . . . called conscience" (I, 162). The visits to Benjamin Franklin and Thomas Paine, inserted partly to increase the verisimilitude of the work, serve a patriotic purpose as well. Franklin is praised (chapter 23) for his democratic rise from a lowly position by his own efforts (and for the inevitable qualities of frugality and wisdom, illustrated with anecdotes); Paine, on the other hand, a "spare man, rather under size," whose "bodily presence was both mean and contemptible" (I, 176), is a "missionary of vice" and a "modern vandal" who has "vilified a great prophet, the saviour of the Gentiles," and has "railed at Washington, a saviour of his country" (I, 183–184). Updike delights in telling a story (chapter 28) in which Paine is defeated in a clash of wit by Peter Pindar, Paine's point of view being that the United States would be better off if it were still a colony, without a Washington as the great leader.[28] Finally, at the end of volume I, when Updike is in the dungeon of the Algerine ship, he exclaims, "Grant me . . . once more to taste the freedom of my native country, and every moment of my life shall be dedicated to preaching against this detestable commerce" (I, 213). The humanitarianism and didacticism of the work, then, are a function of its patriotism, for the existence of slavery anywhere in the world is an affront to a free American. As Updike says of his role on the slave ship, "I thought of my native land and blushed" (I, 190).

This relation between freedom and patriotism is particularly clear in volume II. As early as the second chapter, Updike declares that any American citizen who, "in the warmth of . . . patriotism," condemns him for lack of spirit in submitting to Algerine slavery should have been there to "avail himself of a noble opportunity of suffering gloriously for his country" (II, 25). In the fourth chapter he continues in the same vein:

Judge you, my gallant, freeborn fellow citizens, you, who rejoice daily in our federal strength and independence, what were my sensations. . . . Let those of our fellow citizens, who set at nought the rich blessings of our federal union, go like me to a land of slavery, and they will then learn how to appreciate the value of our free government. (II, 35, 39)

At the public spectacle, one look at a tortured slave is "enough to appal a New England heart" (II, 76). Updike's homesickness for New England is revealed in his many allusions to native foods, customs, or language and in his eagerness to see another American: "the idea of embracing a fellow citizen, a brother christian, perhaps some one, who came from the same state, or had been in the same town, or seen my dear parents" (II, 187). But his own feelings are less important than the lesson he hopes to impart:

A slave myself, I have learned to appreciate the blessings of freedom. May my countrymen ever preserve and transmit to their posterity that liberty, which they have bled to obtain; and always bear it deeply engraven upon their memories, that, when men are once reduced to slavery, they can never resolve, much more achieve, any thing, that is manly, virtuous, or great. (II, 79)

It is this sentiment which Tyler gives the final position of emphasis in his closing chapter. Updike, who has been restored to the "rights and protection" of "the freest country in the universe," intends to support the "excellent government" which he "learnt to adore, in schools of despotism" and thus to be a "worthy FEDERAL citizen":

My ardent wish is, that my fellow citizens may profit by my misfortunes. If they peruse these pages with attention they will perceive the necessity of uniting our federal strength to enforce a due respect among other nations. Let us, one and all, endeavour to sustain the general government. Let no foreign emissaries inflame us against one nation, by raking into the ashes of long extinguished enmity or delude us into the extravagant schemes of another, by recurring to fancied gratitude. Our first object is union among ourselves. For to no nation besides the United States can that antient saying be more emphatically applied; BY UNITING WE STAND, BY DIVIDING WE FALL. (II, 241)

The shift from indirect to direct statement, which begins in the closing chapters of volume I, reaches its culmination here. Tyler seems to have been aware of the changed tone, for he has Updike comment that the doctors in the Algerine infirmary are "more ignorant than those of my own country, who had amused me in the gayer days of life" (II, 81). What was a subject for humor and satire in volume I has become matter for sober reflection and didactic exhortation.

The serious directness of volume II is also evident in the treatment of religion. To be sure, the satire of religious pedantry and of hypocritical ministers is balanced, even in volume I, by more direct assertions of faith, as when the physician who restores sight has a pleasure surpassed only, "with reverence be it spoken, by the satisfaction of our benevolent Saviour, when, by his miraculous power, he opened the eyes of the actually blind, made the dumb to sing, and the lame and impotent leap for joy" (I, 93). Of his role as doctor on the slave ship, Updike observes:

I have deplored my conduct with tears of anguish; and, I pray a merciful God, the common parent of the great family of the universe, who hath made of one flesh and one blood all nations of the earth, that the miseries, the insults, and cruel woundings, I afterwards received, when a slave myself, may expiate for the inhumanity, I was necessitated to exercise, towards these MY BRETHREN OF THE HUMAN RACE. (I, 193–194)

However much such references to God are discounted as conventional expressions, the subject of slavery and captivity, as opposed to freedom, has religious, as well as patriotic and political, implications. It is also evident, by the end of the first volume, that the discussion of religion will not be so one-sided as that of patriotism, for Updike remarks of the Algerines on shipboard, "the regularity and frequency of their devotion was astonishing to me, who had been taught to consider this people as the most blasphemous infidels" (I, 214).

The religious element in the second volume takes the form either of a dramatic clash between Christianity and Mohammedanism or of an exposition of practices and customs in Mohammedanism — the first more likely to occur in the opening and closing sections of the volume, the second in the middle expository section. Chapters 5, 6, and 7 offer the best example of the dramatic conflict. In chapter 5 Updike encounters an Englishman who has adopted Mohammedanism, and he clarifies the connection between liberty and religion:

I looked at him with astonishment. I had ever viewed the character of an apostate as odious and detestable. I turned from him with abhorrence, and for once embraced my burthen with pleasure. Indeed I pity you, said he. I sorrow for your distresses, and pity your prejudices. I pity you too, replied I, the tears standing in my eyes. My body is in slavery, but my mind is free. Your body is at liberty, but your soul is in the most abject slavery, in the gall of bitterness and bond of iniquity. (II, 43)

But Updike does consent to give a hearing to the Mohammedan priest, so that, as the Englishman says, his decision will be based on reason, having a knowledge of both systems. Updike is taken to the luxurious palace of the priests, or mullahs, in chapter 6 and is treated very courteously for eleven days. His reactions well illustrate the mixture of tone in volume II, for he is still capable of wry commentary, but within a few paragraphs he is verging on the sentimental:

I have often observed that, in all countries, except New England, those, whose profession it is to decry the luxuries and vanities of this world, some how or other, contrive to possess the greatest portion of them. (II, 47)

Though I viewed his [the mullah's] conduct as insidious, yet he no sooner retired than, overcome by his suavity of manners, for the first time I trembled for my faith, and burst into tears. (II, 51–52)

When Updike is in this frame of mind the mullah comes to

debate the relative merits of the two faiths. Chapter 7 summarizes in dialogue form their five days' discussion — it is this chapter which was criticized in contemporary discussions of the book. The *Monthly Anthology* objected to the fact that the mullah came out much better in the argument than Updike.[29] While the total context makes it impossible to believe that Tyler is attacking Christianity here, one must admit that the course of the debate does not lead very logically to Updike's final reaction: "disgusted with his fables, abashed by his assurance, and almost confounded by his sophistry, I resumed my slave's attire, and sought safety in my former servitude" (II, 65). In long and eloquent speeches, the mullah attempts to prove that the Koran is of divine origin and that Mohammedanism has multiplied more than Christianity, has greater miracles, was not promulgated by force, and does not have a sensual paradise; by comparison Updike's replies seem weak. Tyler's rationale, however, lies in the statement of the Englishman two chapters earlier: if his readers are brought to see that a good case can be made out for other religions, they will approach their own more thoughtfully, with more knowledge and with less bias. But whether Updike has set a better example of the thoughtful approach to religion or of Yankee stubbornness is debatable.

Tyler has created in Updike, for those of his readers able to see it, a subtle characterization of the typical New Englander with his prejudice and narrowness. In the expository chapters, when Updike is supposedly reporting facts, his preconceptions are obvious. He may praise a Mohammedan sermon (chapter 27) and say that it "was received . . . with a reverence, better becoming christians than infidels" (II, 172), but his very use of the term "infidels," and his conception of the relative worth of the behavior of the two, negates the seeming praise. Or, at the beginning of the three chapters on Algerine religion (chapters 22–24), Updike's assertion that he will "endeavour to steer the middle course of impartiality" is belied in the same paragraph by his reference to Mohammed as a "fortunate impostor." Mohammed's rise is depicted as the result of a calculated plan to gratify his ambition:

Mankind are apt to impute the most profound abilities to founders of religious systems, and other fortunate adventurers, when perhaps they owe their success more to a fortunate coincidence of circumstances, and their only merit is the sagacity to avail themselves of that tide in the affairs of men, which leads to wealth and honour. . . . The system of Mahomet is said to have been calculated to attach all these. To gratify the Arian and the Jew, he maintained the unity of God; and, to please the Pagans, he adopted many of their external rites, as fastings, washings, &c. . . . The stories of Mahomet's having retired to a cave with a monk and a Jew to compile his book; and falling into fits of the epilepsy, persuading his disciples that these fits were trances in order to propagate his system more effectually, so often related by geography compilers, like the tales of Pope Joan and the nag's head consecration of the English bishops, are fit only to amuse the vulgar. (II, 144–146)

The pose of impartiality is strengthened by mentioning certain points that one proceeds to deny, for the sake of getting those points on record, and by appearing to treat allegedly parallel situations in one's own religion in the same light.

This passage illustrates another aspect of Tyler's persona — Updike's Yankee common sense. Throughout the chapters on Algerine religion, it is the natural, rather than the miraculous or romantic, explanation that appeals to him. There were stories, he says, of Mohammed's being poisoned by a monk, but, "when we consider his advanced age and public energies, we need not recur to any but natural means for the cause of his death" (II, 149). Later, in the narrative chapters on the pilgrimage to Mecca (chapters 31–35), Updike constantly denies the supernatural explanations favored by the leader of the group, only to make this observation in the same breath:

We passed near the north arm of the red sea, and then pursued our journey south, until we struck the same arm again, near the place where the learned Wortley Montague has concluded the Israelites, under the conduct of Moses, effected their passage. The breadth of the sea here is great, and the waters deep and turbulent. The infidel may sneer, if he chooses; but, for my own part, I am convinced beyond a doubt, that, if the Israelites passed in this place, it must have been by the miraculous interposition of a divine power. I could not refrain from reflecting upon the infatuated temerity, which impelled the Egyptian king to follow them. Well does the Latin poet exclaim; *Quem Deus vult perdere, prius dementat.* (II, 210–211)

Either the satire has turned upon Updike himself, or he is directing his sarcasm toward Christian as well as Mohammedan miracles. But if the latter is the case, it is difficult to reconcile Updike's purple eloquence at other times, as when he describes a dream:

That Beneficent Being, who brightens the slumbers of the wretched with rays of bliss, can alone express my raptures, when, in the visions of that night, I stepped lightly over a father's threshold; was surrounded by congratulating friends and faithful domestics; was pressed by the embraces of a father; and with holy joy felt a mother's tears moisten my cheek. (II, 72)

It is true that Updike does approach the sarcasm of volume I in most of his description of the pilgrimage — he ridicules the practice of visiting the holy shrines by proxy, the ceremonial connected with the shrines, and the economic motive of the pilgrims. These cynical observations, however, are consistent with his tendency to seek the rational or practical explanation and do not (in conjunction with the sentimental statements of faith) constitute evidence of such impartiality that Christianity could also be ridiculed.

It is more reasonable to see Tyler here casting a few rationalistic doubts about religious extravagances through the less broad-minded attitudes of Updike. Volume II, while perhaps not so intrinsically interesting to an American, does have a form and consistency of its own, for it shows a New Englander trying to report foreign customs accurately and exhibiting his own prejudices in the process. The flaw in *The Algerine Captive* may best be expressed in terms of a satiric shift. In volume I, Updike, though naïve at times, is aware of the stupidities and hypocrisies around him and consciously satirizes them; in volume II, he is still willing to satirize certain things occasionally, but in the main he is explaining unfamiliar customs and in so doing displays his own hypocrisies and becomes the chief satiric object. If it was Tyler's plan, as it presumably was, to expose certain follies in the American scene through the eyes of a shrewd New Englander, and then to reveal the provinciality of the New Englander himself by placing him on a larger stage, it would have been to his advantage to consider the difficulties inherent in changing the stance of the narrator. This is not to say that we are witnessing a different Updike in the two volumes; rather, in volume I, Updike was in with us on a joke from which he seems to be excluded in volume II.[30] The question has to do, not with the plausibility or justice of Updike's portrait as a New Englander, but with the artistic method of producing that portrait. *The Algerine Captive*, quite simply, fails to achieve a unity of tone that would hold both volumes together.

Language

The book is most successful in individual satiric sketches, rather than in the fusion of the whole, and that success is partly accounted for by the skillful handling of language. Irony is the principal device, both verbal and dramatic — sometimes through direct statements of Updike's which are obviously the opposite of what he means, at other times through the contrast between his expectations and actuality. Updike is at one moment the naïve observer, overly impressed with strange customs, and at another the objective historian, whose own bias is clear. Professions of objectivity occur from the beginning. In the second chapter Updike says that he hesitates to present anything which will reflect on his ancestors, but he has "the impartiality of a historian" (I, 43); two chapters later he observes, "I only relate facts, and leave the reader to his own comments" (I, 51). The supposed factual quality of the book is also supported by the frequent recording of detail, as when Thomas Paine appears before Updike "dressed in a snuff coloured coat, olive velvet vest, drab breeches, coarse hose. His shoe buckles of the size of half a dollar" (I, 176).

Another source of irony is the title and the epigraph to each chapter — usually incongruous with the contents. Thus, the chapter describing Updike's unpleasant experience as a schoolmaster is headed with a quotation from Thomson's *Seasons* beginning, "Delightful talk! to rear the tender thought" (volume I, chapter 7); the account of the Harvard museum begins with two lines from Mrs. Barbauld, "A hornet's sting, / And all the wonders of an insect's wing" (volume I, chapter 17); the absurd consultation among the different types of doctors starts with Pope's "For man's relief the healing art was given" (volume I, chapter 21); four lines from Cowper on beauty form the epigraph for the dismal picture of London (volume I, chapter 26); a Biblical verse, "The heaven of heavens cannot contain thee," is placed at the head of the description of Mecca (volume II, chapter 34); and a quotation from Blair's *Grave* adorns "The Infirmary" (volume II, chapter 12). One of the best examples of this technique occurs in chapter 16 of volume I: the epigraph, from *Tristram Shandy*, is "The lady Baussiere rode on," and the title is "Doctor Underhill visiteth Boston, and maketh no Remarks." As one might expect, most of these humorous headings occur in the first volume and, when they are found in the second, come in the less straightforward chapters near the beginning and end. Similarly revealing, there are six quotations from Pope in volume I and only one in volume II, while Shakespeare is called on more in volume II (six times, as compared with three in volume I), and Tyler resorts to verses which he himself has composed (in a serious vein) more frequently in the second volume (nine times; four in volume I).

This interest in playing with language (as well as the familiarity with English poetry) is not unexpected from the author of the "Colon & Spondee" poems and manifests itself not only in the discussion of the Algerines' lingua franca or in the ungrammatical challenge to a duel but in the balancing of sentences and the ability to produce fluent prose on several stylistic levels. There are the oversentimental excesses (laden with adjectives) of some of the references to God and family — these to be placed next to the straightforward, generally unadorned style of the expository chapters, contrasted in turn with the elaborate prose poem which Tyler allows himself as an example of a Mohammedan sermon.[31] On the omniscience of deity, the Mohammedan priest presents Tyler's best metaphorical and balanced style: "Michael, whose wings are full of eyes, is blind before him, the dark night is unto him as the rays of the morning; for he noticeth the creeping of the small pismire in the dark night, upon the black stone, and apprehendeth the motion of an atom in the open air" (II, 174). For a concentrated example of the stylistic devices that make up Tyler's satiric skill, the best choice would be one of the final chapters of volume II, here quoted entire:

Chapter 32

The Author is blessed with the Sight and Touch of a most holy Mahometan Saint

Procul! O procul! este profani. — Virgil

When we were within one day's journey of Medina, we halted for a longer time than usual; occasioned, as I found, by the arrival of a most holy saint. As I had never seen a saint, being bred, in a land, where even the relics of these holy men are not preserved, for I believe all New England cannot produce so much as a saint's rotten tooth or toe nail, I was solicitous to see and converse with this blessed personage. I soon discovered him, in the midst of about fifty pilgrims, some of whom were devoutly touching their foreheads with the hem of his garment, while others, still more devout, prostrated themselves on the ground, and kissed the prints of his footsteps in the sand. Though I was assured, that he was filled with divine love, and conferred felicity on all, who touched him; yet, to outward appearance, he was the most disgusting, contemptible object, I had ever seen. Figure to yourselves, my readers, a little decrepit, old man, made shorter by stooping, with a countenance, which exhibited a vacant stare, his head bald, his finger and toe nails as long as hawks' claws, his attire squalid, his face, neck, arms, and legs begrimed with dirt and swarming with vermin, and you will have some faint idea of this Mussulman saint. As I was too reasonable to expect that holiness existed in a man's exteriour, I waited to hear him speak; anticipating, from his lips, the profoundest wisdom, delivered in the honied accents of the saints in bliss. At length he spake; and his speech betrayed him, a mere idiot. While this astonished me, it raised the respect of his admirers, who estimated his sanctity in an inverse ratio to the weakness of his intellects. If they could have ascertained, that he was born an idiot, I verily believe, they would have adored him; for the Mahometans are taught by their alcoran, that the souls of saints are often lodged in the bodies of idiots; and these pious souls, being so intent on the joys of paradise, is the true reason, that the actions of their bodies are so little suited to the manners of this world. This saint however did not aspire to the sanctity of a genuine idiot; though, I fancy, his modesty injured his preferment, for he certainly had very fair pretensions. It was resolved, that the holy man should go with us; and, to my great mortification and disgust, he was mounted behind me on the same camel; my Mahometan friends probably conceiving, that he would so far communicate his sanctity by contact, as that it might affect my conversion to their faith. Whatever were their motives, in the embraces of this nauseous being, with the people prostrating themselves in reverence on each side, I made my entry into the city of Medina.

Here one finds the matter-of-fact pose, the specificity of detail, the exaggeration, the incongruity, and the solemnity of logic misapplied that give satire its richest double meanings. Occasional flaws in syntax (as in the first and ninth sentences) do not obscure the control in diction and structure of the whole movement, ending with an appealing flourish in the final periodic sentence.

A passage of this sort indicates both the strengths and the weaknesses of *The Algerine Captive*. The merits of the book are found in such individual sketches, which rarely fail to be amusing and effective, but the work seems less impressive when viewed as an artistic entity. Tyler's very skill in the restricted form of journalistic squibs was perhaps his undoing in the longer form. At any rate, *The Algerine Captive* can hardly be called a novel, except in the sense that it is a narrative recounting fictitious incidents. The whole intent of the work, from its preface to its final patriotic paragraph, is nonartistic. Tyler, a true Federalist and devout Christian, is writing to impress upon his readers the advantages of their new government and the greater importance of inner faith than of ritual. He does find a metaphorical approach useful at times, but the mixture it creates is at the heart of the dissatisfaction which a modern reader must feel about the structure of the book. Updike is Tyler's mask, but without the dimensions of a real character (he is never described physically); he is the mouthpiece for certain ideas, but the way in which that mouthpiece operates in volume II (with the exception of a few passages like the one just quoted) is different from its mode of operation in volume I. The factual material about the Algerines in volume II is not in itself inappropriate, since it becomes the vehicle for Tyler's indirect exposure of provinciality; but neither is it the basis for a coherent metaphorical structure, like the cetological information in *Moby-Dick*. It would be foolish to search for a symbolic reading of

Royall Tyler

The Algerine Captive, with Updike, "lost . . . and now found" as he says at the end, charting the course to spiritual rebirth after a trial of faith and a dark night of the soul. The subjects of freedom and slavery — political, spiritual, and physical — do unite the material of the book; but the embracing context of direct exhortation prevents a final dramatic unity. While the value of the book as a historical and literary document is not disputed, there is no reason to be patronizing about its artistic qualities either. Its quaintness is of slight importance compared to the firmness of mind inherent in it, the realism of its approach, and the undeniable skill of which it gives evidence if not fulfillment.

❧ VI ❧

Essayist

IF Tyler had completed all the works he planned, the proportion of nonfiction prose in his output would be considerably larger than it is, for most of his projected writings fall into this category. In addition, Tyler of necessity did a great deal of writing in the course of his profession, and his legal reports and transcripts of jury charges add to the bulk of his prose writings, though they can hardly be classed as literary essays. His speeches, like the Washington oration in 1800, are only extensions of his role as lawyer and public servant, as are his contributions to official documents of the University of Vermont, the "Laws and Regulations," for example, which he and William C. Bradley drew up on 28 July 1811.[1] Further, certain ideas which he mentioned to publishers grew out of his professional interests; he wrote to Isaac Riley in 1810 to suggest the publication of an "American Law Dictionary," which he had been compiling for some time.[2] Other ideas, not directly related to law, reveal his love of learning and of factual information; he approached Joseph Nancrede in 1800 with a proposal for a "Cosmography," which, he said, he had thought about for such a long time that it was almost written.[3]

One unfinished prose work, which missed completion by only a slim margin, was entitled "The Touchstone, or a Humble Modest Inquiry into the Nature of Religious Intolerance." In 1817 the well-known printer Simeon Ide, of

Brattleboro, began setting this tract in type before Tyler had finished writing it. When, by 26 January 1818, Tyler had not yet furnished the complete copy, Ide drew up a formal agreement, which Tyler signed, whereby Tyler agreed to provide copy for a seventy-two-page work by 4 March, or else pay Ide twelve dollars to cover the cost of the paper already used. It seems likely that Tyler never completed the work, for no copy of the book can be located, and the only copy which has ever been noted in print was an incomplete one of thirty-six pages. What Tyler had to say about religious intolerance in 1817, then, must remain conjectural.[4]

That Tyler esteemed these serious works more highly than his lighter and more "literary" productions is suggested in one of his letters to Nancrede about some children's tales he had written: the only reason for publishing the tales, he says, is to make his name better known before the "Cosmography" appears. These "Moral Tales for American Youth" were a series of stories intended to amuse and instruct at the same time; according to Tyler, nothing of the kind had been produced in America, though many such books had been imported from England. The work contained a story about Dr. Franklin and his mother, "A Philosophical Experiment"; a Green Mountain tale entitled "Home"; a story about a "tub woman," adapted from a British magazine; a parable illustrating the folly of believing gossip and of embroidering the truth — and so on.[5] Dennie wrote enthusiastically in 1797, "Vose has read your 'Moral Romances;' and, he assures me, it rendered a gloomy and snowy Fast day pleasant, He declares it more uniformly pure than Updike, and, in elegance, greatly its superior. For myself, I have always assured you of the sure and certain hope of popularity & profit." [6]

With such encouragement Tyler envisioned a large sale for the book and even planned further volumes to take advantage of the same market, "a little library," as he called it. The second volume would contain dialogues reminiscent of Berquin and character studies like those of La Bruyère and Theophrastus; the third would be a "Comic Grammar," in which the rules were to be illustrated not only by entertaining quotations from authors of the past but by amusing stories of Tyler's own invention which would bring the meaning home to a child. In describing the idea to Nancrede, Tyler explains that he once had to teach grammar to a young lady reluctant to study:

I accordingly wrote a grammar in *usum puellae*, and being forwarded in twelve letters, folded as billet doux, she condescended to read. . . . A lover at the feet of his mistress, gave a passionate example of interjection; a lady crowned her favored lover's virtuous wishes in the passive voice, and dismissed an unsucessful admirer in the imperative mood. Thus every rule of syntax was associated with some pleasing anecdote, brilliant quotation, or quaint observation, which familiarized the stubborn rule to a mind open only to the amusing and pleasing.[7]

Tyler perhaps anticipated modern educational ideas; certainly his plans for books took a practical and utilitarian direction.

On the question of publishing the "Moral Tales," Tyler had some difficulties with Nancrede. In a fascinating series of letters,[8] which reveal the kind of bargaining that took place between author and publisher in 1800, Nancrede argued that he expected a work twice as long and that he could not pay $200 for one hundred pages which cost the author "eight days' amusement." He claimed on 7 March, however, that the work had gone to press, but it is unlikely that the negotiations were ever straightened out sufficiently for the printing to be completed; at least, no copy of the book is known to exist today. Tyler sent three more stories in an attempt to lengthen the work, but he emphasized that he was not primarily a writer. "You certainly misconceived me," he had written on 14 February, "if you concluded that I was anyways anxious to have the work published. . . . So far from this, it is with [a] great degree of reluctance I have consented to its publication." The most significant part of the letter may stand as a remarkable summary of Tyler's entire position as a writer:

> I have a profession, and my abilities in the exercise of it in this wooden world are esteemed above mediocrity. This profession affords me the comforts and conveniences of life, for myself and family; and I have learned that great secret of felicity to find enjoyment at home. From certain disgusts perhaps uncharitably admitted, I had renounced the ambition of authorship. Your charming plausibility drew me from my retreat and made me willing — not anxious — to write again for the press. I rely upon your uprightness; and am ready to believe that what you offer is all that you can afford to give for this little work: but if writing for the public is attended with no more profit, I had rather file legal process in my attorney's office, and endeavor to explain unintelligible law to Green Mountain jurors; and when the *cacoethes scribendi* assails me, I will write sonnets to rustic loves, and tales for children; and look for my reward in the exhilarating smiles of partial friends round my own fireside.

Tyler had stated the case eloquently, not only for himself, but for many others as well. Literature, in the United States of 1800, was not a profession, and one wrote, when the urge came, between the rounds of business.

Periodical Essays

In a day when newspapers and magazines were filled with Addisonian essays, it is inevitable that Tyler, as a member of an informal club of writers and a facile versifier, should have tried his hand at light essays. The problem of determining just which ones he wrote, however, is even more difficult than in the case of the newspaper verse. Since prose was generally Dennie's province in the "Colon & Spondee" partnership,[9] the attribution to Tyler of particular essays under this heading requires especially strong evidence. In point of fact, Tyler probably wrote a sizable number of these essays, just as Dennie contributed poems from time to time (signed "C." in the early columns). But the graceful, polished style and the ubiquitous allusions to English literature do not serve to distinguish between the prose of the two men, and it is probable that some essays result from a collaboration of both, given the conditions of composition in Crafts Tavern and the pressures of the printer's deadlines. The safest course, therefore, is to take the few pieces linked to Tyler by contemporary evidence and allow them to serve as examples of his work in the informal periodical essay.

Tyler's prose contributions to the *Farmer's Museum* ranged from short notes — largely puns, anecdotes, and quotations — to brief paragraphs and essays for the "Colon & Spondee" column, according to the annotations which Joseph Dennie made in a copy of *The Spirit of the Farmers' Museum* (1801).[10] Most of his topics are predictable: quack doctors, the law, the Bible, fashions, language. He wrote "Colon & Spondee" essays with such headings as "Fine Comb Points," "Between You and I," "State of Literature in England and America, at Different Periods," and "Oilnut, or Butternut." [11] On one occasion he satirized the handbooks which oversimplify complex material by announcing a similar work for children, to be called "The Pap of Science; or, Goody B——'s Nursery Gift"; its contents, with nursery rhymes under such divisions as "Geographical Lullabies," "Cypher Candy," "Biographical Bon Bon," and "Political Sugar Plumb," recall Tyler's plans for a comic grammar.[12] Of the twenty-six "Colon & Spondee" essays in the *Spirit*, Dennie credits Tyler with fifteen, and, if the selection is at all representative, he may have written even more of the prose than is usually thought. But the sample is large enough to show that these pieces, sufficiently entertaining for space-fillers in a newspaper, do not represent Tyler's satire at its height.

Although most of Tyler's essays seem to have been literary in content, the Hall files of the *Port Folio* attribute one political satire to him.[13] Entitled "Logic," [14] it begins by announcing that "those profound logicians, Colon and Spondee," deny the effectiveness of majority rule in carrying out the will of the people. The position is not an unlikely one for a Federalist, but the ensuing argument shows that Tyler's wit transcended party lines. He "proves" in four ways that the minority should always prevail: from reason (fools make up the bulk of mankind); from experience (witness the blunders of British ministers); from expediency (the masses of men could then stay out of public affairs and tend to their own business); and from religion (only the few are to be saved, the majority damned). The essay, like others of this class, involves a triple satiric mask: the writer is seemingly serious; he constructs his argument to reveal that he is after all being playful; but there is point to the playfulness, and he does mean part of what he says.

Tyler's other prose contributions to the *Port Folio*,[15] according to the Hall files, are three essays in early 1802 in the "Colon & Spondee" series called "An Author's Evenings." [16] This series was designed (partly as a filler) to accommodate random remarks on literary figures of the past, usually accompanied with copious quotations from their works. It had begun, under the "Colon & Spondee" rubric, in the *Farmer's Weekly Museum* in 1799, and Dennie continued it for several years in the *Port Folio*. Like the "Colon & Spondee" label, it inspired imitations and parodies, such as "An Author's Moonlight Nights, from the Garret of Messrs. Lunatic and Lumbago." [17] Tyler begins his column for 21 January 1802 in the spirit of the title: "To night, after my return from the theatre, into which I sometimes saunter, to smooth the wrinkles of my brow, to surrender myself to the illusions of imagination, and derive fresh spirits for my lucubrations, I could not help reflecting. . . ." And he launches into a discussion of the "new pantomime of *Obi*," which leads into reflections on the power of magic over men's minds, references to a related magazine article, quotations from Jonson's *Masque of Queens* and from *Macbeth*, and a comparison of sorcerers' charms in different cultures.

This literary wandering is repeated on 27 February when he first quotes an "exquisite" poem from a British magazine, then quotes British critics on the subject of Sir William Jones, and finally gives a prose translation by W. Ouseley of an ode of Hafiz. He pays attention to diction and parallelism in prose no less than in poetry: Jones, he says, had the good fortune "to resist the sleep of sloth and withstand the blandishments of pleasure." Tyler also comments in this essay that he is "too laboriously engaged in *reading* poetry to have any leisure to combine a couplet." In the third of these essays (on 15 May), he is prompted, by taking up a volume of Chesterfield, to consider the usefulness of proverbs and to lament their current lack of fashion. He points out many parallels between ideas in Chesterfield and old adages and ends with a final thrust at Chesterfield: "Much more might be added, but the printer's boy calls, and I much fear, by tracing the sentiments of this polite writer to so unfashionable a source, I may destroy that relish for his works, which gives the true zest to most of his readers." As in *The Contrast*, Chesterfield represents the extreme of vicious artificiality, Tyler's perennial subject of attack, whether it occurs in the Della Cruscans or in the courtroom.

One other series of essays, under the title of "Trash," Tyler contributed to Buckingham's *Polyanthos* in 1806 and 1807.[18] In his opening column, he explains the title of this "department" as inspired by a friend who bound miscellaneous sermons and pamphlets together and labeled the spine "Trash":

Royall Tyler

Those who are too wise, grave, and learned to be *amused*, when they see my *title*, may pass my humble lucubrations — they can regale themselves on the *ripened* fruits of science; but there are many, who may wish to cheer the gloom of a stormy evening, or relieve the tedium of busy life, with what may relax without tainting the mind; and such may have a relish for TRASH.

The amusement which he offers is not without a satiric bite. After commenting on the habit of giving scriptural names to babies and after quoting an English and Latin poem signed "B.," he turns to current stage pronunciation. His own "Yankee utterance," he claims, has been "wonderfully corrected in various important particulars" during his attendance at the theater, and he composes a poem in which he attempts through spelling to "delineate the elegant tones of our more polished players." The ensuing thirty-six lines, "Love Varses to the Bucheous Daffodel," have a glossary "for the benefit of the *unlearned* reader," explaining such words as *ajore* ("adore") and *churn* ("turn").

The other "Trash" columns proceed in the same rambling way. The second is a poem, "The Town Eclogue," but the third and fourth are again essays. They illustrate Tyler's familiarity with English literature, for in the third he draws on Chaucer, Drayton, and Shakespeare as he attempts to construct realistic and unsentimental portraits of Jane Shore and Edward IV; in the fourth he surveys famous riddles of the past and quotes Wyatt's "Riddle of a Gyft by a Ladie." There is very little explicit literary criticism here, but occasionally Tyler does express a judgment, as when he comments that "Drayton seldom rises above mediocrity as a poet, and these epistles [to Jane Shore] are not among the most excellent of his labours." The most revealing passage occurs in the fourth "Trash" essay, in which Tyler recalls that Dr. Johnson found certain lines without rhyme in Dryden's Cecilia ode:

Now this is the case with all of us when we set down to criticise. We are forced to discover some defects in order to evidence that we have some penetration. But yet, great as the Doctor is, I, who am an enthusiastick admirer of the Ode, would no more thank him for his discovery, than I would the officious person who should approach me at dinner, and point out something disgusting in my favourite dish. At the literary feast, I wish to cater for myself, and an austere, captious critick is as disagreeable to me as the Physician in Don Quixotte was to Sancho Pancha, when he criticised away the best viands from the table of that governour in the island of Barataria.

Using the dining metaphor (with its allusion to the subject of his *Barrataria* play), Tyler sets forth "the acknowledged triumph of publick taste over the fastidiosity of referred criticism."

This attitude — as well as all the other elements of Tyler's newspaper essays: the random associations, the literary allusions, the graceful but detached manner — is suggestive of the gentleman who dabbles in literature, the littérateur rather than the writer. But Tyler's love of literature was real, his acquaintance with it extensive, and his concern for its standards sincere; the gentlemanly approach did not preclude satiric attacks on patent absurdities like the Della Cruscans, and the "publick taste" that would triumph was to be an informed one. For Tyler, like Dennie and other serious writers of newspaper prose, the Addisonian manner lent dignity to a calling that was not highly regarded in a new country; they could not avoid being artificial in that sense, but the basic integrity of their efforts, at the same time, was laying the foundations for an authentic native tradition.

The Yankey in London

The Yankey in London, a small volume of 180 pages printed in New York by Isaac Riley, appeared in early October 1809. Like *The Algerine Captive*, the book was issued not only anonymously but under a mask — in this case concealing Tyler even from his publisher. Throughout the spring and summer of 1809 Tyler was in correspondence with Riley about the first volume of the Vermont *Reports*, and he casually mentioned another work which he could procure; in June he sent it:

Captain Holbrook will communicate the work I mentioned some time since. He is instructed and empowered to agree with you on the terms of publication. The copy sent will, I am sensible, make but a small book; but, from the preface, you will learn it may be enlarged. The present object of those concerned is merely to feel the public pulse, by the publication of a small edition. If the thing takes, it can be extended to any size: and even the present edition, if you should so agree with Captain Holbrook, can be enlarged by a few more letters; say, ten or fifteen more pages of the manuscript. The remainder of the letters are not in Vermont, but can be commanded. To give it currency among the class of readers who will most probably purchase, the edition must be elegantly edited. If you cannot agree upon terms, I have every reliance on your word, that any concern I may have in ushering this little work into public notice, through the medium of some other press, will be scrupulously concealed.[19]

Riley pushed the work through the press ahead of the *Reports* and wrote optimistically to Tyler on 7 October:

By the mail I send you one copy of "The Yankee in London" hastily put up. Some, more handsomely bound, I shall forward soon. . . . I have to ask you to aid me in procuring the future Letters to make a more enlarged edition. I did not print but few of this, merely to get it into notice. I believe the work will have a good sale: it is however but this week before the public.[20]

The following spring, when Tyler had further ideas to suggest to Riley, he included in his letter a comment on the book: "I am exceedingly pleased with the elegant impression of the Yankee, but can say nothing as to another edition until the beginning of July, when I will write you on the subject."[21]

The secret seems to have been kept better than with Tyler's other writings, for even a Brattleboro friend, William Wells, was completely fooled, thinking that the book was an authentic account of a visit to England.[22] Tyler's wife, however, in her reminiscences, openly asserted her husband's authorship.[23]

The mask, intricate enough in Tyler's dealings with Riley, was preserved throughout the book, which becomes a kind of parody of the Tocqueville tradition of travel writing. Giving no hints, the title page merely reads, "By an American Youth." A preface, signed "The Friends of the Writer," purports to explain that the author is "a native of Boston, in Massachusetts, known to his fellow-townsmen as a young man of modest merit, and only known to a few particular friends as a gentleman of an active and inquisitive mind, and of quaint, and ofttimes original remark." He has supposedly written a series of letters from London which these "friends" have persuaded him to consent to have published, "upon the express condition of expunging such passages as might lead to a discovery of the author." The "friends" give the impression that, out of a large number of letters, the present ones have been selected so as not to offend the English; but they hope that "the approbation of the public will give confidence to our friend to publish the remainder of his letters" under his own name, and they label the collection "Volume I" (causing librarians, ever since, to stamp the card "No more published").

The pretense is even more elaborately carried out by choosing random numbers to identify the letters, suggesting that many have been left out in the intervals. Consisting of thirteen letters, the book begins with "Letter III" and ends with "Letter XLV." All but one are addressed to a friend named Frank (see pp. 27, 28, 48, 64, 150), usually referred to as "My excellent Friend," and the remaining one, on fashions in clothing, is directed to his sister. There are allusions to an Amelia (pp. 98, 99, 132), who is presumably his sweetheart, and memories of his home at Brookline (pp. 85–86). He is established as a character, whose personality reveals itself in the course of the letters as intelligent, patriotic, and somewhat naïve — not unlike Updike Underhill, though the author of these letters rarely seems to be the object of Tyler's satire, as Updike sometimes was. A final element of the mask is the appearance of editorial ellipses: proper names are given with asterisks, and, at the end of Letter XLII, there appears a note in brackets (signed "The Editors"), to the effect that "it was deemed expedient to omit" the remainder of this letter, since it "contained certain pointed observations" on English political figures (p. 143).

The epistolary device permits Tyler to write individual essays on a wide range of subjects and yet achieve unity and dramatic interest through the cumulative reactions of his letter writer. The book is sometimes classified as a novel since there is a main character visiting London and writing to a friend about it; but there is no further plot, and the emphasis of the work — a direct, not a metaphorical, exposition of ideas — is such that the more meaningful label is "essay." A quick glance at the sequence of chapters suggests the diversity of materials. Letter III discusses traits of the English character and literary fashions, followed by two (V and VIII) on the Houses of Parliament and one (XI) on English biographical writing. This leads, in Letter XIX, to the subject of books and etymology; Letter XX returns to the House of Commons, with remarks on the merits of seriousness. The next two letters deal with fashions — in clothing (XXIII) and in language (XXX) — and the following two with deception (literary forgery in XXXIII and quacks in XLII). Finally there are further strictures on the English character (XLIII), on travelers (XLIV), and on the English language (XLV).

Essayist

The unity of the book comes not only through the constant presence of the letter writer but through his interest in two dominant concerns. In the vein of *The Contrast* and *The Algerine Captive*, every subject discussed in *The Yankey in London* contributes directly or by implication to two propositions: first, that America is a glorious place, with a proud heritage and a promising future; second, that hypocrisy and artifice irrationally govern the lives of many supposedly rational beings. The satirist's exposure of man's folly is again joined with the patriot's desire to improve his country. English habits and institutions are compared unfavorably with those of Americans; and the existence of quacks, of slang, and of rapidly shifting fashions is testimony to the sway of artificiality over naturalness. Letter VIII could perhaps furnish the motto: "let us, my friend, endeavour to guard against the delusions of forms, and look to the essence of that national liberty for which our fathers successfully fought" (p. 45).

Rarely does the application to the United States have to be inferred. When a London bookseller discovers that the author can quote the classics, he is prompted to observe that "the country of Franklin, Adams, and Jefferson, must produce scientific men. Sir, you were born in a new world; every thing there evinces the vigour of youth; Europe, sir, I fear, is in her dotage. — You have withstood our arms, and, I fear, will soon rival us in the arts and sciences" (p. 72). The patriotism is broad enough to encompass England as part of the American heritage; yet current practices in the British government make one ashamed: "I felt the dignity of my nature violated. I felt more — I remembered I was of English descent, and I blushed for the land of my ancestors" (pp. 27–28). This patriotism, however, should not be blind; it is natural, the author says, to be patriotic, but there are proper limits, and English vanity goes beyond them in assuming that people in all other countries must be wretched. He takes his illustration from the weather: the English are proud of their climate (which, to an American, "presents, every day, an apology for suicide"), but a bright, sunny American day "is one of those few common blessings which the Bostonians have sensibility to relish" (pp. 157–158). To argue that the superiority of America extends even to its atmospheric conditions may suggest that the letter writer has a touch of the national vanity he is condemning; but he is generally frank in acknowledging America's faults and here implies that Americans often do not have the perception to recognize their strengths.

As one might expect, the British government is one of his prime examples to show, by contrast, the superiority of the United States. Letter V, describing his visit to the House of Commons, provides one of the best instances of the naïve approach. "I justly expected," he says, "to find the talents, the learning, the wisdom and political science of a wise nation collected in one brilliant focus" (p. 18), but he is disappointed. When he overhears one member say, in reference to a horse race, "Creeper against Sweeper, feather weight," he reacts with a characteristic comic device: "I was so simple that, at first, I thought the learned Creeper might have written a commentary on Smith's wealth of nations, and that the erudite Sweeper had illustrated Dr. Price's essay on finance, by the negative quantities of algebra. *Feather weight*, I naturally concluded, alluded to the balance of power in Europe" (p. 20). His uncertainty "whether to laugh or weep" is repeated when he gets to the House of Lords (Letter VIII), where he also manifests a certain objectivity about American institutions. Although the idea of a hereditary legislature contains "something essentially ludicrous to the mind of a republican" (p. 35), a hereditary court (the Lords were judging a case at the time) "might provoke the risibility of even

Littleton himself": "This baronial bench seemed to me even more absurd than the court of errors in the state of Connecticut, where the council of that state, composed generally of plain farmers, correct the judgments of their supreme court, composed of men of the first legal talents" (pp. 35–36). This is a natural point of view for Tyler the lawyer, but he has his letter writer recommend such a common-sense court for England, where an exaggerated respect for precedents and forms is destroying the spirit of the common law, the Britons' "richest legacy, to their posterity" (p. 45). When his correspondent objects that he has been too harsh, he replies (Letter XX) that the frivolity and facetiousness found in the House of Commons are never among the qualities of great men; decorum and gravity are the essential marks of greatness, and for proof he has only to point to the dignified group of men who produced the American Declaration of Independence (p. 81).

If the British government deserves criticism, so do the British national traits, but again not without some penetrating comments on the American character. The author remarks, in his opening letter (III), on British "national reserve and hauteur," shyness, and class consciousness (pp. 4–6), but proceeds as usual to make the comparison with America explicit:

> The difference between the English and their American descendants, in this particular, is — the Englishman is shy and suspicious, grows more suspicious, and is surly. The New-England man is suspicious and inquisitive, grows more suspicious, and is familiar and troublesome. When once the Englishman's suspicions are dissipated (no matter how) he is unbounded in his confidence; while the Yankey shews very little distrust, is never silent or surly to the stranger, but his suspicions never leave him. (p. 6)

Vanity, however, is the most prominent trait applicable to all classes in England (Letter XLIII), and government is "the

gas which inflates the full-blown bladder of English vanity"
— a government, based on "commercial aggrandizement,"
with laws too complex to guide behavior and with a criminal
code so harsh that it "violates the moral sense of justice"
(p. 154). Despite these weaknesses, the English expect all
other countries to see the superior merits of their form of
government and imagine that other countries cannot win
battles without their support. One Englishman, proud of
Britain's "dense and sombre" fogs, was made ill by Boston's
clear weather and had to shut himself in a room with a damp
coal fire (p. 160). This vanity is also seen in such phrases as
"English courage," but Tyler's writer finds "English bull
dogs" the most apt illustration. The trait, he says, leads to
prejudice against foreigners and the association of certain
habits with particular nations.

The generalizing in this letter has been doing that very
thing — classifying a nationality; but the letter writer explains
that he would not be above the level of the English traveler
if he had intended all his comments seriously. This awkward
conclusion to Letter XLIII raises more problems than it
solves, for the contradiction, obviously, is still there. Either
Tyler is engaging in subtle irony at the expense of his letter
writer; or he is identifying himself with the letter writer at
the cost of the logic and forcefulness of his argument. Here
is the same confusion in the use of a persona that came up in
The Algerine Captive. But part of the irony directed at Updike was based on his behavior in various episodes, as he reported it; in the present instance one has only the comments,
not the behavior, to look at, for the letter writer tells us not
what he has done but only what he thinks. Since his opinions
at most times are straightforward expressions of Tyler's own,
there is no reason, in the context of the book, for not accept-
ing at face value these closing remarks in Letter XLIII. The
letter writer says that he has made friends among the English

and that England does have things to be proud of. Tyler no doubt imagined that a show of broadmindedness would strengthen his other criticisms; but, having created a mask, he at least opened the possibility for a moment that he was also exposing American narrowmindedness.

The subject of national traits leads to the third major topic of the book — fashions — when we are told that one of the Englishman's desires is not only national glory but individual glory. He attempts to achieve personal distinction by adopting eccentricities, which eventually are imitated by others. One man "cut off the skirts of his coat, close to his waistband, and set the fashion you now have in Boston, called the spencer," while another "*eat a live cat*" (p. 9). The principal discussion of fashion, in Letter XXIII, emphasizes its changeability and unnaturalness. The writer predicts that, if he should attempt to describe the current styles, the information would be obsolete by the time the letter arrived; but such changes are essential since many people's incomes depend on them. Fashions pass down from the upper classes to the lower, and then to the United States; when a manufacturer wants to revive something, he persuades the royal family to wear it and it becomes common. This entire diatribe is part of a larger concern with artificiality, and chief among the criticisms of fashion is that it seems unrelated to beauty and to climate. Tyler's gift for comic elaboration helps him to explain the appearance of a modish, but excessively thin, shawl by comparing it to wet drapery in statuary, at the same time pointing out the dearth of statuary in America:

Next washing-day, if you will quit your piano-forte and follow Betty into the clothes'-yard, and direct her to cover one of the old red posts with muslin dripping from the wash-tub, you will have a distinct idea of wet drapery, and, if you have the eye of a connoisseur, will certainly notice that, although the post is completely enveloped, yet, none of the beauties of its fine form are lost. (p. 92)

Fashion is the "conqueror of decorum, modesty, beauty, and health," and the letter writer tells his sister that she could come to London dressed as an Indian and "set the fashion at court." He has had some suits sent to her, along with "a turban or cap which, as it is very gaudy, very odd, and extremely homely, I conclude must be very fashionable" (p. 99). As a parting thought, he cautions her, when wearing the new clothes, not to expose herself to the evening air, "especially after dancing."

There are fashions in all things, not merely clothing, and in every case they result from a thoughtless preference for the artificial over the natural. Quacks of all kinds (Letter XLII) flourish by appealing to man's irrationality, and in England "the belief in panaceas is a national weakness" (p. 133). For example, there are mechanical quacks who insist, "with grave effrontery," that their arms and legs are superior to natural ones and are so eloquent that they "had almost persuaded me to submit to amputation" (p. 139). One manufacturer of glass eyes asserts that "they excel the natural in displaying the finer and nobler emotions of the soul" (p. 136), and cites the testimonial of a man who met his wife through the attraction to such eyes:

[He was] peculiarly impressed with the fascinating glances of her brilliant eyes: upon after acquaintance, although he was not insensible to the expression and good sense which beamed from her right eye, yet, the mild serenity of the left gave such happy presage of that suavity of temper which promised a plenteous harvest of conjugal peace. (pp. 137–138)

Tyler is unrelenting in his ridicule of affectation, whether it is Dimple worshiping Chesterfield, the Bishop of Cloyne drinking tar-water, or a West Indian praising his cork leg. There are even culinary quacks, and a cookbook by John Perkins, linking alphabetically foods and diseases ("Apple-pye and Asthma," "Pickles and Piles," "Ragouts and Rheumatism"),

Tyler's letter writer wittily imagines to be "an ethical work, exhibiting the dreadful consequences of a life devoted to intemperance" (p. 142). But the evils of affectation are not overlooked when they occur in an American, and the brief Letter XLIV exposes the folly of a young Bostonian in London, dressed in the latest fashions, spending a great deal of money, and visiting all the tourist attractions ("he went to see a man who eat himself, but found this was a joke," p. 169). This young man is important enough, as an illustration of the superficiality of most travelers, that he is referred to again (spending his money) in the final lines of the book, a postscript to the last letter.

A fourth main topic of the volume — language and literature — perhaps bulks largest and is by no means unrelated to the question of fashion. There are literary quacks (forgers and perpetrators of hoaxes); there are slang phrases adopted by everyone as the proper things to say; there are styles of writing, decidedly not natural, which make their authors popular. Enough is said on these subjects here, even if we did not have the satire in *The Contrast*, *The Algerine Captive*, and the newspaper poetry, that we should still know where Tyler stands on literary questions. His position emerges obliquely from the cynical discussion of literary "larceny" in Letter XXXIII. After relating the stories of Chatterton, Ireland, and Ossian, he asks why, if they had such genius of imitation, they are not honored. These men, he says, were more modest than Michaelangelo, since he revealed his imitation of classic work; but literature is a trade in England, and the English do not want to admit that their great writers can be equaled. Furthermore, "as most of their modern books are made up by plagiarisms from old works, the English book-makers are admirably qualified to detect literary fraud" (p. 126). After this double irony, he turns, still with tongue in cheek, to "our happy land," where Americans "prize books, as the principles of our excellent republican government teach us to value men, not for their origin but their intrinsic merit" (p. 132).

Tyler's interest in writing manifests itself throughout his work in a concern with language, and his keen observation of linguistic habits appears again and again in *The Yankey in London*.[24] He tries to record dialect (p. 39) and observes several differences in diction between England and New England (pp. 104–109); he remarks on phrases like "certain people" (p. 7), "smoked the quiz" (p. 141), and "Yankey" — a corruption of "Yorkshire," as pronounced by the Indians (p. 75) — in letters that are otherwise not on linguistic subjects. But two letters in particular, XXX and XLV, show that Tyler gave a good deal of serious thought to language. At first glance they seem to contradict one another. The first attacks current slang phrases as "*scoria* floating on the English language" (p. 101) and deplores the fact that "there are a number of words now familiar, not merely in transient converse, but even in English fine writing, which are of vulgar origin and illegitimate descent, which disgust an admirer of the writers of their Augustan age, and degrade their finest modern compositions by a grotesque air of pert vivacity" (p. 103). Among such words, the most objectionable is "clever," "not derived from those pure and rich sources which have given all that is valuable in the English language." To set against this prescriptive attitude are the sentiments of Letter XLV:

Indeed, the perfectibility of language is as ridiculous as the perfectibility of man. Language, as pertaining to man, partakes of the laws of our nature: it is ever changing; it has the incoherency and simplicity of youth, the vigour of manhood, and the decline and decrepitude of old age. This has been its fate in all ages: it has begun in barbarism; had its age of elegance and refinement, and became nerveless and weak. (p. 175)

Here are the rudiments of a scientific approach to language, not disentangled from prescriptive considerations. Though modern linguists would not agree with Tyler that his own period represented a "decline" in language, they could join him in pointing out the futility of national academies and in saying, "New discoveries will call for new terms to express novel ideas" (p. 177). Tyler is aware of the way in which language changes (even if his discussion is occasionally confused), and his earlier strictures on slang are more concerned with the slavish and unthinking repetition of fashionable phrases than with an attempt to keep language "pure" — directed more at warning writers to avoid clichés than constructing a theory of language.

His comments on language are part of his argument against artificiality and are related to matters of literary taste. One of the marks of the deplorable taste of the English, according to the letter writer, is the kind of biography they currently produce (Letter XI). He believes that lives of great men should be instructive and inspiring; he admires Dr. Burnet's account of the Earl of Rochester because every sentence is a "homily" (p. 53). Recent biographies, however, follow their subjects in their most trivial daily activities, reveal their infirmities, and are "not only disreputable to the subjects of them but injurious to the cause of virtue" (p. 56). One might guess that "the lives of most of the eminent men in England were written by their valets, or rather by their grooms or scullions" (p. 54); it is as if West, instead of painting William III mounted on his horse, had chosen to show him in his water closet with a bellyache: "Oh, it is vile! it is descending from the dignity of the biographer, to expose the infirmities of the wise for the gratification of the idle; to patch the venerable garb of wisdom with the motley of Harlequin, and hold it forth as a laughing stock for folly" (p. 58). Dr. Johnson, the writer continues, set the fashion for such "gossiping biography" and has now been paid back with three of the same kind written about him, the one with the largest amount of irrelevant material being Boswell's. The *Gentleman's Magazine* also furnishes an illustration of the trivial when it publishes the life of a man who "was remarkable for having never used but one pen during this period [of forty years], which was made of a gray goose-quill" (p. 62). This moralistic theory of biography therefore condemns the memoirs of prostitutes and suggests that prosecution of the printers of "these apologies for pollution" makes more sense than the imprisonment of those who publish pamphlets against the ministry, since their crime, "in the next administration, may be considered a virtue" (p. 66).

Such a remark shows that, however much Tyler approved of the didactic in biography, his major concern was with the devastating effects of fashion on taste and discrimination. His most energetic efforts were always, as in the satiric poetry, directed against the sentimentalists, the Della Cruscans, and the structure of fashion that supported them. "I ask for elegant wit," he says in Letter XLV, "and they hand me Peter Pindar — I inquire for sublimity, and they present me Della Crusca" (p. 179). This is placed at the end of the book to recall the reader to a brilliant passage at the beginning that sums up the criticism, social as well as literary, of the whole work:

Then, my dear Chum, if you wish an introduction, carry with you no letter of civility, but hasten to your ink-pot, tag me a hundred lines to some languishing Anna Matilda, or dying Dorinda; spangle them well with bland metaphors and love-lorn similies; drop a word or two in some lines, and insert others in capital letters, so as to render the meaning unintelligible, and then, of course, you know it must be sublime: or write a lugubrious sonnet to some captive mouse, or pretty pathetic ode to a sportive mouser,

Essayist

> Who on the bosom of the spangled eve,
> With velvet step and deeply dulcet breath,
> PURS for his attic love! —

select some sweet fanciful name . . . such as Valentina Orsona, Assenella Crusca, or Idiotilla, or any other name more significant of the attributes of your muse; carry the soft effusions of your melancholy muse to the editors of the most fashionable magazine; and, after you have *love-lorned* enough to make a little volume of verse, publish your works, boldly, under your own name . . . and then inscribe your volume to the honourable, or right honourable, Mrs. ———, the patroness of some blue-stocking club, beginning your dedication thus: — "Madam, your exalted genius, correct taste, and elegant knowledge of ancient and modern learning, so richly displayed in that incomparable poem, your devine ode to the sleeping Cicada," &c. &c. &c. . . . Then, if you are not the most unfortunate wight of a poet who ever attempted the temple of fame, you will be invited to the club, be enrolled as a member, and, perhaps, have your name immortalized in the next Ladies' Day. (pp. 12–14)

The reader is provided at the outset with a frame of reference, a set of values, and all the succeeding letters fall in place. The arrangement of material may seem casual, as it should in a book of letters, but a plan is there.

When one reads of wits as "the cicada of literature, who chirp away the summer and starve in the winter of life" (p. 79), the word "cicada" has taken on added associations from the opening passage; and when one hears a politician "point out this defective plank in the vessel of the commonwealth, and drag from their lurking-holes those pestiferous worms who are gnawing the foundations of the constitution" (p. 24), one knows that Della Crusca has become a statesman. There is not a great deal of formal organization of the individual essays, and like actual letters they may introduce secondary subjects, more briefly treated, near the end; the over-all arrangement, too, from government through books to clothing and back to literary matters and national character, is intended to suggest the random order of selected letters rather than formal argument. What is carefully planned, however, is that the seeming casualness shall add up to something in the end: all the letters do contribute toward a consistent and coherent point of view. The book's brevity is part of its effectiveness, for the letter writer's attitude has been so firmly established in those pages that one can infer what his reactions would be to other topics not discussed.

In this process, the style, no less than the attitudes themselves, is central. Some of Tyler's best flights of humorous fancy, with brisk and lively movement, occur in these pages. Every letter unobtrusively furnishes its epigram or flash of wit: "After a while [in the House of Commons] something like silence (which, however, would be called an uproar in any decent assembly) was produced" (pp. 25–26); the Lords discussed "a subject abstruse in itself, and rendered more so by the eloquence of the learned counsel" (p. 40); "let precedents govern if justice is trampled upon" (pp. 42–43); in regard to biographies of prostitutes, Constantia Philips is "the mistress of this school," but her followers have gone so far that "her infamous memoirs may be considered, in a comparative view, as an ethical work written expressly for the promotion of virtue" (p. 65). Tyler's similes are fresh and occasionally arise from his own interests — the theater and the law. The House of Lords, compared to the House of Commons, is "what the Opera-house is to Drury-lane theatre. . . . but, then, even an opera is not without its absurdities. . . . [exhibiting] heroes in recitative, dancing princes, and British lions" (p. 34). Boswell's inclusion of trivial details reminds Tyler of the question of immaterial facts in court: "Were a man called to testify to a contract . . . he would not be guilty of perjury should he omit to relate that one of the contracting parties, on his way to the court, had fallen into a jakes" (p. 56). Tyler's literary knowledge appears in classical allusions (as on pp. 26, 78, 112) and quotations from Pope (pp. 29, 88, 105), Stern (p. 78), Addison (p. 4), Shakespeare (pp. 49, 86), and other English authors. That the style is functional the letter writer himself suggests in Letter VIII, describing lords speaking:

> If the first was Somnus, the second was father Nox himself; — eldest night — ere Satan, that Brindsley of Milton, had canalled chaos, and built a bridge and rail-way o'er the "wide abyss," for the transportation of original sin into paradise. — Pardon the magnificence of my metaphor, my excellent friend; remember I am in training for the honours of a blue-stocking club. (p. 39)

If a dull and imitative style is indicative of a lack of taste and judgment, reflecting ultimately on the character of a whole people, then a series of letters addressed to a young republic must be particularly careful, not simply to assert, but to demonstrate what is good and what is bad. For that reason, the letter writer more effectively expresses the same ideals as Jonathan, Manly, and Updike, and his book deserves the labels which have been applied to it: "tour de force" and "minor classic." [25] The style and content of *The Yankey in London* are one.

"The Bay Boy"

If *The Yankey in London* illustrates Tyler's perennial experimentation with ways of revealing the native American character, one of his unfinished manuscripts gives even greater evidence of his progression toward a more direct portrayal of the American experience. Entitled "The Bay Boy," this work is a revision of the early chapters of *The Algerine Captive*, making more extensive use of details drawn from Tyler's own youth in Boston. Such a book had been promised in the sixteenth chapter of *The Algerine Captive*:

> The remarks I made upon this hospitable, busy, national, town born people; my observations upon their manners, habits, local virtues, customs, and prejudices; the elocution of their principal clergymen; with anecdotes of publick characters, I deal not in

private foibles; and a comparative view of their manners, at the beginning, and near the close of the eighteenth century, are pronounced, by the partiality of some friends, to be original, and to those who know the town, highly interesting. If this home-spun history of private life, shall be approved, these remarks will be published by themselves in a future edition of this work. (I, 124–125)

An accurate description of the content of "The Bay Boy," this passage also suggests that at least parts of it were already written in 1797. But it was this manuscript which occupied much of Tyler's time during his last years, and whether his labors were then revision or original composition is difficult to say. Tyler's wife, in her diary entry for 22 April 1825, wrote, "Began copying *Bay Boy* for the press." [26] The version which survives is not complete, consisting of thirteen main sections (119 pages) and five smaller fragments, only roughly arranged into chapters and often without transitions between them. Much of the material presented in *The Algerine Captive* in short chapters is consolidated, much reappears verbatim (chapters 5–11), some (the first four chapters, for example) is omitted, and a great deal (in local detail) is added.[27] Whatever the course of composition, Tyler recognized the greater value of volume I of *The Algerine Captive* and saw in it the only path that a native literature could take.

"The Bay Boy" perhaps should be considered a novel rather than an essay, for it does repeat episodes from an earlier novel and presents a larger number of characters. But it is more accurately an autobiography written in the third person — "this home-spun history of private life." Updike is still the hero, but the focus is not so much on what he does as on what he sees; the account is descriptive first and narrative second. The reader remembers, not the activities Updike engages in, but the flavor of a New England Sunday, the celebrations of Thanksgiving and Christmas, a Twelfth Night ball, a Commencement Day, a Revolutionary political discussion, and the hazards of early theatrical productions in Bos-

ton; he remembers detailed portraits of historical figures, like
Dr. Sylvester Gardiner or the Reverend Henry Caner,[28] and
vivid sketches of types, such as the young boy in love or the
hypochondriac old lady. Satire is still present, but there are
two additional elements which mark an advance over *The
Algerine Captive*. One is deeper characterization, involving
both psychological insight and precise detail; the other, possibly the result of Tyler's late revisions, is a mellowness and
warmth, a nostalgia mixed with amusement. Updike's mother,
for example, before her marriage "began to show evident
signs of veteran maidenhood, was more and more attentive
to her Parrot, made daily assignations with the tabby cat, and
could not abide the noise of children." Another woman, Mrs.
Diaway (whose parlor is described in concrete detail) spent
her time in bed, "her head covered by mob caps tier over
tier and the whole surmounted by a cambrick handkerchief
which she occasionally shifted, as if to guard against the rude
contact of some wandering zephyr"; she "languidly pointed"
to a chair and "ordered the servant with a shiver to close
the door immediately" when Updike visited her on his first
professional call as a physician.

Tyler retains the fictional thread of a physician-hero, which
gives the account an emotional distance that might have been
difficult in a straight autobiography. The nostalgic passages are
by no means sentimental: witness the description of the drowsy
congregation at a Sunday afternoon service (quoted in Chapter 1) or of the young hero when he thinks he is in love. Updike watches a girl each Sunday in church, only to find when
he returns home to eat that "the first mouthful of goose stuck
in my throat, could no more swallow than if a whole dumpling was sticking in my gullet — could not think what ailed
me, never suspected I was in love." But soon he visits the family that employs the girl and sees her in old clothes, "her hair
unkempt and the big drops of perspiration occasioned by her
labors, standing upon her forehead or trickling in dingy chan-

nels down her neck. . . . The charm of first love was broken." This realism is constantly present, and it rests on a solid foundation of physical details, set forth in language full of colloquialisms.[29] These fragments suggest that Tyler was well on his way toward producing an organically American work, native in content, attitude, and expression. It is entirely possible that "The Bay Boy," if completed as begun, would have ranked with *The Contrast* in reputation; at any rate it represented the next step. Tyler knew where *The Contrast* was leading, even if he never arrived there.

One reason for the relative success of "The Bay Boy" is undoubtedly that it was revised late in Tyler's life and could benefit from a more mature point of view, a knowledge of human nature gleaned from several decades in the courtroom; but another reason is that it was revised at all. Most of Tyler's work was hastily written, dashed off at a moment's notice. The legend of Tyler's speed in composing *The Contrast*, and Nancrede's reference to the "Moral Tales" as "eight days' amusement," are suggestive of a central fact about Tyler's literary labor. Dennie, no deliberate worker himself, continually admonished Tyler to be less hasty:

You appear to proceed in any literary undertaking with a lover's ardor. Be not too impatient; hurry in writing and over-weening zeal with the fair, are both dangerous. Horace, and the rest of those dull fellows, advise slowness in composition; but I know thy pride, and the naughtiness of thy heart. . . . you shall give me your Royal word not to write a play in less time than I have dictated this sentence. If you are determined to Lope-de-vega it, and write 100 lines upon one leg — why then, to conclude dramatically with Capt. Cape, "Dam'me, I'm off."

In another of his charming letters, Dennie referred to Tyler's "galloping consumption of ink." [30] The productions of Tyler's pen, it is all too evident, are not the carefully wrought creations of a painstaking craftsman, and it is both superfluous and irrelevant to criticize them for failing to meet the highest tests of literary art. Their importance lies elsewhere, and it is the very speed of their composition, curiously enough, which points the direction.

Tyler's writings are the products of brief idle moments between the rounds of circuit-riding and legal business. "The Bay Boy" is instructive because it shows the older man with leisure changing the proportions and emphases of what he had written hastily in his younger years. Tyler's whole career is similarly instructive because it epitomizes the position of the writer in the early years of the republic. Dennie put the problem in these terms: "I think it hard, Royall, when I am actually industrious & disposed to exercise regularly peculiar talents, that I can not obtain bread and wine." [31] Tyler was more successful than Dennie in solving the dilemma, since he was more willing to put writing in second place and devote his energies to interpreting "unintelligible law to Green Mountain jurors"; but this solution was hard-won, and more doubts crossed his mind than Mary Tyler was ever aware of. He did find time to write fiction, drama, verse, and essay, but he was not a man of letters. He was an intelligent man, however, with an active and vigorous mind, and when he wrote he expressed the spirit of his own time and place. To such a man, it seemed only the natural thing to do, but for that reason he could not fully comprehend that his Jonathan and his Updike were of greater significance for the cultural development of the nation than all the self-conscious pleas for a native literature which he, and others before him, had uttered. If his "abilities . . . in this wooden world" are to be "esteemed above mediocrity," it is precisely because of those "sonnets to rustic loves, and tales for children" which he disparaged. He could not avoid speaking in the idiom of the age, but he instinctively sensed what lay beyond it. In this is his proper praise.

Chronology

1757 Royall Tyler born in Boston on 18 July, second son and fourth child of Royall and Mary Steele Tyler; originally named William Clark Tyler.

1776 Graduated from Harvard; also received B.A. from Yale. Began study of law with Francis Dana.

1778 Served as aide to General Sullivan, with rank of Major, in the Battle of Rhode Island, August.

1779 Received M.A. from Harvard.

1780 Admitted to bar, 19 August.

1785 Love affair with Abigail Adams ended.

1787 Served as aide to General Lincoln in the attempt to capture the insurgents in Shays' Rebellion, January–March; arrived in New York on this mission, 12 March.
      The Contrast performed at John Street Theatre, New York, 16 April.
      May Day in Town performed, 19 May.

1790 *The Contrast* published, May.
      Moved to Vermont, settling in Guilford in 1791.

1793 *The Origin of Evil* published.

1794 Became State's Attorney for Windham County (through 1801). Married Mary Hunt Palmer at Framingham, Massachusetts, May.
      Literary partnership with Joseph Dennie, as "Colon & Spondee," began, July; contributions to Dartmouth *Eagle* and *Federal Orrery*.

1796 Contributions to *Newhampshire and Vermont Journal* began.

1797 *The Algerine Captive* published, August.
      The Georgia Spec performed in Boston, 30 October.

1800 *Oration* on George Washington published, March.

1801 Moved to Brattleboro, 3 March.
      Became an Assistant Judge of Vermont Supreme Court.
      The Spirit of the Farmers' Museum published, containing many of Tyler's periodical contributions.

Chronology

Selected Bibliography

PRIMARY SOURCES

Books, Pamphlets, and Broadsides

The Contrast. A Comedy. Philadelphia: Prichard & Hall, 1790. Reprinted by the Dunlap Society (New York, 1887), with an introduction by Thomas J. McKee, and in a limited edition (Boston: Houghton Mifflin, 1920), edited by James B. Wilbur, with an introduction by Helen Tyler Brown (reviewed by H. S. Wardner in *Vermonter*, XXVI [February 1921], 40–41). Reprinted also in Arthur Hobson Quinn, *Representative American Plays* (New York: Appleton, 1917); Montrose J. Moses, *Representative Plays by American Dramatists* (New York: Dutton, 1918); Robert E. Spiller, *The Roots of National Culture* (New York: Macmillan, 1933); Allan G. Halline, *American Plays* (New York: American Book Company, 1935); Edwin H. Cady, *Literature of the Early Republic* (New York: Rinehart, 1950); Alan S. Downer, *American Drama* (New York: Crowell, 1960); Milton R. Stern and Seymour L. Gross, *Viking Portable Library American Literature Survey*, volume I (New York: Viking, 1962); and Richard Moody, *Dramas from the American Theatre 1762–1909* (Cleveland: World Publishing Company, 1966).

The Origin of Evil. An Elegy. N.p., 1793.

A Christmas Hymn . . . Sung at Claremont, N.H. 1793. Broadside.

The Algerine Captive; or, the Life and Adventures of Doctor Updike Underhill: Six years a prisoner among the Algerines. 2 vols. Walpole, N.H.: David Carlisle, 1797. Reprinted in two volumes by G. and J. Robinson (London, 1802); in the *Lady's Magazine* (London), XXXV (1804); and in one volume by Peter B. Gleason (Hartford, 1816).

Convivial Song, Sung at Windsor, on the Evening of the Fourth of July. Broadside, 1799.

An Oration, Pronounced at Bennington, Vermont, . . . In Commemoration of the Death of General George Washington. Walpole, N.H.: Printed for Thomas & Thomas by David Carlisle, 1800.

The Trial of Cyrus B. Dean, For the Murder of Jonathan Ormsby and Asa Marsh. Burlington, Vt.: Samuel Mills, 1808.

Selected Bibliography

The Yankey in London, Being the First Part of a Series of Letters Written By an American Youth, During Nine Months' Residence in the City of London. New York: Isaac Riley, 1809.

Reports of Cases Argued and Determined in the Supreme Court of Judicature of the State of Vermont [1800–1803]. 2 vols. New York: Isaac Riley, 1809–1810. Reprinted, with annotation, by the West Publishing Company (St. Paul, Minn., 1888).

A Valedictory Address . . . at the Quarterly Examination of Miss Peck's Select School. Broadside, 1823.

The Chestnut Tree, Or a Sketch of Brattleborough (East Village) At the Close of the Twentieth Century, Being an Address to a Horse Chestnut Presented to the Author by the Rev. A. L. Baury. North Montpelier, Vt.: Driftwind Press, 1931.

Four Plays, ed. Arthur Wallace Peach and George Floyd Newbrough (volume 15 of "America's Lost Plays," ed. Barrett H. Clark). Princeton: University Press, 1941. Reprinted by the Indiana University Press (Bloomington, 1965), bound with volume 16 of the series.

The Verse of Royall Tyler, ed. Marius B. Péladeau. Charlottesville: University Press of Virginia, 1967. Issued also in the *Publications of the Colonial Society of Massachusetts,* XLIV (1967).

Contributions to Periodicals

Because Tyler's many poems and essays appeared anonymously in scattered newspapers and magazines over a number of years, no entirely satisfactory record of them has yet been compiled. The fullest is the list of Tyler's poems in the Péladeau thesis (pp. 266–272), or its revised version in his 1967 edition. Periodical references to the poems and essays mentioned in the present study are given in the Notes. The principal periodicals to which Tyler contributed (with the years, roughly, of his original contributions) are as follows: *Eagle, or Dartmouth Centinel* (1794); Boston *Federal Orrery* (1794–1795); Boston *Tablet* (1795); Walpole (N.H.) *Newhampshire and Vermont Journal, or The Farmer's Weekly Museum* (1796–1799); *Port Folio* (1801–1804); *Polyanthos* (1806–1807).

A large selection of Tyler's poems and essays (particularly in the "Colon & Spondee" column) is reprinted in *The Spirit of the Farmers' Museum* (Walpole: Printed for Thomas & Thomas by D. & T. Carlisle, 1801). Periodical pieces have also been included in the following: Samuel Kettell, *Specimens of American Poetry* (3 vols.; Boston: S. G. Goodrich, 1829); Joseph T. Buckingham, *Specimens of Newspaper Literature* (2 vols.; Boston: Redding, 1850); E. A. and G. L. Duyckinck, *Cyclopaedia of American Literature* (2 vols.; Philadelphia: Rutter, 1855); A. M. Hemenway, *Poets and Poetry of Ver-*

Selected Bibliography

mont (Rutland: Tuttle, 1858); E. C. Stedman and E. M. Hutchinson, *A Library of American Literature*, volume IV (New York: Webster, 1888); Burton E. Stevenson, *Poems of American History* (Boston: Houghton Mifflin, 1908); Walter J. Coates, *Favorite Vermont Poems, Series One* (North Montpelier: Driftwind, 1928), *Series Five* (1934); W. J. Coates and Frederick Tupper, *Vermont Verse: An Anthology* (Brattleboro: Stephen Daye Press, 1932); Louis Untermeyer and Carter Davidson, *Poetry: Its Appreciation and Enjoyment* (New York: Harcourt, Brace, 1934); Louis Untermeyer, *Early American Poets* (New York: Library Publishers, 1952); Karl Kroeber and John O. Lyons, *Studying Poetry* (New York: Harper & Row, 1965); George F. Horner and Robert A. Bain, *Colonial and Federalist American Writing* (New York: Odyssey Press, 1966).

Manuscripts

The only extensive collection of manuscript material relating to Royall Tyler is the Tyler family papers at the Vermont Historical Society. The Royall Tyler Collection (Gift of Helen Tyler Brown) consists principally of ten boxes, some of the contents of which are as follows:

Box 45 — typescripts of "The Bay Boy," the sacred dramas, the Washington oration, a Christmas sermon, "Utile Dulci," and miscellaneous poems, along with correspondence about *Grandmother Tyler's Book* and *The Chestnut Tree*, Mary Tyler's later diary, and copies of some Tyler letters.

Box 46 — material gathered by Helen Tyler Brown in her research, and letters from Mary Tyler to Royall.

Box 47 — notebooks and scrapbooks of Thomas P. and Gertrude Tyler.

Boxes 48–49 — mainly printed material.

Box 50 — letters and papers of Helen Tyler Brown, a typescript of *The Island of Barrataria*, and a handwritten copy of Thomas P. Tyler's memoir of his father.

Box 51 — galley proofs and other material connected with the publication of *Grandmother Tyler's Book*, and Tyler family correspondence of the nineteenth century.

Box 52 — Brown family papers.

Box 77 — Helen Tyler Brown's Boston researches, and another typescript of "The Bay Boy."

Box 78 — correspondence of Helen Tyler Brown in the 1910's and 1920's.

The Vermont Historical Society has certain other Tyler material — notably a typescript of the T. P. Tyler memoir, a handwritten copy of *The Chestnut Tree*, a group of documents relating to Shays' Rebellion, and numerous photostatic copies of relevant papers.

Other libraries have a few Tyler letters or documents:

The Boston Public Library — four letters from Tyler (to John S. Tyler, May 1814, 1 December 1814; two others to unidentified correspondents, probably of 1807); ten letters to Tyler (from Joseph T. Buckingham, 14 March 1820; Stephen R. Bradley, 27 January 1810; Martin Field, 28 October 1816; Samuel L. Knapp, 7 January 1820; Jonathan Robinson, 31 January 1811; David Tracy, 25 October 1808, 19 July 1812; J. S. Tyler, 11 December 1811; Mary Tyler, 30 December 1810, 28 January 1811); four juvenile poems in manuscript; four legal documents signed by Tyler (November 1796, 15 October 1807, 30 July 1808, 25 October 1810).

William L. Clements Library — two documents signed by Tyler (11 February 1808, 1–2 February 1809).

Columbia University Library — one letter from Tyler (to Jonathan Robinson, 5 June 1812); one letter to Tyler (from Jonathan Robinson, 1 December 1811); two documents signed by Tyler (March 1794, 5 March 1802).

Dartmouth College Library — one letter from Tyler (to Jonathan Hunt, 24 December 1798).

Haverford College Library — one letter from Tyler (to an unidentified correspondent, 21 February 1787).

Houghton Library, Harvard University — one document signed by Tyler (2 August 1808).

Massachusetts Historical Society (Adams Papers) — four letters from Tyler (to Abigail Adams, 13 October 1785; to John Adams, 13 January, 27 August 1784, 15 October 1785); three letters to Tyler (from Abigail Adams, 4 January 1785; John Adams, 3 April 1784, 12 December 1785).

Massachusetts State Archives — one letter from Tyler (to Benjamin Lincoln, 18 February 1787); three reports by Tyler about Shays' Rebellion (13, 17 February, 6 March 1787).

New Hampshire Historical Society — two letters from Tyler (to Joseph Dennie, 9 September [1794], 7 October 1795); one letter to Tyler (from Jonathan Robinson, 21 July 1811).

The New-York Historical Society — one letter to Tyler (from Russell Fitch, 15 January 1811); one document signed by Tyler, about "The Touchstone" (26 January 1818).

New York Public Library — one letter from Tyler (to Israel Tefft, 24 November 1820); one document signed by Tyler (30 October 1804).

Pennsylvania Historical Society — two letters from Tyler (to David G. Barnet, 12 February 1810; to Mary Tyler, 9 October 1807); one

Selected Bibliography

letter to Tyler (from Jonathan Robinson, 8 January 1810); three documents signed by Tyler (26 October 1802; 3, 4 February 1809).

University of Vermont Library — one letter to Tyler (from Jonathan Robinson, 25 April 1809); eight documents signed by Tyler (23 October 1798; 2 June 1803; August 1805; June, 27 September 1806; 28 May, August, 29 August 1812).

University of Virginia Library — four letters from Tyler (to William Griffith, 18 May 1824; Jonathan Jones, 16 February 1812; P. C. Merril, 26 March 1810; Cornelius S. Vanness, 23 November 1812); one document signed by Tyler (22 February 1808).

Still other manuscript material is in private collections; for example, the present writer has one document signed by Tyler (26 January 1810).

SECONDARY SOURCES

Bibliographies

There has been no full bibliography. The principal checklists are those in the 1920 edition of *The Contrast*; in *Driftwind*, VI (March 1932), 27–31 (by Walter J. Coates); in the bibliography volume of the *Literary History of the United States* (New York: Macmillan, 1948); and in the Péladeau thesis. A descriptive bibliography of Tyler's works, prepared by the present writer, is "Some Uncollected Authors XLII: Royall Tyler, 1757–1826," *Book Collector*, XV (1966), 303–320.

Biographical and Critical Studies

Listed here are articles exclusively on Tyler and books which devote entire sections or chapters to him; other works, with briefer comment on Tyler, are referred to in the Notes.

Burnham, Henry. *Brattleboro, Windham County, Vermont*, ed. Abby Maria Hemenway. Brattleboro: D. Leonard, 1880. A pioneer effort to publish the facts of Tyler's life (pp. 83–101); draws heavily and uncritically on the manuscript Tyler memoir; the most important and comprehensive early account, and the source for most later sketches.

Butterfield, L. H., Wendell D. Garrett, and Marc Friedlaender. "Introduction" to *The Earliest Diary of John Adams* (Cambridge: Harvard University Press, 1966), pp. 1–42. Includes an account of Tyler's relations with the Adamses ("The History of the Manuscript Reconstructed," pp. 16–32).

Cabot, Mary R. *Annals of Brattleboro 1681–1895*. 2 vols. Brattleboro: E. L. Hildreth, 1921–1922. Contains a general sketch of Tyler (I, 251–271), often repeating Burnham verbatim.

Selected Bibliography

Chapman, Bertrand William. "The Nativism of Royall Tyler." Master's thesis, University of Vermont, 1933. A discussion principally of *The Algerine Captive* and "The Bay Boy," useful for its examination of sources.

Cowie, Alexander. *The Rise of the American Novel*. New York: American Book Company, 1948. The most extensive critical discussion of *The Algerine Captive*, stressing its satire and "crisp, classic prose" (pp. 60–68).

Crane, Charles Edward. *Pen-drift: Amenities of Column Conducting*. Brattleboro: Stephen Daye Press, 1931. Contains a general summary of Tyler's career based on secondary sources ("Royall Tyler," pp. 118–125).

Halline, Allan Gates. "Main Currents of Thought in American Drama." Ph.D. dissertation, University of Wisconsin, 1935. Includes, in chapter I ("Nationalism: Royall Tyler," pp. 15–30), a discussion of the historical background and importance of *The Contrast*.

Lauber, John. "*The Contrast*: A Study in the Concept of Innocence," *English Language Notes*, I (September 1963), 33–37. An analysis of the play as a precursor of the Jamesian international theme, with American innocence opposed to European sophistication.

Nethercot, Arthur H. "The Dramatic Background of Royall Tyler's *The Contrast*," *American Literature*, XII (1941), 435–446. Carefully examines Tyler's sources and preparation as a dramatist.

Newbrough, G. F. "Mary Tyler's Journal," *Vermont Quarterly*, XX (1952), 19–31. A selection of entries (between 1821 and 1826) from Tyler's wife's journal, important for an understanding of Tyler's last years.

Péladeau, Marius B. "The Verse of Royall Tyler: Collected and Edited." Master's thesis, Georgetown University, 1962. A valuable attempt to establish the canon of Tyler's poetry, with extensive annotations and bibliographical citations; the introduction (pp. 1–38) includes a general survey of Tyler's career. (For the published edition, see the list of primary materials above.)

Quinn, Arthur Hobson. *A History of the American Drama from the Beginning to the Civil War*. Second edition. New York: Appleton-Century-Crofts, 1943. The standard discussion of *The Contrast* (pp. 64–73).

———"Royall Tyler," *Dictionary of American Biography*, XIX (1936), 95–97. A scholarly account, based on the Tyler manuscripts as well as the published material.

Riese, Teut. *Das englische Erbe in der amerikanischen Literatur: Studien zur Entstehungsgeschichte des amerikanischen Selbstbewusstseins im Zeitalter Washingtons und Jeffersons* ("Beiträge zur

Selected Bibliography

Englischen Philologie," 39). Bochum-Langendreer: Heinrich Pöppinghaus, 1958. Concentrates, in the section about Tyler (pp. 139–149), on *The Algerine Captive* and its relation to the English picaresque tradition.

Rourke, Constance. *The Roots of American Culture and Other Essays*, ed. Van Wyck Brooks. New York: Harcourt, Brace, 1942. Contains an important evaluation of Tyler's concern with the Yankee character (pp. 114–124).

Seilhamer, George O. *History of the American Theatre*. 3 vols. Philadelphia: Globe Printing House, 1888–1891. Includes a detailed account of the reception of *The Contrast* (II, 225–239), largely unfavorable to Tyler.

Stein, Roger B. "Royall Tyler and the Question of Our Speech," *New England Quarterly*, XXXVIII (1965), 454–474. A suggestive analysis of *The Contrast* as an early treatment of the search for an authentic native idiom — a search that continues to the present, fluctuating in its emphases between the Jonathan and Manly types.

Taft, Russell. "Royall Tyler," *Green Bag*, XX (January 1908), 1–5. A general biographical sketch, with emphasis on Tyler's legal career (cf. *Green Bag*, VI [1894], 72–74).

Tanselle, G. Thomas. "Early American Fiction in England: The Case of *The Algerine Captive*," *Papers of the Bibliographical Society of America*, LIX (1965), 367–384. A collation of the various editions of the novel, showing the care with which the text was treated in England.

Tupper, Frederick. "Royall Tyler, Man of Law and Man of Letters," *Proceedings of the Vermont Historical Society*, IV (1928), 65–101. An estimate of Tyler's entire career, giving biographical facts but emphasizing his literary productions.

Tyler, Mary Palmer. *Grandmother Tyler's Book: The Recollections of Mary Palmer Tyler*, ed. Helen Tyler Brown and Frederick Tupper. New York: Putnam, 1925. The autobiography of Tyler's wife, of obvious importance for first-hand information about the family. Reviewed by H. S. Wardner in *Vermonter*, XXIX (1924), 181–182; by G. H. Busey in New York *Tribune*, 10 May 1925; in *Saturday Review of Literature*, I (28 March 1925), 633; in Boston *Transcript*, 16 December 1925.

Tyler, Thomas Pickman. "Royall Tyler," *Proceedings of the Vermont Bar Association*, I (1878–1881), 44–62. A general survey of Tyler's life, based on his son's long memoir.

White, Pliny H. "Early Poets of Vermont," *Proceedings of the Vermont Historical Society, 1917–1918* (1920), pp. 93–125. The earliest substantial commentary on Tyler's verse (pp. 108–119), originally read on 18 October 1860.

Notes

I. *Lawyer and Wit*

1. The best account of this Royall Tyler (1724–1771) is in Clifford K. Shipton, *Sibley's Harvard Graduates*, XI (Boston, 1960), 313–318. His standing (determined mainly by the social position of the family) was sixteenth in a class of thirty-nine (p. 176); he received his Master's degree in 1746 and a degree from Yale *ad eundem* in 1750 (see the Quinquennial Catalogues). After graduation he studied law for a time with the great Edmund Trowbridge (1709–1793); cf. Shipton, *Harvard Graduates*, and *Commonwealth History of Massachusetts*, ed. Alfred B. Hart (New York, 1928), II, 179. For more information on the pamphlet episode, see *Extract from the Journal of the Honorable House of Representatives . . . Relating to the Imprisonment of Daniel Fowle and Royall Tyler* [Boston, 1756]; for an unfavorable estimate of his character, see *The Conversation of Two Persons under a Window on Monday Evening the 23rd of March* [Boston, 1765]; for his relationship to Otis, see William Tudor, *Life of James Otis* (Boston, 1823), p. 92, and Shipton, *Harvard Graduates*, XI, 254–255; for his activities in demanding withdrawal of British troops, see Edward L. Pierce, ed., "Diary of John Rowe," *Proceedings of the Massachusetts Historical Society*, 2nd ser., X (1895–96), 67 (entry for 14 June 1768), and George G. Wolkins, "The Seizure of John Hancock's Sloop *Liberty*," *ibid.*, LV (1921–22), 250n (the *Romney* affair, 16 June 1768); for his later services to Harvard, see Josiah Quincy, *The History of Harvard University* (Boston, 1860), II, 101, 488; for the repercussions of his remarks after the Boston Massacre, see *Proceedings of His Majesty's Council . . . Relative to the Deposition of Andrew Oliver* (Boston, 1770) and William Gordon, *The History of the Rise, Progress, and Establishment of the Independence of the United States of America* (London, 1788), I, 288–289; and for a detailed account of his last hours, told by his physician Thomas Young, see the Boston *Evening Post*, 3 June 1771. He is also mentioned, as Shipton indicates, in the Massachusetts *Archives* (see especially XXIV, 303, and XXVI, 213), the *Records* of the Province Council (XV, XVI), and John Adams' *Works* (Boston, 1850–1856), II, 247. Specific dates of his numerous offices and committee appointments can be ascertained in

the *Reports of the Record Commissioners of the City of Boston* (39 vols.; Boston, 1876–1909), XIV, XVI, XVIII, XIX, XX, XXIII (his marriage is recorded in XXVIII, 265); and in *The Acts and Resolves, Public and Private, of the Province of Massachusetts Bay* (21 vols.; Boston, 1869–1922), III, IV, V, XV, XVI, XVII, XVIII. He is listed as one of the Sons of Liberty who dined at the Liberty Tree, Dorchester, on 14 August 1769, in *Proceedings of the Massachusetts Historical Society*, XI (1869–70), 142. Henry Burnham, in *Brattleboro, Windham County, Vermont* (Brattleboro, 1880), says (p. 87) that Tyler went into the mercantile business with his brother-in-law, Samuel Phillips Savage (husband of his sister Sarah). In the Boston Public Library there are two letters (1760, 1761) written to Tyler in his capacity as a member of the committee to look after victims of the Boston fire.

2. The most detailed treatment of the genealogy is in *Grandmother Tyler's Book*, ed. Frederick Tupper and Helen Tyler Brown (New York, 1925), esp. pp. 327–357, with charts on pp. 329, 331, 333; see also Thomas Bridgman, *Memorials of the Dead in Boston . . . Inscriptions on the Sepulchral Monuments in the King's Chapel Burial Ground* (Boston, 1853), pp. 288–291, and the *New England Historical and Genealogical Register*, VIII (1854), 102. Thomas Tyler's name appears in the list of inhabitants of Boston in 1695 in the *Reports of the Record Commissioners*, I, 169; his sons, besides William, were named Thomas (born 15 August 1685), John, and Andrew (who married the sister of Sir William Pepperell), and they appear in the Boston records, VIII–XII, XIV–XVII (the source for the dates in the text). These records suggest (IX, 167, 182) that Thomas, not William as in *Grandmother Tyler's Book*, was the eldest of the brothers. William's portrait, painted by John Smibert, was presented to the New England Historic, Genealogical Society in 1874; see its *Register*, XXIX (1875), 119. William's children, besides Royall, included another Thomas, William, Joseph, and Sarah. See further references to the Tylers in the Boston records, XXII, XXV, XXVIII, XXX. Willard I. Tyler Brigham's *The Tyler Genealogy* (Plainfield, N.J., and Tylerville, Conn., 1912) deals with an entirely separate line of Tylers, though it mentions Thomas Tyler (and the "Thomas Tyler Boston Line") on p. v, in pointing out the number of original Tyler immigrants in the Boston area.

3. "An Act to change the Christian name of William Clark Tyler from William Clark to Royall," passed 23 April 1772 (*Acts and Resolves . . . of the Province of Massachusetts Bay*, VI, 213, and see further references given there; the act is also listed at V, 181, where the date is reported as 25 April 1772).

4. Quoted from p. 9 of an unpublished memoir of Tyler by one of his sons, Thomas Pickman Tyler, now in the Vermont Historical

Society (Royall Tyler Collection, gift of Helen Tyler Brown). Page references will be made to a typewritten copy consisting of 233 pages (numbered 1–232, with one page skipped), then a brief gap, followed by 69 more pages (with new pagination, from 47 to 115, hereafter prefixed with a superscript 2 to distinguish them from earlier pages with the same numbers); though Helen Tyler Brown did not finish her renumbering of this copy, it is still more convenient for reference than the handwritten fair copy. The memoir has been drawn upon extensively for several published accounts, notably Burnham's. It is here quoted by permission of the Tyler heirs and the Vermont Historical Society.

5. For this reconstruction I am indebted to the researches of Bertrand W. Chapman, "The Nativism of Royall Tyler" (master's thesis, University of Vermont, 1933), pp. 55–61. For information about the Latin School at this period, see Henry F. Jenks, *Catalogue of the Boston Public Latin School* (Boston, 1886), esp. pp. 35–40 (a letter from Harrison Gray Otis describing the school in the 1770's); references to Tyler and to his father (who had entered in 1732) are on pp. 87, 47. Cf. Arthur W. Brayley, *Schools and Schoolboys of Old Boston* (Boston, 1894), esp. pp. 33–35; and Kenneth B. Murdock, "The Teaching of Latin and Greek at the Boston Latin School in 1712," *Publications of the Colonial Society of Massachusetts*, XXVII (1932), 21–29 (Tyler's father, p. 26). A typescript of "The Bay Boy" is in the Vermont Historical Society, Box 45, Envelope 29.

6. Details of this period of Harvard history are drawn from Samuel Eliot Morison, *Three Centuries of Harvard* (Cambridge, Mass., 1936), pp. 133–163; Quincy, *Harvard University*, II, 148–181; Samuel F. Batchelder, *Bits of Harvard History* (Cambridge, Mass., 1924), pp. 37–76, 243–258; Albert Matthews, "Harvard Commencement Days, 1642–1916," *Publications of the Colonial Society of Massachusetts*, XVIII (1916), 354–355; *The Cambridge of 1776*, ed. Arthur Gilman (Cambridge, Mass., 1875); and George Gary Bush, *History of Higher Education in Massachusetts* (Washington, 1891), esp. pp. 60–61, 71, 80.

7. Reprinted in the *Publications of the Colonial Society of Massachusetts*, XXXI (1935), 358; the earlier quotation from the laws occurs on p. 347.

8. Tyler is listed on p. 32 (and his father on p. 19) of the *Catalogus eorum qui in Collegio Harvardino, quod est Cantabrigiae Nov-anglorum, ab Anno MDCXLII, ad Annum MDCCLXXVI* (Boston, 1776) and also on the 1776 broadside *Proceribus Politiae Massachusettensis Honoratissimis*; for his Yale degree, see p. 22 of *Catalogus eorum qui in Collegio-Yalensi . . . ab anno MDCII ad Annum MDCCLXXVIII, alicujus Gradus Laurea donati sunt* (New Haven, 1778).

9. Tyler's father died intestate, and the size of the estate is generally

reported as £4100 (cf. Shipton, *Harvard Graduates*); however, Abigail Adams in 1782 declared Tyler's patrimony to be £7000, though he could not then realize more than half that amount because of the depreciation of the paper currency; he was his mother's favorite, she says, and his mother insisted that the elder brother John Steele share equally with Royall (letters from Abigail to John Adams, 23 and 30 December 1782, Adams Papers Microfilms, Reel 359).

10. Tyler memoir, p. 10; Burnham, *Brattleboro*, p. 87.

11. According to Francis Dana, Tyler had studied with him "but a short time, two or three months" and then continued his study with Hichborn; see letter from Dana to Adams, 23 May 1783, Adams Papers Microfilms, Reel 360 (in answer to Adams' letter of 24 March 1783, inquiring about Tyler's character). Abigail Adams, however, in her letter to her husband on 30 December 1782 (Reel 359), says that Tyler studied with Angier after Dana left. Another tradition makes him one of the pupils of John Adams himself — an impossibility since it is clear from the extensive correspondence relating to Tyler's courtship of Adams' daughter (1782–1786) that Adams had never met Tyler (see, for example, letters from Abigail to John Adams, 23 and 30 December 1782, Reel 359; from Richard Cranch to Adams, 20 January 1784, Reel 362; from Tyler to Adams, 15 October 1785, Reel 366). Cf. *Legal Papers of John Adams*, ed. L. Kinvin Wroth and Hiller B. Zobel (Cambridge, Mass., 1965), I, lxxxi, note 182. Adams had, however, known Tyler's father and on one occasion in 1770 had borrowed some books he recommended; see the *Diary and Autobiography of John Adams*, ed. L. H. Butterfield (Cambridge, Mass., 1961), I, 362.

12. The group occasionally asked distinguished outsiders to join them; when Dr. Korant, "a man of extensive learning," came to Boston from South America, they felt impelled to become acquainted with his views on government. See *The Autobiography of Colonel John Trumbull*, ed. Theodore Sizer (New Haven, 1953), pp. 44–46, 56–57. Biographical sketches and further references for Francis Dana (1743–1811), William Eustis (1753–1825), and Rufus King (1755–1827), as well as John Trumbull (1756–1843), may be found in the *Dictionary of American Biography*; Thomas Dawes (1757–1825), Aaron Dexter (1749–1829), and Christopher Gore (1758–1827) are less well-known. Trumbull painted portraits of some members of the group, and he described one as "Head of Royal Tyler, with both hands — a respectable portrait." This portrait, like the one of Dawes, is now lost; but, according to family tradition, it hung for years in the office of Tyler's brother at the Boston Custom House and was either burned in a Custom House fire or destroyed when removed at the time of the fire (Tyler memoir, p. 13). Trumbull's autobiography also includes information about his friendship with John Steele Tyler

in France in 1780 and about the danger the two found themselves in after the André affair (pp. 58–59, 63–72).

13. See the Records of the College Faculty, IV, 70, 74–75 (in the meetings for 20 October and 18 November 1777). The Quarter Bill Books show that Tyler did not remain in residence at Harvard as a tutor after his graduation, but Sewall did (through the quarter ending 12 December 1777); in any case the faculty had announced that "Bachelors of Arts in particular, whether residing at the College or not, who are guilty of any Scandalous immorality, are accountable therefor, whenever they come to ask for their Second Degree" (Records, IV, 70). Two years later (at the meeting of 10 July 1779) the faculty reaffirmed its stand, insisting that the three men could not be awarded their masters' degrees unless they apologized (IV, 110–111). Cf. *The Earliest Diary of John Adams*, ed. L. H. Butterfield *et al.* (Cambridge, Mass., 1966), p. 23, note 50. The only other references to Tyler in the faculty Records occur at III, 207 (entered as a freshman in July 1772), 225 (fined seven shillings on 15 March 1774 for absence from recitation), 228 (excused from commons for a brief period, recorded 1 April 1774); IV, 11 (fined sixpence on 4 April 1775 for abusing a library book; excused from commons for half a week, recorded 7 April 1775). See also Corporation Records, II, 481 (petitioned to use the college library in 1777). It should be noted that references to "Tyler 1^{mus}" during this period are to Tyler's classmate Dean Tyler, two years older, and that Royall Tyler is "Tyler 2^{dus}"; in the 1777 episode the chief basis for equating "Sr Tyler" with Royall rather than Dean is that King and Sewall are known to have been friends of Royall. Quotations from material in the Harvard Archives are made by permission of Clifford K. Shipton for the Harvard University Library.

14. Jeremiah Mason, *Memoir and Correspondence* (Cambridge, Mass., 1873), p. 32.

15. This statement occurs in the manuscript Private Journal of the antiquarian John Langdon Sibley (now in the Harvard Archives). His entry for 15 October 1856 (p. 109) begins, "Mr Royal Morse, (illegitimate son of a woman who was sweeper for very many years in the college buildings by a student, Royall Tyler)." The woman, one year older than Tyler (she was born 24 October 1756 — see *Records of the Church of Christ at Cambridge in New England, 1632–1830*, ed. Stephen P. Sharples [Boston, 1906], p. 165), was Katharine Morse, who for over forty years worked in the Harvard dormitories, as her mother had before her; she was a familiar figure in Cambridge, mentioned in Augustus Peirce's *The Rebelliad* (1842; written in 1819), eulogized in verse by B. D. Winslow (1835), and depicted with her broom in a cartoon — see Batchelder, *Bits of Harvard History*, pp.

278–280. Her mother may be the Mrs. Morse reported to have "2 Rooms" available at the time Burgoyne's men were in town (Samuel F. Batchelder, *Bits of Cambridge History* [Cambridge, Mass., 1930], p. 58). Her son Royal was born 6 June 1779, according to his obituary in the Cambridge *Press* on 10 February 1872 (signed with Sibley's initials); he was baptized on 12 January 1782 (at which time his mother was admitted to full communion), according to Sharples, *Records*, pp. 240, 243, and *Vital Records of Cambridge, Massachusetts, to the Year 1850*, ed. Thomas W. Baldwin (2 vols.; Boston, 1914–15), I, 502. Royal Morse, during his long life of nearly ninety-three years, was a prominent and respected figure in Cambridge. It was Morse to whom James Russell Lowell referred in his sketch of "Cambridge Thirty Years Ago" in *Fireside Travels* (Boston, 1864): "Long may R.M. be spared to us, so genial, so courtly, the last man among us who will ever know how to lift a hat with the nice graduation of social distinction!" (p. 35). (This identification is made by Thomas Wentworth Higginson in "Life in Cambridge Town," in *The Cambridge of Eighteen Hundred and Ninety-Six*, ed. Arthur Gilman [Cambridge, Mass., 1896], p. 40.) In 1792 Katharine Morse bought the Lamson-Francis-Gamage-Richardson house, and Royal continued to live there for many years — cf. *An Historic Guide to Cambridge* (rev. ed.; Cambridge, Mass.: Hannah Winthrop Chapter of the Daughters of the American Revolution, 1907), p. 158. He married Hannah Rand on 25 May 1800 (Sharples, *Records*, p. 491), and at least two children are recorded in the *Vital Records*, in 1800 and 1803 (Baldwin, I, 501; II, 668); his mother died on 23 February 1835 (Baldwin, *Vital Records*, II, 669; William Thaddeus Harris, *Epitaphs from the Old Burying-Ground in Cambridge* [Cambridge, Mass., 1845], p. 165). He became a well-known auctioneer (listed, for example, as one of five in the *Cambridge Directory for 1848*), and he was an assessor for a time (Lucius R. Paige, *History of Cambridge, Massachusetts* [Boston, 1877], p. 468; cf. pp. 231, 450). In his later years he was a fund of information about earlier days in Cambridge, and he contributed his recollections both to Sibley (for use in his biographies of Harvard graduates) and to Paige (for his history of Cambridge); according to Paige, his "memory of events which occurred during his life was remarkably comprehensive and accurate," and his "traditional lore was almost equivalent to authentic history" (p. 413). In regard to Tyler's paternity of Morse, it seems highly unlikely that Sibley, himself a student of local history and a friend of Morse, would be incorrect; at the same time, an extensive search has failed to produce any corroboration of Sibley's remark.

16. Mercy Otis Warren, *History of the . . . American Revolution*

(Boston, 1805), II, 45–46; see also Batchelder, *Bits of Cambridge History*, pp. 3–113.

17. *Massachusetts Soldiers and Sailors of the Revolutionary War* (17 vols.; Boston, 1896–1908), XVI, 240; *Acts and Resolves . . . of the Province of Massachusetts Bay*, XIX, 710–711. In the fall of 1779 John Steele Tyler and others resigned because of the depreciation of currency and petitioned for their payment (*Acts and Resolves*, XXI, 130, 254).

18. Tyler memoir, pp. 14–15; Burnham, *Brattleboro*, p. 86. Information about the Newport campaign may be found, among other places, in Francis Vinton Greene, *The Revolutionary War and the Military Policy of the United States* (New York, 1911), pp. 150–154 (which includes a map).

19. A copy of Tyler's admission to the bar is in the Tyler Papers, Box 45, Envelope 20. It had been voted, upon Hichborn's motion, at the 18 July 1780 meeting, according to George Dexter's transcript of the "Record Book of the Suffolk Bar," *Proceedings of the Massachusetts Historical Society*, XIX (1881–82), 154. See also note 29 below.

20. William Willis, *A History of the Law, the Courts, and the Lawyers of Maine* (Portland, 1863), p. 105; repeated in Burnham, *Brattleboro*, p. 88. Willis dates Tyler's arrival in Falmouth as 1779 and says that the privateer episode took place during Tyler's practice in Cumberland.

21. Abigail to John Adams, 30 December 1782, Adams Papers Microfilms, Reel 359. Abigail dates Tyler's "excursion" to Falmouth as "18 months ago." According to her letters of 23 December 1782 and 10 January 1783, he had then been in Braintree for nine months. All quotations, here and below, from the Adams Papers (microfilm edition) are made by permission of the Adams Manuscript Trust.

22. Abigail to John Adams, 23 December 1782, Adams Papers Microfilms, Reel 359. This letter also quotes from a reply Tyler made to a note of Abigail's informing him that he was not yet well enough established in business to think of marriage.

23. Abigail to John Adams, 30 December 1782, Adams Papers Microfilms, Reel 359. She added that Tyler had "opened his mind" to her and "declared his attachment" for her daughter.

24. Abigail to John Adams, 10 January 1783, Adams Papers Microfilms, Reel 360.

25. His letters to Abigail of 8 April–9 June 1783 and 11 April 1783 (Adams Papers Microfilms, Reel 360) and of 13 July 1783 (Reel 361) contain further anxious allusions to the affair.

26. Abigail to John Adams, 7 April 1783, Adams Papers Microfilms, Reel 360.

27. Abigail to John Adams, 7 May 1783, Adams Papers Microfilms, Reel 360. She had expressed the same opinion more briefly in a letter to Adams on 28 April 1783.

28. Abigail to John Adams, 20 June 1783, Adams Papers Microfilms, Reel 361. A few days earlier, on 14 June, she had written to Tyler an encouraging but restrained letter, giving him advice on how to overcome a tendency toward dissipation (see Tyler memoir, pp. 20–23; Tyler Papers, Box 45, Envelope 4).

29. His admission to the Supreme Judicial Court was recommended in February 1783 (Records of the Supreme Judicial Court, 1783, f. 29, in Suffolk County Court House); the action was approved on 30 July 1783, according to the "Record Book of the Suffolk Bar," *Proceedings of the Massachusetts Historical Society*, XIX (1881–82), 156. Tyler is also listed as being present at the quarterly meetings of the bar on 12 October 1784, 11 January 1785 (p. 160), and 12 July 1786 (p. 161).

30. According to Abigail Adams' letter of 27 December 1783 (Adams Papers Microfilms, Reel 362), the farm included fifty acres of wooded land and the best collection of fruit trees in Braintree; according to Joseph Palmer's letter of 16 June 1784 (Reel 363), Tyler paid £1000 for it. The "Vassall-Borland" farmhouse was later owned by the Adamses (1788–1927) and is now the Adams National Historic Site in Quincy. (See note 55 below.)

31. Cf. Abigail's letters of 20 June and 19 October 1783 (Adams Papers Microfilms, Reel 361), 27 December 1783 (Reel 362), and 3 January 1784 (Reel 362).

32. Quoted in Adams' *Diary*, III, 156n.

33. John to Abigail Adams, 25 January 1784, Adams Papers Microfilms, Reel 362.

34. *Diary*, III, 160–161, in a passage taken from Abigail's diary (entry for 1 July 1784). In *Grandmother Tyler's Book* we are told that "Mrs. Adams appeared as much afflicted as her daughter" (p. 79).

35. *Grandmother Tyler's Book*, p. 80. Cf. the account given by Mary Cranch in her letter to Abigail Adams of 8 October 1786 (Adams Papers Microfilms, Reel 369).

36. Cranch to Adams, 20 January 1784, Adams Paper Microfilms, Reel 362. Another testimonial to Tyler's character came from General Joseph Palmer, writing on 16–18 June 1784: "Previous to his coming to Braintree, I knew not any thing of him, but 'tis said that he scattered some wild Oats; be this as it may, since he came hither, his conduct, so far as I know, has been unexceptionable, & he is generally respected, & has, I believe, his full share of business" (Reel 363).

37. Adams to Tyler, 3 April 1784, Adams Papers Microfilms, Reel 362.

38. Tyler to Adams, 27 August 1784, Adams Papers Microfilms, Reel 363.

39. Mary Cranch to Abigail Adams, 16 January 1785, Adams Papers Microfilms, Reel 364. Cf. the references to Tyler in her letters of 7 August, 10 October, 6 November 1784 (Reel 363), and 25 April 1785 (Reel 364), and in her daughter's letter of 6 November 1784 (Reel 363).

40. Mary Cranch to Abigail Adams, 4 June 1785, Adams Papers Microfilms, Reel 364.

41. For Abigail had been making inquiries on her own into Tyler's conduct; see, for example, her letters to her uncle, Dr. Cotton Tufts, on 2 May 1785 (Adams Papers Microfilms, Reel 364) and to her son John Quincy on 26 June 1785 (Reel 364) and 23 August 1785 (Reel 365).

42. *Grandmother Tyler's Book*, p. 76. This note and the letters were delivered by Charles Storer, a friend of Tyler's and a cousin of young Abigail's, who, with Colonel Smith, escorted the Adams ladies frequently during their stay in Europe; *Grandmother Tyler's Book*, p. 81, gives at second hand Storer's account of Abigail's making her final decision. Her mother and Storer exchanged numerous letters commenting on Tyler — such as those of 12 February, 23 March, 13 April 1786 (Adams Papers Microfilms, Reel 367); 22 May, 15 August, 12 September 1786 (Reel 368). Cotton Tufts (who looked after the Adamses' business affairs in their absence) was appointed to collect Nabby's letters and other Adams possessions from Tyler, but it was not until late summer of 1786 that he succeeded in getting a part of them (Tufts to Adams, 15 August 1786, Reel 368; cf. his letter of 13 April 1786, Reel 367, and Mary Cranch's letter, 28 September 1786, Reel 368). Whether or not Tyler kept the Adams letters, his memory of their detailed descriptions of life in England no doubt served him well in making the national contrasts which are so important in *The Contrast* and *The Yankey in London*.

43. The connection between Tyler and the Adamses was given national publicity in the summer of 1965, when John Adams' Harvard diary (beginning in June 1753, earlier than any previously known diary of Adams) was discovered among the Tyler Papers. Presumably Tyler had picked it up in Adams' library (which Adams had invited him to use) and had never returned it; he could have found it either before Abigail's departure (for her letter of 23 December 1782, on Reel 359 of the Adams Papers Microfilms, shows the freedom with which he removed items from the library) or after she had sailed for Europe (since she included among her last instructions the stipulation that only Tyler and Richard Cranch were to be given access to the library

— see her letter of 18 June 1784 in the Clements Library). Wendell D. Garrett, an associate editor of The Adams Papers, made the discovery; his own account appeared in the *Boston Sunday Globe*, 4 July 1965, p. 7, accompanied by an article on the Tyler love affair by Mary Meier (pp. 1, 7). The news release was widely reprinted all over this country and abroad. This "diary" (containing lecture notes, notes on legal cases, and the like) has been published as *The Earliest Diary of John Adams*, ed. L. H. Butterfield *et al.* (Cambridge, Mass., 1966), with an introduction tracing the relationship of Tyler with the Adamses (pp. 16–32). It is possible that this document had been unknowingly mentioned in print thirty years earlier, for among the lists of gifts received, in the *Proceedings of the Vermont Historical Society* for 1936, occurs this statement: "Nearly three-fourths of the Royall Tyler diary, written in 1753 while he was a student at Harvard, has been typed as far as it could be deciphered" (IV, 39). Neither Tyler nor his father was at Harvard in that year, and no Tyler diary is now known.

44. The Tyler account occurs in *Grandmother Tyler's Book*, pp. 75–82; a retelling based on it is in Katharine Metcalf Roof's *Colonel William Smith and Lady* (Boston, 1929), pp. 33, 35, 46–50 (chapter 9), 90–101 (chapter 14), 132–133, 308 (including the "suspicion that Mr. Adams found himself exhilarated by denunciation"). Accounts based on the Adams Papers are found in Adams' *Diary*, III, 192–193n, and *Earliest Diary*, pp. 18–28; Janet Whitney, *Abigail Adams* (Boston, 1947), pp. 167–171; Page Smith, *John Adams* (New York, 1962), pp. 531–532, 559–560, 572–573, 591–593, 614–615, 658–662, 665–666 (emphasizing Tyler's "disconcerting instability," his "streak of morbidity and melancholy introspection," and his "reputation for being fast"); Lida Mayo, "Miss Adams in Love," *American Heritage*, XVI (February 1965), 36–39, 80–89; and Irving Stone, *Those Who Love* (New York, 1965), pp. 387–393, 398–402, 404–406, 409, 429, 446, 457, 463–464, 469–470, 481, 484. According to the Tyler version, even Tyler's participation in the balloon craze was enough to cause a report about his frivolous behavior to reach Adams' ears (*Grandmother Tyler's Book*, pp. 80–81; Roof, *Smith*, pp. 98–100). It is also claimed that Tyler, to prove the Cranches responsible for the malicious gossip, once planned with the Adamses to give exclusive attention to the Cranch girls for a few days, whereupon Tyler, in the eyes of the Cranches, became a model of virtuousness — but, understandably, all the more wicked when the trick was discovered (*Grandmother Tyler's Book*, pp. 78–79; Roof, *Smith*, pp. 46–50).

45. Tyler to Adams, 15 October 1785, Adams Papers Microfilms, Reel 366. Tyler's letter to Abigail is dated 13 October 1785. Adams replied on 12 December 1785 with a friendly letter, which did not

mention his daughter's prospective union with Smith but did allude to a change in circumstances (Reel 107, pp. 447–448). According to Abigail's letter to Mary Cranch on 15 August 1785 (in the American Antiquarian Society), Tyler had written young Abigail only four letters.

46. On 9 February 1786, for example, she wrote, "I am more thankful than ever that I have been so cautious in what I said about him." This letter and those of 10 January and 22 March–9 April 1786 are on Reel 367 of the Adams Papers Microfilms; those of 8 November and 10 December 1785 are on Reel 366.

47. John Quincy to Abigail Adams, 28 December 1785, Adams Papers Microfilms, Reel 366. Cf. his letter of 15 May 1786 and Abigail's to him of 13 June 1786 (Reel 368). Letters from John Quincy (who had returned to the United States to study at Harvard) to his sister occasionally refer to his associations with Tyler — as those of 29 August–7 September, 8–18 September, and 19–30 September 1785 (Reel 365).

48. Eliza Shaw to Abigail Adams, 18 June 1786, Adams Papers Microfilms, Reel 368. She had earlier expressed dissatisfaction with Tyler's conduct, on 6 November 1785 (Reel 366); more favorable references are in her letters of 12 June 1785 (Reel 364) and 22 July 1786 (Reel 368).

49. Mary Cranch to Abigail Adams, 7 May 1786, Adams Papers Microfilms, Reel 368. That the Cranch daughters delighted in tormenting Tyler is suggested by Betsy Cranch's account of their posting, by the side of a letter for Tyler, the calling card of "Mr. and Mrs. Smith"; see her letter to Abigail, 20 May 1786 (Reel 368).

50. Mary Cranch to Abigail Adams, 2 July 1786, Adams Papers Microfilms, Reel 368.

51. See her letters of 8 July (Tyler neglecting the Cranches' invitations) and 28 September 1786 (Tyler in debt for £200 and speaking slightingly of Colonel Smith) on Reel 368 of the Adams Papers Microfilms; 8 October (Tyler defending himself at the Cranches' expense) and 9 October 1786 (Tyler criticizing Smith and encouraging Negroes to stay in the Adams house) on Reel 369. Her remark on 21 December 1786 (Reel 369) makes it clear that Abigail had asked her not to discuss Tyler further; Abigail had made the same request over a year earlier, on 15 August 1785 (letter in the American Antiquarian Society). Tyler's name did briefly recur in their correspondence at the time of the production of *The Contrast*: Mary Cranch alluded disapprovingly to his play-writing (22 April–20 May 1787, Reel 369), and Abigail thought that the contrast was probably between his own character and that of Smith (16 July 1787, privately owned, and quoted in Adams' *Earliest Diary*, p. 29).

52. Mary Cranch to Abigail Adams, 8 July 1786, Adams Papers Microfilms, Reel 368; cf. her letter of 22 March–3 April 1786, Reel 367.

53. Tyler to Abigail Adams, 13 October 1785, Adams Papers Microfilms, Reel 366; *Grandmother Tyler's Book*, p. 96.

54. This chronology is based on a letter from Mary Cranch to Abigail Adams, 2 July 1786, Adams Papers Microfilms, Reel 368; it differs somewhat from Mary Tyler's retrospective account in *Grandmother Tyler's Book*. For references to Tyler's positions on committees or as moderator of Braintree town meetings, between 1784 and 1786, see *Records of the Town of Braintree*, ed. Samuel A. Bates (Randolph, Mass., 1886), pp. 547, 549, 552, 553, 558–560, 564, 565.

55. See especially Mary Cranch's letter to Abigail Adams, 28 September 1786, Adams Papers Microfilms, Reel 368. The house and farm reverted to the Borlands in 1787, and the Adamses, upon the advice of Mary Cranch, purchased it (Mary Cranch to Abigail Adams, 22 April–20 May 1787, Reel 369).

56. See the accounts of Lincoln in the *Dictionary of American Biography* and in Francis Bowen, *Life of Benjamin Lincoln* (in the *Library of American Biography*, ed. Jared Sparks, 2nd ser., XIII [1847], 207–434), which mentions Tyler on p. 404. See also J. G. Holland, *History of Western Massachusetts* (Springfield, 1855), I, 230–302; Joseph Parker Warren, "The Confederation and the Shays Rebellion," *American Historical Review*, XI (1905–06), 42–67; and John H. Lockwood *et al.*, *Western Massachusetts: A History 1636–1925* (New York, 1926), I, 113–206.

57. Tyler memoir, p. 29; Burnham, *Brattleboro*, p. 89; *Grandmother Tyler's Book*, p. 105.

58. Letter in the Vermont Historical Society; printed in Burnham, *Brattleboro*, p. 90.

59. Burnham, *Brattleboro*, p. 91; *Records of the Governor and Council of the State of Vermont*, ed. E. P. Walton (8 vols.; Montpelier, 1873–1880), III, 119, 125, 375–376 (with pp. 357–380, an appendix on "Vermont at the Period of Shays's Rebellion — 1784 to 1787"). A few months later, on 28 August 1787, Ethan Allen wrote Tyler, pointing out that amicable relations now existed between Vermont and Massachusetts in regard to fugitives and asking whether Tyler could procure enough subscriptions for the publication of the appendix to Allen's *Reason the Only Oracle of Man* (Burnham, *Brattleboro*, p. 92). Tyler apparently could not, for it was not published until 1873 (in the April through August issues of the *Historical Magazine*); see John Pell, *Ethan Allen* (Boston, 1929), p. 264.

60. Letter of 17 February 1787, in Tyler memoir, pp. 44–45.

61. The "Memorial" of 6 March 1787, read in the Massachusetts

House and Senate on 7 March, is now in the Archives of the Secretary of State, Boston, along with a letter to Lincoln of 18 February 1787 and some earlier reports about Shays.

62. Tyler memoir, p. 51.

63. Burnham, *Brattleboro*, pp. 89–92, and Tyler memoir, pp. 29–57, give detailed accounts of Tyler's role in Shays' Rebellion and quote documents written by Tyler and Lincoln. There are also documents relating to Shays' Rebellion in the Tyler Papers at the Vermont Historical Society, including Tyler's letter to Governor Chittenden, 23 February 1787. Some of the state histories, like Ira Allen's *The Natural and Political History of the State of Vermont* (London, 1798), p. 248, allude to Tyler's place in the Shays affair. Further information and references can be found in the sketches of Shays (c. 1747–1825), Shepard (1737–1817), Bowdoin (1726–1790), Sedgwick (1746–1813), Allen (1738–1789), and Chittenden (1730–1797) in the *Dictionary of American Biography.*

64. *Grandmother Tyler's Book*, p. 107; Burnham, *Brattleboro*, p. 93.

65. Burnham, *Brattleboro*, p. 92; Tyler memoir, p. 58.

66. "Biographical Sketch of Gen. Joseph Palmer," *New Englander*, III (January 1845), 2; this article (pp. 1–23), in a magazine edited by one of Tyler's sons, Edward Royall Tyler, is one of the most detailed treatments of Palmer, printing a number of letters and documents, especially in connection with the Rhode Island affair.

67. See Samuel A. Bates, ed., *Records of the Town of Braintree* (Randolph, Mass., 1886), esp. pp. 453–454, 511–512; William S. Pattee, *A History of Old Braintree and Quincy* (Quincy, 1878), esp. pp. 475–482 (purchase of land in Germantown), 486–490 (biographical sketch of Palmer, with a portrait), 490–492 (sketch of Cranch). In addition to the *New Englander* article and the sketch in *DAB*, references to Palmer's work in the Provincial Congress may be found in the *Journals of the Provincial Congress of Massachusetts* (Boston, 1838), *passim*, and the New Hampshire *Provincial Papers*, ed. Nathaniel Bouton, VII (Nashua, 1873), 457. He is also alluded to in the sketch of Robert Treat Paine in George A. Ward, *The Journal and Letters of Samuel Curwen* (4th ed.; Boston, 1864), p. 586. Background for the Rhode Island incident is in Alden Bradford, *History of Massachusetts*, II (Boston, 1825), 125–137, 160–166. It is undoubtedly Palmer's glassworks that Edwin Atlee Barber is referring to in *American Glassware* (Philadelphia, 1900) when he says that thick greenish bottles were made in Germantown in 1760 (p. 12).

68. Adams, *Diary*, I, 233 (1 February 1763).

69. For genealogical trees setting forth these relationships, in both the Palmer and Hunt families, see *Grandmother Tyler's Book*, p. 329. The Palmers are discussed in that book on pp. 20–110 *passim* and in

such books about later branches of the family as Julian Hawthorne, *Nathaniel Hawthorne and His Wife* (Boston, 1884), I, 39–81, and Louise Hall Tharp, *The Peabody Sisters of Salem* (Boston, 1950), pp. 11–19, 341–342. A sketch of J. P. Palmer, as a member of the Boston Tea Party, is included in Francis S. Drake's *Tea Leaves* (Boston, 1884), pp. cxxxviii–cxxxix. For the Hunts, see *Grandmother Tyler's Book*, pp. 5–19, and citations in T. B. Wyman, Jr., *Genealogy of the Name and Family of Hunt* (Boston, 1862–1863), pp. 286–287. The Hunt daughters formed other interesting associations, since Katherine had Elbridge Gerry as a suitor and Mary's second husband (Richard Perkins) was earlier married to John Hancock's sister. Since John Hunt (as well as three of his sons) graduated from Harvard (1734), a sketch appears in Shipton, *Harvard Graduates*, IX (1956), 414–418. One of the sons, Samuel, was for thirty years Master of the Boston Latin School, following John Lovell (see Jenks, *Latin School*, p. 7).

70. The chronology here is confused and is partly a matter of conjecture, for the dates in *Grandmother Tyler's Book* are not always consistent. A comparison of the published book with the manuscript of Mary Tyler's memoirs (in the possession of Edward Royall Tyler — a microfilm copy in the Library of Congress and a handwritten copy in the Vermont Historical Society) shows that numerous small omissions were not indicated by ellipsis marks; but the confusion in dates is in the original as well, the natural result of the tricks of memory after sixty years.

71. This visit to New York is fully described in chapter 4 of *Grandmother Tyler's Book*, pp. 111–137. Mary Tyler mistakenly says that *The Contrast* "was acted every night for some weeks" in 1789 (p. 118).

72. The move to Framingham is described in *Grandmother Tyler's Book*, pp. 138–157. J. H. Temple, in his *History of Framingham, Massachusetts* (Framingham, 1887), says that William and John Hunt operated a tavern at the Phinehas Rice (Nat. Hardy) place, which Joseph P. Palmer took over about 1789 and which his wife kept until 1797 (p. 360).

73. *Grandmother Tyler's Book*, p. 151.

74. *Grandmother Tyler's Book*, p. 180. Constance Rourke, in *The Roots of American Culture* (New York, 1942), comments on Tyler's "obscure and complicated inner life" — reflected in his moodiness, his formality, and his secrecy — and remarks, "Surely he was not in love with little Mary Palmer" (pp. 120–121).

75. According to the *Gazetteer and Business Directory of Windham County, Vermont, 1724–1884*, comp. Hamilton Child (Syracuse, N.Y., 1884), p. 304 (the source also for the figures on Brattleboro

below). The population of Guilford had been only 436 twenty years earlier, in 1771, and it was to fall from its 1791 population to 2256 by 1800. Tyler is mentioned in the sketch of Guilford in Zadock Thompson's *History of Vermont* (Burlington, 1842), III, 83.

76. Burnham, *Brattleboro*, pp. 94–95. In the June term of 1793, Tyler had 62 cases, 32 of them new; in November 48 cases, 22 of them new.

77. The New Lebanon visit is taken up in *Grandmother Tyler's Book*, pp. 157–176, and an incident involving the bracelet on pp. 201–203.

78. This is another point at which the chronology is difficult. The relevant passage of *Grandmother Tyler's Book* (pp. 177–192) first suggests that the proposal came during Tyler's visit just after Mary's return from New Lebanon in the winter of 1792–93; but when Tyler left, after the proposal, he took Mary's father with him, and Joseph Palmer's letters en route to Vermont are dated February 1794. Either Tyler did not propose quite so soon after Mary's return or else Mary is combining her memories of two separate occasions.

79. For the story of the secret marriage, the months of waiting, and the eventual entry into Guilford, see *Grandmother Tyler's Book*, pp. 204–232. The house in which the Tylers lived in Guilford was on land bought by James Fosdick from James and Edward Houghton; see *Official History of Guilford, Vermont*, ed. Broad Brook Grange No. 151 (Guilford, 1961), pp. 196, 368. Other references to Tyler's activities in Guilford are on p. 110 (report of the December town meeting in 1794, when Tyler received eleven votes, more than the other candidates, for the position of representative to the legislature) and pp. 159–160 (brief biographical sketch). See also *Vermont Historical Gazetteer*, V (1891), part 3, pp. 42, 46 (where John Phelps is named as a "warm friend and admirer of Judge Tyler" in Guilford).

80. Joseph Pearse Palmer, who spent his last years away from home, tutoring in Woodstock and Windsor, Vermont, was killed on 25 June 1797, when he fell from a bridge that was under construction at Woodstock. Edward Palmer, through Tyler's influence, had been apprenticed to the Brattleboro printer Benjamin Smead; on 2 July 1797 he drowned and caused the friend who was trying to save him to drown, too. William Wells, the pastor of Christ's Church in Brattleboro, delivered the funeral sermon, which was printed in 1798 by Smead as a twenty-page pamphlet: *A Sermon, Preached at Brattleborough, Vermont, July 3, A.D. 1797 . . . at the Interment of Mess. Pardon Taylor and Edward Palmer, Who the Day Before Were Drowned in Connecticut River*. The story of the drowning is recounted in a four-page preface; the sermon takes Job 1:21 as its text. Tyler's mother was declining in health during the winter of 1799–

1800, and John Steele had written urging Tyler to visit her, but he did not go; see *Grandmother Tyler's Book*, pp. 244–245, 270–271.

81. The letter, written on 18 March 1801, appears in *Grandmother Tyler's Book*, pp. 278–282, in Burnham, *Brattleboro*, p. 97, and in Mary R. Cabot, *Annals of Brattleboro* (Brattleboro, 1921–1922), I, 265–267. Because of its associations (as site of the first meetinghouse in Brattleboro and home of Micah Townsend, first lawyer in the state), the history of this property has been described by Martha Votey Smith in "On Meeting-House Hill," *Vermonter*, XXVI (January 1921), 22–25. See also the *Records of the Council of Safety and Governor and Council of the State of Vermont*, I, 519.

82. The Brattleboro years are described in more detail on pp. 272–326 of *Grandmother Tyler's Book*.

83. Tyler, in the course of his correspondence with Riley about *The Yankey in London* and the Vermont *Reports*, mentioned his wife's work, on 22 May 1810: "Captain Holbrook will show you the manuscript of a little Treatise upon the nurture and management of Infants. You will please not to mention through what channel this work comes to you; but if you incline to print a first edition, upon such terms as Captain Holbrook and you can agree upon, you can keep the manuscript, and the remainder, which will be about as much more, shall be sent to you by the middle of June. I have no doubt it will sell, as it is upon an interesting topic, and written by an American Lady. It must, however, be printed tastily as it is calculated for sale in cities. You can show it to any of your medical friends" (Tyler memoir, p. 280). According to the memoir (p. 286), Mary Tyler refused to have her name on the title page, even though Riley was willing to pay more if the work were signed. There are a few internal hints of her authorship: the preface is signed "Mary"; on p. 17 the author says she has brought up eight children, the number the Tylers had in 1811; on p. 170 she refers to "little Joseph," and Joseph Dennie Tyler would have been not quite seven at the time. The book is discussed briefly by Frederick Tupper in "Royall Tyler, Man of Law and Man of Letters," *Proceedings of the Vermont Historical Society*, IV (1928), 99–100; Tupper originally made the suggestion that Tyler may have supplied his wife with the poetical quotations.

84. *American Modern Practice* (2nd ed.; Boston, 1826), pp. 706, 726, 706, respectively.

85. Mary Tyler died at the age of ninety-one on 7 July 1866, having outlived four of her children. An obituary appears in the *Vermont Phoenix* for 13 July 1866; see also Cabot, *Annals*, I, 271–272, where "Madam Tyler" (as the village called her) is described as "a light and center to society, giving warmth and enjoyment to all who came within her sphere."

86. For example, in a letter to Jonathan Hunt on 24 December 1798 (now in the Dartmouth Library), Tyler mentions that a Mr. Smead has just begun to study in his office.

87. Jacob served as Assistant Judge with Tyler from October 1801 to September 1803, when he was replaced by Theophilus Harrington. In October 1807, when Tyler became Chief Justice, the third place was filled by Jonas Galusha (later Governor), who was replaced in 1809 by David Fay. Tyler was succeeded as Chief Justice by Nathaniel Chipman. James Benjamin Wilbur, in *Ira Allen: Founder of Vermont* (New York, 1928), says that Tyler had been since 1787 an "intimate friend" of Isaac Tichenor, "to whom he undoubtedly owed his appointment" to the Supreme Court (II, 357). For the report of Tyler's election (and taking of the oath — pages given below in parentheses) each October from 1801 through 1812, see the *Records of the Governor and Council of the State of Vermont*, IV, 293 (299), 337, 373; V, 12, 71 (73), 108, 155 (157), 205 (212), 248–249, 286–287, 321 (325), 353 (375); other duties of Tyler are recorded at IV, 97; V, 192, 298, 316; VI, 16, 25.

88. Stephen Row Bradley wrote to Tyler on 27 January 1810, suggesting the possibility that Tyler take over his Senate seat; the letter is in the Boston Public Library and has been published in the Library's *Bulletin*, VII (1903), 70–71. See also the letter (in the Columbia Library) from Jonathan Robinson to Tyler, 1 December 1811.

89. Evidence of one of Tyler's University services is the manuscript copy of the University laws, dated 28 July 1811 and compiled by Tyler and William Czar Bradley; see *UVM Notes*, XVII (December 1920), 8. Jonathan Robinson wrote Tyler on 21 January 1811, congratulating him on his new position as Professor of Law and praising him for his attitude that the law is not infallible and often needs correction (letter in New Hampshire Historical Society). The minutes of the corporation show that Tyler attended meetings on 12 June 1802, 13 October 1804, 11 September 1807, six meetings in October 1810, 2 January 1811, 12 July 1812, and 21 October 1813, and that his main function was to represent the University at the state legislature; his Vermont M.A. was granted 30 June 1811. (See record in Tyler Papers, Box 46). Julian I. Lindsay, in *Tradition Looks Forward: The University of Vermont, A History* (Burlington, 1954), points out that Tyler, soon after he took the oath as trustee (2 January 1811), was asked, on 14 January, to work with President D. C. Sanders in preparing a public address to announce the new administration (pp. 91–92).

90. *Grandmother Tyler's Book*, pp. 183–184. When Thomas P. Tyler tells the incident in his memoir, he says that Tyler's method in the sermons was one of logical argumentation, as if he were presenting a case to a jury; the memoir also suggests that the Reverend Mr.

Wollage was angry upon discovering that Tyler had spoken in his absence.

91. Tyler's connection with the ministry can be overemphasized if, as sometimes happens, he is confused with another Royal [S.] Tyler (1763–1826), who was pastor at Andover, Connecticut, from 4 July 1792 to 20 May 1817 (see Brigham, *Tyler Genealogy*, I, 184–185). This Tyler published *A Family Discourse* (Boston, 1817), which has at times been attributed to the dramatist, as has a letter (17 December 1792) now in the Dartmouth Library, despite the fact that it is signed as "Pastor" of the church at Andover.

92. *Grandmother Tyler's Book*, p. 105.

93. Tyler memoir, pp. 112–114. In the memoir the letter is dated at Bennington, January 1800, but, according to the title page of the *Oration*, the speech was delivered on 22 February. Furthermore, Tyler writes that he wishes his wife were present, but she says, in *Grandmother Tyler's Book* (p. 105), that the only occasion on which she ever heard him speak in public was to deliver the Washington oration. It is perhaps possible that he gave the speech twice, just after Washington's death in December and again on Washington's birthday.

94. The oration has also been discussed by Tupper, "Royall Tyler," pp. 98–99.

95. The two passages are, respectively, from letters of 4 February 1810 and 15 June 1812 (Burnham, *Brattleboro*, pp. 99, 100). From the time Robinson first went to the Senate in 1807 he wrote frequent letters, often weekly, to Tyler describing the political situation in Washington, valuable for their first-hand accounts of events leading up to the War of 1812. See the Tyler memoir, pp. 174–203, 209–220, ^{2}49–54, ^{2}93–115; Robinson's letters to Tyler may also be found at the Boston Public Library, New Hampshire Historical Society, Pennsylvania Historical Society, University of Vermont, and Vermont Historical Society.

96. John A. Graham, *A Descriptive Sketch of the Present State of Vermont* (London, 1797), pp. 154–155. An illustration of one of the traits mentioned here, championing the underdog, is furnished in the correspondence of Roger Vose and Joseph Dennie; it seems that, in a 1789 case in which two of Dennie's Harvard classmates were accused of assault, Tyler was counsel for the defense — see H. M. Ellis, *Joseph Dennie and His Circle* (Austin, Tex., 1915), p. 66; and *The Letters of Joseph Dennie*, ed. Laura G. Pedder (Orono, Me., 1936), p. 57n. Though Graham calls Tyler a resident of Ryegate, there is no mention of Tyler in Edward Miller and Frederic P. Wells, *History of Ryegate, Vermont* (St. Johnsbury, Vt., 1913).

97. Tyler memoir, pp. 107–108.

98. A series of Tyler's letters to Riley is included in the Tyler

memoir (pp. ²54–81 *passim*). The correspondence seems to have begun (on Riley's part) on 10 October 1808, and Tyler first replied on 8 November. On 22 July 1809 he sent the last batch of material for the first volume, and on 13 December 1809 Riley wrote: "The Reports are out, and will be shipped to Mr. Fessenden on Monday." Tyler sent the copy for 360 pages of volume II on 22 May 1810. The copyright deposit date for volume I is 27 October 1809; for volume II, 30 November 1810.

99. A similar attitude is reflected in Tyler's own comment that "at a not far distant period the bar of *Vermont* will be viewed in a light not unfavourable by the more eminent of the profession in the elder States" (2 Tyl. 135). The reception of the *Reports* is discussed in the Tyler memoir, p. 81; these two letters, of 21 July and 3 August 1810, are quoted from that source.

100. The People v. Douglass, 4 Cowen 26 (1825); he made the remark in connection with a citation of 1 Tyl. 252. The comment is repeated by John William Wallace in *The Reporters, Chronologically Arranged* (3rd ed.; Philadelphia, 1855), p. 343. Nine small corrections of Tyler's work are listed in Guy B. Horton, *Notes on the Vermont Reports* (Montpelier, 1941), pp. [5–6]. Perhaps it was Savage's remark which lay behind the comments in the Boston *Courier* obituary of Tyler: "The two volumes of reports which bear his name, were prepared with almost as much haste and lack of labor as his light literary articles, and are of course meagre abstracts of Decisions, the majority of which are of no permanent value."

101. Statements by Tyler appear in the reports of the following cases: Pearse v. Goddard, 1 Tyl. 373 (1802); Adams v. Brownson, 1 Tyl. 452 (1802); Robbins v. Windover and Hopkins, 2 Tyl. 11 (1802); Harris v. Huntington et al., 2 Tyl. 129 (1802); Selectmen of Windsor v. Jacob, 2 Tyl. 192 (1802); Rich v. Trimble, 2 Tyl. 349 (1803); State v. White, 2 Tyl. 352 (1803); Browne et al. v. Graham, 2 Tyl. 411 (1803). Tyler is listed as *dubitante* or *hesitante* in the following: Doe v. Whitlock, 1 Tyl. 305 (1802); Sherwood v. Pearl, 1 Tyl. 319 (1802); Hawley v. Clerk and Hazletine, 2 Tyl. 20 (1802); Wallace v. Farnsworth, 1 Tyl. 297 (1803); Cushenden and Rutherford v. Harman et al., 2 Tyl. 431 (1803). Tyler did not sit for the case of Houghton v. Jewett and Martin, 2 Tyl. 183 (1802), because he was counsel for the plaintiff.

102. 1 Tyl. 454; 2 Tyl. 141.

103. See H. S. Wardner, "Judge Jacob and His Dinah," *Vermonter*, XIX (May–June 1914), 80–88. The case is one of the few that Horton singles out for brief comment in *Notes on the Vermont Reports* (no pagination). It is also referred to in two biographical sketches by Russell Taft which emphasize Tyler's legal career: *Green Bag*, VI

(1894), 72–74 (part of a series on the Supreme Court of Vermont, V, 553–564; VI, 16–35, 72–91, 122–141, 176–192); and "Royall Tyler," *Green Bag*, XX (1908), 1–5. Tupper ("Royall Tyler," p. 67) assigns to Tyler the famous statement that the only valid claim to a slave is "a quit-claim deed of ownership from the Almighty," but Horton attributes the remark to Tyler's fellow-judge Theophilus Harrington. (Tupper's main discussion of Tyler's legal career is on pp. 79–82.)

104. The denial of the appeal for Dean is on pp. 36–48 of the pamphlet; the quotation from the jury charge is taken from the Tyler memoir, pp. 228–232. In addition to these sources, two detailed accounts of the affair are in Walter Hill Crockett, *Vermont: The Green Mountain State* (New York, 1921), III, 3–15, and *Vermont Historical Gazetteer*, ed. A. M. Hemenway, II (1871), 342–347 (which includes another passage from the jury charge). Less complete are Walter Hill Crockett, *A History of Lake Champlain* (Burlington, 1909), p. 237, and Ralph Nading Hill, *The Winooski: Heartway of Vermont* (New York, 1949), pp. 127–132 (which quotes from a ballad on the subject). Mary Tyler wrote to her husband on 3 March 1809, "Mr. Buckingham has sent us the *great trial*" (Tyler Papers, Box 46).

105. This chronology of the circuit is derived from Tyler's *Reports*.

106. These letters are included in the Tyler memoir, pp. 138–151. The specific quotations given here are, respectively, from the letters of 2 February, 8 February, 11 January, and 11 February 1802. A similar sentiment occurs in a letter of January 1800: "I enjoy myself as well as I could wish or expect away from you" (p. 114); in the same letter he tells of declining an invitation because "I have religiously resolved never to participate in the evening social circle without the presence of my wife." The Pennsylvania Historical Society has a three-page letter from Tyler to his wife, written at Woodstock on 9 October 1807. It expresses the same concern with the health of his family, gives advice about the tenant, and promises money. Some letters to Tyler from his wife, during these years, are in the Tyler Papers, Box 46.

107. The salary of the Vermont Chief Justice was $1000 and of the Assistant Judges $900 (the Governor received only $750), according to *Walton's Vermont Register and Farmer's Almanack* for 1819 (Montpelier), p. 97. Graham (*Descriptive Sketch*, p. 179) gives the salary for 1792 as 27 shillings per day on the circuit for the Chief Justice and 22 shillings for the Assistant Judges. After Tyler's retirement from the bench, he no longer had any right to the state's collection of statute books, and the *Records of the Governor and Council of the State of Vermont* report that George Worthington was asked, on 8 November 1814, to move these volumes from Tyler's house in Brattleboro to the statehouse in Montpelier (VI, 99–100).

108. Burnham, *Brattleboro*, p. 101. Burnham credits the story to Justice Daniel Kellogg, who was a young law student at the time and who was present in the courtroom.

109. Letter of 22 May 1810, in Tyler memoir, p. 79.

110. The fullest account of the accomplishments of Tyler's children is in appendix B of *Grandmother Tyler's Book*, pp. 337–357. For Edward Royall, see also the obituary notice in the *New Englander*, VI (October 1848), 603–608, which lists his articles and published sermons; for Amelia, see also Cabot, *Annals*, I, 382–384. Royall (Charles) published a legal work, *A Book of Forms*, in Brattleboro in the early summer of 1845; George Palmer wrote an elegy on Lincoln, *The Successful Life* (Brattleboro, 1865), and revised the *Encyclopedia of Religious Knowledge* in 1858.

111. Denison's son Henry, a classmate of young Royall's, wrote an elegy on his friend's death; he, too, was to die as a young man (in October 1819). Undoubtedly it was this association which made Denison one of the few persons to whom Tyler would talk in the months just after the tragedy (*Grandmother Tyler's Book*, p. 325). For a fuller account of Henry Denison, see the *Official History of Guilford, Vermont*, pp. 171–172. Twenty-six of Denison's poems (with a biographical sketch) are included in *The Columbian Lyre* (Glasgow, 1828), pp. 245–284; the "Elegy on the Death of Royall Tyler, jun." (pp. 280–282), in forty-eight iambic pentameter lines, contains a reference to Tyler's grief: "That eve, that saw a hapless father weep." There is a letter in the New York Public Library, from Tyler to Israel Tefft (editor of the Savannah *Georgian*), 24 November 1820, which shows that Tyler had agreed to contribute to a biography of young Denison (for an edition of his works), and was doing research into Denison's ancestry; in the letter, he apologizes for not having finished his part, and he quotes from a letter of James Rousseau which discusses the whereabouts of Denison's manuscripts. Tefft was responsible for getting Denison's poems into *The Columbian Lyre*, and he wrote an explanation of the delay in publication to be inserted at the front of the volume; the Boston Public Library copy is inscribed to his son, Henry Denison Tefft. See G. T. Tanselle, "*The Columbian Lyre*, 1828," *Transactions of the Edinburgh Bibliographical Society*, IV (1966), 159–165.

112. The moves to five different Brattleboro houses, after the family left the farm, are recorded in *Grandmother Tyler's Book*, p. 326, note 1. *Walton's Vermont Register* for 1819 lists the Register of Probate fees: the charge for recording or copying a will was eight cents; for drawing up an administration bond, thirty-four cents; and for drawing the probate of a will thirty-four cents (for estates up to $166), and forty-two cents (over $166). Tyler is listed as Register of

Probate from 1815 to 1821 in Leonard Deming's *Catalogue of the Principal Officers of Vermont* (Middlebury, 1851), pp. 81–83. Though Tyler was not able to transact much legal business in his last years, he was listed in the *Vermont Register* as one of the attorneys in Brattleboro to the very end of his life; see, for example, the *Registers* for 1819 (p. 82), 1820 (p. 63), 1822 (p. 87), 1824 (p. 69), 1826 (p. 99).

113. This journal begins on 2 December 1821 and continues until 1843, providing a contemporary record for the years following those covered in the retrospective *Grandmother Tyler's Book* (written 1858–1863). Selections for the years 1821–1826 have been published by G. F. Newbrough in "Mary Tyler's Journal," *Vermont Quarterly*, XX (1952), 19–31, from which the present quotations are taken (cf. Tyler Papers, Box 45, Envelope 10). The continually recurring motif is faith in God despite adversity; the journal is important for its detailed references to current prices (apples at 10¢ a bushel, a quarter of beef at $3.25), household chores (such as making pies, knitting, mending shirts), social activities (visits from Judges Denison and Whitney, games of backgammon), and medical knowledge, as well as to Tyler's decline. There are letters of Mary Tyler's from this period mentioning financial difficulties (12 January 1823) and the low state of Tyler's health (10 August 1825), in the Tyler Papers, Box 46.

114. According to Dr. Gordon N. French of the Green Mountain Clinic, Northfield, Vermont, Tyler's disease was melanosarcoma, tumor of the choroid layer of the eye (Newbrough, "Journal," p. 31).

115. Burnham, *Brattleboro*, p. 101.

II. *Dramatist:* The Contrast

1. Quoted from Tyler's unpublished and unfinished work, "The Bay Boy," from a section entitled "First Theatrical Presentation in Boston," describing an amateur production of *Cato*; quoted, by permission of the heirs and the Vermont Historical Society, from a typescript in the Tyler Papers, gift of Helen Tyler Brown.

2. Constance Rourke, "Rise of Theatricals," *The Roots of American Culture* (New York, 1942), pp. 88–108. The standard history of the early American theater is Arthur Hobson Quinn's *A History of the American Drama from the Beginning to the Civil War* (2nd ed.; New York, 1943), pp. 1–135; for greater detail see the first volume of George C. D. Odell's *Annals of the New York Stage* (New York, 1927) and Hugh F. Rankin's *The Theater in Colonial America* (Chapel Hill, N.C., 1965).

3. Dunlap, *History of the American Theatre* (New York, 1832), p. 71. The 1786 date is repeated by (among others) Benrimo (referred

to below); Henry A. Beers, *Initial Studies in American Letters* (New York, 1895), pp. 63–64; Julian W. Abernethy, *American Literature* (New York, 1902), pp. 98–99; William B. Cairns, *A History of American Literature* (New York, 1912), pp. 138–139.

4. See *Argus and Patriot*, n.s. XXIX (5 November 1879), 1; M. D. Gilman, *The Bibliography of Vermont* (Burlington, 1897), p. 282; Tyler memoir (cf. Chapter 1, note 4, above), p. 60. This date is followed by (among others) Henry Burnham, *Brattleboro, Windham County, Vermont* (Brattleboro, 1880), p. 93; and Walter Hill Crockett, *Vermont* (New York, 1921), V, 73.

5. Joseph Ireland, *Records of the New York Stage* (New York, 1866), I, 76. Among the early historians, George O. Seilhamer also gives the correct date, in his *History of the American Theatre* (New York, 1888–1891), II, 215, as does Oscar Wegelin, in *Early American Plays 1714–1830* (New York, 1900); but T. Allston Brown, in *A History of the New York Stage* (New York, 1903), I, 9, dates the first performance as 18 April 1787.

6. Because the reviewer refers to the performance "last evening," Barnard Hewitt, in *Theatre U.S.A.: 1668 to 1957* (New York, 1959), p. 34, gives the opening date as 17 April 1787. However, one must assume, I think, that the reviewer was doing the actual writing of the review on the day after the performance and that it did not get printed until the second day. It seems safer to rely on the advertisements. If a performance were to be held on the 17th, it is unlikely that the notice on the 17th would mention only the one for the following evening, when the issue for the 16th does say "This Evening."

7. The companion piece on 18 April was O'Keeffe's *The Poor Soldier*; on 2 May, Colman's *The Deuce Is in Him*; and on 12 May, Inchbald's *The Widow's Vow*. See the advertisements in the *Independent Journal*; this paper also reports the 18 April performance as "with some alterations." There is no evidence for a 5 May performance of *The Contrast*, as listed by Seilhamer (*History*, II, 215) and Odell (*Annals*, I, 255): no such performance is announced in the New York newspapers; 5 May 1787 was a Saturday, and plays were normally presented only on Monday, Wednesday, and Friday; and the play for Friday, 4 May, was *Romeo and Juliet*.

8. Quoted by Montrose J. Moses, *Representative Plays by American Dramatists* (New York, 1918), p. 436. After the publication of the play in 1790, it was given a number of unauthorized productions in Southern cities by Charles McGrath, who continually pirated copyrighted works; in 1790 and 1791 audiences in Alexandria, Frederick, Georgetown, Hagerstown, Williamsburg, and perhaps other cities saw *The Contrast*. It was performed in the first regular Boston season, on 29 October 1792; in Alexandria in 1793; in Charleston on 25 Feb-

ruary 1793 and 11 February 1794; in Boston again on 11 May 1795; and in Philadelphia on 27 June 1796. Cf. Thomas C. Pollock, *The Philadelphia Theatre in the Eighteenth Century* (Philadelphia, 1933), pp. 45, 141, 158, 303; and Eola Willis, *The Charleston Stage in the XVIII Century* (Columbia, S.C., 1924), pp. 163, 196. In Charleston the play was advertised as by "Major Tyler," and it was given the subtitle, "The American Son of Liberty."

9. See the article on *Androboros* and text by Lawrence H. Leder, *Bulletin of the New York Public Library*, LXVIII (1964), 153–190. As early as 1894 Paul Leicester Ford, in "The Beginnings of American Dramatic Literature," *New England Magazine*, n.s. IX (1894), 673–687, tried to correct the misconceptions about *The Contrast* by pointing out some of these other firsts.

10. A. Benrimo, "The First American Play," *Dramatic Magazine*, I (May 1880), 57–59; Andrew P. Peabody, "The Farmer's Weekly Museum," *Proceedings of the American Antiquarian Society*, n.s. VI (1889), 115; "Early American Dramatists," *Theatre*, XXIV (October 1916), 208, 250; *Official History of Guilford, Vermont* (Guilford, 1961), p. 160. Katharine Metcalf Roof, in *Colonel William Smith and Lady* (Boston, 1929), declares, "*The Contrast* was the first play by an American dramatist to be produced in the American theatre" (p. 133n); but she also assigns its production to 1786 (p. 133) and its composition to Tyler's stay with his mother at Jamaica Plain, where "between outbursts of despair he unquestionably wrote dramas" (p. 132).

11. Dunlap, *History*, p. 71; Ireland, *Records*, I, 76.

12. Hewitt, *Theatre U.S.A.*, p. 36; Rourke, "Rise of Theatricals," p. 115.

13. See Evert A. and George L. Duyckinck, *Cyclopaedia of American Literature* (New York, 1855), I, 432; and Joseph T. Buckingham, *Specimens of Newspaper Literature* (Boston, 1850), II, 203. Thomas P. Tyler, in giving the 1789 date for the production of the play, sets the winter of 1788–89 as the time of its composition (see note 4 above).

14. This whole argument is set forth clearly by Arthur H. Nethercot in "The Dramatic Background of Royall Tyler's *The Contrast*," *American Literature*, XII (1941), 435–446.

15. Frederick Tupper, "Royall Tyler, Man of Law and Man of Letters," *Proceedings of the Vermont Historical Society*, IV (1928), 71.

16. *Worcester Magazine*, III (May 1787), 61; Seilhamer, *History*, II, 234–235; *Independent Chronicle*, 30 October 1797.

17. Dunlap, *History*, pp. 71–72; Duyckinck, *Cyclopaedia*, I, 432; Odell, *Annals*, I, 256; Oral Coad and Edwin Mims, *The American Stage* (New Haven, 1929), p. 33; Robert E. Rogers, "Our Dramatic

Past," *New Republic*, X (21 April 1917), 10–11 sup. (review of Quinn's anthology); Moses, *Representative Plays*, pp. 435, 437; Grenville Vernon, *Yankee Doodle-Doo* (New York, 1927), p. 23; Russell Blankenship, *American Literature* (New York, 1931), pp. 703–704; Quinn, *History*, pp. 294–303; Glenn Hughes, *A History of the American Theatre* (New York, 1951), pp. 57–58.

18. Arthur Hornblow, *A History of the Theatre in America* (Philadelphia, 1919), I, 171. Some of the other roles were taken by prominent actors also: Manly by John Henry, Dimple by Lewis Hallam, Van Rough and Charlotte by Mr. and Mrs. Morris, Jessamy and Maria by Mr. and Mrs. Harper. In the Baltimore cast (followed in the 1789 New York performance) Hallam took the role of Manly and Harper of Dimple. For information about the casts see Odell, *Annals*, I, 257, 274; Seilhamer, *History*, III, 211, 250. On Wignell, see W. B. Wood, *Personal Recollections of the Stage* (Philadelphia, 1854).

19. Perley Isaac Reed, *The Realistic Presentation of American Characters in Native Plays Prior to Eighteen Seventy* (Columbus: *Ohio State University Bulletin*, May 1918; Contributions in Language and Literature, No. 1), p. 136. He points out further that after the years 1787–1789 the Yankee type rarely appears for twenty years, but particularly after 1815 it becomes very prominent.

20. Reed, *Realistic Presentation*, pp. 136–137.

21. See Albert Matthews, "Brother Jonathan," *Publications of the Colonial Society of Massachusetts*, VII (1901), 94–122; "Brother Jonathan Once More," XXXII (1935), 374–386. Matthews reports the story that the term originated as a friendly nickname applied by Washington to Governor Jonathan Trumbull of Connecticut but rejects the account because it can be traced back no farther than 1846.

22. The discovery of this first Jonathan play was announced by Marston Balch in "Jonathan the First," *Modern Language Notes*, XLVI (1931), 281–288. Balch points out a number of parallels between Tyler's figure and Atkinson's and believes that in both cases the Yankee "remains at the end the most clearly defined figure of all." Atkinson's play would have attracted more attention if it had been played in London, but Mrs. Inchbald's version of Patrat's work was already established there (as well as in America, where Tyler could have seen it on 23 March 1787).

23. This is not to disagree with Constance Rourke in considering Tyler's depiction of Jonathan an event of prime historic significance, but only to change the emphasis. When she asserts that the Yankee sprang "almost full blown" from *The Contrast*, with not even a prose sketch preceding it ("Rise of Theatricals," p. 117), she is speaking,

I take it, of the appearance of a satisfactory literary embodiment of a particular attitude, not the appearance of the attitude itself — though, of course, the nature of a literary symbol is such that it often makes this kind of separation difficult. Reed has the same point in mind when he says that Jonathan was "reproduced fundamentally from the very substance of American civilization" (*Realistic Presentation*, p. 46); Allan G. Halline, however, in his anthology *American Plays* (New York, 1935), finds the nationalism of the play a much greater contribution than the creation of Jonathan (pp. 4–6). For further discussion of Yankee characters, see Walter Blair, *Native American Humor* (New York, 1937), pp. 17–37; Richard M. Dorson, "The Yankee on Stage," *New England Quarterly*, XIII (1940), 467–493; James J. Quinn, "The Jonathan Character in American Drama" (unpub. diss., Columbia, 1955).

24. Vernon, in *Yankee Doodle-Doo* (pp. 23–24), says that *The Contrast* "gave to us the version of 'Yankee Doodle' which most of us know"; Reed (*Realistic Presentation*, p. 48) considers it the first dramatic use of the text; Balch ("Jonathan the First," p. 287n) traces the "authentic" version, not printed until 1815, to Edward Bangs, a Harvard undergraduate with Tyler. See also *Living Age*, LXX (10 August 1861), 382–384; and O. G. T. Sonneck, *Report on "The Star Spangled Banner," "Hail Columbia," "America," "Yankee Doodle"* (Washington, 1909), pp. 79–156.

25. This tradition (including "Alknomook") has been discussed by Frank Edgar Farley, "The Dying Indian," in *Anniversary Papers by Colleagues and Pupils of George Lyman Kittredge* (Boston, 1913), pp. 251–260.

26. Thomas J. McKee in his introduction to the Dunlap Society edition of *The Contrast* (New York, 1887), p. x; Quinn, *History*, p. 71n. Richard Moody, in *America Takes the Stage* (Bloomington, Ind., 1955), mentions a "*Death Song of a Cherokee Chief* (1790)" as one of Tyler's works (p. 86).

27. *The Poems of Philip Freneau*, ed. F. L. Pattee (Princeton, 1903), III, 313–314; Pattee did append a note saying, "The authenticity of a poem suspected to be Freneau's may always be gravely doubted if it is not found to be included in his collected works, for he hoarded his poetic product . . . with miserly care." It was still credited to Freneau by W. B. Cairns in *Early American Writers* (New York, 1909), p. 440, and Annie Russell Marble, *Heralds of American Literature* (Chicago, 1907), pp. 95–96, among others. But Harry Hayden Clark did not include it in his 1929 edition, and Lewis Leary, in *That Rascal Freneau* (New Brunswick, N.J., 1941), says that the *American Museum* "mistakenly" attributed the song to Freneau (p. 152).

28. Anne Home Hunter, *Poems* (London, 1802), pp. 79–80; *British*

Critic, XX (1802), 409–413; *Gentleman's Magazine*, XCI (part 1; January 1821), 89–90. She says that the lyrics were suggested by a man who had resided among the Cherokees. The song appeared in Joseph Ritson's *Select Collection of English Song* (London, 1783), I, ii, and in sheet music of the early 1780's. In America, after the *American Museum* appearance (I, 90), it was included in *The Philadelphia Songster* (Philadelphia, 1789), p. 8; the American sheet music came later, about 1800. The songs from *Tammany* are reprinted in *Magazine of History*, XLIII (1931), 59–69. McKee noted its use in a British play, John Scawen's *New Spain*, but the date he gave, 1740, is a misprint for 1790. For further discussion, see *Musical Antiquary*, III (1912), 166–170; Tom Peete Cross's review of Henry A. Burd's *Joseph Ritson* (1916) in *Modern Philology*, XVII (1919), 233–238; and G. T. Tanselle, "The Birth and Death of Alknomook," forthcoming in the *Newberry Library Bulletin*.

29. All quotations are from the first edition of 1790. Act and scene (rather than page) numbers are given to facilitate reference to later editions (which are not always, however, very accurate; a dependable one, despite a few changes in punctuation, is in Arthur Hobson Quinn's anthology *Representative American Plays* [New York, 1917]). The first edition used inverted commas around lines and passages "omitted in the representation"; within the passages quoted in this chapter, then, single quotation marks indicate words not spoken on the stage.

30. The reading of a letter (III.i) is a common device to accomplish the same ends, but at least it makes the exposition more plausible in a framework that emphasizes externals.

31. Herbert R. Brown, in "Sensibility in Eighteenth-Century American Drama," *American Literature*, IV (1932), 47–60, discusses *The Contrast* in terms of the sentimentality, the didacticism, the sympathy for humanitarian reform, and the "prevailing moral tone" characteristic of both the drama and the fiction of the time; he shows some parallels between Manly and Bevil in Steele's *The Conscious Lovers* (1722). Nethercot ("Dramatic Background," pp. 444–446) suggests a possible influence in Hugh Kelly's *False Delicacy* (1768), which exposes excesses of sentiment and has a character similar to Maria; he also points to George Colman's *Polly Honeycombe* (1760) for its references to the circulating libraries. For a fuller discussion of the sentimental tradition, see Ernest Bernbaum, *The Drama of Sensibility* (Boston, 1915).

32. Nethercot ("Dramatic Background," p. 442) suggests possible sources for some of the names: Manly in Vanbrugh's *Provoked Husband* (1728) and Wycherley's *Plain Dealer* (1677); Transfer in Samuel Foote's *The Minor* (1760).

33. Van Rough's phrase, however, is not so much a speech habit as an expression of a ruling philosophy with him.

34. Marie Killheffer, in "A Comparison of the Dialect of 'The Biglow Papers' with the Dialect of Four Yankee Plays," *American Speech*, III (1928), 222–236, analyzes Jonathan's language in *The Contrast*, particularly III.i. Tyler's method, she says, is to use "a few localisms against a background of standard English" (pp. 230–231); *The Contrast*, among the plays she studied, "shows the slightest attempt to indicate dialect but by far the largest proportion of dialect words used are localisms" (p. 235). She gives a summary of the traits of the Jonathan-figure on p. 222. Another discussion of the language in *The Contrast* is in George H. McKnight and Bert Emsley's *Modern English in the Making* (New York, 1928), pp. 479–480; one of the contrasts in the play is shown to be the difference between "the American countrified mode of speech and the refinements of speech in American urban life" — for Jonathan uses older forms no longer current in cultivated conversation. That the play is "thematically concerned with questions of language" has been perceptively argued by Roger B. Stein, in "Royall Tyler and the Question of Our Speech," *New England Quarterly*, XXXVIII (1965), 454–474. He suggests that the heart of the drama is a satiric exposure of the weakness or falsity of various speech patterns, which become masks to hide character; the search for an honest, authentic native speech produces an unresolved dilemma, he says, from which Tyler is forced to extricate himself by resorting to a conventional plot line in the last part of the play.

35. "Rantipole," first used about 1700, appears in Vanbrugh's *Provoked Husband* and provides a further reason for believing that this play may have influenced Tyler; it was performed in New York two weeks before *The Contrast*, on 29 March 1787. Tyler's use of "penseroso" is discussed by B. Sprague Allen in *Tides in English Taste, 1619–1800* (Cambridge, Mass., 1937), II, 176.

36. The idea that the play is important as an early treatment of the "international theme," contrasting American innocence with Old World corruption, is discussed by John Lauber, "*The Contrast*: A Study in the Concept of Innocence," *English Language Notes*, I (1963), 33–37. He compares the Dimple-Maria-Manly relationship with that of Osmond-Isabel-Goodwood in *The Portrait of a Lady*; in Manly, he says, Tyler almost provides an instance of R. W. B. Lewis' "American Adam." The first American play with international contrasts, according to Halline's *American Plays*, is John Leacock's *The Fall of British Tyranny* (1776).

37. *Daily Advertiser*, 18 April 1787; *Independent Journal*, 5 May 1787; *Worcester Magazine*, III (1787), 61; *Pennsylvania Herald*, 13 November 1787 (see Seilhamer, *History*, II, 233).

38. The *Pennsylvania Journal*, after the Baltimore production, also praised the sentiments of the play, speaking of the "vices it corrects" and the "pernicious maxims of the Chesterfieldian system" which it exposes (Seilhamer, *History*, II, 233).

39. The volume was advertised for sale by Thomas & Andrews' Bookstore in the *Massachusetts Centinel*, 22 May 1790; it was entered for copyright in the Pennsylvania district court on 15 June 1790. The subscription list in the published volume contains 371 names, including Aaron Burr, David Humphreys, Isaiah Thomas, Jonathan Trumbull, and George Washington; some persons subscribed for more than one copy, and the list thus accounts for 658 copies, 311 of which were to go to persons in Maryland. See Seilhamer, *History*, II, 234–237, for a discussion of the list and for an exposition of the theory that publication was held up because of jealousy aroused by Wignell's success as Jonathan.

40. *Universal Asylum and Columbian Magazine* (Philadelphia), V (August 1790), 117–120.

41. "Scenes from the Contrast," *Massachusetts Magazine*, II (October 1790), 581–583.

42. Dunlap, *History*, pp. 71–72; Buckingham, *Newspaper Literature*, II, 203; Duyckinck, *Cyclopaedia*, I, 432.

43. Charles F. Richardson, *American Literature 1607–1885*, II (New York, 1888), 18; *A Library of American Literature*, ed. Edmund C. Stedman and Ellen M. Hutchinson, IV (New York, 1888), 92–97. Other late nineteenth-century references to the play, besides Seilhamer (1889), *History*, II, 225–239, are in Washington Frothingham and Charlemagne Tower, *Our Book*, 2nd ed. (New York, 1892), pp. 380–382; Donald G. Mitchell, *American Lands and Letters* (New York, 1897), pp. 220–224; Katherine Lee Bates, *American Literature* (New York, 1898), pp. 82–83 ("Dull, trivial, and shapeless"); Henry A. Beers, *An Outline Sketch of American Literature* (New York, 1887), p. 79 ("very low comedy").

44. Despite the myth that only one or two copies survive, there are at least a dozen copies of the first edition now in institutional collections. George Washington's copy sold for $2800 in the Avery sale of 1919 and for $3100 in the Wilbur sale of 1933. See Wilbur's preface to his 1920 edition of *The Contrast*, pp. v–xviii; L. E. Chittenden, *Personal Reminiscences* (New York, 1893), pp. 288–293; and G. T. Tanselle, "Some Uncollected Authors XLII: Royall Tyler, 1757–1826," *Book Collector*, XV (1966), 303–320.

45. For example: Marble (1907), *Heralds*, pp. 238–242; Carl Holliday, *The Wit and Humor of Colonial Days* (Philadelphia, 1912), pp. 295–301; William J. Long, *American Literature* (Boston, 1913), p. 93 (Tyler's "crude plays"); William P. Trent *et al.*, *Cambridge History of American Literature* (New York, 1917), I, 218–219; Hornblow

(1919), *Theatre in America*, I, 170–172; Quinn (1923), *History*, pp. 64–73; Mary Caroline Crawford, *The Romance of the American Theatre* (Boston, 1925), pp. 91–94; Montrose J. Moses, *The American Dramatist* (Boston, 1925), pp. 72–74; Odell (1927), *Annals*, I, 255–257; Coad and Mims (1929), *American Stage*, p. 33; Charles Angoff, *A Literary History of the American People* (New York, 1931), II, 372–376 ("worthless as drama"); Fred Lewis Pattee, *The First Century of American Literature 1770–1870* (New York, 1935), pp. 218–221; Van Wyck Brooks, *The World of Washington Irving* (New York, 1944), pp. 148, 160; Robert E. Spiller *et al.*, *Literary History of the United States* (New York, 1948), pp. 186–187; Hughes (1951), *History*, pp. 57–58; A. H. Quinn *et al.*, *Literature of the American People* (New York, 1951), pp. 198–200; Walter F. Taylor, *The Story of American Letters* (rev. ed.; Chicago, 1956), pp. 60–61; Hewitt (1959), *Theatre U.S.A.*, pp. 34–37.

46. Some of these performances are as follows: 6–8 June 1912: Brattleboro pageant; 16, 18 January 1917: Players of the University of Pennsylvania; 22–23 January 1917: Drama League of America (New York); 7 April 1917: Drama League of Boston; 19–21 November 1925 and 11–12 June 1926: Cornell Dramatic Club; 30 October 1926: Columbia Laboratory Players (reviewed in *Billboard*, XXXVIII [October–December 1926], 39); 7–19 March 1927: Pasadena Community Playhouse; 1932: Marquis Players of Lafayette College (Easton, Pa.); 15–17 December 1937: Bennington College Theatre Guild; 25 March 1940: Dock Street Theatre, Charleston (version arranged by Charles H. Meredith); 11–16 November 1940: Senior Players, Pasadena; 5–6 December 1941: Curtain Callers, Manse Barn, Tappan, N.Y. (Meredith version); 3–12 November 1943: Catholic University of America (directed by Walter Kerr); 20 July 1948: On-Stage, New York Academy of Vocal Arts (reviewed by Richard Watts in *New York Post*, 22 July; by William Hawkins in *World Telegram*, 23 July); July 1954: Hyde Park (N.Y.) Players; 26–27 March 1958: Boston University Division of Fine Arts (directed by Priscilla Bussan); 17 February –8 March 1959: Fair Park Arena Theatre, Dallas; December 1960: Hofstra College Drama Department; July 1966: O'Neill Conference, Waterford, Conn. (produced and directed by Worthington Minor). Photographs of productions appear in *Theatre Arts*, XVI (July 1932), 570; XXIII (July 1939), 526; XXXVIII (September 1954), 31; and in *Life*, XXXVII (2 August 1954), 73.

47. The articles by Killheffer (1928), Balch (1931), Brown (1932), Nethercot (1941), Lauber (1963), and Stein (1965) have already been referred to, as has the dissertation by Reed (1918). Among the other relevant dissertations are Allan G. Halline, "Main Currents of Thought in American Drama" (Wisconsin, 1935), and Josef A. Elfenbein,

"American Drama 1782–1812 as an Index to Socio-Political Thought" (New York University, 1952).

48. See, for example, "Our First Truly National Play: How a Young Harvard Graduate Was Inspired to Create 'Brother Jonathan,'" *Delineator*, LXXXV (July 1914), 7; J. L. Hornibrook, "America's First Comedy," *Landmark*, XIV (1932), 391–392.

49. Anthologies edited by Quinn (1917), Moses (1918), Spiller (1933), Halline (1935), Cady (1950), Downer (1960), Stern and Gross (1962), and Moody (1966) — see Bibliography. Excerpts from the play have been reprinted in numerous biographical sketches of Tyler and in other anthologies.

50. Before its publication in the 1790 volume, the prologue had been published in the New York *Daily Advertiser* on 20 April 1787.

III. *Dramatist: Later Plays*

1. New York *Daily Advertiser*, 19 May 1787. The prologue was to be spoken by Mrs. Morris.

2. The New York *Journal and Weekly Register* of 17 May 1787, for example, advertised the play for "tomorrow"; but the New York *Packet* the next day was still announcing it for "tomorrow," with a note about its unavoidable postponement. Cf. George C. D. Odell, *Annals of the New York Stage* (New York, 1927), I, 259.

3. Odell, *Annals*, I, 259. Arthur Hornblow, in his *History of the Theatre in America* (Philadelphia, 1919), similarly says that the play "probably had little merit" (p. 172).

4. The letter is in volume VII of the Madison Papers, Library of Congress; it has been published by Worthington C. Ford, in "The Federal Constitution in Virginia, 1787–1788," *Proceedings of the Massachusetts Historical Society*, 2nd series, XVII (1903), 461; and it is quoted by Helen Tyler Brown in her introduction to the 1920 limited edition of *The Contrast* (p. xxx).

5. *The Letters of Joseph Dennie*, ed. Laura G. Pedder (Orono, Me.: University of Maine Studies, 2nd series, no. 36, 1936), pp. 150–151; the five letters from Dennie to Tyler given in this edition are taken from the Tyler memoir (cf. Chapter 1, note 4, above).

6. Tyler memoir, p. 84; T. P. Tyler says that a fragment of the play was found among his father's papers. For announcements of the play, see Boston *Columbian Centinel*, 4 May 1796, and *Independent Chronicle*, 5 May.

7. Dennie to Tyler, 14 April 1797, in *Letters*, p. 156.

8. See also, for other announcements, *Massachusetts Mercury*, 27 October 1797; *Columbian Centinel*, 28 October; Boston *Gazette*, 30 October.

9. See *Columbian Centinel*, 12 March 1796, where part of the poem

is quoted; this speculation, it is said, "has been made the sport of wit, in prose and verse."

10. See, for example, *Massachusetts Mercury*, 3 October 1797.

11. *Columbian Centinel*, 28 October 1797; quoted by Frederick Tupper in "Royall Tyler, Man of Law and Man of Letters," *Proceedings of the Vermont Historical Society*, IV (1928), 82.

12. See the notices in the New York *Time Piece*, 20 December 1797 and 12 February 1798; *Daily Advertiser*, 19, 20, 22, 23 December 1797. Although there is no evidence that the play was ever printed, it is treated as a published volume (octavo, Boston, 1797) in Evans entry 32946 and Sabin 97618.

13. John Steele Tyler to Royall Tyler, 11 December 1811 (letter in Boston Public Library). For information about J. S. Tyler as manager of the Boston theater, see W. W. Clapp, *A Record of the Boston Stage* (Boston, 1853), pp. 24–35; Clapp says that he took over "more from a desire to advance the cause of the drama than from any pecuniary motives." Tyler's 1795 poetical "Address" is in the *Federal Orrery*, 9 November 1795 (see Chapter 4, below). The *Vermont Historical Gazetteer*, I (1867), 559, in a list of Tyler's works, includes "An Author's Evenings — a Comedy repeatedly performed in Boston," but the writer is seemingly confusing Tyler's newspaper columns with a play.

14. Tyler, writing to Dennie on 7 October 1795, quoted from a letter he had received from his brother John Steele, commenting that Tyler's "Mock Doctor" would probably be a success in Boston (letter in New Hampshire Historical Society). Perhaps both Tyler and one of his sons wrote a play on this subject, for Julian I. Lindsay, in *Tradition Looks Forward* (Burlington, 1954), reports that Royall Tyler, Jr., wrote an adaptation of Molière (entitled "Quackery") while he was attending the University of Vermont (pp. 102–103).

15. Stanley T. Williams, in *The Spanish Background of American Literature* (New Haven, 1955), traces the influence of Cervantes in America, at its height near the turn of the century (I, 44–46); he dates Tyler's play at about 1800 (I, 408). Quotations from *Four Plays* are by permission of Norbert Towne, attorney for Mrs. Arthur Peach.

16. Though it is superfluous to find a source for this in Cervantes, Sancho in chapter 45 does ridicule the affectation of nobility immediately upon his arrival in Barataria, when he learns that "Don" has been attached to his name.

17. Although episodic, Sancho's adventures in Barataria in *Don Quixote* are set in the larger framework of the plot devised by the Duke and Duchess, and the Sancho chapters alternate with those about Don Quixote. Whether or not Tyler expected his audience to fill in the background of the trick on Sancho from a knowledge of

Don Quixote is a debatable question that does affect the texture of the play. In Cervantes the reader knows how Sancho got to be governor and enjoys watching him outwit those who expected him to look more foolish than ever; in Tyler this dimension is lacking, for Sancho seems to be presented as a legitimate governor, possibly to make stronger the satire on unqualified rulers. Perhaps the two references to "Duke Don Cosmo Jokeley" indicate that we are to assume the *Don Quixote* background; on the other hand, the battle at the end is more realistic than in Cervantes — Tyler's stage directions do not indicate that the soldiers are performing purely for the effect to be produced on Sancho.

18. This speech is foreshadowed by Sancho's last one in III.i: "I can but marvel why so many men wish to be Governour when they get nothing but abuse for their pains — but the world will never lack Sancho's."

19. In the same conversation Sancho makes a number of other puns: "a word for your private ear" — "Which ear is that?"; "the belle of Barrataria" — "Hope she has a short clapper." In III.ii a Courier is announced, and Sancho says, "I'll curry him . . ." (p. 26). He also engages in more elaborate plays on words: Don Formal refers to the preceding governor who was called "the Skeleton of the Law & the Shadow of Justice"; Sancho answers, "I had rather be called the fat squab of the Law and the Substance of Justice. Let him have all the Honour — and let me have the Dumpling" (p. 10). Like Jonathan, he often has unusual exclamations, sometimes related to the meaning of the statement, such as "Snuff my peepers — how it vanished!" (p. 23).

20. It seems safe to take this as a reference to the American Presidency, though of course such a comment is dramatically inappropriate in the play; if this reading is correct, then the *terminus a quo* can be pushed forward to the time of Washington's death in 1799.

21. Tupper, "Royall Tyler," p. 101.

22. Quoted, by permission, from a typed introduction to the sacred dramas in the Tyler Papers (Box 45, Envelope 33) in the Vermont Historical Society, the gift of Helen Tyler Brown. This brief introduction, another statement of American literary independence, asserts, "The unrivaled excellence of the parent Country in any art or science should not be permitted to confound us into inactivity, but should rather excite to emulation."

23. For example, the King James version reads, "I believed not the words, until I came, and mine eyes had seen it; and, behold, the half was not told me. . . . Happy are thy men, happy are these thy servants, which stand continually before thee, and that hear thy wisdom" (10:7–8). In Tyler this becomes:

Slow was I to believe, but now I've come
And with mine eyes thy glory do behold.
Well may I say that not one half was told.
Happy the men, thrice happy they who stand
Before thee, and continually do hearken
To thy wisdom. (p. 119)

24. Baanah was one of Solomon's twelve commissariat officers (cf. I Kings 4:12 and 4:16); Chalcol was noted for his wisdom (as in I Kings 4:31); Shimei, of the house of Saul, cursed and stoned David (II Samuel 16:5–8), later begged forgiveness (II Samuel 19:16–23), and was eventually executed by Solomon (I Kings 2:8–9, 36–46); "Liba" is an error (whether made by Tyler or a later copyist) for Ziba, to whom David gave the possessions of Mephiboseth (II Samuel 9:1–13; 16:1–4); Solomon's daughters, Taphath and Basmath, and their husbands, Abinadab and Ahimaaz, both among Solomon's twelve officers (all mentioned near the beginning of Act II), are referred to, respectively, in I Kings 4:11 and 4:15. The name Maachah, which Tyler assigns to the scheming mother, does occur in the Bible but not in that connection; sometimes a male name (I Kings 2:39), it is given as the name of a king's mother in I Kings 15:2. Belkis (or Balkis), though not Biblical, is the name sometimes ascribed to this particular Queen of Sheba; for a discussion and further references, see A. J. Wensinck and J. H. Kramers, *Handwörterbuch des Islam* (Leiden, 1941), under "Bilkis," p. 81.

25. For a rare example of alliteration, see Esther's soliloquy at the end of III.iii in *The Origin of the Feast of Purim* (pp. 57–58).

26. The first epigraph is Proverbs 16:18: "Pride goeth before Destruction and a haughty spirit before a fall"; the second is Psalms 58:11, which asserts that "there is a reward for the righteous"; and the third is Proverbs 31:30, stating that "a woman that feareth the Lord, she shall be praised."

27. Compare, for example, Haggai 2:6–7, 22 ("For thus saith the Lord of hosts; Yet once, it is a little while, and I will shake the heavens, and the earth, and the sea, and the dry land; And I will shake all nations. . . . And I will overthrow the throne of kingdoms") with Tyler's chorus on p. 36 ("Thus saith the Lord: / 'Yet once — and yet it is a little while / And I — the Heavens, and the earth — the sea / And the dry land will shake; before my face / The nations of the earth shall quake and fear. / The thrones of kingdoms I will overthrow' ").

28. Though Tyler says in the first stage direction that the "Time chorus" is composed of women (as opposed to the group labeled simply "Chorus," which is made up of men), at the end of the play

he has a "Chorus of Jewish Women" alternate with the "Time Chorus." The male Chorus is listed in the dramatis personae as "Elam Chorus."

29. The names in this play are again Biblical, but (as with Liba-Ziba in the Solomon play) someone has had trouble reading Tyler's z's: the name of Haman's wife should be Zeresh (see Esther 5:10, 14), not Geresh, and the leader of the returning Jews, referred to in Act I on p. 35 and twice on p. 38 as Gerababel, should be Zerubbabel (see Haggai 1:12; 2:2, 4, 21, 23). Carshena, who speaks in III.i, is one of the seven princes of Ahasuerus mentioned in Esther 1:14, as is Memucan, referred to in I.ii (p. 39). Meres, another of the seven princes, is identified in the cast as "friend of Haman"; though no speech is assigned to him, perhaps the short one on p. 55, labeled "One of Haman's Friends," is his. Harbonah and Carcas are two of Ahasuerus' seven eunuchs (Esther 1:10), and Hatach is another eunuch appointed to attend Esther (Esther 4:5). Luzzi and Elam, who speak in I.ii, are not listed in the cast. Elam is the head of a family that returns to Palestine (see Ezra 2:7; Nehemiah 7:12), and Luzzi, not a Biblical name, is perhaps related to the town of Luz (Bethel), close to Jerusalem. Shushan is the Biblical name of Ahasuerus' palace (Esther 1:2). Haggai appears four times on p. 35 as "Haggia," but, though there is a Biblical Haggiah (I Chronicles 6:30), obviously the prophet Haggai is meant throughout.

30. There is no division marked "Act III" in the printed text, but it may be assumed that Act III begins on p. 85; the preceding scene is labeled "Act Second — Scene Third," and the one following ends with "End of the Second Scene," presumably of Act III — thus the intervening scene must be the first of Act III. The editors point out (p. 63) that, in the case of this one play, they have not found the original manuscript and have based their text on "what seems to be a carefully made copy."

31. Of the eleven brothers of Joseph, enumerated in Genesis 49:3–27, those who have speaking parts in the play are Simeon, Levi, Reuben, Zebulon, Issachar, Judah, Dan, and Benjamin. The only other characters, besides Joseph and Jacob, are Jacob's wife Leah, Joseph's steward, and his interpreter. As in the Bible, Reuben is the brother who defends Joseph from the others' anger, but Tyler describes his efforts in much greater detail.

32. For example, Genesis 42:13 reads: "Thy servants are twelve brethren, the sons of one man in the land of Canaan; and, behold, the youngest is this day with our father, and one is not." The Tyler passage (p. 80) is as follows: "Thy servants, O my Lord, are brethren twelve, / Sons of one man, who in Canaan dwells / And behold the

youngest with our Father / Is this day — and one is not." Not only single speeches but large passages are taken almost verbatim from Genesis — cf. Genesis 43:1–13 with II.ii (pp. 82–84).

33. There are times, however, when Tyler's elaboration of a sentiment is less successful because it does not blend in with the diction and syntax of the paraphrased verse. An example is Joseph's praise of home, "where first he felt a Mother's kiss / And a fond Father's love" (p. 80).

IV. *Poet*

1. There had been virtually no scholarly work on Tyler's poetry before Marius B. Péladeau wrote his master's thesis at Georgetown University in 1962, entitled "The Verse of Royall Tyler: Collected and Edited." Though I do not always come to the same conclusions as he does about the attribution of particular poems, I wish to express my gratitude to Mr. Péladeau for generously allowing me to consult both his thesis and a revised version of it which he prepared for publication. Walter Muir Whitehill of the Boston Athenaeum very kindly offered to let me examine the galley proofs of the Péladeau edition, prior to its appearance in the *Publications of the Colonial Society of Massachusetts*. These proofs, however, did not become available before the time when the page proofs of the present book had to be returned. I have therefore not seen the Péladeau edition in its final form and am not able to give page references to it for the poems discussed in this chapter.

2. H. Milton Ellis, *Joseph Dennie and His Circle* (Austin: University of Texas Studies in English No. 3, 1915), p. 43. Ellis' work is the most detailed source of information about Dennie. But of particular interest is Tyler's own memoir of Dennie's courtroom manner in the *New England Galaxy*, 24 July 1818.

3. A brief account of the *Eagle* is in John King Lord, *A History of the Town of Hanover, N.H.* (Hanover, 1928), pp. 265–266; see also Clarence S. Brigham, *History and Bibliography of American Newspapers 1690–1820* (Worcester, 1947), I, 462.

4. See, e.g., *Port Folio*, II (19 June, 14 August, 9 October 1802), 191, 249, 313. Cf. "Conserves from the Cookshop of Adeona," *Farmer's Weekly Museum*, 16 January and 15 May 1798.

5. See the *Port Folio*, I (14 March 1801), 87: "When the Editor [Dennie] and a literary friend first projected the scheme of writing miscellaneous essays in conjunction, the prose was generally understood to be the province of the Editor, and the poetry that of his associate." Earlier, on 28 February 1801 (I, 69), Dennie had referred to the work of his "associate and *principal*" as "the *poetry of Spondee*."

6. However, Dennie did occasionally contribute poetry and Tyler prose; in some of the early columns, for example, there are poems signed "C."

7. For further information about the *Orrery*, see Joseph T. Buckingham, *Specimens of Newspaper Literature* (Boston, 1850), II, 221–250; cf. Brigham, *American Newspapers*, I, 296.

8. On the *Tablet*, see Ellis, *Joseph Dennie*, pp. 69–83.

9. See George Aldrich, *Walpole as It Was and as It Is* (Claremont, N.H., 1880), pp. 76–82. The *Farmer's Museum* has been discussed in various places; see, especially, Andrew P. Peabody, "The Farmer's Weekly Museum," *Proceedings of the American Antiquarian Society*, n.s. VI (1889), 106–129; Ellis, *Joseph Dennie*, pp. 84–109; Buckingham, *Newspaper Literature*, II, 174–220; Brigham, *American Newspapers*, I, 486–489. Jeremiah Mason's *Memoir and Correspondence* (Cambridge, Mass., 1873) includes a first-hand account of the Walpole group (esp. pp. 28–32) and suggests that in Walpole was "more motion, life, and bustle" because it was in transition between the "rude and boisterous manners" of the original settlers and a more "civilized, orderly" condition.

10. Buckingham (*Newspaper Literature*, II, 179) says, "For three years . . . , the Museum was more richly supplied with original communications of a literary character than any other paper, that had then, or has since, been published in the United States." Peabody asserts that "it is not too much to say that this paper had a larger amount and variety of original matter of a high character than there has been in the same number of issues of any American paper before or since" ("Farmer's Weekly," p. 109).

11. The most extensive account of the *Port Folio* is by John Queenan, "*The Port Folio*: A Study of the History and Significance of an Early American Magazine" (unpub. diss., University of Pennsylvania, 1955). See also Frank Luther Mott, *A History of American Magazines 1741–1850* (New York, 1930), pp. 223–246; Albert H. Smith, *The Philadelphia Magazines and Their Contributors* (Philadelphia, 1892), pp. 86–151 (which credits Tyler with all the "Colon & Spondee" papers, p. 125); and Ellis P. Oberholtzer, *The Literary History of Philadelphia* (Philadelphia, 1906), pp. 168–188.

12. Some writers, including Péladeau in his thesis, assign much more poetry in the *Port Folio* to Tyler on the ground that all the contributions signed "S." are his. I am inclined to be more cautious. To begin with, we have a reasonably reliable basis for attributing ten items to Tyler in the annotations in the file that belonged to John E. and Harrison Hall, the later editor and publisher of the *Port Folio*; see Randolph C. Randall, "Authors of the *Port Folio* Revealed by the Hall Files," *American Literature*, XI (1940), 379–416. Of the ten items

there recorded for Tyler, five are prose (either signed "Colon &
Spondee" or not signed at all) and two are "Colon & Spondee" poems
reprinted from the *Museum*; only three original poems are left, and
these are unsigned. To these we may obviously add "Love and Liberty" (IV, 336), which is signed in print with Tyler's name. But the
Hall file provides no justification for associating all "S." work with
Tyler; Dennie's own comments in his editorial column would furnish
better justification, since he is still (in 1801 and 1802) referring to
Tyler as "S.", but his remarks all have to do with the fact that "S."
has been neglecting his poetry and sending nothing in. The two early
poems (I, 24, 39) which have prefatory notes signed "S." may be by
Tyler despite what the notes say, but in view of the fact that Dennie
soon after laments Tyler's absence, they may very well not be his.
Dennie's next comment on Tyler comes at the same time that he
reprints an old "Spondee" poem; and his three pleas in 1802 begin
two months after the last 1802 contribution marked as Tyler's in the
Hall files. The one poem in 1803 (Hall files) and the one in 1804
(Tyler's signature) cause little trouble. But early in 1804 there is
indication that "S." may no longer stand for Tyler, even in Dennie's
mind. His message to "S." on 11 February 1804 (IV, 48) is a curt
dismissal, in sharp contrast to his earlier tone when addressing Tyler;
and prose contributions signed "S." begin to appear under the "Samuel
Saunter" heading (IV, 57). Poems signed "S." occur with some frequency in the early part of 1805, but again Dennie's note does not
lend credence to the equation of "S." with Tyler, for on 20 April
1805 he writes, " 'S,' whose penmanship is not familiar, but whose
poetry is of a character so agreeable to us, that we wish for farther
specimens, is, we are convinced, a writer, endowed with such ability,
that we shall always welcome him in the shape of a contributor to
our poetical stock" (V, 118). As for the second series of the *Port
Folio*, if "S." is not automatically assumed to be Tyler, the kinds of
poems signed "S." do not seem characteristic of him; in at least one
case (n.s. V, 64) the "S." might be an abbreviation of "Stanley," the
signature of the poem just above, and on 15 August 1807 (n.s. IV,
110–111) "S." is identified as the author of political essays in the
Boston *Gazette*. By the time of these later "S." poems, Dennie's
health was not allowing him to spend as much time with the magazine
as before, and Tyler was at the height of his legal activity — both
circumstances lessening the chances of Tyler's poetry appearing in
the *Port Folio*. In the Tyler Papers at Montpelier is a file of the *Port
Folio*, but the numerous markings in it are not contemporary and
represent only later guesses at what may conceivably have been
Tyler's work. All this is not to say that Tyler may not have contributed a great deal to the *Port Folio*; it is only that we do not yet

have a firm way of knowing. If one is looking for items of Tyler's, it seems to me that such remarks by Dennie as the following carry more weight than the letter "S.": "The well-known wit, who favoured us with the sensible satire against 'Fanaticism,' published in vol. IV. No. 50, is sure to be always warmly welcomed by his affectionate friend. We shall omit no opportunity of doing honour to a man for whose head and heart we entertain a well-founded partiality" (V, 7). The poem "Fanaticism" (IV, 400), though unsigned, may possibly be Tyler's.

13. Joseph T. Buckingham, *Personal Memoirs and Recollections of Editorial Life* (Boston, 1852), I, 56; Tyler memoir (cf. Chapter 1, note 4, above), p. 169. Buckingham seems to have kept up a contact with Tyler; Mary Tyler wrote to her husband on 3 March 1809 saying that Buckingham had sent a letter "in which he seems to anticipate *more good things in the Spring*" (Tyler Papers, Box 46).

14. On the *Centinel*, see Buckingham, *Newspaper Literature*, II, 58–117.

15. These have been published, respectively, in Mary R. Cabot, *Annals of Brattleboro* (Brattleboro, 1921–22), II, 834; *Favorite Vermont Poems, Series One*, ed. W. J. Coates (North Montpelier, 1928), p. 6 (and in *Driftwind*, September 1926); *ibid.*, p. 5; *Series Five* (1934), p. 19. Another poem, "A Valedictory Address," was published only as a broadside during Tyler's lifetime (the unique copy is in the possession of Marius B. Péladeau) but was reprinted in Henry Burnham, *Brattleboro, Windham County, Vermont* (Brattleboro, 1880), pp. 84–85; it is a poem of 160 tetrameter lines (based on the metaphor of children as flowers in a garden) written for his son, Thomas Pickman, to recite at the closing of Rebecca Peck's school for the summer of 1823.

16. In the Tyler Papers are typed copies of many poems, some of them apparently unpublished (before Péladeau's edition); Box 45, Envelope 36, contains "The Inimitable Fair" (36 anapaestic lines), "Say is it height, or shape, or air" (36 iambic lines), and "The Colt" (16 lines, dated 1796), among others. In the Boston Public Library are four manuscript poems, supposed to be juvenilia of Tyler: a 16-line jingle (plus a 6-line "chorus") about a "jolly cobler," with the inevitable pun on mending soles; an 8-line "Song" about a merchant anxiously looking to sea; 8 lines beginning "Oh, like a storke among the Rush"; and 8 lines on "Our old Moll" who hands out "a Mug of foaming Flip." The copy of "The Bay Boy" in the Tyler Papers (Box 45, Envelope 29; cf. Box 77, Envelope 13) contains original epigraphs, not included in *The Algerine Captive*, at the beginnings of most sections; three of them, amounting to more than 60 lines of tetrameter couplets, are labeled as from "The Doggerel Romaunt," and one (of

8 lines) is said to be from "The Pleasures of Pain." Other verses appear in the typescript of "Utile Dulci" (Box 45, Envelope 35), particularly a 111-line poem on the wisdom of Darius.

17. "Anacreontic to Flip," *Eagle*, 11 August 1794 (signed "Colon & Spondee"; 36 lines); reprinted in *Newhampshire and Vermont Journal*, 5 September 1794, and *Columbian Centinel*, 4 October 1794. All quotations are from the earliest publication of each poem.

18. *Eagle*, 25 August 1794 (signed "S."; 56 lines); reprinted in *Tablet*, I (19 May 1795), 4, and in *Port Folio*, I (14 March 1801), 87–88. Though this poem praises the "rural beauty," Tyler at other times celebrates the city, as in "The Town Eclogue," *Polyanthos*, II (June 1806), 181–184 (54 lines of tetrameter couplets), where he says, "Her rustick coz let others sing, / But let me taste the town bred Spring."

19. "A Reputation Vindicated," *Farmer's Weekly Museum*, 11 April 1797 (16 lines); reprinted in *Port Folio*, I (24 October 1801), 339. Another poem about marital relations with an unsentimental — even bitter — conclusion is "The Test of Conjugal Love," *Eagle*, 29 December 1794 (36 lines), reprinted in *Farmer's Weekly Museum*, 27 March 1798, and in *The Spirit of the Farmers' Museum* (Walpole, N.H., 1801), pp. 258–259. All poems which were reprinted in this anthology and are here credited to Tyler have been endorsed with a "T" or "Tyler" by Joseph Dennie in the copy (now in the Boston Public Library) which he presented to James Abercrombie on 26 December 1801. See also Chapter 6, note 10, below.

20. "Epigram," *Farmer's Weekly Museum*, 25 September 1797 (14 lines).

21. "The Mechanick Preferred: An Epigram Founded on a Recent Fact," *Polyanthos*, II (April 1806), 56 (signed "S."; 12 lines).

22. *Polyanthos*, V (April 1807), 49–50 (signed "S."). Another "Epigram" on clothes and poverty is in the *Eagle*, 17 November 1794 (6 lines), reprinted in the *Federal Orrery*, 27 November 1794 (signed "S.").

23. *Farmer's Weekly Museum*, 1 May 1798 (44 lines); reprinted in *Spirit*, pp. 227–228.

24. See Mark Longaker, *The Della Cruscans and William Gifford* (Philadelphia, 1924); Roy B. Clark, *William Gifford: Tory Satirist, Critic, and Editor* (New York, 1930), pp. 36–80; Edward E. Bostetter, "The Original Della Cruscans and the *Florence Miscellany*," *Huntington Library Quarterly*, XIX (1956), 277–280, 288–290, 293–300. For the influence of the Della Cruscans in America, see Fred Lewis Pattee, *The First Century of American Literature 1770–1870* (New York, 1935), pp. 107–115, and M. Ray Adams, "Della Cruscanism in America," *PMLA*, LXXIX (1964), 259–265 (which quotes 46 lines of Tyler's "Address to Della Crusca"). Adams suggests that the reference

to "Criticus," who "bids instructed taste to scorn / The sound of Della Crusca's horn," in the *Farmer's Weekly Museum* of 2 January 1798, may be to Tyler (p. 262).

25. Reprinted in *Spirit*, pp. 223–225.

26. *Farmer's Weekly Museum*, 16 May 1797 (signed "Della Yankee" in a "Colon & Spondee" column); reprinted in *Spirit*, pp. 221–223.

27. *Farmer's Weekly Museum*, 11 September 1797.

28. *Farmer's Weekly Museum*, 1 April 1799; reprinted in *Spirit*, pp. 289–292, and in *Port Folio*, I (24 October 1801), 339. The prose comment which introduces the poem announces that Messrs. Colon & Spondee "Have, at a great expense, erected an Epithet Jenny, with which they card, spin, and twist all kinds of epithets" and with which, therefore, they may be able to compete against European productions.

29. *Farmer's Weekly Museum*, 15 April 1799; reprinted in *Spirit*, pp. 311–314.

30. *Farmer's Weekly Museum*, 20 May 1799; reprinted in *Spirit*, pp. 218–219.

31. *Newhampshire and Vermont Journal*, 14 March 1797 (24 lines); reprinted in *Spirit*, p. 234, with the heading "Fond Frederick to Fanny, False Fair." On p. 186 of *Spirit* is an epigram written in reply, entitled "Frighted Fanny's Faithful Friend, to Frederic, Fictitiously Fond."

32. *Farmer's Weekly Museum*, 3 June 1799 (64 lines); reprinted in Haverhill *Federal Gazette*, 28 June 1799, and in *Spirit*, pp. 243–245. The poem also contains some good descriptions of contemporary scenes, such as farmers sending vegetables to Boston. Other poems have literary sources, like the popular "Spondee's Mistresses," which refers at the beginning to Cowley's description of his mistresses and then takes up Miss Conduct, Miss Chance, Miss Take, and so on; *Farmer's Weekly Museum*, 15 April 1799 (42 lines), reprinted in *Port Folio*, I (28 March 1801), 104, in *Spirit*, pp. 225–227, in *Farmer's Museum*, 5 January 1802, and in Brattleboro *Reporter*, 12 September 1803. Another is "The Widower," which has as its subtitle "A Parody on Pope's Ode to Solitude" (actually a serious poem praising marriage); *Eagle*, 24 November 1794 (signed "S."; 20 lines), reprinted in *Newhampshire and Vermont Journal*, 5 December 1794.

33. *Farmer's Weekly Museum*, 25 April 1797; reprinted in *Spirit*, pp. 229–232.

34. *Farmer's Weekly Museum*, 2 October 1797; reprinted in *Spirit*, pp. 239–243.

35. *Eagle*, 6 January 1794; the unique copy of the later broadside version (with a revised last stanza) is at Dartmouth (cf. Vermont Historical Society *News and Notes*, II [December 1950], 1–2).

36. Another occasional religious poem, "Hymn to the Supreme

Being," written for Good Friday 1803, contains the line, "A nation's voice we raise"; *Port Folio*, III (21 May 1803), 168 (identified in the Hall file).

37. Besides the original publication, the poem has appeared in *Spirit*, pp. 235–236; in the anthologies edited by Kettell (1829), Stedman and Hutchinson (1888), Stevenson (1908), Coates (1928), Coates and Tupper (1932), and Untermeyer (1952) — see Bibliography; and in *Theatre Arts*, XXIX (July 1945), 417, and *Collier's*, CXXVIII (7 July 1951), 20.

38. *Port Folio*, IV (20 October 1804), 336; reprinted in the *Columbian Centinel*, 24 July 1805. Cf. Thomas Paine's poem "The Great Republic; Or, The Land of Love and Liberty" in the *Columbian Centinel*, 13 July 1796.

39. The first on 29 July 1799, and the second on 5 August 1799 (reprinted in Haverhill *Federal Gazette*, 8 August 1799, and as a broadside, the unique copy of which is in the University of Vermont library).

40. *Federal Orrery*, 29 December 1794 (signed "R. Tyler, Esq."); reprinted in *Newhampshire and Vermont Journal*, 10 February 1795.

41. *Federal Orrery*, 9 November 1795 (signed "By a Gentleman of Vermont"); the poem is quoted by W. W. Clapp, *A Record of the Boston Stage* (Boston, 1853), in his account of the opening of the third season (p. 26).

42. *Polyanthos*, II, 62–70, 197–202. For the literary context, see Agnes Marie Sibley, *Alexander Pope's Prestige in America 1725–1830* (New York, 1949).

43. The line between occasional verse and reflective poetry is of course not clear-cut. Tyler's "Elegy: Occasioned by the Death of the Rev. Samuel Stillman, D.D., Pastor of the First Baptist Church in Boston," in the *Polyanthos*, V (April 1807), 45–49, is both occasional and reflective; it also illustrates the degree to which Tyler sometimes echoed English poetry, for its twenty-six iambic pentameter quatrains continually remind one of Gray's "Elegy": "Mute is that warning voice, whose power awoke / The sleeping conscience from its dread repose" (lines 17–18); "The sculptured urn, let polished Europe raise" (line 26); "What though no massy fanes his dust inclose, / No brass or marble his loved form supply; / Yet, not forgotten shall his dust repose, / Nor yet unhonoured shall the good man die" (lines 33–36).

44. *Eagle*, 21 July 1794 (signed "T."); eleven stanzas reprinted as "The Cave of Chastity" in *Columbian Centinel*, 2 August 1794.

45. *Tablet*, I (11 August 1795), 50–51 (signed "S."; 88 lines); reprinted in *Newhampshire and Vermont Journal*, 14 February 1797, and in *Farmer's Museum*, 26 January 1801.

46. *Polyanthos*, V (May 1807), 127–132 (signed "S."; 162 lines).

Tyler quotes this poem in one of the fragments of "The Bay Boy," where he has Updike submit it for inclusion in the poets' corner of the *Massachusetts Spy*.

47. *Farmer's Weekly Museum*, 6 May 1799; reprinted in *Port Folio*, I (14 November 1801), 368. See also "Fluttering lovers, giddy boys," *Newhampshire and Vermont Journal*, 6 December 1796 (30 lines), reprinted in *Spirit*, pp. 219–220.

48. *The Algerine Captive* (Walpole, N.H., 1797), I, 49.

49. Respectively, II, 21, 69, 130, 141, 227. The blank verse passages appear as epigraphs to chapters 2, 4, 10, and 29 in the first volume (I, 37, 49, 94, 182) and chapters 2, 9, 15, 16, 19, 22, 23, and 35 in the second (II, 21, 69, 97, 117, 130, 141, 150, 227). Two other epigraphs are by Tyler: an iambic quatrain at chapter 20 of the second volume (II, 132) and eight lines of iambic tetrameter couplets (paraphrasing Horace) at chapter 21 (II, 135).

50. *Polyanthos*, II (April 1806), 52–53.

51. Though the lines are not numbered in the Driftwind edition, the line numbers here and below are based on that text. It should be pointed out, however, that this numbering will not serve for references to the manuscript copy of the poem (not in Tyler's hand) at the Vermont Historical Society (the copy from which the Driftwind edition was taken), for there are a great many differences between the two versions. In the printed edition there is a note explaining that line 23 has been altered from "Thy homely sarcophagus burst" to "Shall burst thy rough sarcophagus" because of "false accent on word 'sarcophagus.'" But there is no indication that the poem has been silently changed for publication at nearly a hundred other points as well. There are three kinds of editorial alteration involved: (1) omission of stanzas—four stanzas are omitted in the published version, following lines 376, 456, 468, and 644; (2) rearrangement of stanzas—three stanzas originally following line 600 are inserted (along with one other) in the published version after line 692 (thus becoming lines 693–708); (3) revision of single words or phrases—ninety lines contain substantive variants, ranging from insignificant errors (such as *ah-oh* in line 33) and minor changes (e.g., *which-that*, 124, 162) to revisions in diction (as *view-see*, 36; *whim-chance*, 38; *immense-dull*, 55; *bounding-bouncing*, 147; *boisterous-roistering*, 301; *drive-send*, 308; *walls-halls*, 345; *path-task*, 350; *barb'rous-cruel*, 586; *sweat-brow*, 591), changes in number of noun, verb, and pronoun (99, 132, 150, 518, 520, 574, 677), and the recasting of an entire stanza (the last, 741–744). In some cases the changes are no doubt correct (as in lines 486 and 513, where lost rhymes are restored), but in others they produce inferior readings (as in line 328, where *As* replaces *And*). If these revisions do not greatly affect a total evaluation of the poem, one

should at least be aware of their existence. Quotations from this poem are made by permission of Mrs. Dorothy Sutherland Melville and Dr. Allan D. Sutherland.

52. Donald G. Mitchell, *American Lands and Letters* (New York, 1897), p. 221.

V. Novelist

1. *Independent Chronicle*, 24, 31 August 1797. Part of this chapter was read at a meeting of the Midwest Modern Language Association in Normal, Illinois, on 8 May 1964.

2. It was advertised in the *Farmer's Weekly Museum* on 31 July and 7 August 1797 as "Now in press"; as "Just published" on 14, 21, 28 August, 4 September, and 2, 9 October. It was also labeled as "just published" in the advertisement for Blake's Book Store, in the Boston *Independent Chronicle*, 28 September and 5 October. The price was $1.50. The source for the size of the edition is a preface Tyler later wrote for a proposed new edition, quoted in the Tyler memoir (cf. Chapter 1, note 4, above), pp. 98–100. Two excerpts appeared in the *Farmer's Weekly Museum* on 14 August 1797 (volume I, chapter 18) and on 21 August (volume II, chapter 14).

3. Nancrede's advertisement is dated 21 September 1797 and appears in the *Independent Chronicle* for 5, 12, 19, 26 October and in the *Columbian Centinel* for 27 September and 4 October. Knowledge of Tyler's identity underlies a statement in the *Columbian Centinel* for 25 October 1797: "It is said that the presumptuous editor of the Walpole paper [Dennie] is helped to all his native poetry by Dr. Updyke Underhill, who was six years a prisoner among the Algerines." As late as 1937, W. Roberts could write to *Notes and Queries* (CLXXII, 282) asking who the author of *The Algerine Captive* was; he deduced that the author was American from the reference to Dilworth's *Spelling Book*. Roberts' query was answered twice, first briefly by Albert Matthews (p. 374) and then in more detail the following week by Robert S. Forsythe (pp. 389–390). Many readers must have taken the book as a true account of adventure: William Czar Bradley, in a letter of 7 December 1857 (now in the Vermont Historical Society), tells of "an honest Westmoreland farmer" who came into his father's office soon after the publication of the book, talking about "Dr. Underhills adventures"; when the truth was explained, the "indignation of the farmer on hearing what he called the gross imposition was almost uncontrollable and would have delighted the author." The letter also gives indication that Pliny White at this time was planning to prepare a new edition of *The Algerine Captive*.

4. Dennie to Tyler, 30 August 1797, in *The Letters of Joseph Dennie*, ed. Laura G. Pedder (Orono, Me.: University of Maine Studies, 2nd series, no. 36, 1936), p. 165.

5. Coleman to Tyler, 24 September 1797, in Tyler memoir, pp. 103–104.

6. See *Farmer's Weekly Museum*, 17, 24, 31 July, 6 August, 1 October 1798.

7. Tyler memoir, pp. 98–99.

8. For a detailed account, see especially Gardner W. Allen, *Our Navy and the Barbary Corsairs* (Boston, 1905), pp. 11–58; Ray W. Irwin, *The Diplomatic Relations of the United States with the Barbary Powers 1776–1816* (Chapel Hill, N.C., 1931), pp. 1–81; and H. G. Barnby, *The Prisoners of Algiers: An Account of the Forgotten American-Algerian War 1785–1797* (London, 1966). (I am indebted to Richard Colles Johnson for assistance with this documentation.)

9. The *Newhampshire and Vermont Journal*, which Tyler certainly read, devoted much space in the issue of 29 March 1796 to the text of the 1795 treaty with Algiers and letters of Humphreys and Washington about it. As examples of the various kinds of attention given to Algiers in the newspapers, see the issues of this paper for 23 August 1796, 29 October 1798, 4 February 1799, and 25 August 1800; see also the Boston *Independent Chronicle*, 20 October 1785, 27 April 1786, 16 October 1788; the Hanover (N.H.) *Eagle*, 13, 20 January 1794, 9 February, 27 August 1795; the Boston *Federal Orrery*, 26, 29 January, 30 November 1795.

10. There were other poetic references, if not whole poems, as in David Humphreys' *On the Happiness of Americans* (1786) and Joel Barlow's *Columbiad* (1807).

11. In *The Algerine Captive* Tyler himself refers to such authorities as Shaw (II, 100), Sales, and Prideaux (II, 141–142). For further discussion of several possible sources and of the book's historical accuracy, see Bertrand W. Chapman, "The Nativism of Royall Tyler" (master's thesis, University of Vermont, 1933), pp. 24–26, 32–4.

12. This pamphlet of twenty-four pages, printed in Boston for N. Coverly, does not usually quote from Tyler verbatim but is often extremely close, especially in the "Concise Description of Algiers" (pp. 18–22) — compare, for example, the sixth sentence of chapter 16 of Tyler's second volume (II, 118) with the opening of Nicholson's description ("Algiers is situated in the bay of that name, and built upon the sea shore an eminence, which rises above it"); or the concluding anecdote of chapter 25 (II, 164) with Nicholson's version. The beginning of the pamphlet is based on the first chapter in Tyler's second volume; the phrase "Six Years a Prisoner among the Algerines"

appears in the titles of both works. For other books about Algerine captivity, after 1797, see the bibliographies in Allen, *Our Navy* (pp. 305–311), and Irwin, *Diplomatic Relations* (pp. 205–214).

13. *Port Folio*, II (16 January 1802), 8.

14. See Dorothy Blakey, *The Minerva Press* (London, 1939), p. 196. Cf. *Anti-Jacobin Review*, VI (1800), 451.

15. Roland L. Shodean, in "English Editions of American Authors 1801–1863" (master's thesis, University of Chicago, 1958), says that only eight American novels of the 1801–1820 period were published in England before 1863 (p. 26); the Robinsons published only one American work during that time (p. 180).

16. Tyler memoir, p. 99.

17. It is unlikely that the changes in punctuation are authorial, nor is it characteristic of Tyler to make the kind of careful verbal revision reflected in the Robinson edition; and in 1802 he was occupied with legal matters. On the other hand, Tyler was interested later in revising the work, and perhaps he made some revisions as early as 1802. The tradition of asserting that the English edition grossly altered the book began with Dennie, who commented on the treatment of American novels in England in the *Port Folio*, IV (1 September 1804), 277; of *The Algerine Captive* he said, "Some London *Lethe* had washed away every American trace," and he assured his readers that he "actually sat by the American author, while he was writing the above adventures, and know, that, *at this present writing*, he neither prescribes nor compounds in the city of London, but administers the justice of his country from the supreme courts of Vermont." For a more detailed collation of the various editions, see G. T. Tanselle, "Early American Fiction in England: The Case of *The Algerine Captive*," *Papers of the Bibliographical Society of America*, LIX (1965), 367–384.

18. *Lady's Magazine*, XXXV (1804), 37–43, 68–75, 134–142, 198–204, 247–254, 289–296, 345–352, 401–408, 457–465, 513–521, 569–577, 625–6??, ??1–690.

19. *The Algerine Captive* (Walpole, N.H., 1797), I, 35–36. All quotations are from the first edition.

20. *Monthly Review*, XLII (September 1803), 86–93.

21. *Port Folio*, III (4 June 1803), 181; IV (28 April 1804), 134. Tyler is here referred to as "a favourite friend of the Editor of the Port Folio."

22. *Monthly Anthology and Boston Review*, IX (November 1810), 344–347. The review was written by Nathaniel Appleton Haven, according to the entry for 13 November 1810 in the *Journal of the Proceedings of the Society Which Conducts the Monthly Anthology &*

Boston Review, introd. M. A. DeWolfe Howe (Boston, 1910), p. 242.

23. The text was set from a copy of the Robinson 1802 edition, but further changes — usually omitted letters or words — were made accidentally. Typographical errors, for example, appear on pp. 70, 82, 87, 101, 108, 164, 197.

24. It has been reissued in Publication No. 64 of the Augustan Reprint Society, *Prefaces to Three Eighteenth-Century Novels*, ed. Claude E. Jones (Los Angeles, 1951); the editor says that the preface and dedication may well be the most important parts of *The Algerine Captive*. The preface was also reprinted by Frederick C. Prescott and John H. Nelson in *Prose and Poetry of the Revolution* (New York, 1925), pp. 253–255. Attention was drawn to the preface from time to time in the nineteenth century — for example, by G. P. Lathrop, "Early American Novelists," *Atlantic Monthly*, XXXVII (April 1876), 404–405, and by W. J. Fletcher, "An Early Call for 'the American Novel,'" *Critic*, XVI (15 February 1890), 83.

25. Cf. Tremaine McDowell, "Sensibility in the Eighteenth-Century American Novel," *Studies in Philology*, XXIV (1927), 383–402. Lillie D. Loshe, in *The Early American Novel* (New York, 1907), contrasts the romantic and sentimental approach of *Fortune's Football* (which also involves Algerine piracy) with the "iconoclastic realism" of *The Algerine Captive* (pp. 24–25).

26. A wholly fictitious genealogical tree has grown up around Tyler's invention of the names Benoni and Updike, and certain persons have claimed their descent through this line, asserting that Updike had three children after his return from captivity. But these two names were inventions of Tyler's, and the Benoni line has no authenticity, as shown by Josephine C. Frost in *Underhill Genealogy* ([Boston]: Underhill Society, 1932), II, 43–50. On p. 50 of that work is a letter from E. R. Tyler, equating the captured ancestor with Tyler's great-grandfather; but the chart in *Grandmother Tyler's Book* (New York, 1925) labels the great-uncle as the "Algerine Captive" (p. 331). The Underhill family owned the house in Stratford which Shakespeare bought in 1597; see J. H. Morrison, *The Underhills of Warwickshire* (Cambridge, 1932), pp. 31, 76–77, and Mark Eccles, *Shakespeare in Warwickshire* (Madison, Wis., 1961), pp. 88–89. The activities of John Underhill are recounted in Belknap's *History of New-Hampshire* (rev. ed.; Dover, N.H., 1831), I, 23–27, in *Underhill Genealogy*, I, 28–33, and in H. C. Shelley's *John Underhill* (New York, 1932); Whittier's poem on Underhill appears in the *Atlantic Monthly*, XXXII (December 1873), 668. *Newes from America* was reprinted in the *Collections of the Massachusetts Historical Society*, 3rd series, VI (1837), 1–28. The first three chapters of *The Algerine*

Captive were reprinted as "An Account of Captain John Underhill" in the *Marvellous and Entertaining Repository* (Boston), II (1827), 229–238.

27. Chapter and page numbering begins anew with volume II.

28. Paine argues that the minority should always govern; Peter Pindar replies that, since most of the crowd present had been swayed to Paine's viewpoint, it automatically is defeated, by Paine's own reasoning. Paine, pictured as a moody man, then "retired from the presence of triumphant wit, mortified with being foiled at his own weapons" (I, 181). Updike finds it hard to understand why Paine wrote such a book as *The Age of Reason* unless as a "sacrifice to save his life from the devouring cruelty of Robespierre" or as an outlet for his "passion for paradox" (I, 183); yet he did not recant. In this, Tyler's most vehemently hostile portrait, there is also reference to Paine's drinking; and a Peter Pindar epigram is quoted (said to have been written in a copy of *The Age of Reason* and not included in Peter Pindar's works), ending with the pun that "the Devil's in Paine" — reprinted in *Notes and Queries*, CLXXII (1937), 390.

29. *Monthly Anthology*, IX (1810), 346. Tyler, in his later proposed preface, said: "The Algerine Captive was reviewed in a Boston Magazine by some one who had the sagacity to discover that it savored of infidelity. The Author was prepared to meet severe criticism on his style; and various other imperfections; but certainly he never imagined it was objectionable on the score of infidelity, or even scepticism. The part objected to, as far as the Author recollects, was written with a view to do away the vulgar prejudices against Islamism. He never thought that in adopting the liberality of the good Sale, the translator of the Koran, he was even jeopardizing the truths of Christianity: for the Author considered then, and now considers, that, after exhibiting Islamism in its best light, the Mahometan imposture will be obvious to those who compare the language, the dogmatic fables, the monstrous absurdities of the Koran, with the sublime doctrines, morals and language of the Gospel Dispensation" (Tyler memoir, pp. 99–100). Cf. *Diary of William Dunlap* (New York, 1930), p. 174.

30. It is customary to find the second volume inferior to the first, but for a discussion of further merits in volume II, see Teut Riese, *Das englische Erbe in der amerikanischen Literatur* (Bochum-Langendreer, 1958), pp. 139–149.

31. Alexander Cowie, in *The Rise of the American Novel* (New York, 1948), describes Tyler's "finished prose" as "swift, well-balanced, allusive but comparatively unembellished." He says, "In maturity of observation and in command of language, Tyler was far superior to the average popular novelist" (p. 67). Frederick Tupper compares Tyler's prose to the "plain unvarnished style" of Defoe, in *Proceedings of the Vermont Historical Society*, IV (1928), 84.

VI. *Essayist*

1. See *UVM Notes*, XVII (December 1920), 8.

2. Letter of 22 May 1810, in Tyler memoir (cf. Chapter 1, note 4, above), p. ²80. Pliny H. White, in "Early Poets of Vermont," *Proceedings of the Vermont Historical Society, 1917–1918* (1920), p. 119, says that four quarto pages of the dictionary were printed.

3. Letter of 14 February 1800, in Tyler memoir, p. 119.

4. The agreement between Tyler and Ide is preserved at The New-York Historical Society; there is a reproduction of it in the Tyler Papers at the Vermont Historical Society. The document goes on to say that if Tyler does finish the work, Ide will pay him $24 for the copyright. The title was entered by Ide for copyright on 26 April 1817. The 36-page copy of the book was once in the library of the University of Vermont, but no trace of it can now be found. The work was listed as Tyler's in M. D. Gilman's *Bibliography of Vermont* (Burlington, 1897), pp. 282–284; it is also recorded in R. W. G. Vail's list of Ide imprints in Louis W. Flanders and Edith F. Dunbar, *Simeon Ide* (Rutland, Vt., 1931), p. 146.

5. Tyler later hoped to collect these tales and his other unpublished works into a volume with the title "Utile Dulci"; a typed copy of some of the contents is in the Tyler Papers (Box 45, Envelope 35). The proposed title page was to read as follows: "UTILE DULCI / Being / A Collection compiled / from the more Juvenile and unpublish'd / Works / of the Author / embracing Dialogues Sacred Dramas Fables in Prose / and verse, Tales, / &c / Design'd to allure the youth / of both Sexes / To Profitable Studies. / By / Royall Tyler, A.M." (Quoted, with permission, from the Royall Tyler Collection, gift of Helen Tyler Brown.) The surviving fragments include "Five Pumpkins," "Historiette of the Tub Woman," and a poem on Darius' rule by intellect rather than force.

6. Dennie to Tyler, 14 April 1797, in *The Letters of Joseph Dennie*, ed. Laura G. Pedder (Orono, Me.: University of Maine Studies, 2nd series, no. 36, 1936), pp. 155–156. Dennie also refers briefly to "your historical labors," still another project (or perhaps the "Cosmography").

7. Tyler to Nancrede, March 1800, in Tyler memoir, pp. 126–127; it is also quoted, from the memoir, in Henry Burnham, *Brattleboro, Windham County, Vermont* (Brattleboro, 1880), p. 96.

8. These letters are transcribed in the Tyler memoir, pp. 115–127; they are published in G. T. Tanselle, "Author and Publisher in 1800: Letters of Royall Tyler and Joseph Nancrede," *Harvard Library Bulletin*, XV (1967).

9. See Chapter 4, note 5, above. The two men have therefore been referred to as "Damon and Pythias Among Our Early Journalists" by

S. Arthur Bent in *New England Magazine*, n.s. XIV (August 1896), 666–675. Cf. E. C. Coleman, *The Influence of the Addisonian Essay before 1810* (Urbana, Ill., 1936). Further information about the periodicals to which Tyler contributed is found in Chapter 4 above, on Tyler's poetry.

10. This copy is now in the Boston Public Library. One must use even these annotations with caution because some items are marked only with a "T" and others with "Tyler"; some of the "T's" occur in parts of the book where other pieces are labeled "Thomas," and they could logically stand for "Thomas" as easily as for "Tyler" (see pp. 61–62, 65, 151–158). Brief items labeled either "T" or "Tyler" appear on pp. 53, 55, 56, 57, 58, 59, 61, 65, 151, 153, 188, 252, 253; of the longer "Colon & Spondee" prose pieces, the name "Tyler" is written on the following: pp. 256–258, 266–269, 271–274, 277–281, 286–314. There is a copy of the *Spirit* at the University of Vermont with similar annotations, in pencil; the annotator is not indicated, but the distinction between "T" and "Tyler" exactly follows the Boston copy. Cf. G. T. Tanselle, "Attribution of Authorship in *The Spirit of the Farmers' Museum* (1801)," *Papers of the Bibliographical Society of America*, LIX (1965), 170–176.

11. *Farmer's Weekly Museum*, 11 April 1797, 3 May 1796, 27 May 1799, and 31 July 1797 (reprinted in *Spirit*, pp. 277–281, 288–289, 302–303, 309–310).

12. *Farmer's Weekly Museum*, 18 February 1799 (reprinted in *Spirit*, pp. 271–274).

13. See Randolph C. Randall, "Authors of the *Port Folio* Revealed by the Hall Files," *American Literature*, XI (1940), 379–416.

14. *Port Folio*, I (21 November 1801), 371.

15. In addition to one item (partly prose and partly verse, incorporating the "Mouser" sonnet), reprinted from the *Museum*; see Chapter 4, note 28, above.

16. *Port Folio*, II (21 January, 27 February, 15 May 1802), 9–10, 57–58, 148.

17. In William Duane's Philadelphia *Aurora*, 20 June 1803.

18. This series is identified as Tyler's by Joseph T. Buckingham in his *Personal Memoirs and Recollections of Editorial Life* (Boston, 1852), I, 56. The four "Trash" numbers appeared in the *Polyanthos* for May and June 1806, and April and May 1807 (II, 92–97, 181–184; V, 14–19, 86–89). The third was unsigned, but the others were signed "S."

19. Tyler to Riley, 16 June 1809, in Tyler memoir, pp. 263–64. "Captain Holbrook" was probably a member of the firm of booksellers in Brattleboro, Holbrook & Fessenden — see *Grandmother Tyler's Book* (New York, 1925), p. 298. Tyler also sent the manuscript

of *The Maternal Physician* by Holbrook, and Riley (in a letter of 13 December 1809) mentioned shipping a supply of the *Reports* to Fessenden.

20. Riley to Tyler, 7 October 1809, in Tyler memoir, p. [266]. The book was entered for copyright on 23 September 1809.

21. Tyler to Riley, 22 May 1810, in Tyler memoir, pp. [279]–80.

22. See *Grandmother Tyler's Book*, pp. 294–295, and Tyler memoir, p. [267].

23. *Grandmother Tyler's Book*, pp. 265, 294.

24. As it had in *The Algerine Captive*.

25. The first by Frederick Tupper in "Royall Tyler, Man of Law and Man of Letters," *Proceedings of the Vermont Historical Society*, IV (1928), 90; the second by Constance Rourke in *The Roots of American Culture* (New York, 1942), p. 123. Miss Rourke says that in *The Yankey in London* the "humor is keen, the style silvery-sharp: the little book is close to being a minor classic." A contrary view was expressed by the contemporary reviewer William Tudor, Jr. (identified in the entries for 24 October 1809 and 16 January 1810 in *Journal of the Proceedings of the Society Which Conducts the Monthly Anthology & Boston Review*, introd. M. A. DeWolfe Howe [Boston, 1910], pp. 209, 220): in the *Monthly Anthology and Boston Review* for January 1810 (VIII, 50–58), he called the book "a very useless addition to the almost innumerable books of travels, which crowd the shelves of libraries" (p. 50). He took the work as an authentic account of a visit to London (and quoted the complete chapter on the House of Commons) but recognized the lack of first-hand observation: "There is a degree of smartness and some humour in this writer, that would induce us to think he might do better. The fault of his work is, that it gives nothing new, nothing but what a man, with some knowledge of English history, and the habit of reading English newspapers and magazines, might write in this country. The account of the English bookseller and the remarks on the House of Lords are really too stale even for a magazine" (pp. 57–58). Whether or not the title was derived from Tyler, David Humphreys' play *The Yankey in England* (1815) makes dramatic use of the conflict of ideas present in Tyler's book and carries on the tradition of *The Contrast*.

26. G. F. Newbrough, "Mary Tyler's Journal," *Vermont Quarterly*, XX (1952), 28.

27. This typescript of "The Bay Boy" is in the Tyler Papers, Box 45, Envelope 29 (and a second copy is in Box 77, Envelope 13); quotations are here made, by permission of the heirs and the Vermont Historical Society, from these papers in the Royall Tyler Collection, gift of Helen Tyler Brown. Of the larger sections, four of them are labeled with the chapter numbers 5, 6, 7, and 9, but the position of the

others is not indicated; all have epigraphs (mainly of Tyler's own composition) except the one which quotes "The Wolf and Wooden Beauty." Of the smaller fragments, one is a preface of two pages (pointing out that the work is "designed not so much for the entertainment of the existing generation" as "for the gratification of their descendants"); two are marked as fragments of chapters 3 (2 pp.) and 4 (3 pp.); and two, unnumbered, deal with Updike's birth (2 pp. and 1 p.). The fragment of the third chapter of "The Bay Boy" consists of part of chapter 5 of *The Algerine Captive*; the sixth incorporates chapter 6, on Updike's education; the seventh consists of chapters 7 and 8, on his teaching and his return home; and the ninth is made up of chapters 9–11, on his early medical study. Though these papers were not available for many years, Bertrand W. Chapman had access to them in writing his 1933 master's thesis at the University of Vermont on "The Nativism of Royall Tyler," and he includes an extensive discussion of "The Bay Boy" on pp. 52–98. It is his belief that "The Bay Boy" contains "many of the elements of a literary masterpiece" (p. 97), and that it could have been "the first realistic work of fiction to be produced in the United States" (p. 98).

28. For a good discussion identifying the historical figures Tyler refers to, see Chapman, "Nativism," esp. pp. 75–80, 92–93.

29. The concrete details can be illustrated by a passage from the description of a Boston street in the evening: "The streets were now almost deserted, nothing was seen except the tardy footsteps of some belated labourer, or the cautious tread of some conscientious beau who was returning from the barber's shop under the shade of the projecting pent house, with his chin smoothly shaved, his toupee nicely craped his side curls neatly bound over leaden wires, and the whole as white as the powder puff and caster could make them. At length the old South Clock struck eight and all was silence." But the language can occasionally partake of all the worst features of Tyler's style: "When the gloom of vexation or the thunder gusts of anger and revenge are rapidly succeeded by the bright beams of hope which reflect their glittering rays on the watery bubbles that hang pendent from every Shrub and Spray in the Youngsters Horizon. . . ."

30. Dennie to Tyler, 14 April and 22 April 1797 respectively, in *Letters*, pp. 156, 157.

31. Dennie to Tyler, 2 October 1795, in *Letters*, p. 151.

Index

273

Index

Chamberlain, John Curtis, 115
Chapman, Bertrand W., xi, 272
Charlestown, N. H., 30, 35, 111
Chase, Dudley, 34
Châteillon, Sébastien, 135
Chaucer, Geoffrey, 188
Chesterfield, Philip Dormer Stanhope, Earl of, 76, 187, 198
Chipman, Daniel, 40
Chipman, Nathaniel, 237
Churchill, Charles, 131
Clapp, W. W.: quoted, 252
Claremont, N. H., 112, 125
Clough, Molly, 29
Coad, Oral: quoted, 56
Coates, Walter J., x, 136
Coleman, William: quoted, ix, 141
Colman, George, 247
"Colon & Spondee." *See* Dennie, Joseph; Tyler, Royall
Columbian Centinel (Boston): review of *Georgia Spec* quoted, 85; mentioned, 118
Concord, Mass., 5, 7
Cooper, T. A., 120, 130
Courier (Boston), 239
Cowie, Alexander: quoted, viii, 268
Cowley, Hannah, 121
Cowper, William, 176
Crafts Tavern, 114, 115, 185
Cranch, Betsy, 10
Cranch, Mary (Smith): opinion of RT quoted, 16, 18, 231; mentioned, 10, 15, 16, 17, 19, 24
Cranch, Richard: opinion of RT quoted, 14–15; mentioned, 10, 15, 16, 24, 229

Daily Advertiser (New York): review of *Contrast* quoted, 77, 78; mentioned, 51
Dana, Francis, 7, 224
Dawes, Thomas, 7
Day, Luke, 20
Dean, Cyrus B., 43
Della Cruscan movement, 121–124, 187, 189, 202, 203
Denison, Gilbert, 47, 242
Denison, Henry, 241

Dennie, Joseph: "The Farrago," 111, 112, 114; edits *Tablet*, 114; "The Lay Preacher," 115; edits *Farmer's Museum*, 115; "Colon & Spondee," 30, 112–113, 114, 115, 116, 184–185, 256; edits *Port Folio*, 30, 116, 257–259; laments RT's absence from *Port Folio*, 116–117; comments on *Algerine Captive*, 144–145, 147–148, 266; letters to RT quoted, 83–84, 140–141, 182, 208; mentioned, xi, 113, 114, 121, 122, 189, 209, 238
Dexter, Aaron, 7
Donaldson, Joseph, 142
Drama League of America, 80
Drayton, Michael, 32, 188
Driftwind (North Montpelier, Vt.), 136
Dryden, John, 188
Dunlap, William: quoted, 53, 79; mentioned, viii, 51, 56
Dunlap Society, x, 79
D'Urfey, Thomas, 86
Duyckinck, Evert A.: quoted, ix; mentioned, 56, 79
Duyckinck, George L.: quoted, ix; mentioned, 56, 79
Dwight, Timothy, 30, 122

Eagle (Hanover, N.H.), 30, 112, 113, 125, 135
Elliott, James: quoted, viii
Emsley, Bert, 248
Estaing, Charles Hector, Comte d', 8
Esther (Biblical character), 101–105
Eustis, William, 7
Everett, David, 115

Falmouth, Me., 9
Farmer's Weekly Museum (Walpole, N.H.): opinion of *Algerine Captive* quoted, 143–144, 145; mentioned, 30, 34, 114, 122, 128, 185
Farquhar, George, 82
Fay, David, 21, 37, 38, 237

Index

Index

Index

Index

Index